ALSO BY KIRK DOUGLAS

The Ragman's Son

DANCE WITH THE DEVIL

RANDOM HOUSE NEW YORK

RANDOM HOUSE NEW YORK

KIRK DOUGLAS

DANCE WITH THE DEVIL

Manufactured in the United States of America

Quality Printing and Binding by:
Berryville Graphics
P.O. Box 272
Berryville, VA 22611 U.S.A.

To Stolz, with love and gratitude

AUTHOR'S NOTE

The country I have described in the pages of this book can be found in the margin of the San Sabba Concentration Camp in Trieste, Italy. Tha Jen, who sculpted it, died there. Nothing is known about him, and the story I have told here is entirely imaginary. All scenes, characters, places, and incidents are also fictitious, or are used fictitiously, and any resemblance to actual persons, living or dead, is entirely coincidental.

X. D.

DANCE WITH THE DEVIL

PROLOGUE

1987 | London, England

ncomfortably perched on metal folding chairs, the six young women fidgeted nervously, their anxiety magnified by the mirrored walls of the barren rehearsal hall. They kept darting quick glances at the door until, finally, he walked in.

Danny Dennison was striking—six feet two, muscular, with a head of thick black curls here and there reflecting steel gray, high cheekbones, intense brown eyes. The eyes could intimidate, make him seem unyielding, especially when, deep in thought, he narrowed them, tensing the muscles of his firmly set jaw. But when he smiled, his face relaxed, creasing with dimples and projecting a disarming boyish charm, though the eyes always stayed just a little sad. With his good looks, he certainly didn't appear fifty-five, and he was often taken for the star actor, not the director.

Danny scratched his head. He had to choose one of these young women for a bit part. Another director would have left this chore to his casting chief, but Danny never sloughed off even the little things; he cared about details. It was one of the reasons he was so highly respected by his peers.

He gave each of them a chance, patiently watching as they strutted about, swinging their hips, bending down to show the curve of their asses, pushing their breasts up in their bras, anything to draw his interest. They all tried too hard. Except one. She just sat there quietly waiting. Her name was Luba. Something about her silent self-confidence attracted him. He gave her the part, and dismissed the group.

As he watched her walking out with the others, he heard himself call out, "Luba . . ."

She turned and slowly came close to him. She was only five-two, and, standing before him like a pupil before a teacher, she seemed girlish, with a child's round cheeks and glowing pink skin. But the full mouth was too sensuous for a young girl, and her large, very dark eyes were adult, steady, slightly intimidating. He tried to be nonchalant. "I'd like to talk to you—would you be free tonight?"

"Sure."

Her answer was so simple he almost didn't know how to continue. "How about dinner—eight o'clock?"

"I can't make it until ten. How about a nightcap?"

"All right. I'm staying at the Dorchester. Meet me at the bar."

She smiled with her eyes, then walked away.

Behind him someone said in a loud voice, "Now there goes a great little ass."

Danny turned to face his star. Bruce Ryan had a glazed, vacant stare, probably from too much coke. Danny wondered if the actor had heard him make the date. "Bruce," he said good-naturedly, "just keep your mind on *London Rock.*"

"Yeah," the actor slurred, "rhymes with *cock.*"

Walking back to his trailer, Danny mumbled to himself, "*London Rock* also rhymes with *crock.* What a stupid script!"

He hated it, but he had a contract with Ace Films, and Art Gunn, the head of the studio, didn't worry about critics or reviews. "I want a film that will make *gelt*—you understand?" he had told Danny, rubbing his fingertips together. "Don't worry about anything else."

"But this is a piece of shit."

Art squinted at him from behind his huge mahogany desk and took another puff on his cigar. Then he leaned forward, let the smoke drift out of his mouth, and said very softly, "I *want* a piece of shit."

He sure was going to get it, Danny thought, passing Bruce Ryan's trailer, which was twice the size of his own, as befitted the new young star of today; Bruce Ryan was hot.

"Keep Bruce happy" were the last words of advice Art Gunn gave him before he boarded the polar flight for London.

Danny sighed. It wasn't going to be easy.

When he got back to the Dorchester at the end of the day, the concierge handed him two letters with his key. Going up to his room, he glanced at the first one. He recognized his wife's handwriting—the postmark, Reno, Nevada, divorce capital of the world. He could guess the contents; he didn't need to read it. The other was from his daughter—the postmark, Long Island. That one made him nervous; he put both in his inside pocket.

He finished his room-service dinner quickly and then took a long shower. His bedside clock said nine. "God, a whole hour!" He pulled back the heavy velvet curtains and peered across the street at Hyde Park; in the dim glow of park lights the swaying trees cast eerie shadows through curly wisps of fog.

He tried to study the scene for the next day, but it bored him. He checked the clock again—nine-forty. Too early to leave yet.

Luba bothered him. Why did he choose her? Why did he make the date? He would keep it short—one drink; he definitely wouldn't ask her to his room.

When he arrived at the bar a minute after ten, she was already waiting for him in a corner booth, looking very pretty in an ice-blue jumpsuit. He tried to look composed as he summoned the waiter, but he was a little nervous. She was not.

Something about her—her calm manner, her steady gaze—drew him to her. After a couple of drinks, he began to feel a warm glow. Maybe he would ask her to his room. . . .

"Will you take me home?" she said suddenly.

A feeling of disappointment washed over Danny, but he said, "Of course," immediately reaching for his wallet.

The cab took them to an unfamiliar part of London and stopped before a three-story brownstone.

She got out, then turned, her eyes locking on his. "Come on," she said.

Intrigued, he followed her up the winding staircase to the top floor. She unlocked the door, and, without turning on the lights, led him by the hand down a hallway. He caught a glimpse of a cat's yellow eyes glowing in the dark. Inside a bedroom she lit a small candle on the nightstand. "Something to drink?" she asked, and disappeared without waiting for his answer.

Danny sat down on the bed. He wondered if he should begin to undress, but took off only his sports jacket. She returned with two ice-filled glasses and a bottle of vodka, which she placed on the bureau. He watched her pour the liquor. Bruce was right, he thought—she has a lovely ass.

Moving toward him, she took a long sip. Slowly she leaned over, put her mouth on his, and let the liquid trickle down his throat. For Danny, it was a new, erotic sensation.

She looked at him with those large eyes. "I'm glad you picked me." "So am I."

Her full lips were soft, their touch tender. Her mouth felt very cool —maybe it was the ice from the drink—as the moist tip of her tongue sought his. He pulled her closer, his excitement mounting, but she broke away. "I'll be right back," she whispered, vanishing again. He took off the rest of his clothes and waited on the bed, but lying there in the buff made him uncomfortable. He was putting his shirt on just as the door opened.

She stood there nude, silhouetted by the hall light behind her. Her soft brown shoulder-length hair, which she had unpinned, fell loosely down the sides of her face.

She came over to the bed and, opening his shirt, caressed his body with her fingers. Then she moved onto her knees, straddling him. She slowly brushed her round, firm breasts back and forth across his chest, and he could feel her nipples harden. Gently, she touched the inside of his thighs. She kept looking at him. What was it about those eyes that mesmerized him?

He couldn't remember when he had last been so strongly aroused. He felt like a teenager—eager to plunge into her, unable to hold back. He rolled her over and slowly moved inside her, watching her face. She was beautiful. In the candlelight, those large eyes seemed bottomless. Her mouth was wide open, reaching toward him. He began pushing harder and faster, and her eyes seemed to get larger and larger. He was staring down deep into them, and suddenly, as he came, his vision blurred. He felt dizzy. He looked around the room, straining to clear his head, but everything seemed strange.

It was a different room that was slowly turning around him—heavy, ornately carved pieces of furniture moved past his eyes. He saw a large bookcase filled with leather-bound books; he could make out their gold titles inscribed in German. The dim light glanced off silver picture frames holding portraits of uniformed soldiers, their faces blurry.

He turned back to Luba and saw Rachel.

Her eyes—Rachel's eyes—were bulging. She was hanging, suspended from the ceiling beam, a braided satin rope around her neck. Her body was swaying slightly. An overturned chair lay under her on the floor. Her hair hung loosely down each side of her face. He couldn't utter a sound. He lifted the chair upright and stood on it, but his twelve-year-old hands were too short to reach the taut rope around her neck. He almost toppled over, and had to clutch her waist to steady himself. He was startled to find his hands touching her belly, very round, firm, and distended under her full skirt. He looked up again at the staring eyes. Then he felt something, a movement against his hand. He jumped off the chair and backed away from the swaying body, realizing with horror that an unborn infant was within, struggling against the inevitability of death.

CHAPTER 1

1944 | San Sabba Concentration Camp, Trieste, Italy

is large brown eyes full of intense admiration, twelve-year-old Moishe watched the sparks flying from his father's blowtorch as another sculpture, welded together from pieces of scrap iron, took shape before him.

The Italian guards were amused by his father's artistic efforts; the Germans were indifferent. Often Tateh made miniature sculptures for the Italians, and they permitted him to putter in the basement machine shop as long as his daily work was finished. From the scraps of iron, he was now forming a little boy in short pants, pulling a small wagon. To the boy's head he welded delicate curlicue shavings of steel like the black curly hair of Moishe.

The torch illuminated the sculptor's deeply lined, gaunt face, reflecting the silver in his wavy hair. The silver strands weren't there when they came to this place a year ago; now only his beard was still black. Tateh was tall, powerfully built, a strong man with muscles that rippled as he moved heavy iron pieces closer to the fire. Only lately did he seem a bit stooped over, somewhat smaller, weaker, not as alive as he had once been, and he coughed continuously.

Perched on the basement windowsill, Moishe was level with the gravel roadway that led to the main courtyard, the center of the camp's activities. That was where the daily executions took place. Moishe couldn't see the bullet-scarred wall, nor the long, sloped wooden trough to catch the blood, nor the bodies being carted away by wheelbarrows to the crematorium. But he could hear the rifle shots and the screams of the dying, which the blaring music unsuccessfully attempted to cover.

He pressed his cheek to the steel bars and watched the different feet going past—the clean, high-stepping boots of the SS men, the sauntering, dusty boots of the Italian guards, the slow-shuffling, worn-out shoes of the inmates. And he remembered the carefree sound his sister Rachel's clogs used to make, their wooden soles clattering against the farmyard cobblestones as she hurried to the barn, just when he was waking up.

On the straw-thatched roof of that barn was a sculpture of a stork that his father had made years ago. It stood with one foot raised and wings outstretched. Tateh told Moishe that when he turned thirteen and became a man on his Bar Mitzvah, the iron bird would fly away.

Moishe hoped the stork was still there. He hoped the barn was still there. And what had happened to all the other sculptures his father had created?

After his day's work in the fields was over, Tateh used to sculpt for hours into the night. Moishe would sneak into the workshop and watch, fascinated by his father's skill, puzzled by his sorrowful expression as he melded scraps into pieces of art. "Don't come too near or you might get burned," Tateh warned, his acetylene torch emitting long white flames and sending sparks into the darkness.

But why, Moishe wondered, did Tateh seem unhappy—doing what he loved to do? Often tears trickled down his cheeks as he mumbled a prayer in Hebrew. Was he dissatisfied with his work? Praying for its success? Moishe wasn't sure, but it hurt him to see his father crying.

The sculptures were placed all over the farm. Little David, with arched back and slingshot poised, faced the giant Goliath, who protected himself with a large, round shield; a shoulder strap from a broken chain crossed Goliath's chest, and he aimed a long, pointed spear at his tiny adversary. For hours, Moishe would sit, captivated, waiting for David to hurl the rock. He would not have been surprised to wake up one morning and see the giant stretched out at David's feet.

Don Quixote, mounted on a rearing steed with its front legs pawing the air, guarded the big wooden gate framed by hazelnut trees at the farm's entrance. Moishe remembered picking the hazelnuts and trying to crack them with his teeth the way his father did. Only Tateh could do it.

His parents had moved to the farm in 1935, when Moishe was three and Rachel eight. Both schoolteachers from Munich, Jacob and Leah Neumann had been disturbed by a wave of anti-Semitism fueled by the Nazi party, and they had decided to escape the turmoil. They took up farming not far from the Swiss border, where they believed they would be safe until the trouble had passed.

The place wasn't much—half a dozen stuccoed, straw-roofed buildings all set around a cobblestoned square; one was the farmhouse, and the others housed the chickens, sheep, cows, and the four horses to plow the twenty hectares of hay and wheat fields beyond the large wooden barn. But even if small, the farm was self-sufficient, which gave them little need to interact with outsiders. They grew enough fruit and vegetables to put away for the winter, and when they needed staples the farm could not supply, their hired hand, Hans, the only person who knew they were Jewish, brought these from the nearby town of Ravensburg.

Hans—jolly, fond of German beer songs, with a pot belly to prove how he had learned them—lived a few kilometers down the road and bicycled over to the farm every morning. Moishe liked Hans, who promised to teach him to ride a bicycle as soon as his legs got long enough. Hans did the heavy work, Tateh and Mameh did the rest; and, as they grew up, Rachel and Moishe were expected to carry their load of the lighter chores. Rachel had a special touch with the animals; she loved all living things, and the creatures seemed to sense it. Moishe would watch apprehensively from a distance as she opened the beehives that stood between the barn and the orchards. She would come out, her face and arms covered with bees, approach

Moishe teasingly, and laugh at him as he ran away, scattering the chickens underfoot.

Moishe followed Rachel wherever she went; he felt safe with her around. And she treated him like one of the little calves she looked after. If Mameh caught him getting into trouble, she could be very stern, but Rachel would only look at him with her soft brown eyes and say, "Moishe, you mustn't do that," and her full lips would curl into a hint of a smile. He couldn't resist sliding down the sloping straw-thatched roof of the barn—something strictly forbidden by Mameh—because he knew Rachel would pretend she didn't see him. Playing on the roof, he once fell to the cobblestones below. As usual, Rachel was there to save him; she brought him, battered and bawling, into the house, then washed off the scrapes and bandaged his bleeding hand. That day, she looked to him like an angel he had seen in a picture book. She promised she wouldn't tell Mameh.

His mother was always quiet. Short, compact, with a round face made the more so by the twin braids she wound around her head, Mameh kept away from the animals, preferring the solitude of her flower garden. Her eyes often had a faraway look behind their wire-rimmed glasses as she went about tending her white roses. She never complained, dreaming of the time when they would go back to Munich. She missed the big city—the museums, the theater, the opera. For now, she had to be satisfied with books and records.

The years went by uneventfully, the quiet routine of the farm a sharp contrast to the turbulence outside. Moishe, now seven, was becoming aware that disturbing events were taking place in the world beyond. Mameh and Tateh frequently listened to the radio, which always seemed to be broadcasting angry voices. And sometimes he overheard things that he could not understand.

"If the international Jewish financiers should again succeed in plunging the nations into a world war—the result will be the annihilation of the Jewish race throughout Europe," the voice on the radio shouted. But Moishe never got the whole story; whenever he walked into the room, Mameh abruptly turned the radio off. Once, as he was helping Rachel carry the milk into the kitchen, he heard his parents arguing:

"Jacob, your friend Dr. Goldman is an alarmist—planning to leave for America just because he lost his license to practice. Why doesn't he appeal to the courts?"

"Leah—"

"This is a civilized country," Mameh went on, refusing to be interrupted, "full of decent, law-abiding people. Kind people, fair, hardworking, like our Hans."

"But Leah, different people are leading the country now." Tateh's voice was tense.

"It cannot be taken over by a group of hooligans," she insisted. "We were born here. We are German citizens."

"You choose to forget—they took away our citizenship years ago. Hysteria has taken over. I think the Goldmans are right—"

"Nonsense, Jacob. I refuse to believe it. It will be over soon and we will be back in Munich."

Moishe nudged Rachel and whispered, "Are we going back to Munich?"

"Not right away," she whispered back.

"Rachel, tell me again—what was it like?"

They put the milk pails on the bench by the kitchen door and went outside.

"I don't remember much, Moishe. It was very pretty and we lived in a nice little house . . . painted yellow, with red flowers out front in the yard."

"Where did the cows and horses live?"

"It wasn't a farm—Munich is a city. We didn't get animals until we moved here. Mameh and Tateh were teachers in a big school."

"I wish we could go to a big school. I bet we wouldn't have as much homework as Mameh makes us do here."

"Stop complaining, Moishe—it's important to learn things."

Any questions Moishe had were forgotten when he lay in bed beside his sister, listening to her read his favorite Hans Christian Andersen story. It was the one about the mirror that the Devil had created to make everything look ugly and distorted.

" 'The Devil was so pleased with his creation that he decided to take the mirror up to heaven to mock God. But as he flew higher and higher, the mirror slipped from his grasp and crashed to earth. The billions of pieces, some as tiny as grains of sand, scattered all over the world.' " Rachel's voice was soft; the music of Mozart from Mameh's gramophone gently drifted in. " 'If a sliver got in your eye it made you see everything as twisted and ugly. If a piece entered your heart it made you evil and cruel, and your heart turned to ice.' "

Suddenly Moishe interrupted, "Rachel, you've got bumps on your chest."

Rachel did not look up from the page.

"Rachel, can I feel your bumps?"

Rachel slammed the book shut. "I'm not going to read any more if you keep interrupting."

Perplexed by her anger, Moishe kept quiet.

Rachel picked up the book again, pulling her nightdress tightly around her.

Moishe was disappointed—if *he* had bumps he'd let Rachel touch them.

―――――――

Every evening, after Tateh unhitched the horses and put away the hay wagon, he let Moishe help him clean and oil the many leather straps that made up the harness. Moishe constantly asked, "When can I drive the team, Tateh?" and constantly heard the same answer: "When you can figure out how to harness the horses." Moishe never could.

After supper, he watched Tateh sculpt. In the distance Rachel would be singing a lovely song, "Roshinkes mit Mandlen"—"Raisins and Almonds"—as she helped Mameh wash the dishes, her high sweet voice tinged with sadness.

Moishe would later remember the night Tateh stopped, removed his goggles, and wiped the tears from his eyes. "Tateh, are you crying?"

His father brushed away the tears.

"Why, Tateh, why?"

Tateh took a long look at his son and smiled. "In God's eyes, what I'm doing is a sin."

"A sin?"

"Someday I'll explain it to you." Tateh put on his goggles again and flamed the torch.

Moishe wanted to ask a hundred questions. Sculpting was a sin? How could it be? God sure was strange. He wanted Abraham to sacrifice Isaac, and now He didn't want his father to sculpt beautiful things. But Moishe kept his thoughts to himself; he didn't want Tateh to cry again.

―――――――

During the day, when they had finished the lessons Mameh assigned, they did their chores, which Moishe always preferred to math problems. They were menial tasks—feeding the chickens, spreading clean straw in the stables, helping Hans unload the hay wagon.

One day he asked Rachel to teach him how to milk a cow. She was good at it. Sitting on a little stool, she expertly squeezed milk into the pail. As he leaned over her shoulder to watch, he could see down her dress. The bumps were bigger now.

"Rachel, can I see the bumps on your chest?"

She squirted milk from the cow's udder—right in his face. Moishe wiped off the warm liquid with his sleeve and persisted. "Please, Rachel, just a little peek."

"No," she said firmly. "Help me with that other pail."

As they walked out of the barn, Moishe muttered, "I show you everything. When I found the dead snake . . ."

Suddenly he stopped, distracted by the excited thunder of horses' hooves. They looked over the picket fence. Behind the orchard, in the pasture, the new gray stallion, his tail up like a pennant, was circling the chestnut mare—he was prancing as if dancing on air. The mare had her neck arched, and when he broke his dance and came nearer, she nuzzled his mane. Then she turned around, lifted her tail up, and spread her hind legs. The stallion reared up, and now Moishe and Rachel saw his enormous cock. The stallion's hooves came down on the mare's haunches, then he covered her with his body. All they could see was the shudder of his deep thrusts.

"He's hurting her!" Moishe cried out.

"No, no . . . she likes it," Rachel said softly, her eyes riveted to the scene.

They watched in silence until Mameh's voice broke the spell: "Please bring in the milk before it turns sour."

———

After finishing the chores, Moishe coaxed Rachel to play hide-and-seek. He crouched down behind the coats outside the kitchen door, gleeful as she walked off in another direction in search of him. Then he heard Tateh in the kitchen; he peeked in through the crack of the half-open door.

"*Liebchen,* why aren't you listening to the radio?"

"I don't want to hear any more," said Mameh, darning socks at the table. "I want to talk to you."

"What about?"

Mameh took a few more stitches. "The stallion and the mare were mating this morning."

"Good," said Tateh. "I'm glad to hear that life still goes on in this crazy world."

"Rachel and Moishe were watching—"

"So?"

"With great curiosity."

Tateh chuckled. "Innocent curiosity. Children need to learn that there is more to life than existing and dying. There is also sex—all kinds of sex. Don't you think they should learn that, Leah?"

Mameh didn't look up from her darning. "What I think is that Moishe is big enough now to have his own bed. He should sleep in the loft."

A loud laugh like a rumble came out of Tateh. "Yes, that's part of life, too."

Moishe didn't grasp everything that was said, but he didn't like what he had heard. He didn't want to be banished to the loft, away from Rachel.

That evening, a crestfallen Moishe carried his few belongings up the wooden ladder. The loft was a dark, musty room with a tiny, cell-like window that looked out onto the farmyard and stables beyond. It might as well have been a gloomy dungeon. The heavy, rough-cut roof beams seemed to loom ominously over him as he sat on his cot, hunched under their oppressive weight. A spider ran across his hand, and Moishe, never afraid of spiders before, flinched involuntarily. He wanted so badly to be downstairs again, curled up safely against Rachel on that big straw mattress.

As he lay there trying not to weep, he heard someone slowly climbing the ladder. Rachel's head peeked through the trapdoor, and Moishe had to clasp his hand over his mouth to stifle a happy cry. His eyes never left her as she carefully lit a small candle she had hidden in her apron pocket. She sat on the bed beside him and read his favorite story—the one about the Devil and the broken mirror:

" 'Greta and her little boyfriend Kay were in a beautiful rose garden, smelling and admiring the flowers. Suddenly, a gust of wind blew something into Kay's eye. Greta tried to get it out, but Kay insisted it was gone. He squinted, looking at the roses. "They're ugly!" he said. He broke the stem of the rosebush, kicked the flowerpot, and ran away.' "

"Rachel," Moishe interrupted, "the wind was blowing today. Look in my eyes—" and he opened them wide.

Rachel leaned over, smiled, and kissed him on the forehead. "You have no evil slivers. Now go to sleep." And she blew out the candle.

On Friday evening Tateh did not work on his sculptures. The family washed thoroughly, put on their best clothes, and sat around the kitchen table, which was covered with a white cloth for the occasion. Mameh made the blessing over the lighted candles that greeted the Sabbath, while Rachel repeated the prayers along with her. Moishe felt very grown up when his father let him make the blessing over the breaking of the *hallah,* the Sabbath bread that his mother and Rachel had made: "Blessed art Thou, O Lord, who giveth us the fruit of the earth."

While the women cleaned up the dishes from a meal of broth, roast chicken, potatoes, and carrots, Tateh took Moishe by the hand and led him into the farmyard. Looking up to the heavens—inky black and heavy with stars—Tateh prayed softly. Then he said, "Moishe, it's not easy to be a Jew."

Moishe waited; he didn't know what to say.

"My son," Tateh continued, "making idols, even out of scrap iron, is a sin before our Lord. I pray that God will forgive me, and permit me to fulfill my obsession."

"But I love the statues you make, Tateh."

"It's wrong, Moishe, it's wrong. It's against the Commandment 'Thou shalt not make graven images.' I'm a sinner, Moishe, a sinner." So that was why his father cried.

Tateh looked down at Moishe with a sad smile. "I know you don't understand me now. But when you grow up, son, you'll find there is torment in being a Jew."

Hans saw him first. Moishe was helping the hired hand gather up hay in the fields when a young man carrying a knapsack walked over the brow of the hill.

"Who are you?" Hans yelled.

"A friend—looking for Mr. Neumann."

Hans surveyed him suspiciously.

"I used to be a student of his," the young man added, coming nearer and showing straight white teeth in a sincere smile. He was of medium height and stocky build, with light brown hair, brown eyes to match, and a neatly trimmed beard.

"Mr. Neumann is very busy," Hans answered brusquely.

Moishe was surprised that friendly Hans was acting so rudely. "But Hans, we never get any visitors. I think my father would like to see him."

Hans grumbled an incoherent reply, so Moishe offered, "I'll take you." He led the way to the barn, Hans following without a word. Tateh was tending a mare's hoof that had been punctured by a nail a few days before. As they approached, he slowly lowered the hoof and stared intently at the stranger's face.

"Don't you remember me? David Meyer. Your worst student."

Tateh's face broke out in a wide grin. He engulfed the young man in a tight embrace. "David, David—is that you behind the beard? The last time I saw you, you weren't shaving yet."

"I'm still not shaving."

Tateh laughed heartily. "How long has it been—five, six years?"

"More like seven or eight, Mr. Neumann."

"You're right—we moved here when Moishe was three and he's almost eleven now. How did you find me?"

"Dr. Goldman sent me with a message for you."

"How are the Goldmans getting along?"

"They've left the country."

"It's that bad?"

David, no longer smiling, glanced over his shoulder at Hans. "I must talk to you—in private."

"Oh, don't worry," Tateh said. "We are all friends here. But let's go inside and give you some refreshment after your travels."

Hans followed them up to the house, still eyeing the stranger with suspicion, Moishe noticed.

Once inside, the family sat around the kitchen table listening to David. "All the Jews from the cities are gone, and now Eichmann has 'Jew hunters' combing the small towns and farms for anyone who's managed to hide."

In the silence that followed, David gulped down a few mouthfuls of the soup Mameh had put before him, occasionally throwing admiring glances in the direction of Rachel, who flushed each time. "On the way here, I saw Gestapo trucks loaded with people—men, women, children."

"Where are they taking them?" Mameh asked. Moishe was bewildered by the tremor in her voice.

"I'm not sure," David answered, again looking over at Rachel. "I hear they are being shipped to camps in various countries."

"Camps? What sort of camps?" Moishe asked excitedly, thinking of tents and campfires.

They looked at him, and Moishe was embarrassed that he had interrupted grown-ups talking.

"I don't know, Moishe," said David with a faint smile.

"Don't you think we are safe here, until it's over?" Mameh asked, her voice still unsteady.

Moishe almost jumped at David's sharp response. "No! I'm on my way to Lake Constance—if I can cross over into Switzerland, there are ways of getting out to Palestine or America. Come with me."

"Yes." Tateh nodded. "You are right. We must leave."

"But when, Jacob?" The panic in Mameh's voice was increasing.

"Now, Leah, now." Tateh put his arm around Mameh, and she hid her face against his shoulder. "Moishe," Tateh said hoarsely, "why don't you and Hans give the animals enough hay to last a couple of days."

Moishe ran out calling, "Hans! Hans!" but the hired hand was nowhere to be found. Then Moishe noticed that his bicycle was gone. What made him leave? What was happening? Moishe tried to make some sense of it as he ran to the barn.

They packed their belongings hastily that evening. Moishe was in the loft putting his few things in a satchel when he heard the rumble of an approaching truck. He rushed to the little window, and through the web of tree branches he saw blazing headlights enter the farmyard. Dogs were barking. He recognized Hans sitting next to the driver. He wanted to call out to him, but then two uniformed men carrying rifles jumped off the truck.

He would never forget the sound of their fists pounding against the door.

––––––

Some of the soldiers ransacked the house as others herded them to the truck. Moishe saw one soldier pocket Tateh's gold watch. Another grabbed Mameh's hand. She backed away, trembling and pleading, "No, no, let me go." He roughly yanked the wedding ring off her finger. When Tateh tried to intervene, the soldier rammed him in the side with a rifle butt. Rachel started to cry. David put his arm around her while Tateh held Mameh, soothing her and repeating, "It'll be all right, it'll be all right, *Liebchen.*"

Moishe tugged on his father's sleeve. "Why is Hans with them?"

Tateh patted his curly head. "People do many strange things out of fear . . . or greed."

Moishe tried to figure out what Tateh meant as the truck lurched away.

At the depot, a freight train was waiting. They were ordered to get into a car with three other Jewish families. One of the men said he had been on the train for four days, and had heard rumors it was bound for Italy, where a new concentration camp had been opened.

When the train stopped occasionally to pick up more Jews, the last remnants left in Germany and Austria, tin cups of water and hunks of black bread were handed to them through a narrow slot in the door, then the slot was tightly latched. They were not allowed to get off and had to relieve themselves in the corner of the car, where some straw had been piled up, the women shielding each other for a little privacy. The car was always in semidarkness, the only light filtering through small openings near the roof.

Over the three days of travel, David was the cheerful one, trying to engage others in conversation and word games to pass the time. He took special care to look after Rachel, putting his coat around her shoulders when it was cold, making a place for her to sit when she tired of standing, insisting she share his food rations.

They all bore up fairly well through the ordeal, except for Mameh, who only stared ahead in a sort of trance. Tateh had to coax her to eat some of the bread, but she seemed oblivious to everything around her, humming a Chopin sonata and rocking back and forth as if she were a metronome marking time.

Moishe took his cue from Tateh, who seemed calm and unafraid. Tateh lent him a penknife, and Moishe kept himself busy trying to chisel a hole through the thick car wall. It wasn't easy, and he wished he was as strong as Tateh.

Once they arrived in Trieste, the men and women were separated and taken by trucks from the train station to the edge of the town. There, they were ordered to get out in front of a large iron gate set in a high stucco wall that enclosed several brick buildings. A sign above the gate read LA RISIERA DI SAN SABBA.

"What does it mean?" Moishe asked.

"*La Risiera* means rice factory," said David. "Maybe we'll get something good to eat."

Nobody laughed.

As they walked through the gate, Moishe saw a tall chimney billowing black smoke into a clear blue sky. He reached out and grasped Tateh's hand, and was surprised to find that it was shaking; he looked up into his father's face and saw his chin quivering. For the first time since their trip began, Moishe felt something terrible was about to happen.

They were marched double-file down a narrow gravel roadway between the buildings and made to line up in the courtyard for the camp commandant's review. The commandant—tall, slim, not more than forty—walked back and forth, spinning gracefully on his heels, studying the collection of prisoners with electric eyes. His slender gloved hand impatiently flicked a crop as he gave orders to his adjutants.

The Jews, too frightened to object, were quickly divided into different groups. The eerie silence that hung in the air was interrupted by an occasional stifled sob. The ones to be led away first were the women with babies, the sick, and the elderly; Moishe saw Mameh in that group, shuffling along like a sleepwalker.

"Where is she going?" he asked, but Tateh just stared at Mameh and mumbled a prayer in Hebrew. Men who seemed fit to work were next, and Tateh, Moishe, and David were put with them. Moishe looked over to where Rachel stood with other young women and saw the commandant talking to one of his adjutants as he pointed in her direction. The officer took Rachel politely by the arm and led her to a waiting car. Startled by a muffled cry next to him, Moishe turned to see David, his eyes wide with horror, biting down hard on a tightly clenched fist.

That was the day this unbelievable existence began. They were housed in cramped quarters, six men to a compartment that used to hold stores of unbleached rice. Often, at night, Moishe would be awakened by the clanging of steel doors and the cries of prisoners being dragged out. During the days, loud music blared—Strauss waltzes were the commandant's favorite. Black smoke constantly billowed from the tall chimney.

In the beginning, Moishe barely slept at all, jumping at each new, horrifying sound, then quivering uncontrollably for hours. Now, after a year, an invisible coating covered his emotions, and he didn't even cry anymore when he thought of Rachel and Mameh. The continuous nightmare seemed routine. At least he and Tateh were together.

David was with them for a while, until he was assigned to work in the wood shop. Tateh was given welding work, and Moishe was allowed to help him, to sweep up and stack materials. The Italian guards even let the two of them sleep in the basement machine shop instead of returning to the crowded cell at night.

Moishe wore only the clothes he had come in, now tattered and very dirty. His pants were way too short for his long legs. He had grown much taller in a year, but Tateh seemed to have shrunk. Tateh was very thin now; he coughed constantly and seemed caught up in a world of his own, far away from reality.

When they first came here, Moishe endlessly watched the passing feet, hoping to see the brown walking shoes with yellow laces that his mother had worn on the day they arrived. After a while he gave up—he knew he would never see them again.

Moishe sat at his usual spot peering through the bars of the basement window. He heard the rumble of trucks in the distance and then saw the wheels of motorcycles speed past, followed by many pairs of tired, shuffling feet. This meant a new group of inmates had arrived. His father was oblivious to what was going on outside. The music kept playing and he didn't seem to hear anything. He was engrossed in creating a new piece of sculpture.

"Moishe, what are you looking at?"

"I was watching the birds, Tateh."

"Yes, birds are beautiful. They are so free. I like to watch them too." His hands never stopped working on the scraps of iron. "Do you remember the stork I made?"

"Yes, Tateh—you put it on the roof of the barn."

His father smiled sadly and then doubled over in a spasm of coughing.

"Are you all right, Tateh?"

His father nodded, still trying to catch his breath. "I'm fine, I'm fine." And he went back to work.

He had welded together a base of nuts, bolts, and gears. This, he said, represented the machinery of the Nazi regime. Emerging from the base was a skeletal torso of a man. His arms were outstretched and nailed with large spikes to a wooden cross; one of the arms wore a white canvas band with the blue Star of David. His head tilted upward, poignant with the agony all Jews had suffered at the hands of the Nazis. Through the dull strips of steel that formed the rib cage could be seen a shining piece of copper, his soul.

The work seemed to exhaust Tateh. Moishe was worried about him, but what could he do? He sighed and turned back to the window.

Suddenly, out of nowhere, a towheaded toddler came running, and stumbled on the gravel by the window. Moishe instinctively reached out through the bars to help him. Just then a black hobnailed boot swung like a hammer at the child's head. The little skull exploded, blood and brains splattering out.

Moishe felt sharp needles racing through his skin. He closed his eyes.

Slowly he eased down from his perch and went back to picking up the scraps lying around the sculpture, while his father, still coughing, stenciled on the board next to one of the outstretched hands the Hebrew word *Adonai*—God.

"Tateh, why doesn't God stop people from doing bad things?"

His father put down his stenciling tool. "God relinquished His power over man when He gave him free will. Man chooses good or evil."

"But the good people get punished!"

"They don't, Moishe—sometimes they suffer."

"Aren't we God's chosen people?"

"Of course—you know that."

"Then why doesn't He protect us?" asked Moishe, his voice rising.

Tateh stared at his sculpture. "He will, he will," he said very softly.

Moishe walked away. For the first time he wasn't certain that Tateh was right.

———

A prisoner's legs stopped in front of the basement window. When the legs squatted down, Moishe looked into a smiling face.

"David!"

"How are you, little Moishe?"

"Fine."

"And your father?"

"He coughs all the time."

"I'm sorry to hear that. Take care of him, Moishe. You know what happens when a man can't do his work."

"I'm trying."

"Listen . . ." David quickly looked around. "This will cheer him up. I overheard the Italians—the Allies are advancing. Tell him the war is almost over! We should be out of here—God willing—in a few months."

Moishe grabbed both bars and pressed his eager face closer. "Are you sure?"

David nodded, grinning from ear to ear. "And tell him . . . Rachel is fine."

"Did you see her?"

"Yes—I'm building bookshelves in the commandant's house this week. She sends her love."

"Oh, that'll make Tateh happy."

"And Moishe . . ." David hesitated. "When it's all over I want you to be my best man."

"Best man?" Moishe repeated, unsure what that meant.

"Yes, at my wedding." He threw a quick glance over his shoulder again. "I'm going to marry your sister." And then his face disappeared from view.

Moishe rushed into the back room, yelling, "Tateh! Tateh! David just—"

He gasped.

Two German guards were dragging away his father's inert body. Tateh had always been so strong and protective. How weak he seemed now, helplessly staring, his eyes never leaving Moishe's face.

"NO!" Moishe screamed, hurling himself against one guard, who, with a sweep of his arm, sent him reeling into the iron sculpture.

Dazed, Moishe waited for the hobnailed boot to come crashing into his skull. He blacked out.

When he came to, Tateh was gone. He put his hand to his throbbing head and felt a sticky substance. He was lying in a pool of blood. The face of the crucifixion seemed to be staring at him.

———————

David was carefully fitting the bookcase into the niche in the commandant's bedroom. It was to house leather-bound collections of Goethe, Nietzsche, and Schopenhauer. The room was spacious, and furnished with heavy, ornately carved German pieces, its tall casement windows draped in dark-brown velvet tied back by thick satin sashes.

David put down his hammer when Rachel walked in with the silver picture frames she had been polishing in the kitchen. She went directly to the table beside the canopied bed and carefully began to arrange the stiffly posed photographs of uniformed officers in the specified order.

"Rachel," David whispered.

"Shhh—someone could hear."

David closed the door and came over to her.

"David, please." She tried to push him away. "It's too dangerous."

Ignoring her entreaty, he cupped her face in his hands and kissed her. "You look beautiful."

Nervously, Rachel clutched the apron covering her blue-striped maid's uniform. "No, David, no . . ."

He smoothed away her long brown hair. "I've told Moishe how I feel about you. It's easier to tell him than to tell you."

Her large dark-brown eyes filled with tears as she looked up into his sincere face.

"Don't cry, Rachel." He took her hands in his and squeezed them tightly. "I love you. I'll take care of you. Just believe we will be together. It won't be long."

Just then the door was flung open, and they jumped apart. "Ar you through with your work?!" The commandant was standing in the doorway, his personal aide behind him.

"No, sir." David quickly crossed back to the bookcase. "It will take me just a few more hours." His voice was a bit unsteady.

"You are finished *now*."

David left the room without looking back, and the aide followed him, closing the door behind. The commandant and Rachel were alone.

The commandant took off his hat and gloves, laid them on his desk, sat down, and began leafing through documents.

"Herr Commandant." Rachel approached him, her hands folded as if in prayer and trembling violently. "I apologize for David."

"Apologies are not necessary. I understand—it's difficult for a man to resist a pretty girl."

"No, no—David was only telling me he had seen my brother."

"If you have any questions about inmates in the camp, Rachel, you should ask me." His tone, no longer commanding or harsh, was almost pleasant.

"Yes, Herr Commandant."

"Rachel—" He put aside his papers. His hard blue eyes seemed softer as he leaned back in his chair. "Don't look so frightened. I am not a monster. Haven't I treated you well?"

"Yes, Herr Commandant."

"Tell me, how old is your brother?"

"Twelve, Herr Commandant."

"Well—old enough to work in the kitchen?"

"Yes, Herr Commandant. Yes, he is, Herr Commandant." She was laughing through the tears that were now flowing freely down her face. The commandant smiled.

––––––––––

Moishe was given a clean shirt, a pair of overalls, and a cot of his own in Rachel's tiny room next to the kitchen. She let him crawl in beside her, and then they were together as they used to be on the farm. He told her about Tateh. They talked about Mameh, who was never seen after that first day. They knew what had happened to both of them.

"I could have saved them," Rachel whispered.

"You? How?"

"I could have got them to work here."

"Why didn't you?"

"I didn't know I could then . . ."

In bed with Rachel, Moishe caught glimpses of two full breasts that had replaced the bumps. But he said nothing for fear of being sent back to his cot.

"Rachel?"

"What is it now, Moishe?" she sighed.

"Are you getting married?"

She rolled over to face him. "What are you talking about?"

"David said I'm going to be the best man."

Rachel laughed and kissed him on the forehead. "Yes," she said, "if the rumors are true, and we get out of here. We'll be together. David and I will take care of you, Moishe."

Often, Rachel would get up during the night, throw a shawl around her nightgown, and leave the room, quietly closing the door behind her. Moishe was usually asleep before she came back. He wondered what work she would be doing so late, but when he asked her, she never gave him an answer.

During the day, while Rachel was upstairs tending the commandant's quarters, Moishe worked in the kitchen. It was a large room with a brick floor and cast-iron stoves, and he sat at the long pine table peeling potatoes. He also cleaned pots and pans and scrubbed the floor. He liked being in the kitchen. The smell of food was comforting, and he felt safe.

Rachel warned him never to go past the fence that surrounded the commandant's house. But whenever he went to the woodshed, he couldn't help peering through a knothole in the fence. He would watch the emaciated Jews of the camp as they shuffled about in their rags. Often, he would throw pieces of bread that he stole from the kitchen over the fence, and then quickly run back into the house.

One night, he asked, "Rachel, do you think the commandant has a piece of the Devil's mirror in his heart?"

"No, Moishe, I don't think so." Rachel paused, as if weighing what to say next. "He's really a good man. I feel sorry for him. He's a soldier—from a long line of military officers. He is only following orders."

"But they're killing people here."

"This is war, Moishe—that's what they do when they capture enemy soldiers."

"But we're not enemy soldiers," Moishe persisted. "What about people like us?"

Rachel's voice was hardly above a whisper: "We're here because we're Jews."

For a long time nothing was said, then Moishe broke the silence. "Let's not be Jews."

"What are you talking about?"

"You just said it—we're here because we're Jews. So let's not be Jews."

"We were born Jews. You were named after Moses, our great leader. We will always be Jews. Now go to sleep."

Moishe pulled the covers tightly around him. He looked up into the darkness and thought, I don't want to be a Jew. He hoped that Rachel couldn't hear his thoughts.

———

Made more and more comfortable by the security of his new surroundings, Moishe felt bolder. One night, when Rachel crept out of their room, he jumped out of bed and followed her. He held his breath as he saw her leaving the kitchen, closing the door behind her.

He waited a moment, then opened it a crack. He couldn't believe his eyes. Rachel was quietly walking up the forbidden staircase. Moishe poked his head out and saw a German guard standing at the top of the steps. Rachel kept going up. Doesn't she see him? Moishe thought. He's right in front of her. He wanted to cry out, "Come back, Rachel!" but he was frozen with fear.

Rachel walked right past the guard, who didn't move or say anything to her.

Moishe hurried back to bed, but he could not go to sleep. He lay there for hours, his heart thumping. It was getting light outside when he heard Rachel quietly come in again. Moishe couldn't piece the puzzle together, but he now knew that Rachel was doing something that he shouldn't question.

Then she stopped leaving the room at night, and she wouldn't let him crawl in bed with her anymore. Moishe missed the warmth of her body, but he knew that Rachel wasn't feeling well. Several times in the morning, he saw her rush out in the yard to throw up.

———

It was spring 1945. David had been right: The Allies were near. The Italian guards were tense, whispering among themselves. Friction developed between them and the Germans. The commandant speeded up the schedule of executions. The crematorium was now in operation around the clock and smoke billowed out day and night.

Moishe's routine continued. He was planting tomatoes in the garden, patiently digging a little hole for each individual seedling, when the usual quiet of the camp was interrupted by the din of loud voices.

He peered through the hole in the garden fence and saw prisoners scurrying from one barracks to another. What was happening?

Frightened, Moishe grabbed his basket of seedlings and hurried back toward the kitchen. He was almost knocked down by two Italian guards, babbling and gesticulating as they rushed toward a truck at the camp gate. The commandant's Mercedes-Benz was waiting in front of the house, the motor idling, the driver behind the wheel.

Suddenly, David was running toward Moishe, yelling, "We're free! We're alive! The Americans are down the road!" He grabbed Moishe, still holding his basket, picked him up, and kissed him on both cheeks. "We're free, Moishe! We survived!"

Putting him down, David asked, "Where is Rachel?"

"She must be inside."

David rushed toward the front of the house, but just then the door opened and the commandant emerged. Rachel was behind him in the hallway. The two men confronted each other. Moishe stood transfixed. David said something to Rachel, which Moishe couldn't make out. The commandant looked at her over his shoulder. Then, turning back, he raised his arm and pointed it at David. A gun exploded. David teetered on his feet and fell backward; his body shuddered, then lay still.

The commandant calmly stepped over David and got into his car. Moishe jumped as the car roared past; his heart was pounding. He started for the house, then stopped, unable to pass the bloody corpse. Rachel was gone. In a panic, he ran around back to the kitchen. Inside, prisoners were laughing, crying, holding each other. Moishe dropped his basket of seedlings. "Rachel!" he called out above the commotion. She wasn't there. Their little room was empty too. He ran down the main hallway. "Rachel!" he called again. No answer. This part of the house seemed filled with a heavy silence. From the camp, he could hear the happy cries of the Jews who had escaped the ovens.

He hesitated at the bottom of the forbidden staircase, then raced up, taking two steps at a time. At the top, he hesitated again: He was facing two doors, both closed. Slowly he turned the knob. The first room was empty. Then he opened the second door—the commandant's bedroom.

And that's where he found her, hanging from a ceiling beam, a heavy braided curtain sash around her neck. His anguished scream echoed through the empty house.

"RACHEL!"

Moishe's little hand seemed lost in the strong grasp of the big black soldier with the smiling face who led him out of the camp. The American tried to communicate with him, pointing his finger at Moishe's chest: "Jew? *Jude?*"

No, Moishe shook his head. The soldier stared at him questioningly. Moishe pointed at himself: *"Tzigan. . . .* Gypsy."

"Name?" the soldier asked. "NAME?"

"Daniel," said Moishe, remembering one of the gypsy boys at the camp.

"Oh, Danny boy!" The soldier grinned.

Moishe left all of his family behind, dead. He was almost thirteen—time for Bar Mitzvah, the ceremony that would make him a man. But he was no longer a Jew.

CHAPTER 2

1980 | San Sabba Refugee Camp, Trieste, Italy

 girl with a body suggesting a maturity well beyond her thirteen years walked up to the high fence that separated the men from the women. She clutched the wire, pressing her forehead against the steel links. Her features were fragile, sensual, her overly large black eyes full of worry. Where was Valentine? They had escaped from Poland together, and now, for almost a week, they had been apart.

Valentine was tall—she hoped she could spot his light-blond head towering above the others. She peered through the fence and called out to a man passing by, "Do you know Valentine?" He shrugged his shoulders, but came nearer. She showed him a sketch of Valentine she had drawn on her pad. He shrugged his shoulders again.

She sighed mournfully. She had been walking up and down the path next to the fence every day since they had arrived at this refugee camp.

One of the Italian overseers tapped her on the shoulder. "*Andiamo!* Get back to your quarters."

She walked away slowly, reluctantly obeying. Looming ahead were the bizarre remains of the ovens that had been used to cremate Jews forty years ago. She shuddered—to think what had gone on here once, and now this strange place was a refuge for people like her. She passed a building marked OFF LIMITS and noticed that a side door was ajar. Inside, a dark hallway led her into a room filled with benches facing a table on a podium. A courtroom? She was about to leave when her eye caught something glistening in the far corner. She walked nearer. It was a rusty, dust-covered piece of iron, a kind of crucifixion. It reminded her of Christ on the cross, back in the church in Brodki. Ugly, heavy spikes fastened the elongated arms to the board. Strange letters that she could not read were written above one arm, and there was a faded blue star wrapped around the other.

She flipped open her sketch pad and started to draw. She was absorbed by this curious object until she heard a voice call out, "Luba!"

Reluctantly, she closed her pad and went outside. Her mother, a young woman not much taller than Luba and strongly resembling her daughter, stood there, arms akimbo. "I've been looking everywhere for you. Why can't you stay put for once? I've got good news."

Luba didn't respond, still engrossed in her own thoughts.

"Did you hear me? I've finally arranged to contact your father in Australia. We have a chance to get there."

"I have no father."

"Stop that talk." They walked back toward their quarters, the overseer's gaze following, glued to the mother's voluptuous figure. "What were you doing—still looking for Valentine?"

"Yes."

"Oh Luba, forget that circus tramp."

"Never. I love him."

"You don't love him—it's the circus. You've been in love with carnivals and carousels ever since you were a little girl."

Luba turned away from her mother. Then she said very softly, "I only wish I had run away with the circus when I had the chance."

The chance had come four years before.

That spring a circus caravan arrived in Brodki. The bare patch of ground on the outskirts of the small Polish town was transformed into a miniature fantasyland with colorful wagons and banners and costumed ladies and gents, the rollicking calliope music drawing people from all the surrounding villages. The carousel went round and round and children squealed with delight.

Luba spent all her time watching the tightrope troupe rehearse. They skipped across the wire, sat on precariously balanced chairs, jumped over each other. She was fascinated, and they adopted her, charmed by her enthusiasm. Sometimes they walked her across the wire, holding her gently as she swayed from side to side.

She was determined to try it alone, but when she looked down from the platform, fifteen feet above the ground, she was afraid. She bit her lip and gripped the balancing rod tightly.

She placed one foot on the wire, then the other. It swayed a little. With her very next step, she wobbled, slipped, and fell—into the arms of Josef, the father of the troupe. Panic left her as he cuddled her against his chest.

"Try again," he said firmly. "And never look at your feet." He helped her climb up the platform. One of the others handed her the pole.

This time she stayed relaxed. She looked straight out, just as he had told her. *Never look at your feet!*

She couldn't see Josef walking below her, looking up with admiration. But she could sense his presence, and it made her feel secure. She knew he would catch her if she fell. The rest of the family watched from the sidelines as Luba, in a leotard too large for her nine-year-old body, the material bagging around her little legs, kept moving.

"Relax," called out Josef in a calm voice. "Don't look down!" he added sharply.

She reached the middle of the wire, excited but no longer afraid. One foot in front of the other. They broke into a cheer when she made it to the opposite platform.

Josef took the pole, helped her down the ladder, and kissed her. The others crowded around, congratulating her and telling her she should join their troupe. She was so happy.

Luba loved the circus, the sound of the calliope—horses in wild stride on the carousel, manes flying, up and down, round and round, going nowhere. She imagined that when the carousel was locked up, the horses would step down softly and race around totally free. Then, just before dawn, they would gallop back to their places. All this without a sound.

She fantasized that she would collect her things and go with the circus when they left town. Of course, she wouldn't say anything to her mother.

She ran home as fast as her little legs would carry her. It was a cold evening, and her breath came out in little gasps of steam. She was always surprised it was never hot like the steam from the tea kettle.

She reached her street and turned the corner heading for the fourth little house from the end, stuccoed gray like the others, with only two rooms, one in front, one in back, and an outhouse in the yard. She rushed into the kitchen and stopped—a bowl of oranges was sitting on the table. She looked at the fruit with wide eyes. Oranges! From the black market! Something wonderful must have happened. Only Dada brought home oranges.

"Dada! Mama!"

There was no answer. She poked her head into the back room that was both the parlor and her parents' bedroom. Her mother was standing at the window staring at a piece of paper in her hand. Dada wasn't with her, only Uncle Felix. He wasn't really her uncle, just her father's best friend. "Don't cry, Magda," Felix was saying, his arm around Mama's shoulders. Magda continued to stare at the note in her hand.

"Mama, what's wrong?"

Before her mother could answer, there was a loud knock and the front door was pushed open. Four policemen—all with mustaches—marched in, their bulk crowding the little house.

"Where is Adam Woda?"

"My husband's not here."

"Where is he?"

"He's with relatives," Magda stammered. "In Warsaw."

"We'll check that. You come with us."

"What do you want with me?" Magda backed away, taking hold of Luba's hand. Luba felt the note being pressed into her palm.

"Come along!"

Magda looked down at her little daughter. Luba was trembling. "Please—let me take my child to my sister's."

One of the policemen roughly grabbed Magda by the arm and pulled her through the door; another scooped up two oranges in his big hairy hand.

"Magda!" shouted Felix. "I'll stay with Luba."

The police car drove off. Her mother hadn't said one word to her. Luba opened her clenched hand and looked at the crumpled piece of paper.

"It's from your father," Felix explained. "He deserted the army and escaped from Poland. He paid someone to bring over the basket of oranges and a message."

Luba read the brief note:

I love you very much. We will be together soon, I promise.

Luba tried to understand what had happened. The police had taken Mama away. Dada was gone. It was all over so quickly. Only a few oranges from the black market were left behind.

"Don't you worry," said Felix. "Everything will turn out fine. I won't leave you alone."

Luba smiled up at Felix. He grinned back, a matchstick poking out between his crooked teeth. She liked him. He played games with her and he always made her laugh.

That night Luba tossed on her cot in what had once been the kitchen pantry. She had begged Mama and Dada to make this a room of her own, so she could feel grown up. Now, with all that had happened, she felt lonely, frightened. It was so cold.

She got up and peeked into her parents' room; Felix had made up the sofa bed and was lying there, awake too. He saw her shivering in her little nightdress and raised a corner of the blanket. She crawled in.

"Why aren't you asleep?" he said.

"I'm afraid. Can I stay here?"

"Sure," he said with a smile, and pulled her little body closer.

"Let's play a game," whispered Luba. He didn't say anything. "Please, Uncle Felix."

"All right," he said sleepily.

He gently tickled her under her arm and she began to giggle. "Now you tickle me," he said.

Luba tickled his armpits. "Your turn," she said and lay back.

Felix pulled up her nightdress and slowly began to tickle her tummy. After a while, he stopped and lay back, and Luba tickled his stomach. Felix laughed. "That's enough!"

"Your turn again," giggled Luba. Now Felix gently touched the inside of her thighs. It was a pleasant feeling. Then Felix's hand slowly moved higher. It didn't make her laugh, but she liked it and just lay there.

"Now you, Luba," said Felix, spreading his legs apart. Luba placed her hand between his legs and felt something long and hard.

"What's that?" she asked.

Felix was breathing heavily. "My thumb," he finally said.

Luba laughed. Of course she knew it wasn't his thumb, but she liked touching it. She felt it get larger. He took her hand in his and kept rubbing it up and down.

"Does it hurt, Uncle Felix?"

"No, no," he gasped.

She felt his thumb thicken and pulsate. And then, as Felix let out a groan, she felt a warm, sticky liquid on her hand. Then he lay quietly; his thumb stopped pulsating and felt softer. Luba was fascinated.

He wiped off her hand with the sheet, picked her up, and carried her back to her cot. She felt drowsy and went to sleep right away.

After a few days, the police released Magda. But they didn't give up hounding her for Adam's whereabouts. That year proved horrible for her—constant poundings on the door at all hours of the day and night, interminable questioning at headquarters. She was grateful that Felix was always willing to look after Luba whenever the police took her away. Little Luba, with her big, dry eyes, never complained and never cried.

Luba was simply bewildered by the strange things that kept happening. One day as she was walking down the street with her mother, a neighbor who was the head of the local Communist party cell came up to Magda and spat at her, "Your husband's a traitor." Another time, a woman slapped Magda's face and hissed, "Stay away from my man."

After a year, the police finally left her alone, but the town didn't. How they gossiped! Magda did nothing to deserve it—she always concealed her ripe body under a loose blouse buttoned to the neck and made sure her shapely legs were covered by a long skirt. She wore no makeup and kept her hair primly pulled back in a bun.

But every wife saw a threat in an attractive woman abandoned by a traitor-husband. It was hard for Magda to find work. They wouldn't have had enough to eat if Magda's sister didn't send them something from the country. It wasn't much—fruit and vegetables, or sometimes a small piece of meat, or a scrawny old chicken.

Kids were cruel to Luba. "Your father's going to be shot!" they taunted her.

At long last a letter came from Adam. He was in a refugee camp in Turkey, near Istanbul.

"Thank God he is alive!" Magda was excited and relieved as she read the note to Luba:

My darling wife, my darling baby—I love you both. Soon I will be leaving for Australia. Find a way to get out. We will be together. And we will have a better life. I love you both and I think of you always.

Adam

Magda hugged Luba. "Let's start making plans. First, we need money—American dollars. We have to go to a big city like Gdańsk or Warsaw or Kraków, where there are jobs, rich foreign tourists. Then we'll find a way to get out."

Magda finally settled on Kraków, and went ahead, leaving Luba behind with her sister in the country. She gave her a new pair of green suede shoes as a parting gift, promising to send for her in a month's time.

But when the time came to join her mother, Luba got on the train reluctantly. The circus was back in town and she felt its hypnotic pull. The train chugged away from the little town of Brodki, where she had spent the first nine years of her life. Filled with a deep sadness, she closed her eyes as the train passed the circus caravans with their gaily painted wagons. She wanted to be with them, with Josef and his family. But soon the train was moving along faster and faster, and the caravans were out of sight.

––––––––

Magda was waiting on the crowded platform in Kraków. When she caught sight of Luba carrying all her belongings in a little cardboard suitcase and wearing her green suede shoes, she rushed over and embraced her.

"My little Luba! My little baby!" Magda was crying with happiness.

Luba wasn't crying; she was staring at the tall buildings up the hillside, so tall the tops of them were lost in a low-hanging mist; she couldn't imagine why they didn't topple over. And so many cars! Her mother was pulling her by the hand down a tree-lined parkway. The streetlamps were coming on in the gathering dusk. There were no streetlamps in Brodki.

Magda kept sniffling. Luba didn't understand. Why was her mother so emotional? She didn't see any reason to cry.

"Oh darling, you're so quiet, you must be tired. Come on—I will get you something to eat, and then to bed."

For the first time, Luba looked closely at her mother. She seemed different, wearing lipstick and mascara. And the neckline of her blouse was cut low, revealing part of her full breasts.

"You look nice," Luba said, impressed.

"Oh, thank you," said Magda, beaming. "And you look wonderful, Luba. I'm so glad you're back with me. What would you like to eat?"

"I'm not really hungry."

"Well then, we'd better get you to bed. Tomorrow we'll have a long talk and I'll show you Kraków."

Luba liked the way Magda spoke to her—more like a friend. As they made their way along the streets, Magda waved to a couple of men; she obviously had many admirers. Luba was proud of her mother. She had not realized how pretty she was.

"It's not far from here," Magda said.

They walked hand-in-hand, passing postwar cement-block high rises built in between old baroque buildings. They came to the Rynek, a cobblestoned market square closed off to traffic and filled with merchants' stalls. In the middle was an ornate building that Magda said was called "Sukiennice," Cloth Hall. That's where Copernicus bought his robes when he lived here, she said. Luba wasn't paying attention; she clutched her mother's hand more tightly as she stared at the grotesquely misshapen heads that leered from the tops of the hall's pillars. "Oh," Magda laughed, "don't be frightened—they're only gargoyles."

Hectic activity, new sights and sounds, engulfed her—dishes clattering in the open-air cafés, the smells of espresso, accordion music, the voices of happy people babbling in Polish, French, English, and many other tongues.

They finally came to a dilapidated three-story apartment building. The wide stone steps were chipped and the wrought-iron balustrade was rusty. Up two flights, they entered a small room. It had an old-fashioned steel-framed bed on one side, a small cot on the other, and in between, a bureau with a hot plate and sink next to it. The shared toilet was at the end of the hall. Magda put Luba's bag on the cot. "You'll sleep here. Let's put your things away. I've got to work tonight."

"Where do you work?" asked Luba.

"It's a small room, but I think it should be comfortable, don't you?" said Magda, as if she hadn't heard Luba's question.

"If you're late, Mama, I can put my things away."

Magda looked at her. "You're sure you'll be all right?"

"Yes."

Again, tears welled in Magda's eyes and she bent down and hugged her tightly. "Ah, my little girl, I'm so glad you're here. I really missed you."

"Me too, Mama."

"As soon as we have enough money, we'll find a way out of here. We'll find Dada, and we'll all be together again."

Luba wanted to respond with enthusiasm, but something held her back.

"Won't it be wonderful, darling?"

"Yes, Mama."

Magda kissed her on the cheek. "You can put your things in this drawer, then go to bed." She kissed her again.

Luba could hear her mother's footsteps hurrying down the stone staircase, fading away. She looked around the room; on the bureau was a picture of her father with a little girl on his knees—the girl was Luba. She sat down on the cot, trying to sort out all that had happened. It was a warm evening, and through the open window she could hear the excitement of the city floating up to her. Listening to the beautiful noises, she held her breath for a moment—there it was, a calliope. How she loved that sound! It gave her a feeling that she was going to like this place.

As she undressed, she caught a glimpse of her body in the cracked mirror above the bureau. She pushed her hands up against her chest and formed two small breasts. Yes! Something was growing there! When would she have nice full breasts like her mother? She put on her nightdress and got into her little cot. She lay listening to the sounds, thinking of Josef. She missed him. Did he miss her too? She thought about Felix, and it made her smile. Would he find someone else to play with his thumb? Somehow, Luba thought, he would. Although she was very tired, she couldn't sleep. She lay with her eyes closed, letting different thoughts tumble over each other. She was excited, apprehensive, but she was glad to be with her mother again. She began to dream—she was falling through a blue sky, and just as she became frightened, she fell into the arms of Josef. Cuddled tightly to his chest, she felt safe.

She heard the door open. She hadn't been aware of any footsteps. She was about to say, "Mama, I'm still awake," when she saw, in the open doorway, two figures, not one. The other figure was Stash, a tour guide who had spoken to her mother in the street.

Magda whispered, "Shhh, don't wake her." In the dim light Luba saw them walk over to the bed. They embraced. She could hear the rustling of their clothes, but could not make out what they said. Occasionally, her mother would giggle. Luba lay there motionless, watching cautiously. They had their clothes off, and her mother was sitting on the edge of the bed, leaning back on her elbows, and Stash was down on his knees with his head buried between her legs. Luba strained to see more through the darkness.

Now they were in bed. She listened to the sounds and watched the strange shadowy movements of their bodies. She heard a sharp sound, like a slap, then she could faintly make out Stash's form covering her mother. Stifled moans and gasps came from the bed. Luba took shallow breaths. She wanted to hear everything.

After a while, all was quiet, and then she heard a slight snore. When Luba opened her eyes, the room was filled with sunlight. Her mother was sleeping—alone. Nothing was said about the nocturnal visitor.

―――――

They spent two days touring Kraków, eating cotton candy, buying trinkets, giggling in the streets. Magda bought Luba a new school uniform—a black shiny apron with a round white collar and a small knapsack for her schoolbooks.

But the little vacation was soon over. Luba dressed hurriedly—she was going to enroll in school, and she was excited about making new friends. Magda helped her braid her hair in two pigtails and tied a white taffeta bow on each end. Then they walked up the street toward the school, which was next to an old Catholic church. A tall, thin young priest in a long black cassock stood by the door like a sentinel. His narrow face was very pale under his thick black eyebrows.

The school building seemed brand-new and four times the size of Luba's school in Brodki. The playground was filled with children of all ages, laughing, running, screaming. In a short time, Luba was enrolled. Her mother kissed her before she hurried off down the street. Luba happily approached the seething mass of children in the play area. Then, a large fat girl jumped in front of her, wrinkled up her nose in disgust, and shouted in her face, "Your mother's a whore!"

―――――

Other men came on other nights. When Magda brought a man into the room, Luba rarely slept. She found those interludes confusing, yet she was always excited by them. But sometimes Magda would not come home at all. Bored, waiting for her mother, Luba would doodle on whatever paper she could find—brown paper bags, mostly. Her doodles grew into elaborate drawings of fanciful carousels and fairy-tale horses with stars for eyes and crescent moons braided into their manes.

Frequently in the morning when Luba woke up, she would find her mother still asleep; she would get dressed quietly, and go off to school. She hated school. History was dull—she didn't care that Madame Curie-Sklodowska discovered radium or that Comrade Yury Gagarin was the first man in space. She detested long division. And she already read and wrote Polish, so why did she now have to learn Russian and the Cyrillic alphabet too? She was bored and lonely. Once a girl invited her to her house—only once. The parents did not want their child associating with the daughter of a traitor and a whore.

Most mornings, to avoid the other schoolchildren, Luba went to the church. She sat quietly in the back pew inhaling the thick smoky incense, planning how to run away—to the circus, to Josef. And yet, every day, she forced herself to walk up the street toward the school.

The chimes from the church clock tolled seven. The playground was quiet in the soft light of the early morning. How deserted it seemed. The last chime drifted up the hillside. She had an hour before school. Luba turned toward the open door of the church and walked in. Far down, in front of the altar, the young priest was praying. Luba sat in the back pew and tried to pray too. But instead, tears began to spill from her eyes.

Then she felt a firm hand on her shoulder, and a quiet voice said, "What is it, my child?"

Luba couldn't answer. She got up and started to leave.

"Come with me," said the young priest.

He put his arm around her shoulders and guided her down the aisle. At the altar he genuflected, then led her into the vestry and closed the door.

The room was small and sparsely furnished with a table, two chairs, and many books. He motioned to a chair and sat down opposite her. "God will help you," he said in a calm voice.

Violent sobs shook her body as she poured out her grief at last. "I want to run away—I hate it here. I want to join the circus. I want to be with Josef!"

The young priest listened calmly.

Luba knelt before him with her head in his lap. He stroked her hair, and she felt safe and protected.

"It's God's will, my child." His voice was very soothing. And then she was drained—no tears, no anger, no bitterness. She let her head rest in his lap and she felt completely relaxed and grateful.

The priest continued to stroke Luba's head, and she felt something hard against her cheek. She smiled—Uncle Felix's thumb. This was an opportunity to repay the priest for his kindness. She moved her head slowly from side to side. A low moan escaped his lips.

Suddenly, he got up, his face flushed. "Go with God," he said, making a sign of the cross on her forehead. She didn't understand. Why had he dismissed her so abruptly? But she left the church and hurried to school.

The next morning, as the chimes were striking seven, she again entered the church. It was empty. The morning sun threw long beams of dusty light along the high narrow arches. Luba sat there waiting. She was anxious to talk to the priest again. He had helped her so much. She waited until the school bell clanged, but he never appeared. She ran out and missed being late by moments.

The following day she came earlier, and this time she found the young priest intensely praying at the altar. Slowly she walked down the aisle toward him. When he saw her, he stood up, crossed himself, and hurried away into the vestry.

Luba was stunned. What had she done wrong? From the large crucifix hanging in the nave of the church, Christ seemed to be staring down at her. She took a deep breath and approached the vestry door. "Father," she said softly. There was no answer. She knocked. She knew he was there. She knocked again. Silence. She turned the handle—the door was locked.

Rejected once again, Luba refused to cry. She walked out of the church toward the school.

———

Magda worried about leaving Luba alone so much; she felt worse when she had to bring customers home, but there was no alternative. She was registered with the authorities as the wife of a traitor. That made her ineligible for employment in any state-run enterprise, which took care of 98 percent of all business establishments in Poland. The few privately run restaurants and shops employed friends

and relatives. There was only one way of making a living. And competition was tough; many women were willing to sell their bodies for
foreign goods and American dollars.

Life was dreary for Luba with no friends. She pestered her mother
to take her to the Rynek, and finally Magda relented. Luba enjoyed it
—the music, the gaiety, the foreigners.

Magda tried to protect her. At first, she slapped the men away when
they grabbed at Luba's nubile body. But she realized that customers
were titillated by the proximity of a young, pretty girl, and were
willing to pay more. Luba didn't mind that they touched a little; she
liked the attention, and Magda realized that it was becoming increas-
ingly difficult to keep Luba, now almost twelve, in a passive role.

Magda was always happy when Stash's tour bus rolled into town. His
customers paid in American dollars, and it meant she didn't have to
stand around soliciting, looking over her shoulder for the police.
This time he would be with them for at least ten days. There would be
good food to eat, maybe new clothes to wear. And some fun!

The first night he took both of them to the best restaurant in
Kraków—the Koń Morski, the Seahorse, just off the Rynek. Luba had
never seen such a place—she had never been to a real restaurant
before. The ceilings were draped with fishing nets and hung with
bright starfish, the rough walls thickly whitewashed. At the entrance
was a small, richly carved old mahogany bar and, above it, a clock
decorated with the signs of the zodiac. The tables were covered with
spotless white linen. A man in a gypsy costume sat in a corner playing
a mandolin and singing love songs.

They ate huge platters of fresh carp, and Luba tried her first sip of
vodka. "It's the best," Stash said, "Wyborowa. You'll get spoiled." He
laughed at her expression as the strong, fiery liquid went down her
throat.

The second night, Magda and Stash went out without Luba. Before
they left, Stash gave her a present, blue jeans from America. Luba
squealed with delight. He scooped her up in her nightdress and
tucked her in bed still clutching her jeans.

Luba couldn't sleep—she had to try them on. They were a little big,
but that could be fixed. She paraded in front of the mirror, admiring
the cowboy embroidered on her bottom. Too bad no one was there to
see her. She went back to her cot. Magda and Stash were at that
restaurant having a good time. She was jealous. It was fun to be with

Stash. As she lay there unable to sleep, an idea formed in her mind. Hours passed.

Finally she heard Magda's voice outside the door: "Not too loud; she's asleep—she has to go to school tomorrow." Luba was pleased to hear Stash say, "I like that little one!"

They were in bed now. She could hear them kissing. She crawled out of her cot, made her way across the floor, and jumped on their bed. "Mama, I'm cold."

"What are you doing here?" cried out a startled Magda. She quickly pulled up the sheet to cover their naked bodies.

"I want to be with you."

"No, you go right back to your bed."

"Stash," Luba pleaded, putting her arms around him, "I want to be here—don't let her chase me out!"

"Oh, let her stay. Come on, Magda, we can all be together."

Magda knew she had lost the battle.

———

The second winter in Kraków was a bad one, very cold, with snow up to Luba's knees and a strong wind blowing down from the north. No tour buses. No Stash. Magda stood in long lines at the baker's and the butcher's and often, after hours of waiting, she was turned away—everything sold out. To get any decent food you had to bribe people, and they all wanted dollars or francs or marks—anything but worthless Polish zlotys. But Magda couldn't risk spending the American dollars she had accumulated and hidden in the bedsprings. She needed every dollar for their escape. Magda always kept her dream alive—to get out of Poland and find Adam. It would happen, she was sure, and they would all be together.

Then Magda got caught trying to sell some stockings on the black market. One of the women, doubtless to eliminate some competition, informed on her to the police. They kept her at the jail overnight.

Luba was frightened and hungry. When Magda got back, they made soup with some potatoes Luba had "borrowed" from the grocer. There was nothing else in the house. The police had taken away the stockings Magda had been trying to sell and the little money she had been carrying.

Mother and daughter didn't say much to each other. They ate the soup quietly and went to their beds to keep warm.

"Mama, I'm still cold," said Luba through the darkness.

"All right," Magda mumbled as she made room for Luba to crawl in.

Luba snuggled against her mother's warm body, thinking how odd that she still felt just like a little girl, even though they shared such womanly secrets now. The wind howled outside, beating against the frosted windowpane.

Luba broke the silence. "Well it won't be long before spring."

"Thank God," said Magda.

"And then Stash will be back . . . won't he?"

"I hope so."

"I like Stash. And you do too, don't you?"

Magda didn't answer.

"You know I watched you," Luba went on. "Many times. You thought I was sleeping."

"Luba!"

"Oh yes. I could tell. You liked Stash the best."

"Luba, I don't want to talk about it. It's enough I have to do these things to make a living."

"Not a bad way to make a living. And it's fun. Remember the night we were all in bed together?"

"Luba! What's wrong with you?!"

"Oh come on, Mama." She started to giggle. "No matter what you say, you liked it."

"Stop that talk," Magda said weakly.

"You got so excited. And I did too."

When Luba opened her eyes, Magda was making coffee at the hot plate. She handed Luba a cup and sat on the bed. They looked at each other and Luba saw that her mother's eyes were moist.

"What have I done to you? I should have left you in Brodki."

Luba's mouth curled into a wry smile. "Stop it, Magda."

This was the first time she called her mother Magda. She would never call her Mama again.

———

As they sat there quietly sipping coffee, each in her own thoughts, there was a knock on the door. The mailman.

Magda tore open the envelope—a letter from Felix. But inside was a second letter. She gasped. "It's from your father!"

She read the note, put it down, and went over to refill her cup of coffee. Her face radiated happiness. Luba waited.

"Adam is in Australia. Brisbane. He is beginning to do well. He wants us with him and he'll send money when he hears we got out."

Luba was sorry the letter had come. They hadn't heard from him in such a long time. She didn't think of Adam as her father anymore. It was too late for that.

"Now's the time. We're going to escape," Magda said. She waved the letter. "This is what I waited for." With growing excitement, she babbled on about a man who could help them get out of the country. She lifted up the mattress and pulled out the dollars, wrapped in an old newspaper and wedged into the springs. She started counting. "We've got enough. We're going to escape!"

Sipping her coffee, Luba watched her mother impassively.

Magda threw a scarf around her head and went out into the cold. An hour later she was back, still excited. "I found him. He'll take us across the border."

"Which border? Russia? East Germany? Czechoslovakia? Maybe we'll walk across the Baltic Sea to Sweden like Jesus," Luba scoffed.

"Don't be a smart aleck. This man is our chance to get to Australia. He knows how to get forged passports and visas."

"Why would he take the risk for us?"

"Because I paid him. He's done it many times."

"You paid him?" asked Luba.

"*Half* the money. Don't be suspicious. Come on—help me get our things together. We meet him at five o'clock."

Reluctantly, Luba helped Magda collect their belongings. They left the flat, each carrying a shawl tied together in a bundle, and made their way down the windy street to the rendezvous point, a little café. Inside sat a surly-looking character sipping a glass of cognac. Between sips he said, "Where's the rest of the money?"

Magda gave it to him without a word. Two policemen with mustaches appeared at the table. It was over before it started.

———

The chestnut trees were in bloom. Spring came to Kraków and with it a carnival troupe. As soon as she heard the sound of the calliope, Luba ran breathlessly to the Wisla River, where the caravan was quartered. But it wasn't Josef's circus—just a tiny band, a couple of clowns, jugglers, acrobats, a carousel, but no high-wire act. She was disappointed. Then she met Valentine.

Valentine was very dashing. He reminded her of Josef, except he was much younger, about twenty-one. He was in charge of the carousel. The first time Luba saw him, he was nonchalantly leaning against a stanchion as the carousel circled, his cap perched on the back of his blond head. She wished she had undone her pigtails and put on some of her mother's makeup. He looked at her—she was sure—each time the carousel went around. Luba was now a beautiful girl-woman, her little breasts pushing against her blouse and her big black eyes looking calmly ahead, those eyes that had seen so much. She was riveted, waiting to get another glimpse of him as he kept going round and round.

She had no money to take a ride. The other girls climbed aboard, giggling and mooning over Valentine, while she stood quietly to one side, listening to the poignant calliope music. It tried to be happy with cymbals clanging, but there was always a sadness, a yearning, a crying out for something to happen. And something did.

Valentine stepped off the carousel and sauntered over to her, his hands behind his back. He looked down at her face and winked. Luba's heart beat faster. She'd never felt this way before. He waved a hand in front of her face, a brass ring in his fingers.

"You won it," he said. "You get a free ride!"

With a rough grip, he took her by the waist and easily lifted her up onto one of the horses.

"Go ahead—try to get another brass ring," he urged. "This is your lucky day!"

Around and around she went, rocking with the up-and-down movement of the horse. She tried to catch the golden ring, but it didn't matter if she missed—Valentine let her ride anyway.

―――――

Now, when Magda needed her help, Luba was always at the carousel. The competition was getting tougher, with more girls around every year. Magda had finally agreed to Luba's more active role, because they needed to recoup the money she had lost in their failed attempt to escape. But Luba let her mother down. Night after night, she promised she would meet Magda on the Rynek, and night after night, she would be riding the carousel, her long brown hair flying, her eyes glued to Valentine. Sometimes he would disappear, and Luba would count the girls milling about. Then she knew which one was in his little room not far from the river. She would wait patiently for him to return, and when he did, he was always pleased to see her. But would he ever take *her* to his little room?

One day, he simply said to her, "Come on," and strode off. Luba followed, hurrying to keep up. Finally, it was going to happen. She had known if she was patient enough, she would end up in his arms, in his room. She was glad that she had waited.

It was difficult to keep up with his long strides. And she was surprised to find they were heading toward the Wawel, the castle of Polish kings.

"Where are we going?" she asked.

"Trust me," he said, and he increased the length of his strides.

They climbed up the old stone steps to the statue of General Kościuszko, then hiked along the fortification wall to the Gothic castle built by King Casimir the Great. Through the slits in the castle walls cannons protruded, standing ready against Poland's enemies. They looked down at the same view that the king had seen—the glistening Wisła River embracing the city, the spires of the cathedrals jutting up like black spikes against the bright sky. Luba tried to find the carousel along the riverbank; it was hidden in the chestnut trees, but in the quiet she could hear the faint sounds of the calliope.

She studied Valentine, his firm chin, high cheekbones, the mouth always ready to break into a sassy grin. His arms were folded across his chest as he stood staring out across the city, lost in his own thoughts. She waited a long time before she broke the silence. "What a beautiful place!"

"I come here once in a while—to get away."

"I've seen you get away from the carousel with some of your girls—"

"They're little *kurvas*—whores!" he laughed.

Luba winced when she heard the word. How much does he know about Magda? she wondered. How much does he know about me?

"I never bring them here," he continued. "This is where I dream."

Luba hesitated, afraid to interrupt. "What do you dream about?" she asked timidly.

"San Francisco."

"San Francisco? Where's that?"

"California. In America. That's where I want to go."

"Why there?"

"I heard a song." And he sang, "*San Francisco, open your golden gates!* Did you ever hear it?"

She shook her head and Valentine continued, "I want to get away from this shitty place—it's a goddamn Communist prison! And these useless Solidarity strikes only make things worse." He leaped up on the parapet. "I want to march through those golden gates!" And in a loud voice that echoed against the castle walls, he sang: "*San Francisco, open your golden gates . . . la la la, la, la la-la . . .*" Those were the only words he knew.

"When I have enough dollars, I'll get to Vienna and then work my way to San Francisco." He jumped down from the parapet.

"There're a lot of countries between here and Vienna," Luba remarked.

"My friend Zbig works in the freight yard. He loads trains—export goods for Austria and other countries. He'll help me." Valentine winked.

Luba had seen Zbig—a short, skinny boy about eighteen—talking with Valentine around the carousel. Zbig always had stolen stuff with him—chocolate, vodka, canned ham—and Valentine would help him sell his booty on the black market.

They strolled around a little longer, then stopped in a shady, grassy grove. Luba's heart quickened. He would make love to her now, she was sure. But he took her hand and said, "Let's go back to the carousel."

Luba was disappointed. Didn't he want her? Oblivious, Valentine was humming. The light of the setting sun shimmered on the gold cupola of the King's Cathedral. Luba's disappointment dissolved. He was still holding her hand. She hummed along with him.

The next day the hours at school dragged by. Finally it was three o'clock! Luba raced to the river.

She walked around the carousel, but there was no sign of Valentine. She didn't dare ask questions of his assistant. Hours passed. Luba waited.

At last she saw him walking with Zbig. They were talking so intensely, they didn't notice her approach.

"This is our chance," Zbig was saying. "Nobody's guarding the freight yard. The army's up north in Gdańsk to deal with the Solidarity strike and—" He stopped abruptly.

Valentine spun around to Luba. She had never seen him so agitated. His face was ashen.

"Take me with you," she said.

"What are you talking about?"

"You're going to escape, I know it."

They stared at her.

"Please."

"It's too risky," snapped Zbig.

"We'll take the chance," said Luba.

"Who is *we*?" Zbig demanded.

"My mother will come with us."

"Are you crazy?!"

"An older woman will make a good cover," she said, looking at Valentine imploringly. "Please—I want to be with you."

Without answering her, Valentine took Zbig aside. Luba couldn't hear their conversation, but it was evident that Zbig wasn't pleased; he was shaking his head violently. Finally Valentine came back to Luba. The church bells were tolling five o'clock.

"Meet us at the Rondo in two hours."

"You won't leave without me?"

"Yes, we will, if you're not there." His voice was hard. "It's the seven o'clock bus for the freight yards in Nowa Huta. And bring *dollars,* not zlotys."

Luba ran home, rushed up the stairs, and burst into the room. Magda was putting on makeup before the cracked mirror that hung over the bureau.

Luba laid out the plan.

"Impossible! It can't work," was Magda's first reaction.

"You're wrong. They know what they're doing."

"It's too dangerous! Next time it's five years in jail for me. And the police will take you away."

Luba was wrapping her belongings in a shawl. "They're going to make it!"

"Stop it!" said Magda, slapping the bundle out of her hands.

Luba picked up the bundle and glared at her mother. "If we don't do it this time, we'll never do it. We're taking the seven o'clock bus from the Rondo."

"Luba, please—we can't take the risk."

"Well, *I'm* going to take it—with you or without you." And she turned toward the door.

Magda gasped, "I should have left you in Brodki!"

Luba gave her mother another hard look. "Then why the hell didn't you?" And she rushed out.

Magda leaned on the bureau and pressed her forehead against the mirror. Could her daughter be leaving—abandoning her? Tears now streaked her face and smudged her mascara. The clock said six, one hour before the bus departure.

Pulling herself together, she quickly repaired her makeup and hurried down to the Rynek. There, she approached a lonely tourist, whispered in his ear. He nodded. She took him down an alley. They would need money.

She paced the crowded Rondo station nervously. Where was Luba? They were calling out the bus departure. Panic gripped her—Luba must already be on her way. Desperate, she quickly bought a ticket for Nowa Huta and boarded the bus just as it took off, stumbling over the passengers' bundles as she made her way down the aisle. Then she caught her breath. At the back was Luba, sitting alone. Across from her were Valentine and Zbig, their eyes closed, pretending to be tired travelers. Magda sat down beside her daughter, but Luba ignored her. Puzzled, Magda was about to speak when she realized Luba was staring straight ahead at a policeman moving through the bus. The policeman sat down. Luba reached over and squeezed her mother's hand.

The bus reached Nowa Huta in less than an hour. As they got nearer their stop they heard people yelling, but they couldn't make out the words. With some apprehension they hurried off behind the other passengers. Then they saw the source of the commotion. Marching toward the central plaza was a large group of steelworkers demonstrating sympathy with the strikers in Gdańsk. ZOMO, the riot police, helmeted and carrying bats and shields, had circled the group. "This will help us," Zbig whispered. "Just follow me." As they circled the plaza to avoid the marchers, Luba looked up at the towering black granite statue of Lenin, six stories high. He seemed to be glowering at them, as if he knew their secret. She shuddered.

Valentine nudged her. "Good-bye, comrade," he chuckled. Luba put her arm around his waist.

As they approached the freight yard, the shouts of the marchers receded in the distance, taken over by the loud clanging of trains as they coupled together, wheels screeching against the tracks. Locomotives, their headlights bright, seemed to be moving in all directions on a maze of glistening steel. Zbig led them to a grassy slope. "Let's have the money," he said.

They all reached into their bundles and extracted the specified amount—their precious American dollars, everything they had—for freedom.

As he disappeared down the tracks in the darkness, Magda asked, "Can we trust him?"

"We'll soon find out," said Valentine with a shrug. They waited quietly, watching the hypnotic movements of the iron behemoths. Zbig's voice startled them: "It's set." He squatted down, pointing to a man shuffling along a row of train cars, his lantern held high. The man stopped, pulled open the door, waved his lantern, and kept walking. "That's our car." They all clambered aboard and Zbig pushed the sliding door shut. In the darkness, they crouched down among crates and boxes, uncertain, waiting.

"What happens—" Luba began.

"Shhh . . . keep your voice low until the train starts moving," Zbig whispered.

Suddenly, the door rattled and then they heard a pounding. Magda and Luba hugged each other, petrified. The noise ceased. "That's my friend sealing the door," Zbig reassured them.

"Sealing us in? Why?" Luba asked.

His voice sounded contemptuous. "All cars are checked at the borders. If the seal is broken, the car is taken off."

"But how do we get out?" Magda asked.

"That's my job," said Zbig.

With a tremendous jerk that slammed them all against the boxes, the train started, very slowly gaining speed.

Valentine shined his flashlight around the car's crates. "Let's see who's traveling with us. Well, I'll be—" He started to laugh. "The best of Polish porkers, Krakus canned hams. It's time for a celebration."

With that he extracted one of the cans, peeled back the tin lid, and started to cut the ham into pieces with his pocketknife.

"Now I know what happens to all the ham we can never find at the market," Luba joked. "It escapes to the free world." They all laughed.

Zbig produced a bottle of vodka from his coat pocket. Before taking a swig he toasted, "To our new home—Vienna."

Valentine grabbed the bottle. "To San Francisco!" He took a large gulp and handed the bottle to Magda.

"To Australia," she toasted, relaxing and catching the spirit.

Luba brought the bottle to her lips and looked into Valentine's eyes. "To San Francisco," she said softly.

Emptying the bottle, they all sang loudly, above the clanging of the train, "*Sto lat! Sto lat!* May you live one hundred years!" in honor of Zbig, who had led them out of captivity.

"How long before we reach the Austrian border?" Luba asked.

"About ten hours. Relax—you've got plenty of time," Zbig said, settling down on top of some crates and rolling his jacket into a pillow.

Luba eased away from her mother and moved to where Valentine had stretched out in front of the door. He made room on his jacket pillow for her head, and they lay cheek to cheek.

In the darkness, Magda could make out the intertwined forms of Luba and Valentine as, alone, she huddled in the corner, wrapped in her own feelings of rejection. Now she knew why Luba had stopped helping her at the Rynek.

"Are you sorry you came?" Valentine asked Luba.

"No," she answered simply.

"Are you afraid?"

Luba's hand reached over and caressed his face. "I love you."

The words sounded so strange to Luba. She had never said them before. They were words that she had heard in the movies, always spoken by a glamorous woman with manicured fingernails and wearing a diaphanous gown to a handsome man sipping cognac in a tailored robe. Here, they were lying on a hard floor among crates of ham, the rattling of the train jarring their tired bones. She felt Valentine's lips on her forehead, her eyebrows, her eyes, her nose, until they met her lips. The kiss Valentine gave Luba was sweeter than any she had ever seen on the screen.

They woke up with a jolt. Wheels screeched and couplings crashed; the train was coming to a stop. Thin shafts of sunlight crept in through the cracks of the car's siding.

Everybody scrambled up.

"Shhh," Zbig cautioned, as they heard voices outside. "This must be the Austro-Hungarian border check."

Valentine pressed his ear close to the crack in the door, trying to make out the words.

"Hungarian?" Zbig whispered. Valentine answered with a shrug; he couldn't understand.

"German?" ventured Zbig.

"No way."

The train started up again and they sighed with relief. Zbig looked at his watch. "Two more hours and we should be in Vienna."

"What do we do there?" Luba asked.

"We open the door and ask for political asylum."

"That's all there is to it?"

"Yeah—I hear they're very nice. They'll put us up at a refugee camp."

Six more hours had passed. Vestiges of daylight still filtered into the car. The train seemed to be going faster than ever before. When would they stop? Where was Vienna? Where were they heading? Everyone darted glances at Zbig, who kept consulting his watch.

"Zbig, where are we?" Luba finally asked point-blank.

"I don't know—we should have been in Vienna hours ago. Maybe the train is late." For the first time Zbig looked scared.

"Or maybe we're going in the wrong direction," she challenged.

"Well, if we are, we're in Moscow by now," Valentine said jokingly.

"Don't be funny," Zbig muttered.

"You're all getting irritated because you're hungry," Magda said, trying to break up the tension. "Let's open up another can."

Luba rolled her eyes. "I never want to eat another ham as long as I live."

Valentine bent down to peer through a crack, trying to determine which way the dimming sun was setting. "I think we're going south."

"To Yugoslavia? Can't be," grumbled Zbig.

"Why don't we open the door and find out where we are before it gets dark?" Luba was trying to stifle her exasperation.

"Yeah," laughed Valentine. "If we see snow it's Siberia."

"Knock it off," said a worried Zbig. "It's crazy to open that door."

Luba stood up and faced him. "Listen, you're the one that's crazy—you set it up, you took our money, and now you don't know where the hell we are."

"But what if we're not out of the Communist bloc yet? It's too dangerous to open the door and break the seal!" Zbig insisted, his voice rising in agitation.

"Calm down," Valentine said placatingly. "No one's blaming you, Zbig. You did everything you could, but I think Luba is right—"

"Right?!"

"Yes—we've been locked up here for a long time. You say we're six hours overdue and this train hasn't been crawling. Let's open the damn door."

"I tell you it's a mistake."

"Let's find out if it is—and then figure out what to do."

Without waiting for a response, Valentine went over to the door. Reluctantly, Zbig joined him, and together they shoved against it, breaking the seal. The door slid open.

The wind rushed in on them. It felt good after so many hours in the stuffy car. The train was passing verdant pastures with sheep and cows grazing peacefully. They saw road signs too far away to make out, a small car at a railroad crossing, a boy herding cows—he waved to them.

"I like it here," Luba said. "Let's get off."

"You're too young to die—the train's going about eighty kilometers an hour," said Valentine.

They crouched down, looking out, feeling the cool breeze, their eyes searching for some sign of hope. As night began to fall, lights flickered in the distance. Suddenly, the train slowed.

"Now's our chance," cried Luba.

"Not yet—it's still too fast," cautioned Valentine. "I'll tell you when." They all huddled around the open door. "Now get ready—and jump in the direction the train's moving. I'll jump first, then you, Zbig, and we'll help Luba and her mother."

He held on to the side of the open door, gave Luba a reassuring wink, then jumped, and, landing on his feet, ran along with the slow-moving train. Zbig followed, stumbled but didn't fall, and then Luba and Magda. They hid in the tall grass, watching the wheels rumble by. When the train's taillights disappeared in the distance, they headed through a meadow, aiming for the lights of a farmhouse on top of a nearby hill. A dog was barking.

"It doesn't look like Paris and doesn't smell like Russia," said Valentine with not too much gaiety. Everyone was tense. "Stay put and I'll go over there and find out where the hell we are."

"Be careful," Luba pleaded.

"Here, take this," Magda offered.

"Ham? What for?"

"A dog of any country should love Polish ham."

They waited apprehensively for Valentine to return. It seemed like an eternity. Then he came running, stumbling through the meadow. When he reached them, he lifted Luba in his arms. "*Aleluja!* We're in Italy!"

"What?"

"I looked through the farmhouse window—they were drinking red wine and eating huge plates of spaghetti. And"—he kissed Magda's cheek—"their dog loved the ham."

———

By midnight they had reached an Italian police station, and there they asked for asylum. It turned out they were in the town of Trieste, just over the Yugoslav border. The police, used to refugees crossing over, were kind; they let them sleep in the prison cells—Luba and Magda in one, Valentine and Zbig in the other.

Luba threw herself on a bunk close to Valentine's adjoining cell. She pushed her mouth against the bars, and Valentine's was there to meet hers. They kissed for a long time, oblivious to everyone around them.

From the other bunk, Magda watched. Tears began to form in her eyes as she whispered softly, "Happy birthday, my baby." It was the morning of Luba's thirteenth birthday, but Luba had forgotten.

———

Later in the day they were put on a bus. The driver told them that their destination was a refugee camp—San Sabba; once used as a place to exterminate Jews and Italian partisans, it was now a haven for those escaping Communist oppression.

At the camp, the new arrivals were separated. Luba could see Valentine's blond head towering above the others as the men filed through a distant door. He seemed to be looking for her.

When her group got inside, an Italian overseer in a rumpled uniform told them to take off their clothes and go into the shower stalls. He didn't leave while they undressed. Many were embarrassed, but didn't dare complain—the fear of being sent back was still with them. Naked, they shuffled down the corridor.

Is Valentine doing the same thing? wondered Luba. Do they have women guards in the men's section?

Once washed and dressed again, they were taken to the quarantine building to be questioned by Italian immigration officials: "Why did you leave the country?"—"Do you have a prison record?"—"Do you have any diseases?"

Luba wondered how Valentine answered these questions.

Luba and Magda were given a small room on the third tier. Their window gave out onto a courtyard divided by a chain-link fence; on the opposite side was the building housing the men. But Luba didn't see Valentine.

That night, as Luba and Magda lay side by side on their cots, Luba thought how strange it was that they brought refugees here, a camp that had housed people waiting to die. She was waiting to live, hoping to end up in Valentine's arms. Her thoughts were interrupted by Magda's voice.

"Forgive me."

"What?"

"Forgive me for everything I've done. I've been a bad mother."

"Stop it," said Luba.

"No! You never had a chance to be a little girl. But everything will change now—you'll see. We will have a different life, a good life together."

Together? thought Luba. She wanted to be together with Valentine, not her mother. She didn't want to be a little girl. She wanted to be a woman—Valentine's woman. She jumped up from the bed and went over to the small barred window. She looked across the silent courtyard, and in a loud voice, she sang out: *"San Francisco, open your golden gates!"*

Magda bolted up in bed. "What's the matter with you?!"

Like an echo, Valentine's voice answered: *"San Francisco, open your golden gates!"*

"What's that?" said Magda.

"Just a song," Luba said, bouncing back on her cot. Magda couldn't see the happy smile on her face as Luba pulled the blanket around herself.

─────────

Magda met with the Red Cross representative. Their immigration to Australia would not be a problem, she was told, since Adam was waiting for them in Brisbane. The only thing needed was a statement from him confirming that he would guarantee their passage. Magda was relieved; that shouldn't take long. But Luba was restless, pacing the fence in the courtyard, still looking for Valentine.

A week later they were ordered to assemble with their belongings in the reception hall. When they arrived, they found about sixty other refugees already lined up. Luba looked around anxiously, and there was Valentine, smiling at her from the other side of the room. Each night she had been praying to see him. Luba now believed in God.

They were led out of the building to two buses. She hoped that they would be on the same bus, but she didn't have time for another prayer. The official checking off the names put Valentine and Zbig on the second bus. No explanations, no information. There had been rumors of a transfer to a camp near Milan. Maybe this was it, and at last they would be together.

The buses started up, and Luba twisted around in her seat, trying to catch a glimpse of Valentine on the second bus.

They traveled down a long dirt road onto the main highway. At the crossing, her bus made a left turn and headed south. Looking out the back window, Luba saw the second bus turn in the opposite direction.

She gasped. North! Back to Poland?! Her bus picked up speed.

The buses were racing apart. What would happen to him? Would he go to jail? Would he go back to the carousel? Would he ever go through those golden gates? She looked again—Valentine's bus had dropped out of sight behind a hill.

Luba crumpled in her seat. Her heart tightened. She was dizzy, queasy. A voice she tried to stifle was saying, "You'll never see Valentine again."

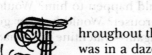

CHAPTER 3

1945 | Syracuse, New York

hroughout the flight from Trieste to Syracuse, "Danny" was in a daze. His fists clenched, he sat tensely aboard the army transport plane, wedged against Tyrone, the black marine who had led him out of San Sabba. The all-black paratrooper squad sang songs and joked, happy to be going home, but Danny wasn't sure what "home" meant. He knew only one thing—he and Tyrone would be separated.

Since the day three months before when Tyrone walked him out of San Sabba, they had been together. At first Tyrone meant to load him onto the big army truck with the other liberated Jews, but Danny clung desperately to the black man's neck.

"You're going to a nice place—don't be afraid," Tyrone tried to reassure him. But Danny, remembering the truck that had taken his whole family away from the farm, just clutched harder. The marine set him down and stooped to reason with him, but Danny's eyes registered terror.

"The hell with it," Tyrone finally said, tossing the boy over his shoulder and jumping aboard his green jeep. He took Danny with him to a small abandoned hotel, where his paratrooper squad was headquartered. The lieutenant in charge pretended not to see this little white stowaway sticking out among his black men.

Danny became the mascot of the squad. The marines laughed at his ravenous appetite, heaping huge portions of corned-beef hash on his plate. They taught him a smattering of English—"Geronimo" and "screw-up" were the first words he learned. Then the squad was ordered back to home base in Syracuse. "Don't worry, Danny boy, you're coming with us," Tyrone insisted, but as the army transport plane revved up its engines, Danny found himself shaking like a leaf. Where was he going? What would happen?

When they finally landed, the men hooted and hollered. Tyrone picked Danny up and carried him down the tarmac to a black station wagon with ST. JOHN'S ORPHANAGE printed on its door. From inside, a pyramid of black cloth emerged. "I'm Sister Mary Theresa," she said. Danny looked up at the pudgy pale face bulging out of her black wimple and spilling over her starched white bib.

Tyrone said, "She's going to take good care of you." He gave Danny a quick hug and yelled, "So long, paratrooper," over his shoulder as he rushed off to join his squad.

———

St. John's was nothing more than a converted warehouse, and the nuns' efforts at decorating—with colorful pictures of suffering saints and martyrs—did little to disguise the dreariness. It was home for 120 boys between the ages of six and ten. Most of them had been given up for adoption as babies, and, after living in foster homes until school age, had been transferred to the institution.

Danny was shown to his room, a stark cell painted white, with six cots lining the wall. The windows were narrow slits so high up you had to stand on a chair to see outside. Something here reminded Danny of San Sabba. He wondered what he would see outside that window.

Sister Mary Theresa explained that since he was older than the others he would have to make sure the room was kept neat and the beds made. He answered, "I won't screw up."

"Holy Mother of God," Sister Mary Theresa gasped, crossing herself. "Don't ever use words like that." From then on, Danny only nodded when given instructions.

The mother superior in charge of the orphanage was less friendly. She expressed dismay when he told her that gypsies had no religious training. Her small eyes, set deep in her pinched face, studied him from behind thick wire-rimmed glasses. "We must correct that," she said, and immediately scheduled catechism classes in order to coach Danny to receive the sacraments—baptism and Holy Communion. He did not resist directly, but he fumbled over his lessons, pretending that he didn't understand enough English. The mother superior finally agreed to put the matter off for a year. Meanwhile, he was enrolled in a nearby high school.

Danny knew he was an oddball. At the orphanage, the boys stayed away from him, mimicking his thick accent behind his back. At school, the kids were more cruel, laughing openly whenever he stumbled over his words in class.

His English teacher, Mrs. Margaret Dennison, was extremely compassionate about his problems. She'd glare at the students who dared to make fun of him. She was a tall, attractive, middle-aged woman with an aristocratic air about her, and she always wore lace collars and smelled faintly of lavender. On his first day she kept him after school, gave him an elementary book in English, and showed him how to use it. The learning process seemed less torturous with her help.

She was his first friend in America. His second was Roy, a six-year-old boy who bunked in his room.

Roy was skinny and frail, with wispy ginger hair, twinkling brown eyes, and freckles across the bridge of his nose; he wore a constant grin that revealed two front teeth with a small space in between. Danny noticed that the other kids picked on Roy and often made him do their chores—like mopping the floor or washing the dishes—in exchange for a brief chance to play on the baseball team. Danny didn't understand the game, but he could see that little Roy wasn't much of an athlete, no matter how hard he tried.

One day, egged on by the other boys, Roy began to make fun of Danny in the shower. "Oh, you got a funny tinkle," he giggled, pointing a finger at Danny's circumcised penis. "Can I see it?"

As the little boy came closer, Danny felt anger well up within him. He shoved him, and Roy slipped and fell against the tile wall. He hit his nose, and blood immediately spurted out. Danny didn't mean to push him that hard, but Roy was so frail, so light, he just flew. The other boys quickly scattered, but Danny, seeing the little body crumpled against the wall, rushed over and tried to stop the flow of blood with his washcloth.

Sister Mary Theresa was outside dispensing towels and checking to see if the boys had scrubbed properly behind their ears. When Roy came out, still bleeding, and tears now running freely down his cheeks, she exclaimed in horror, "Roy, what happened?!"

"Nuthin'," Roy mumbled.

She threw a menacing look at Danny's guilty face and pressed on: "Did someone hit you? Push you?"

"No, no," said Roy. "I slipped and fell by myself."

That night, when the lights were turned out, Danny went over to Roy's bunk. "Thanks a lot," he whispered.

"Will you teach me to be a catcher?" Roy whispered back.

"I don't know how to play baseball," Danny answered.

"Will you read me a story?" Roy persisted.

"I'm not good at that either," Danny said, remembering how much he used to like a bedtime story, "but I'll try."

From that day on they were practically inseparable. They sat together at mealtimes, Danny protecting Roy from the bullies who picked on him. Roy bribed another boy, giving him a dried frog skin —the most precious possession from his cigar box of treasures—in order to sleep in the cot next to Danny. He sneaked in an old baseball and they tossed it back and forth from their cots as he taught Danny the rules of the game.

Then he managed to appropriate a flashlight from somewhere so that Danny could read him bedtime stories after Sister Mary Theresa turned out the lights. For all his trouble, Roy would usually fall asleep before Danny finished the story.

Danny spent hours in the meager orphanage library trying to find interesting stories for Roy. When he found a copy of Hans Christian Andersen's tales, he picked up the richly illustrated book and began leafing through it excitedly. Then he stopped. He was looking at a picture of the Devil and his disciples flying through the clouds with their mirror. As he stared at the drawing, his eyes started to burn. He closed them tightly and slammed the cover shut. He shoved the book back on the shelf so hard it fell behind the book rack.

Danny was making rapid progress in school, and Mrs. Dennison was proud of him. One day she suggested that he go to the movies more often—it was a good way of learning English intonations and thinking quickly in the language.

Danny was embarrassed. "I've never seen a movie."

"Never? Well, of course, I should have realized it—you've only been in this country six months. We'll have to correct that. One of the best memories of my youth was going to a Saturday matinee."

The next weekend the two of them took the bus down to the city. Danny felt almost dizzy from the excitement—he had never seen so many people, all in a hurry, carrying packages, bustling about. Cars whizzed by, splashing sooty slush; horns tooted; trolley bells clanged; lights flashed red, green, yellow; colorful signs, extolling the virtues of soft drinks, detergents, cars, beckoned from every corner. They passed street vendors selling roasted chestnuts and strange twisted pastries that Mrs. Dennison said were called pretzels, and even though it was winter, he saw children eating ice cream cones. Everybody was going somewhere, and they didn't seem confused by the cacophony of sounds or the maze of streets—they belonged.

Mrs. Dennison guided him around a corner, and then Danny saw it. The sign shone a brilliant blue in the afternoon light—RIALTO. They stood in a long line, slowly approaching the ticket booth, which resembled a miniature Taj Mahal. With a smile, Mrs. Dennison handed Danny a quarter to buy his own ticket. He was dazzled as they entered the rotunda. A fountain of multicolored spray danced before him—red, green, and blue water—how did they do it? Mrs. Dennison guided him across an immense round rug to a winding staircase with a heavy marble balustrade. Danny didn't see the cracks in the marble, the frayed edge of the rug, or the peeling paint. All he saw was the magic.

They entered the balcony. Spread before him was a cavernous palace. Huge columns painted with gold filigree soared up to the blue firmament on the ceiling, where a galaxy of stars twinkled. His mouth wide open, still trying to absorb the riot of images, he was led to a red velvet seat. In one corner, a large arrangement of tall golden pipes suddenly erupted in a majestic sound. A shiver went through him. He wasn't even aware of Mrs. Dennison. Straight ahead, a brocade curtain slowly rose as the music softened and the lights dimmed. Behind the curtain, a large white screen was exposed. The theater went completely black, and Danny was frightened. "I hope you like it," he heard Mrs. Dennison say, but he was unable to answer. Then a beam of light pierced the darkness, illuminating the screen with the images of another world. Trumpets blared and knights in armor raced across a hillside—the king was galloping toward his castle, King Henry V, Laurence Olivier. This was Danny's introduction to Shakespeare.

———

It became a weekly ritual. Every Saturday afternoon, Danny and Mrs. Dennison sat side by side, munching popcorn in a half-filled theater, eyes glued to the screen.

Danny wouldn't budge from his seat until the very last credit disappeared; he hated it when the screen went blank and the houselights went on. He now knew everything about the movies, the stars, the directors, the writers, the cinematographers. He didn't know how many stolen bases Jackie Robinson had in 1947 (something that all the boys at the orphanage, Roy included, could recite by heart), but he sure knew that Ronald Colman got an Oscar for *A Double Life* that year.

Danny loved those shadows projected by a beam of light. In awe, he watched Harold Russell in *The Best Years of Our Lives* deftly pouring a cup of coffee with the steel hooks that had replaced his hands. When the lights came on, Danny choked back his tears and was surprised that some of the men leaving were openly weeping.

As they walked out into the world of reality, Danny could see that Mrs. Dennison was also moved. She said quietly, "Movies touch people all over the world—they are a very important form of art, just as important as literature, and perhaps more powerful."

Yes, thought Danny, I feel that power.

The next week he worked harder than ever at his schoolwork and did all his chores at the orphanage, dreaming of Saturday, anticipating the next adventure—Fred Astaire in *Easter Parade*. But Mrs. Dennison couldn't take him.

He was crushed. He spent the morning pacing in his room, restless, lonely; Roy was outside—the baseball team had finally admitted him as a substitute. Danny could hear them yelling to each other. He stood up on a chair and looked out through the narrow window at the game in progress. Roy, a pained expression on his face, was sitting on the bench alone, holding a bat that seemed as big as he was. Danny was not the only one feeling sorry for himself.

He glanced at the wall clock. It was almost twelve-thirty. In a half hour Fred Astaire would be dancing at the Rialto. He had to see it. Putting on the St. John's cap that all the boys were required to wear, he tiptoed past the mother superior's office.

"Where are you going, Daniel?" Sister Mary Theresa's voice startled him just when he reached the front door.

"Mrs. Dennison is waiting for me," he stuttered.

She nodded and waddled back into the office. Weak with relief,
Danny ran out into the street.

He had no money, but he had a plan. When he arrived at the
cinema, he stuffed his cap into his pants' pocket and positioned
himself in line beside a matronly-looking woman; as she approached
the box office, he sauntered up the ramp to the usher. "My mother is
getting the ticket," he said, motioning behind him. Allowed inside,
Danny scurried up the stairs to the balcony, and slinked down in a
corner seat. He didn't relax until the houselights dimmed. But as
soon as the music started he forgot everything, tapping along with
Fred Astaire with such gusto that the woman next to him kicked his
shin.

Before the final credits began to roll, he slipped out a side door and
hurried back. He danced up and down the stairs of the brownstones
he passed, imitating Astaire, twirling a broken tree branch, and singing to himself, *"Stepping out with my honey . . . can't be bad if it feels so
good . . . never felt quite so sunny and I keep on knocking wood."*

As he opened the door, he saw that Sister Mary Theresa was still on
guard duty. "Thank you, Mrs. Dennison!" he yelled into the street.
He nodded politely to the nun and quickly went up to his room.

He decided not to tell Mrs. Dennison what he had done; he didn't
even tell Roy.

Sundays were the worst days at the orphanage. All the boys had to get
up extra early for the 6 A.M. service at the nearby church; the pastor
didn't like them taking up the pews during the more popular mass
hours later on. When they came back, they had to get things ready for
the communion breakfast for prospective parents. The mother superior always addressed the couples, sanctifying the deed of giving an
unfortunate orphan a home, dramatizing the rewards such a generous act would bring in heaven. Then the boys marched in, lining up
four deep on the platform like so much merchandise on display. They
sang hymns while the adults munched on their eggs and toast, studying them with interest. By the time breakfast was over at least one of
the boys would have a new set of parents.

During the time that he had been at St. John's, Danny had often
overheard people saying that he was too old to be adopted. He was
glad of it. He had settled into a routine; he didn't want things to

change again. He was doing well in school, he had lost his accent, and he was accepted by the others now. The only thing worrying him was that little Roy might be taken away. Like so many of the boys, Roy watched the couples with desperate eyes, hoping that this would be his lucky day, and he liked to fantasize what his new home might be like. He told Danny that he was abandoned as a baby and never knew his parents.

"You remember your mommy and daddy, Danny?" he once asked.

But Danny dismissed his question with a curt "I don't want to talk about it."

Sunday nights, after another rejection, Roy had nightmares and sometimes wet his bed. This embarrassed him dreadfully. Punishment for bed-wetting was severe. If any boy was caught, he got no dinner and had to stand in the dining hall with a sign hanging from his neck: I WET MY BED. Several times Danny sneaked fresh linens from the hall closet while the others were still sleeping, and helped Roy remake the bed before Sister Mary Theresa could find out. The wet sheet was tucked into the springs until the next dirty-laundry pickup.

One night Danny was awakened by a whisper in his ear: "I wee-weed in my bed."

"Oh no, Roy, not again." Sleepily, Danny stumbled out of bed and headed to the linen closet. But when he reached inside, the shelf was bare. Momentarily, he panicked. Then, quietly, he returned to the room. "Just keep your mouth shut," he commanded Roy as he stripped off the wet sheet and switched it with his own.

"But you'll get punished," Roy muttered.

"Go to sleep," Danny ordered gruffly, sliding into the damp bed. "You're too skinny to miss dinner again."

Dozing off, he heard Roy's soft voice. "Danny—"

"Now what?"

"Maybe we'll get adopted together."

"Maybe."

His worst time at the orphanage was the evening when he had to stand in the dining hall with that awful sign around his neck.

―――――――

At the close of the school year, there was a recital in the auditorium and Mrs. Dennison had Danny memorize a poem.

"Don't be afraid, Daniel—your English is very good now. I'll be sitting in the first row. If you get scared, just look at me. I'll be whispering the words along with you."

But he did not need to look at her as he recited without an accent:

If you can dream—and not make dreams your master;
If you can meet with triumph and disaster
And treat those two imposters just the same; . . .

The audience applauded; he liked the sound. That night he told Roy all about it. Roy had memorized the poem too; he didn't have much choice, since that's all Danny had read to him for weeks now, until they both knew it perfectly.

Danny urged Roy to recite the poem at the next communion breakfast. Roy did, and got an enthusiastic response—even the mother superior smiled. One chubby couple applauded more loudly than the others. Danny was the first to spot them conferring with the mother superior as the boys cleared the dishes. He guessed it—they wanted to adopt his friend.

Danny had to hide his feelings when he looked at Roy's happy face. He had to admit he liked the looks of Roy's parents—they had wide grins on their round, pink faces. They would be good parents for skinny little Roy; they'd fatten him up for sure. He told Roy that as he helped him pack. It didn't take long; everything Roy owned fit in his cigar box, and he was allowed to take with him only the clothes he wore. His new parents were waiting down below.

Roy bounced toward the door. Danny could not move. He felt short of breath, and he had a sinking sensation as if he were going deeper underwater and didn't have the strength to come up for air.

Suddenly, Roy turned around, a worried expression on his face. "Danny, do you think we could sneak a sheet out of the closet, just one, and fold it real small so it fits in the cigar box, you know, just in case . . ."

"Don't worry," Danny reassured him. "It won't happen again. You'll have a new father, a new mother, a nice house, a room of your own. You won't have nightmares anymore. You'll sleep well."

"But what do I do if . . ." begged Roy.

"Well, just tell your mother to read you a story." Then he commanded sharply, "Come on!"

He carried Roy's cigar box downstairs, where the waiting parents were still smiling. As they led him toward their car, Roy broke away and rushed back. He threw his arms around Danny in a tight hug. His frail body shook with violent sobs. "I love you, Danny—I'll never, ever forget you." Danny stood rooted to the spot. When the car disappeared from view he was still there. And the lump in his throat didn't go away for a long time.

Now, more than ever, he was grateful for his friendship with Mrs. Dennison. He told her that little Roy had a real home now, and how much he missed him.

"Maybe some nice people will come to adopt you," Mrs. Dennison said.

Danny shook his head. "No. I'm too old. I'm fifteen."

The next Sunday, as Danny was singing in the choir, he was surprised to see Mrs. Dennison seated at a table next to a tall, thin man with long strands of gray hair covering a bald spot. Danny thought it was her father, but later learned he was her husband. Mr. John Dennison was the retired principal of the high school, and they had married ten years ago, when he first employed her as the English teacher. It was the first marriage for both of them.

After breakfast, Danny was called into the mother superior's office, where the Dennisons were waiting. He knew something important was going to happen—all of their faces betrayed it.

The mother superior nodded to him from behind her glasses. "Sit down, Daniel. We have something to tell you." Danny sat down slowly and looked questioningly at Mrs. Dennison.

"Daniel," she said, "we have never been blessed with a child, and we would like to adopt you as our son."

"Yes, my boy." Mr. Dennison smiled weakly and cleared his throat.

Danny was overwhelmed. "You do?"

"We do." Mrs. Dennison leaned over and kissed him on the forehead.

———

Before he left St. John's Orphanage, he asked Sister Mary Theresa for Roy's address, but she shook her head. "That is information we never give out, Danny. You know that."

"But he was my best friend—"

"I know. But often in life we have to put such temporal attachments aside and get on with what is important. You remember why we are on this earth, Danny—to love and serve the Lord."

Danny felt the lump in his throat returning. He would never see Roy again. He would never be able to tell him about the farm, about Mameh and Tateh and Rachel. How he wished that he had shared his secret with the only person he could trust to keep it. He had come close, but something always stopped him.

Now he had a new life and a new name. He was Daniel Dennison,

son of Mr. and Mrs. John Dennison. He had a room of his own on the second floor of the Dennisons' little house, very similar to the other houses on the narrow, tree-lined street. His bed, tucked into a niche under the sloping ceiling, faced the window, where Mrs. Dennison piled up flowered pillows to make a window seat. In the drawer under that seat he kept the paratrooper wings Tyrone had given him and the baseball he and Roy had thrown back and forth.

The entire house smelled of lavender soap and reflected Mrs. Dennison's Victorian tastes—the chintz-covered overstuffed sofa, the fringed lamps, the crocheted napkins that Danny learned were called doilies.

Several times Mr. Dennison broached the subject of Danny's background, but Danny always gave the same brief answer: He was separated from his family during the war and ended up at San Sabba. Mrs. Dennison usually changed the subject; she never pressed him. But in warm moments between them she called him "my little gypsy." Such endearments were rare, though, and she didn't even call him Danny, only Daniel, as if he were more adult than his age.

Since Mr. Dennison—whom Danny, somehow, could never call Father—was often sickly, Danny spent much more time with his new mother. Each morning they walked to school together, and she continued to help him with his English at home in the evenings. Every Saturday they still went to the movies.

Mr. Dennison insisted that Danny attend church services on Sunday mornings. They belonged to the First Episcopalian Church, and later Danny learned that Mrs. Dennison had had a hard time persuading the mother superior to allow him to be adopted into a non-Catholic home. Danny found the services no different from the Catholic mass—boring. Fortunately he was soon spared this tedium. When Mr. Dennison became more infirm and began spending much of his time in bed, church services were forgotten.

Danny's interest in movies grew. From time to time, he would go over to the Syracuse University library to read books on cinematography. Now, when he went to the movies with Mrs. Dennison, he paid attention to how the illusion of reality was created, how light and shadow set the mood.

One Saturday Mrs. Dennison took him to see *White Heat.* Danny sat at the edge of his chair, hypnotized, as gangster Jimmy Cagney, pursued by police, raced up a ladder to the top of a huge oil drum. Fire raging all around him, Cagney yelled, "Look at me, Ma, I'm on top of the world." Engulfed by flames, the drum exploded. Danny gasped and Mrs. Dennison clutched his hand.

When they were walking home, Mrs. Dennison was upset. "I'm sorry, Danny. I shouldn't have taken you to such a violent movie."

"But it was well done. Didn't it seem real to you?"

"Too real—it was gruesome."

Danny didn't respond, though he wanted to say, "I wish I could make a movie like that."

———

On Danny's sixteenth birthday the family shared a chocolate cake and a small bottle of champagne. Mr. Dennison sat stiffly at the table in his robe. He didn't drink any champagne, although he made the toast: "Happy birthday to our son." Seized suddenly by a spasm in his chest, he couldn't go on. Mrs. Dennison gave him a pill. She and Danny sipped the champagne and then she brought out a small, gaily wrapped package. He opened it—inside was a stainless-steel wrist-watch with a black leather strap. Danny was so excited he couldn't buckle the strap and Mrs. Dennison had to help him. He had never had a watch before. He thanked them both profusely.

"Well, that's enough excitement for everyone," said Mrs. Dennison. "John, you get back in bed," she instructed, handing him a sleeping tablet with a glass of water.

"You just gave me one," said Mr. Dennison.

"Oh John, you're getting so forgetful." She smiled, putting the tablet in his mouth and the glass of water to his lips.

Danny said nothing as he helped her carry the dishes into the kitchen.

"All right, birthday boy, get ready for bed, but don't forget to finish your homework."

"I won't, Margaret." She liked him to call her Margaret when no one was around.

She kissed him softly on the cheek. "I'll be up to check on you a little later."

After his shower, Danny put on the clean pajamas that were laid out on the bed and looked at his homework. He loved reading the poems he studied in Mrs. Dennison's class. She had often had him read them aloud. His English was flawless now; no one would have guessed his background.

The door opened quietly and she came in. He was surprised to see that she had on a clingy, low-cut nightgown instead of the white terry-cloth robe she usually wore at bedtime.

As she sat on the bed beside him, Danny could not draw his eyes away from her breasts—the outlines of her nipples protruded through the filmy material.

"Happy birthday, Daniel," she said, reaching out to hug him. "You've been such a joy—to both of us."

"Thanks again for the watch," Danny stammered out, hypnotized by her presence.

Her voice had a dreamy quality, and she spoke as if she hadn't heard him. "I'll never forget the time you recited that Kipling poem in the auditorium. You didn't have to look at me once. You just stood there, sure of yourself, tall and handsome—'If you can fill the unforgiving minute/With sixty seconds' worth of distance run—/Yours is the Earth and everything that's in it,/And—which is more—you'll be a Man, my son!'"

As she stroked the curls on his head, he could feel her breast against his cheek. His heart was pounding and he didn't know what to do with his clammy hands.

"Oh look," she said, nodding to the window. "Moonlight." With her other hand she turned off the lamp. "Isn't that much nicer?"

"Yes," he muttered, his body tingling as she lay down beside him. For a split second, he had the urge to jump out of bed and run away, but then she kissed him on his closed lips, gently prying them open with the tip of her tongue. He felt a hot sensation between his legs.

"You're sixteen—do you feel like a man?" she asked with a soft chuckle. Before he could reply, she kissed him again. This time his mouth was open as her tongue probed his. Her hand slid underneath his pajamas and rubbed his stomach.

Danny put his arms around her and held her tightly. Her hand moved down.

"Yes," she whispered, "you are a man."

From then on, making love with Margaret Dennison became part of the Saturday ritual along with the movie matinee. Danny often wondered if Mr. Dennison got an extra pill on those nights.

Now he was more aware of the girls in his class, with their small budding breasts. One pretty girl, Peggy, who sat next to him in biology, invited him to her sweet-sixteen party. After dinner that Saturday, he rushed up to his room, where he had already laid out his best white shirt, navy-blue suit, and maroon tie. As he polished his shoes, he hummed "Steppin' Out with My Baby" and then tap-danced down the steps. At the landing, Mrs. Dennison stood with a frozen smile. "I hope you have a good time at the party, Daniel."

Her tone caught him off balance. "I won't stay out late, Mother . . . ah, Margaret."

Her eyes seemed to pierce his. "Why, Daniel—stay as long as you like. It's Saturday. And don't worry about me."

"Would you rather I didn't go?"

"You are old enough to make your own decision. Do what you think best." She turned and walked away.

Danny stood there fidgeting with his watch. Slowly, his head hanging down, he walked back up the steps.

———

As his graduation approached, Mrs. Dennison pressed him to stay at home and attend Syracuse University, but Danny knew he had to get away. His senior year in high school he felt stifled, unable to have girlfriends of his own, struggling under Mrs. Dennison's resentment even when he went out with other boys.

But there was little she could do once he had received a scholarship to the University of Southern California's Institute of the Arts.

It was 1950. Others would remember it as the year that President Truman escaped assassination or the year Joseph McCarthy started anti-Communist hysteria, but Danny would remember it as the year *All About Eve*, with Anne Baxter and Bette Davis, won the Oscar. It was the last movie that he and Mrs. Dennison saw together, the day before he left for the West Coast.

———

He was surprised how hot California was in the month of September. In Syracuse leaves were changing color and starting to fall from the trees, but here flowers were in bloom and palm trees, so tall he wondered what kept them from falling over, soared toward a flat blue sky.

He walked the crowded USC campus with much trepidation, eyeing the other students, who seemed completely at ease sauntering about in sweaters with Greek letters designating their fraternities. He hesitated to approach anyone, and was tongue-tied when he did. He was eighteen years old, but he felt like the little boy who had just walked into St. John's Orphanage.

He was homesick. He missed the security that Mrs. Dennison had given him. The first week he wrote her every day. But soon he became aware that pretty coeds were whispering, "He's so handsome." He was invited to many parties, and he found he had less time or need to write home so often. His dependency on Mrs. Dennison was broken completely when he got a job as a waiter in a luncheonette, and no longer needed the small weekly allowance she sent him.

As a top scholar, he got invitations to join several fraternities, but when he received a bid from a Jewish fraternity, he was rattled.

"It must be a mistake—I'm not a Jew," he stammered to the fellow who had approached him.

"That doesn't matter; we're not restricted," was the response.

Danny was shattered. Why did they ask *him*? What did they suspect? Back in his dormitory room, he locked the door and looked into the mirror above the washbasin. He studied his black curly hair; he tilted his face so that he could see his straight nose. He didn't look Jewish. Mrs. Dennison once said he looked like Robert Taylor, the actor. And Taylor certainly wasn't Jewish. Or was he?

Danny jumped at the chance to join the Sigma Alpha Epsilon Society—SAE—considered the most sophisticated group on campus. All the members were very smartly dressed, WASPy-looking, and had girlfriends with long, tanned legs and sun-bleached hair. SAE's head-quarters was the most imposing house on campus, large, white, two-storied, with arched windows and tall Doric columns framing a wide veranda.

Nervous about his interview, Danny came to the fraternity house early. He was met by a senior member wearing a dark-blue blazer with the SAE emblem embroidered in gold on the breast pocket, and escorted into a room that looked like a library, with books lining the walls. Seated around a large mahogany table were four seniors dressed in identical blue blazers. Danny was painfully aware that his own brown sport coat was completely out of fashion.

The fraternity president, who spoke with an affected, nearly British accent and puffed on a pipe, asked polite questions, and Danny thought everything was going very well. Then the president leaned back in his chair and held up a piece of paper. "I have a report here that you were asked to join Alpha Beta Gamma."

"Yes, but—"

"Yes, *sir*," prompted one of the seniors.

"Yes, sir—I mean . . . I was just trying to explain that . . . ah . . . they made a mistake."

"So you're not a Jew?"

"No, sir. My family is Episcopalian."

The president exchanged glances with one of the seniors and then said warmly to Danny, "Just a few questions we ask prospective members—I hope you don't mind."

Danny pledged SAE without further problems. Now he, too, wore a blue blazer embroidered with gold Greek letters. He strolled around the campus with a sexy blond girlfriend on his arm, the prettiest girl in the class; she had come from a strict all-girl boarding school and was more than willing to let loose.

Though he always had many invitations, and was considered popular, he wasn't happy—his sexual encounters were momentarily exciting, but none led to lasting friendships. The more desperately he tried to belong, the more lonely he felt. In his room, studying at night, he often fantasized that Roy would magically appear to keep him company. Roy would understand his loneliness. With Roy, he wouldn't have to pretend. He would tell his old friend everything—even his deepest secrets. He wrote a letter to St. John's, again hoping to obtain some clue to Roy's whereabouts, but the curt reply only told him that "disclosure of information concerning adoption is against state law."

At the beginning of the second term there was a meeting of fraternity brothers to review new applicants. Joseph McDermott, a pudgy redhead, made a startling nomination—Zac Abrams, a star basketball player.

"But he's a Jew!" exclaimed the presiding officer amid much rumbling in the group.

"So what?" said McDermott. "Zac Abrams is the basketball star of USC. He's a great guy and would be a terrific addition to our fraternity. Those archaic rules are full of crap. Let's be the first to take a step forward. I nominate Zac Abrams as a member of SAE."

The room was quiet. There was some shuffling of feet, and McDermott looked around contemptuously.

Danny began to sweat, remembering his inquisition just a few months before. He felt that many eyes were looking at him. He stood up, and as soon as he got everyone's attention, he was sorry he did.

"I just wanted to say that . . ." he started, then bit his lip. "That . . . we all took an oath when we joined this fraternity. We swore to uphold the tradition of Sigma Alpha Epsilon. I, for one . . . ah . . . think we should continue a noble . . . tradition that has endured for a long time." He stopped and sat down quickly.

When the vote was called, only McDermott raised his hand in favor of admitting Zac Abrams. In the hubbub that followed, as others slapped him on the back and congratulated him, Danny remained seated, his eyes downcast.

Abruptly, McDermott's voice cut through the din: "You're all a bunch of assholes, and you deserve each other. I resign from this fraternity." As he stalked out of the room, he passed Danny and spat out, "Jew-hater."

Danny just stared at the floor; he did not want to reveal his admiration for McDermott—nor the contempt he felt for himself.

That feeling of confused self-loathing stayed with him through the term, and he was relieved when the school year recessed for summer vacation.

When Danny arrived home, Mrs. Dennison was in the kitchen preparing his favorite meal. They hadn't seen each other in almost a year. He kissed her on both cheeks and babbled on about his school activities and the pressures that prevented him from writing as often as he would like.

She waved his apologies aside. "The first year is a difficult one, Daniel—for everyone."

"Oh, you're so understanding, Mother . . . ah . . . . Margaret," he stammered.

"We're both so proud of you, though I couldn't show your father your last report—he's taken a turn for the worse."

Danny winced—he had forgotten to ask about Mr. Dennison, who had gone into a nursing home a few months back. "Oh, I'm sorry to hear that. I must go visit him right away."

"Of course . . . but don't rush off now. I saw him early this morning. Let's go together tomorrow."

"No, no—I'd feel better if I went today."

When the nurse escorted him into the room, Danny was shocked by the skeletal figure of Mr. Dennison, a maze of green tubes surrounding his head. The old man's eyes were open, but he seemed asleep.

Danny sat beside the bed, studying the face twisted by a recent stroke and watching the saliva drooling out of the side of his mouth. This man adopted me, he thought. He gave me his name. He wanted to be a father to me. I never even thanked him. Danny realized how little communication there had been between them. Now he wanted to talk to him; now he wanted to apologize for having betrayed him. But he just sat quietly. There was nothing else he could do.

Back at home, Mrs. Dennison was waiting for him, dressed in a black velvet skirt and lacy pink blouse. The best china and silver were laid out on the table. During dinner they ate very little, talking constantly, as if afraid of a pause.

Finally she said, "You must be very tired, crossing the country by bus. Why don't you get ready for bed, while I put the dishes away? I'll be up to say good-night in a little while."

Danny studied his coffee cup before taking a long sip. "Yes, I am a little tired."

His room was exactly as he'd left it. He opened the drawer with Tyrone's wings and Roy's baseball and tossed the ball from hand to hand as all kinds of thoughts tumbled in his head.

Through the half-open door he could hear Mrs. Dennison making her way up the stairs. In a moment she would appear. More than anything he wanted not to be there. He moved toward the door, but it was too late to leave; she was coming down the hall. He pushed the door closed and turned the latch.

He stepped back, holding his breath. Slowly he watched the knob turn. He could feel her presence on the other side. The knob turned again. It seemed like a century before her footsteps receded down the hall.

With a sigh, he sat down on the bed. How scared he was when the affair began; now it was over and he was more frightened.

In the morning, no reference was made to the night before. Mrs. Dennison accepted, very graciously, Danny's excuse that he had to go back to school for a special summer seminar. The next time Danny came home was for Mr. Dennison's funeral, but he stayed in a motel. After that he never went back.

CHAPTER 4

1982 | Milan, Italy

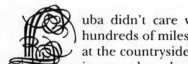 uba didn't care where she was going. Valentine was hundreds of miles away. She stared out the bus window at the countryside. In the distance, horses were galloping up a slope; lost in a thin blanket of mist, their hooves seemed never to touch the ground. In her mind, they became carousel horses with flying manes, disappearing over the hill with Valentine. Her heart was empty.

The bus arrived at a much larger refugee camp near Milan, housing hundreds of people escaped from Communist-bloc countries—Yugoslavia, Czechoslovakia, Romania, Hungary, and of course Poland.

Everyone knew that if you could only get over the border into the free world, the Red Cross would try to find you a home in another country. But the wait, in the army-style barracks with rows of cots jammed close together, could be excruciatingly long.

Aching deep inside, Luba found the place unbearable, even though Magda had cajoled the camp superintendent into giving them a tiny private room, normally reserved for women with small children.

The camp records might have listed Luba as a child, but the fact that she was almost mature didn't escape the men around her. Two Yugoslav youths—Mirek and Franek, one a Serb, the other a Croat—pursued her with special vigor. Mirek, tall and wiry, Franek, short and muscular, were the exterminators of the camp. They roamed the grounds, always slightly drunk, in pursuit of the rats and other vermin that fed on the mounds of garbage. They laughed whenever they saw Luba and made dirty jokes in broken Polish, inviting her to try one of them in the crawl space under the kitchen. Repelled, Luba ran the other way whenever she saw them coming.

Magda got a part-time job cooking in a restaurant in Milan. She was able to bring home leftover food, so they both ate well, and with her salary they could buy some extra clothes. When Luba sneered that they could make twice that much in one night at the Rynek, Magda got angry. That part of their lives was over, she insisted. They were in the free world now, and they must do nothing to jeopardize getting their visas.

Two months later they were still waiting. Their applications could not be processed without a document from Adam verifying that he would guarantee their passage and be responsible for them once they arrived in Australia.

Magda had written twice, explaining what was required. She had sent one letter some time ago from San Sabba, and she wrote again from Milan.

Finally, the reply from Australia arrived. Magda tore open the large envelope with eager hands. Inside was a thick document written in English with lots of legal stamps and seals. Magda grabbed and kissed Luba, then pulled her along to the Red Cross office.

The elderly worker took the document from her. "This is unusual," he said, raising the thick glasses that hung around his neck on a black ribbon. "I've never seen a document like this."

"What does it say?" Magda asked with apprehension.

"I know English, but there are so many legal terms. Let me study it a minute."

Magda sat down; Luba sullenly watched the worker.

After an interminable period of time, he turned to Magda with sympathetic eyes. "These papers say that you and Adam Woda are divorced."

"What?! What?! How can that be?"

"Your husband obviously divorced you." The worker's voice was soft, kind; he was used to giving people bad news. "In Australia these matters are easily arranged."

Magda burst into tears.

"Oh Magda," Luba snapped, "what did you expect after all this time?" She turned to the Red Cross man. "What do we do now?"

"All you can do is wait. We'll put you on a list for several other countries. You'll have to be patient, but one of them will accept you sooner or later."

Magda had struggled so much, endured such pain, all to find her husband, and now she stood there listening silently to the news she never expected to hear—Adam didn't want her. She was destroyed.

From that day on Adam was never discussed, though Luba would hear stifled sobs coming from her mother's cot at night. Somehow, Luba didn't know how to console her mother; she was still grieving for Valentine. Their loss should have brought them closer together; instead, it forced them apart. Each hid behind her own wall of bitterness.

Magda moved through the day like a sleepwalker; some part of her seemed defeated, dead. She cooked all day at the restaurant in Milan, and when she came back to the camp she had to do the kitchen chores assigned to her.

Her mood finally lightened when she met another Polish refugee, a stocky man of fifty with a contagious sense of humor. As they peeled potatoes in the kitchen together, he told her how he had escaped from Poland. He had been active in Solidarity and fled aboard a Baltic freight ship when martial law was declared; he asked for asylum in Naples and was sent to Milan to await his visa for America, where he had some distant relatives.

Magda looked at him humming away as he worked. "And where did you get that?" she asked, pointing to the number tattooed on his arm.

"Oh that. Auschwitz. I was only a boy then."

"My God—Auschwitz!"

He was still humming, as if the name held nothing but pleasant memories. He had a round wide face, made wider by a receding hairline.

"You don't look Jewish," she said.

"Yes I do. Look at my eyes. A Nazi told me that he could tell Jews by their sad brown eyes." He brought his face close to hers and opened his eyes wide. "Are they sad?"

No, they were not sad—they were eyes filled with good humor and good-will. She laughed.

"But how did you survive?" she asked.

"I was meant to live. My name is Chaim—means life." He smiled a warm, ingratiating smile. "Also, I had a good singing voice."

"What?"

"The Nazis were very sentimental. After a day of destroying Jews, they loved to listen to a little boy singing romantic ballads." And in a soft, melodic voice he started to sing: *"Auf der Donau, wenn der Wein blüht, fliegt der Vogel von Haus zu Haus . . ."*

Magda didn't understand the words but loved the sound.

From then on they became good friends. She looked forward to the kitchen chores after a hard day's work in Milan. Chaim always found new ways to make her laugh—he would juggle potatoes, do magic tricks, pull a little onion out of her ear. His cheerful example made her ashamed of herself.

Once, she gently touched his arm and rubbed her fingers over the tattooed numbers. "Chaim, how can you always be so happy?"

"I'm alive," he said with a grin.

"But you've been through so much—a death camp, then living with anti-Semitism, your workers' union destroyed."

"Yes, terrible things."

"But you have no bitterness."

"Magda, if I was bitter I would have been dead a long time ago." He wiped his hands with a towel. "Bitterness eats away at you. Oh, I don't forget; never bury memories—good or bad, they're a part of life. We must accept that." Then he took her hands in his and wiped them too. Magda was mesmerized. "If you don't," he continued, his eyes holding hers, "you lock arms with the Devil, and he makes you dance to his tune." Then he laughed in his wholehearted way, and, putting his arm around Magda, said softly, almost in a whisper, "I don't want to dance with the Devil—I'd rather dance with you."

Magda hid her blushing face against his shoulder.

His simple philosophy affected her deeply. She found herself humming his songs now—and she even taught him her favorite love ballad, "Moje Serce": *"When first you came into my life, I gave my heart to you . . ."* As she recited the words she flushed.

She took an interest in her appearance again, carefully applying makeup, taking trouble with her hair. She even bought a new skirt with sunflowers painted on it and an embroidered yellow blouse to match. And she filed a visa application for America too—who knows what might happen in another country?

Magda had much to look forward to now, but for Luba things were worse than ever. She was constantly alone. In the evening, Chaim would go fishing, which was his passion, and he would take Magda with him. Luba watched them happily strolling toward the river— Chaim carrying the fishing pole and bait box, Magda with a blanket under her arm.

Luba's only recreation was walking around the camp and feeding scraps to the many stray dogs that hung around the camp, skinny, undernourished, frightened. She had one favorite, a dog different from the rest. Someone had told her he was part wolf, and she was drawn to his defiant manner and wild blue eyes that stared at people without fear. She called him Blue Boy.

Besides that, she had nothing to do except go to school, and she hated that. An Italian woman taught English to the refugees in broken Polish. It was difficult to understand her in any language. Luba couldn't wait to rush out of the schoolroom with her sketch pad and find Blue Boy. He would sit quietly while she talked to him and sketched.

One afternoon, when Luba was trying to capture the quality of his almost-human eyes, Mirek and Franek appeared, drunk as usual. They were rounding up the strays. They wore gloves, carried rope, and their belts held long knives to cut the throats of the animals.

Before Luba could stop them, they threw their lassos around the unsuspecting dog's neck and began to pull in opposite directions. "Let him go!" she screamed. Blue Boy was choking. The men only laughed.

"Pretty one," said Franek, swaying on his feet, "we have to do our job."

"Not him!" she cried, wildly beating Mirek with her fists.

Mirek grabbed her around the waist with his free arm, his large hand squeezing her breast as he planted a wet kiss on her lips.

"You're drunk." Luba tried to squirm away.

"I want a kiss too," said Franek. Luba stopped struggling, her attention now on the dog, who was making deathly rasping noises as the ropes tightened.

"Listen," she said in a suddenly calm, provocative voice. "Let go of the dog and I'll give you each a kiss."

"This is worth more than a kiss," Mirek leered.

"OK, I'll take one of you under the kitchen."

They both stared. "Which one?" they asked almost in unison.

"You fight it out." She grinned.

They dropped the ropes, and Luba ran to remove the nooses from the dog's neck. He licked her face, wagging his tail as she kissed his snout.

A shout made her look up. Mirek and Franek were confronting each other, their long knives glistening in their hands.

Clutching the dog, Luba couldn't believe what she was seeing. As they drunkenly circled each other, Franek stumbled on a piece of wood and Mirek thrust his knife into his stomach. With a piercing cry, Franek grabbed Mirek in a bear hug and stabbed him in the throat. The two clung to each other, silently moving in a slow-motion embrace, blood pouring out as they slipped to the ground.

People from the camp rushed over. Something exciting had happened at last. Luba left quickly, Blue Boy following. All she cared about was that she managed to save the dog.

Back in her little room, she opened up one of the tins of smoked salmon that Magda kept under a floorboard along with other delicacies she had squirreled away from the restaurant. Luba began to teach Blue Boy to roll over, rewarding his awkward efforts with bits of salmon.

By the time Magda walked in, the can was empty, and Blue Boy could sit, roll over, and give Luba his paw.

"Get that dog out of here," Magda commanded. She sounded exhausted.

"He's not bothering anybody."

"He's bothering me. This place is hardly big enough for the two of us."

"You're never here anyway."

"I'm out working all day so that you can have good things to eat. I'm doing it for you."

"Are you fucking Chaim for me too?"

A hand cracked against Luba's cheek. Magda was breathing heavily. "Chaim is the only good thing that's happened to me. Adam betrayed me. But you couldn't care less. You haven't cared about me since you met Valentine. You would have left me behind just to go with him."

Luba held her hand to her burning cheek. "I don't have Valentine anymore—and if you don't mind, I'd at least like to have a dog." She opened the door, and saw that Chaim was approaching. "Come along, Blue Boy. We're not wanted here."

She moped around the dusty paths of the camp, feeling sorry for herself, talking to Blue Boy. "Magda is with her lover. Well, good for her. But I'll get even—you watch, Blue Boy."

Sometimes, when Magda was in town, Chaim would go fishing for their dinner alone. One day, Luba and Blue Boy came running after him. "Can we go with you?" Luba panted.

He laughed. "Sure, come along. Carry the blanket."

Chaim assured her that they would have fresh bass on the table when Magda got back. While he was fishing, Luba took off her shoes and socks and waded in. It wasn't long before Chaim was reeling in a fish. Blue Boy barked in excitement and Luba ran toward them in the shallow water. She fell and came up wet and laughing.

"Don't catch cold. Wrap yourself in that blanket." As Luba obeyed, Chaim took the bass off the hook. He expertly gutted it, and, holding it under the gills with his fingers, washed off the blood in the river. Proudly, he presented it to Luba. "Look at that—the biggest I've ever caught. You bring me luck."

"Well, then, give me a good-luck kiss," said Luba. Standing up, she dropped the blanket. He stared at her. She was naked.

She repeated, "My good-luck kiss."

Chaim's mouth hung agape. With a smile, Luba wrapped her arms around him and kissed his open mouth. The fish fell from his hand.

Triumphant, Luba made love to her mother's lover on the bank of a river, next to a dead fish, with Blue Boy barking.

They were still lying in each other's arms when Magda found them. She held a note that Luba had left behind:

Chaim and I are waiting for you by the river.

Even as Chaim scrambled to get up, Luba held him fast. She glared defiantly at Magda, who turned and walked away.

"Oh my God!" Chaim pulled up his pants quickly. "How could I do this? How could I do this?" he kept muttering. He ran after Magda.

Luba stretched out on the riverbank and let her hands move slowly over her breasts—the nipples were still hard—over her flat tummy, and down her thighs. She felt like a woman, a grown-up woman. The dog lay down beside her, wagging his tail and licking her feet.

"Yes, Blue Boy, I'm a woman now," she whispered. "Two men killed themselves for me, and now Magda's man is mine."

Her feeling of triumph rapidly dissipated when she returned to their room and saw the devastation on her mother's face. Magda said nothing about the incident.

Chaim was beside himself; he had tried to beg forgiveness, but Magda wouldn't listen.

A week later, Magda brought home the news that they had been granted visas for England.

"England? It's foggy, wet. I thought you wanted to hold out for America so we could go with Chaim," Luba demanded.

Magda turned and gave her daughter a steely look. "It makes no difference now. I just want to get out of here. We've been waiting for over a year. We are lucky to be accepted somewhere."

"But England? I don't want—"

"Luba—it's too late."

They completed their physical tests and interviews. They would be leaving shortly. But neither felt any excitement.

———

Luba's guilt gnawed at her as she walked around the dimly lit camp, Blue Boy at her heels. In a few days they would be leaving for England and Chaim would be out of their lives. She had been too cruel. Magda needed Chaim's affection. It helped her deal with Adam's desertion. Why did I do it? she berated herself. I humiliated my mother. She sat down on a rock and looked into the adoring eyes of her faithful friend. She patted his head. "Blue Boy, men are stupid, but women are cruel."

She had to make up with her mother and Chaim before they left.

———

Blue Boy didn't want to be left behind. He kept howling and leaping against the side of the bus, specks of white foam dripping from his mouth. Luba and Magda sat stiffly in their seats. Magda was thinking of Chaim, but Luba's thoughts were only on Blue Boy. She was unable to look at this dog, her faithful friend. She had saved his life. Maybe it would have been better to let him be destroyed. He had been an independent, defiant dog who didn't need humans. She had changed all that.

From the corner of her eye, she could see Chaim desperately pulling Blue Boy away. He had promised to take care of him, but how long would Chaim be there?

As the bus drove off, Chaim, holding the dog back, waved a final good-bye. Luba put her hands to her ears in an attempt to block out Blue Boy's poignant yelps.

Magda, crying, reached over and took her hand. That affectionate touch released a knot in Luba's stomach. She bit her lip and closed her eyes tightly to hold back the tears. Suddenly, Luba realized that she was not a woman—she was a little girl, a little girl who had lost her faithful dog. She wanted to bury her head in her mother's bosom and weep. But she didn't.

1984 | Weymouth, England

 hen the wheels of their train screeched to a stop at Victoria Station in London, Luba and Magda were almost afraid to get off, bewildered by all the activity and the strange accents of another language. They were grateful to a big Polish lady, Mrs. Kulik, a representative of the Refugee Relief Foundation, who led them to another train bound for Weymouth, a small seaside town.

There, they were given a flat on the lower floor of a modest two-story house with a little patch of garden out front. Now Luba had her own room; she could close the door and be alone, and she enjoyed that luxury. Other things were not so pleasant. They had to adjust to a normal life, which seemed abnormal. After being in camps for so long, they had to concern themselves with rent, electric bills, gas bills, taxes. It was important that Magda get a job and Luba go to school.

The husband and wife in the flat upstairs were Hungarian refugees who had arrived two years earlier. They worked in a garment factory, she as a seamstress, he as a pattern maker. Ginga was about forty, buxom but not fat; Yanak was much younger, about twenty-five, a bit coarse but very pleasant. They spoke English already and were very helpful; it was good to have someone nearby who shared their experience.

After a few days, with the help of Mrs. Kulik, Magda found a job as a waitress in a hotel restaurant on the beach. Luba took a few hours off from school to take her there and help her fill out the work forms.

Red carpeting led to the entrance. Magda held back. "We can't go in there! We can't walk on that!"

"Sure we can," said Luba hopefully, and they went ahead. Magda was certain someone was going to grab them and throw them out for walking on a carpet put there for some royal guest.

Luba got Magda settled in and went back to school. She was the only foreigner there. She felt out of place, even though her thick accent was disappearing quickly. All her schoolmates seemed so young. She would listen to the girls giggling about being kissed in the back of a movie house. Luba had a strong desire to turn around and ask, "Did he fuck you?" *Fuck* was a word she had learned in Kraków.

She laughed at the oversexed boys who pursued her—they seemed like children, their advances so clumsy as they fumbled to get their sweaty hands inside her underwear. She amused herself by exciting them to orgasm before they could get her panties off.

At seventeen Luba left school and got a job at Woolworth's, not as a salesgirl—the manager didn't like foreigners dealing with the customers—but in the stockroom, a dark, dingy place with lots of shelves, where she spent her time moving crates and boxes. She didn't mind the hard work so much, but she couldn't stand the boredom.

Finally she confronted Magda. "I met a woman on the beach who works for an escort service in London. Her name is Lois. She said she could get us both jobs if—"

"Doing what? You know what those escort services really are."

"Yeah. Sounds like fun, with good money."

"Luba, I told you a long time ago—"

"And I told you that we're going nowhere. I'm getting muscles lifting boxes while you're wiping tables in that lousy little place on the beach."

"We have all we need."

"We've got nothing."

"Be patient. In a few months we'll have enough money to buy a TV set."

"Come on, Magda—I don't want to watch other people's lives. I want to live."

"I want to live too. I have a dream that someday we'll have a little sandwich shop of our own."

"Sandwich shop? That's boring. Don't you remember Kraków? We were good together and we had fun."

"Stop it! We're in a new country. We have a new start. I don't want to hear this again." And she left the room.

Luba was convinced that Magda had blocked out their past life. Whenever Luba brought up Kraków, Magda acted as if she had never heard of the place. She never even mentioned Chaim, although sometimes she would hum one of his songs as she was getting ready for work. Magda wore very conservative clothes now, hardly any makeup. She seemed a different person.

Then Magda met Colonel Stanley Johnson.

Colonel Johnson—African Kings Rifles, Retired—was always immaculately dressed, his suits expertly tailored to fit his short, bony frame, not a wrinkle on him, trouser creases sharp as knives, shoes shined, a handkerchief in the breast pocket carefully folded. On his chest he proudly wore two campaign ribbons earned in the Mau Mau rebellion. He had a pencil-thin mustache above pencil-thin lips. It was hard to tell his age—his narrow face had no wrinkles, though he had to be in his late forties or early fifties. He developed the habit of coming into Magda's restaurant each evening, taking a little table overlooking the sea, and ordering coffee and a scone.

He was extremely polite. From time to time Magda would catch him looking at her. He would smile pleasantly, then go back to his coffee. He always left with a gracious remark.

One night he waited until Magda was finished and then walked her home. He was a widower, Magda told Luba, a military hero who, after retiring from the armed forces, spent many years in very exotic places —Magda couldn't remember them all—Uganda, Tanzania, Kenya. But the politics of Africa had changed too much for his liking and he had recently returned home to England. He now wanted to buy a little hotel or rooming house near Brighton. "I have never met a man like this before. I think he's serious." Magda looked at Luba steadily for a long moment. "I don't want anything to go wrong," she said.

———————

They seem so happy, thought Luba, watching through the window. Colonel Stanley Johnson was walking very stiffly, Magda on his arm, smiling. As they entered the house Magda rushed over to Luba and held out her hand—on her ring finger she wore a very tiny diamond. "Colonel Johnson and I are going to get married," she whispered, tears in her eyes.

Luba didn't move. She glanced at the smiling statue of Colonel Johnson, then back at Magda. She had never seen her mother so blissful, but it was strange—Magda called him *Colonel* Johnson. Would she do so forever?

"Mama, I'm happy for you," said Luba as she put her arms around her mother. It was the first time in years that she had called her "Mama."

Colonel Johnson was still standing at attention in the background. Ill at ease, Luba didn't know whether to shake his hand or kiss him on the cheek. To break the awkward silence, she rushed to the staircase and yelled, "Ginga! Yanak! Magda's getting married!"

They came running down, overwhelming the couple with congratulations. Yanak insisted that they all have a drink. "Let's celebrate! Come on up, all of you!"

"Magda dear, you go on up," Colonel Johnson said. "I want to have a word with Luba."

Yanak led the way, and big, powerful Ginga pulled Magda up the stairs. Luba was left with Colonel Johnson—still smiling. She felt embarrassed and a little nervous.

"Let's sit down," he said as he led her to the sofa. She couldn't look at him; she kept her head down, her eyes on the sharp creases in his trousers.

"I love your mother, and I wish to make her a good husband," he started in his clipped British accent. "I love you too, and I wish to be a good father. I have purchased a little hotel near Brighton. And I'm sure, if we all three strive together, we can make it a success."

The clipped way he spoke made it difficult for Luba to understand him completely. She wondered how much Magda, who knew less English, understood.

"I know that you and your mother have had a hard life," he went on. "I want it to be a happier, easier one. You must have the childhood you never had. Your mother has told me you have a special talent for drawing—that talent should be encouraged. What else do you like? Dancing? I'll send you to ballet school. Swimming? There will be sufficient opportunities for that in Brighton," he said with a tight smile. "I want you to spend a lot of time doing things you like to do and not in a stockroom."

Her tears blocked out the vision of his shiny shoes.

"When you have problems, come to me," he continued. "Let us talk about them. Let us be friends. I want to help. And I want you to help me"—she looked up for the first time—"to make your mother happy."

Luba buried her head in his shoulder. "Thank you. Thank you. I want to help. I promise I'll help."

How could she have doubted this strange, smiling little man? He loved Magda. Her happiness was his main concern. She felt an overwhelming wave of affection for him. She would finally have a father. At last they would be a real family. He would be Dada, not "Colonel Johnson." Yes, she would help him. She would make him proud of her.

———

The wedding took place at the registry office in the Weymouth town hall. Mrs. Kulik was there, and Ginga, towering over Yanak. The local newspaper sent a photographer. It was a romantic story: English war hero weds Polish refugee. A new life begins. The happy end of a long struggle.

After the reception, the bridegroom left for Brighton to sign the deed for the purchase of a small hotel. It bothered Luba that Magda didn't have her wedding night. She wondered if they had ever been in bed together.

Luba looked at her mother—Magda was absolutely radiant. She had just married an English gentleman, charming, polite, intelligent, with immaculate manners. She blushed when anyone called her "Mrs. Johnson." Then the thought hit Luba: She's a whore! It shocked her to think that. Yet it was true. They had both become whores—to survive. But now they would become a normal, happy family. Colonel and Mrs. Stanley Johnson and their daughter, Luba Johnson.

CHAPTER 5

1954 | Hollywood, California

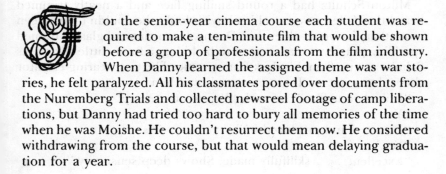

or the senior-year cinema course each student was required to make a ten-minute film that would be shown before a group of professionals from the film industry. When Danny learned the assigned theme was war stories, he felt paralyzed. All his classmates pored over documents from the Nuremberg Trials and collected newsreel footage of camp liberations, but Danny had tried too hard to bury all memories of the time when he was Moishe. He couldn't resurrect them now. He considered withdrawing from the course, but that would mean delaying graduation for a year.

Suddenly it came to him: He would make his movie about Tyrone. It would be the story of a black marine who returns to his home in the South with a little white girl, an orphan from the war. He would call it *Saved.*

Danny had no trouble assembling a cast from among the waiters, all aspiring actors, who worked with him at the luncheonette; they were delighted to act in front of a camera supplied by the university. He had difficulty filling the lead role, since black actors were in short supply, so the cook played the part—and perfectly.

He used the site where homes were being demolished to make way for Dodger Stadium. In the rubble, Fourth of July fireworks simulated a war scene. The first day he stood in front of his cast outlining the scene he had written, he knew he would someday become a director.

The film won first prize.

———

Shortly after, Milton Schultz, a hot young agent from Famous Artists, called him in for an interview. Danny was excited—Schultz had been one of the judges of the student films.

He sat in the waiting room on the sixth floor of the Famous Artists building on the corner of Wilshire Boulevard and Beverly Drive. All around him others were waiting, handsome young actors, sexy ingenues, and a few bearded types, who, Danny assumed, were writers. All eyes turned in unison as Mr. Charles Grossman walked by. On the street you wouldn't have looked at him twice—medium height, black hair, round smooth face—unless you knew, as everyone here did, that he was one of the most powerful agents in Hollywood. Oblivious to the stares of those who had waited hours, or perhaps days, hoping to see him, he closed the door behind him.

The receptionist chirped, "Mr. Dennison, the last office on the left."

Milton Schultz had a round smiling face and a neatly trimmed beard that failed to conceal his boyish looks; he couldn't have been more than five years older than Danny. Horn-rimmed glasses framed sparkling gray eyes that seemed to be hiding a funny little secret. As Schultz got up from his desk Danny noticed he was wearing elevator shoes, but even so, Danny towered over him.

"I liked your film," he said. "You wrote it?"

"Yes."

"Directed and produced it?"

"Yes."

"Excellent . . . skillfully made. Shows deep sensitivity."

"Thank you," Danny answered modestly.

"That scene with the little girl—as a Jew, I was really touched. Brought to mind all those innocent victims of the Holocaust. You Jewish?"

Danny felt the familiar tightening in his stomach. "No, but I have always admired Jewish people. Like many others, I feel a deep compassion for their suffering."

"Not many *goyim* feel that way," muttered Schultz.

"I beg your pardon?"

"*Goyim.* Gentiles. No offense," the agent added with a smile.

Danny took a deep breath and managed a weak smile.

"But in Hollywood, Jewish themes don't sell," Schultz said. "That's just one man's opinion." Then he winked and pointed to a signed photo of a busty starlet. "One of my better clients—she has *no* opinions."

They both laughed, and Schultz motioned Danny to a leather couch in front of which stood a coffee table, a chess set on top.

"You play chess?" the agent asked.

"No, I never have."

"Too bad; it's a great game. But now tell me—what do you want to do?"

Danny had his answer ready. "I want to direct feature films."

Schultz's black eyebrows became two crescents. "Oh, you wanna start at the top, huh?"

"Well, I—"

"You need more than that little piece of film to get your ass in a director's chair."

Taken aback, Danny reddened.

"Let's try to get you started in TV," Schultz went on.

"Move to New York?"

"No—TV is moving out here. I'll set you up with one of the CBS directors. Would you like that?"

"Yes, sir, Mr. Schultz."

"Call me Milt."

"Yes, sir, Milt."

The agent wrote out a name and address. "This guy is a client." He lowered his voice. "Drinks too much . . . old-timer . . . beginning to fall apart. He needs all the help he can get. You understand?"

Danny nodded.

"I'm gonna kill two birds with one stone. Save his job and get you one," Milt burst out in a loud cackle, "and collect a ten percent commission from the both of you." Danny laughed too. He knew he was in good hands. He had his foot in the door.

———

It was a big, heavy door. Above it, a red light blinked and a sign read: DON'T ENTER WHEN LIGHT IS ON. Danny waited with his hand on the knob, and when it stopped blinking, he quickly went in. He was on a Paramount soundstage, a structure big enough to be an airplane hangar, which had been rented to film a TV drama. As he stood there trying to absorb the whirlwind of activities, a young beanpole of a fellow with an unruly shock of blond hair approached him. "Danny Dennison?"

"Yes, sir."

The young man laughed. "Call me Slim. I'm the assistant director —that's a fancy name for gofer." He had a warm smile that relaxed Danny immediately. "Follow me," he said, waving his hand. They wended their way past grips carrying huge hunks of scenery, actors rehearsing scenes, dancers stretching their legs on exercise bars, crew members gossiping around a coffee urn, to a man hunched over a teacup in a high director's chair with MR. ANDREWS stenciled across the back.

"This is Danny Dennison," said Slim as they came up behind him.

Startled, the old man turned around. He removed the dark glasses he was wearing and looked at Danny through hooded eyes as if he were trying to recall where he had seen him before. He scratched a shaggy mane of thick gray hair. Finally he spoke. "Ah yes—the lad Milt sent me."

"I'm happy to be working for you, Mr. Andrews."

"Don't be so sure," came the retort in a low gravelly voice.

Danny wondered if he should laugh.

Mr. Andrews reached down to fill his teacup from a thermos jug. "We'll talk later. For now, you stick with Slim."

As they walked away, Slim smiled at Danny. "He's really a great guy, used to be a big-time director, years ago. Came over from London Films."

"I guess that's why he drinks so much tea."

"Tea?" Slim chuckled. "Oh yes, he loves it." Then abruptly he called out in a loud voice: "Atmosphere—in your places. Musicians, get a move on."

A wave of people noisily moved toward the set, a nightclub scene gaudily lit up. Slim looked at Mr. Andrews, who gave a nod as he sipped. "Roll 'em!" shouted Slim. The cameras started turning. "Action!" There was a sudden blare of dance music through the loud-speakers as everyone started dancing and the band moved their instruments in rhythm. Suddenly the music was cut off but everyone continued gyrating as if it were still playing. The two principals, dancing with great animation, started a conversation, their voices raised above the nonexistent music. Danny was intrigued. At a signal from Slim the music came blaring on again. Slim then glanced at Mr. Andrews and yelled, "Cut!" The music and dancing abruptly stopped. "Take five!" And the extras all noisily shuffled off the set.

Slim leaned over conspiratorially to Danny. "Let me tell you something important. In TV you don't have to be good; you just have to be fast." Then he motioned with his head to Mr. Andrews, still slumped in his chair. "He's *very* good, but he ain't fast. That's why you're here."

After the day's shooting, Danny followed Mr. Andrews up to his office, listening to the steady tap the old man's cane made as he shuffled down the hallway. They sat down and Mr. Andrews offered him a shot of Scotch, which it turned out—and he made no pretense of concealing it—was the major ingredient in his tea. As they both sipped, Mr. Andrews said, "Lad, what do you want to do?"

"Make films, sir—feature films."

Mr. Andrews snorted. "First, learn your craft. The good TV directors and writers of today will be the ones making the feature films of tomorrow."

"You think so, sir?"

"I know so." He removed his dark glasses and wiped them on his shirt sleeve. "Those asshole studio heads scoffed at TV when it started—until they noticed that every Tuesday evening the streets were empty and the people weren't at the movies."

"Where were they?" Danny asked naïvely.

"Home, laddie, watching Uncle Miltie. Mr. Berle, laddie, jolted this industry. Before that, Jack Warner issued an edict that none of the stars in his stable could appear on that little box. Now look—Warner is shooting not one, but three TV series. TV is exciting. The only thing wrong with it is the people who run it."

"You mean the networks?"

"No, no—*they* don't run it."

"Who does?"

"The sponsors. . . . Look, laddie, our sponsor is a cigarette company. Would you believe this—I have orders that all the heroes in our series must smoke cigarettes, and the villains aren't allowed to."

Danny looked at him blankly.

"That's right, laddie—the villains only sneer." With a raspy laugh he continued. "And you want to hear something worse? When they dramatized the Nuremberg Trials, the sponsor, a gas company, wouldn't let them say 'gas.' " Mr. Andrews doubled over in a spasm of laughter. "Get it, laddie? The whole thing was about gassing the Jews and they didn't say 'gas' once." His laughter died. "Now you see what's wrong with this industry?"

Danny sipped his drink in silence.

"You still want to be in this racket?"

"Yes, sir."

"What a mistake." Mr. Andrews took a gulp. "Well, I suppose it's too late to correct the error of your ways. Here's the script of our next episode. Study it carefully and then start working with the actors."

"What do you want me to do?"

"Whatever you can. Help them learn their lines—maybe you'll have a suggestion or two. You think you can handle that?"

"Yes, sir, Mr. Andrews."

"Now run along, lad—don't keep your lassie waiting."

"No, no, I enjoy talking with you, sir. No one's waiting."

Mr. Andrews squinted at Danny. "How old are you?"

"Twenty-two, sir."

"When I was your age . . ." He shook his head with a wry smile. "Now get the hell out of here."

Danny enjoyed working with the actors. At first they resented him, but gradually, imitating Mr. Andrews's quiet way of communicating, he won them over. They could see that he was talented and were grateful for his help.

And the more he observed Mr. Andrews at work, the more his respect grew. He loved the old guy and never tired of listening to him ramble on about his days in the theater, about great literature.

"Laddie, 'to thine own self be true,/And it must follow, as the night the day,/Thou canst not then be false to any man.' "

"Hamlet?"

"Yes, laddie, Hamlet. The classics. All the good plots in English literature have been done a long time ago."

When Mr. Andrews started to pull out a new bottle, Danny usually brought their chat to an end. He worried about the old man. He knew his drinking was getting out of control. Some days Mr. Andrews didn't even bother with his thermos, but blatantly poured Scotch from a bottle wrapped in a brown paper bag.

Danny worked well with Slim too; they became a team and often ate lunch together. Mr. Andrews drank his lunch, seldom leaving his director's chair. But one afternoon, coming back from the commissary, they found his chair empty. "Hunt him up, and I'll get the cast ready," Danny told Slim. A few minutes later Slim reappeared, distressed.

"I can't budge him. He's dead drunk."

The director was slumped over his desk, practically unconscious, and nothing they did would arouse him. Slim threw up his hands. "There is only one thing to do. You gotta take over, Danny, until he comes out of it."

"I can't do that."

"You have to. The front office won't take any more delays."

"I know, but he's the director."

"He is? Look at him."

Danny stared at the man he had come to love. "Slim, help me get him on his feet."

"What for?"

"Once we get him moving and into his chair, he'll be all right."

Reluctantly, Slim helped Danny hoist Mr. Andrews up by his armpits, and they managed to drag him through the side door and into his director's chair. There he sat in his usual pose, seeming to peer through his dark glasses. Danny shook him. "Mr. Andrews!"

Incoherent mumbles escaped the old man's lips.

The cast was waiting.

"Quiet, please!" Slim yelled in the midst of absolute silence.

"Yes, sir," Danny said loudly to Mr. Andrews, and then faced the cast with a warm smile. He took a deep breath. "Ladies and gentlemen . . . uh . . . Mr. Andrews has developed a temporary case of laryngitis . . . and he's asked me to . . . uh . . . transmit the directions he's been whispering in my ear."

Slim stared at him in amazement.

Danny's voice grew stronger. "Mr. Andrews would like to start from your entrance, Joe"—he motioned to the actor—"where you find your wife crying. Let's take it from there."

Slim, still pop-eyed, called out his instructions, the crew answering back.

"Camera ready?"

"Ready."

"Roll 'em."

"Rolling."

The slate boy came in front of the camera. "Scene seven. Take one."

Slim winked at Danny, who tried to appear confident as he stood next to Mr. Andrews's chair, his arms folded across his chest.

The charade worked well. It wasn't until the last shot that Mr. Andrews finally stirred.

Danny leaned over. "Are you all right, sir?"

The old man mumbled something.

"What's that?" Danny bent closer to his face.

"Good work, laddie."

———

At the end of the day Danny was completely exhausted. Slim came over and put his arms around him. "I don't know how we pulled it off —I'm a nervous wreck—but you did a great job, Danny."

"He was sobering up in the end."

"Sure, when the day's work was done. You saved his ass," Slim laughed as he headed toward the exit.

Danny sat down, tired but happy. In the silence of the deserted set, the sharp ringing of the phone made him jump.

It was Milt. "They're gonna pull the plug on the old fart," he told Danny.

"What? What are you talking about?"

"You know what I'm talking about."

"Mr. Andrews wasn't feeling well for a few hours; he's fine now."

"*Boychik*, never crap a crapper. They've wanted to get rid of him for a long time. They know what happened. You did a good job and they want you."

"Me?"

"Why do you think I gave you this chance?"

"He can't lose his job because of me," Danny protested. "He'll never get another. It'll kill him."

"Danny, get tough. You look big and strong, but you're soft. Toughen up!"

"But suppose he stops drinking?"

"He ain't never gonna stop."

"Listen, let me try."

"*Boychik*, I don't understand you. You want to be a director or not? Make up your mind." And Milt hung up.

Ashen-faced, Danny hurried over to Mr. Andrews's office. He walked in without knocking.

"I've been waiting for you, laddie. Here's your drink."

"I don't want a drink, Mr. Andrews." His tone made the director pause in the act of pouring. He looked up at Danny, then calmly filled the glass. As he brought it to his lips, Danny grabbed his hand. "Please. *Please!* You *must* stop drinking."

A bitter laugh escaped the old man.

"Stop drinking!" Danny shouted in his face.

Mr. Andrews leaned back in his chair and looked up at Danny towering over him. "You're a good lad," he said softly. "I like you. But go down to the ocean and command the tide not to come in. You'll have more success." He gulped down the liquor.

Danny stood there helplessly, trying to think of something to say. When the director poured himself another shot, Danny slowly walked out of the office. That was the last time he saw Mr. Andrews alive. The next morning police found the director's mangled body in his car, which was wrapped around a telephone pole on Sunset Boulevard.

For a long time after, Danny couldn't direct a scene unless Mr. Andrews's empty chair was beside him. No one ever sat in it.

Danny was grateful to have Slim working with him. They could almost read each other's thoughts. When they became tense, they kidded each other.

"I tell you, Danny—working for you is making my hair fall out."

"Isn't that hair-restorer stuff doing the trick?" Danny would tease.

"Look at me—it's you who's doing the trick."

Then Danny would put his arm around Slim. "Don't worry—before I'm through it'll all be gone." And they'd laugh.

Slim was a good teammate, but Danny's best friend was Milt. He was the opposite of Danny; nothing bothered him. He was sometimes crude, but he was always honest and direct. For his part, Milt was very proud that his young client was becoming well known and respected in the TV world. He often invited Danny for a home-cooked meal, but Danny tried to keep these evenings to a minimum; they nudged at memories that he had buried long ago.

As he rang the bell, Danny tried not to look at the *mezuzah* nailed to the doorpost. He could hear Kathy, Milt's eight-year-old daughter, hammering away at her piano lessons—one had to admire her tenacity, he thought.

Sarah, her chubby face beet-red from cooking, wiped her hands on a frilly apron over her size-10 hips that were uncomfortably squeezed into size-8 slacks. She kissed him on the cheek, and repeated what she always said: "Come in, Danny. Tonight you eat well—none of that *goyishe* food. We'll fatten you a little. Excuse me . . . ." and she dashed back into the kitchen from which the usual smells of potato pancakes, matzo-ball soup, and chopped chicken liver emanated.

Milt was intently studying the chessboard. "Just in time," he said without looking up. His son, Jonathan, age seven, sat opposite him with the bored expression of a player who knew well the outcome of the game.

"Checkmate," said Jonathan as he contemptuously slapped down his bishop.

"By God, he did it again," said Milt, getting up and shaking Danny's hand. "You try him."

"No, no," said Danny. "I barely know the moves."

"Jonathan will help you," said Milt as he set up the chessboard.

Danny sat down, determined to make it a pleasant experience. After a couple of moves with his pawns, he advanced his bishop and smiled at Jonathan. "How's that?"

"Stupid."

"That's not nice," Milt admonished not too severely.

Danny liked children, but there was something about Jonathan—he didn't quite know what it was. He hated the kid.

He could hear Kathy still laboriously going over the same piece of music. Milt nudged him with pride. "Listen to that, Danny."

Danny tried not to. But he said, "She's great," as he moved the pieces haphazardly, hoping to bring the game to a quick end. He succeeded.

When the meal was finished—Danny didn't dare ask for a bicarbonate—and the kids were, mercifully, sent up to their rooms, Milt whispered to Danny, "I hate Jewish food. Thank God I stopped her from making it kosher."

"Have I got a girl for you, Danny!" Sarah called out from the kitchen. Milt and Danny quickly exchanged glances as she entered with the dessert tray. "She's a jewel—don't you think so, Milt?" Sarah gushed as she poured his coffee. "And she's rich too."

"Thank you, Sarah, but right now, with Milt's help, I want to concentrate on my career."

"The right woman can help your career more than Milt," she said over her shoulder as she headed back to the kitchen to clean up. Her last remark came through the closed door: "Milt, why don't you fix up an evening with her?"

"I will, darling," he shouted, shaking his head "no" at Danny. They both laughed.

"Danny, you haven't seen my office."

"I've seen it—the last one at the end of the hall."

"Wrong—the second one from Mr. Grossman's."

"Congratulations. You must be doing well."

"With clients like you how can I lose? Every one of your TV shows has been a hit. You're brilliant, Danny."

"If I'm so brilliant why can't you get me a feature film to direct?"

"Oh, we're around to that again."

"Well, now that you're two doors away from Mr. Grossman, you got the clout to swing it."

"Yeah, maybe I have. Let me think about it."

"Take your time—I've only been waiting five years."

———

It was 1960. John Kennedy had just been elected, and Chubby Checker and the Twist were the rage, but all twenty-eight-year-old Danny cared about was the meeting Milt had set up with Art Gunn.

Art Gunn had clawed his way up the ladder by making a series of low-budget horror films that had consistently made money for the studio; he was now in line to be the next head of Ace Films. Gunn was tough, Milt warned him. He was made from the same mold as the Russian Jews who had come from New York ghettos to Hollywood to make real their fantasies of America. Gunn's fantasies were cheaper, with less gilt, less glamour—all he cared about was the bottom line.

Milt, dressed in his loudest checkered sports jacket, and Danny, in his usual dark-blue blazer and gray flannel slacks, had lunch at the studio commissary before the meeting. Chomping on a "Humphrey Bogart" steak, Milt mumbled, "Don't say I didn't get you into a studio."

Between bites of his "Greta Garbo" tuna fish salad, Danny watched high-priced directors Willie Wyler and Howard Hawks enter the private executive dining room. "You did, Milt. Now, how do I get in *there?*"

The meeting with Art Gunn lasted five minutes. From behind his oversized desk, punctuating his words with a fat cigar, Gunn told Danny, "You bring me a script that will make me a million and your dog can direct it for all I care."

Danny lost all interest in television, consumed by his search for a script to satisfy the low tastes of Art Gunn. It wasn't easy, but the words of Mr. Andrews—"it's all in the classics"—sent him in the right direction. His first project for Ace Films was a western based on *King Lear*, except the chief character was an old rancher trying to divide his domain among his three daughters. Danny wrote the script himself.

The day of the sneak preview, Milt drove him to the Gondola Theater in the San Fernando Valley, joking that Danny was too nervous to be trusted behind the wheel. Once there, Danny felt nauseous and asked Milt to watch the movie, while he paced in close proximity to the men's room. On the other side of the lobby Art Gunn had placed himself next to the table where the preview score cards and short-stubbed pencils were laid out. Inside, the audience of college students was silent. Danny didn't know how to interpret it.

When, yelling and shoving and blowing bubble gum, they poured out to mark down their reactions, he regarded them with growing despair. As Milt approached, Danny mustered a weak smile. "Does my future depend on what these little idiots think?"

"They paid for their tickets," Milt cackled.

As the audience thinned out, Danny watched Art Gunn rifling through the score cards. The teeth gripping the fat cigar were bared in a wide grin.

Milt had negotiated a good contract with Ace Films that enabled Danny to move out of his modest apartment overlooking Sunset Strip and buy a house he used to think he could never afford. Just off Tower Road, five minutes from the Beverly Hills Hotel, it was a Swiss chalet set against an incline. The garage was underneath the house and the spacious main floor—a large kitchen, living room with fireplace, and a guest room—had a magnificent view of the hills. From the living room a staircase led to the master bedroom, which opened onto a grassy plateau out back. Danny thought he'd someday build a swimming pool and tennis court there. The bedroom was Danny's favorite part of the house. He put his desk in there and loved, while working on scripts, to walk out on the grass and stare at the brown hills.

Classics adapted to westerns were his stock-in-trade. His movies were not Oscar-winning material—intellectuals scoffed at them, saying he corrupted great works of literature to pander to mass taste. But others said he brought the great message of the classics to the common man in an entertaining way. The controversy got him a lot of attention, and even his harshest critics had to admit that his movies were clever. There was no denying that they made money.

Reading articles about himself, he had the feeling they were describing a different person. His success seemed unreal. His life seemed unreal. It was as if he were a character in one of his movies.

His name was frequently mentioned in the gossip columns as one of the most eligible bachelors in town—thirty-three, talented, and climbing. He was considered very good-looking, and was compared to handsome actors like Cliff Robertson or Robert Taylor. He was often linked with one gorgeous starlet or other, but somehow he couldn't make any relationship last longer than a couple of months. Sarah, of course, was undaunted in her efforts to marry him off. Her choices were always described as "decent" and "perfect-wife-and-mother material"—this translated into "overweight and desperate for a husband." Behind her back, Milt went in the opposite direction; the blind dates he sent Danny were voluptuous playgirls hoping to get into movies.

One night after dinner, while Sarah was in the kitchen making coffee, Milt whispered, "How was Nancy last night?"

"Not bad," Danny said with a grin.

"I envy you, *boychik* . . . ahh, to be single again."

"But Sarah is a terrific gal." Danny tried to sound convincing.

"Yeah, she is," agreed Milt with little enthusiasm. "But we've been together since college—we've changed. I love this crazy business, and Sarah would be happier still living in the Bronx."

"Why don't you take her back for a visit?"

"Sure," Milt laughed, glancing quickly toward the kitchen, "but not this weekend. This weekend, let's you and I go to Vegas."

"Vegas? What for?"

"To get away. Come on, you might get lucky." There was an insistence in Milt's voice.

"I wish I could go, but I have to work."

"You work too much—you don't fuck enough."

Danny laughed as Sarah walked in. "Darling, tell Danny about that lovely Gentile girl Rosalind we met at the Rosenbergs' the other night."

"Yeah, that's a good idea," Milt said, rolling his eyes.

When Sarah left the room again, Milt sat on the arm of Danny's chair. "Am I your friend?"

"Yeah, Milt." Danny smiled. "About the only one I have."

"Then you've got to come to Vegas with me."

"But Milt . . ."

Putting a restraining hand on Danny's arm, Milt darted another glance toward the kitchen, where Sarah was making a lot of noise whipping cream for the strawberry tart. "I need an alibi. Sarah's getting suspicious."

"What's in Vegas?"

"Darlene."

"Who?"

"Come on—you remember Darlene. The blond dancer on your last film?"

"Yeah, vaguely . . ."

"Danny, she's terrific. Works in Vegas now. I made a date with her after the show Saturday night."

Danny hesitated.

"I'll tell her to get you a girl," Milt pleaded.

"You don't have to do that. Look, if it means that much to you, I'll go."

Milt looked as if he were going to cry. "You're a real friend, Danny. I won't forget this."

———

They sat together watching the show at Caesars Palace.

"There she is," whispered Milt, nudging Danny and almost knocking the drink out of his hand. "The third from the left. . . . And I got good news for you, *boychik:* Darlene fixed you up with Tina, her best friend." He leaned closer to Danny's ear. "The dark one at the end."

She certainly had a great body. It might be a fun evening, Danny thought.

After the show, they separated, Milt wasting no time taking Darlene up to his room. Danny turned to Tina. "Would you like to have some dinner?"

"Dinner?"

"You must be hungry after the show."

"Sure am," she said gratefully.

He took her to the special restaurant for high rollers in the penthouse. Tina stared blankly at the ornate French menu.

"May I order for both of us?"

"Please," she said with obvious relief.

He studied her. She was probably the beauty queen of some small midwestern town, now ready to do anything to be remembered by a Hollywood director. She was tempting, but so vulnerable. He couldn't go through that routine again.

After dinner, much to her surprise, Danny took her home and caught the next plane back to L.A.

On Monday, Milt came over to the studio. "You left in a hurry, *boychik*—it didn't take you long to score."

"No, Milt, I just bought her dinner and came home."

"I don't believe you."

"Yeah, that's what I did."

Milt scratched his beard and peered at Danny through his glasses. "You know, I think you're a little uptight about sex."

"I am?"

"Yeah, you're damn good-looking, they're all after you, and you don't even notice."

"Come off it, Milt."

"You're not getting your quota."

Danny laughed at how earnestly Milt argued.

"I mean it—pick any star you want, call up, make a date. You'll see. A lot of them stay home most nights, because everyone thinks they're busy and don't ask them. You could be fucking a different star every night."

"Milt, do you want to go to bed with every girl you see?"

"Listen, somebody asked me once, 'You ever have a lousy lay?' I said, 'Yeah.' 'So, how was it?' My answer: 'Terrific!'" And with a cackle Milt put his arm around Danny. "You're crazy, but you're my friend. You covered for me and I owe you one."

"Good. Then keep Art Gunn off my back on my next picture."

"Oh—I'm glad you brought that up."

"Now what?"

"When do you start *Buffalo Land*?"

"Next week."

"Give Darlene a part."

"But it's set. All I haven't cast yet is the herd of buffalo."

"Write something in—unless you want to keep flying with me to Las Vegas."

Danny laughed. "And I thought you were worried about *my* quota."

"Listen—" Milt's voice was unusually serious. "These girls don't go after me for my looks. As Sarah always reminds me, Clark Gable I'm not—so, *boychik*, I gotta deliver."

Danny understood, and he obliged his friend, adding the part of a saloon dancer for Darlene. It was his fifth feature film, an adaptation of *Macbeth*, the story of a greedy rancher and his wife trying to take over the neighboring grazing lands.

Danny parked his new 1967 Porsche and, annotated script in hand, walked briskly onto the soundstage. He greeted Matilda, the script girl, with a kiss on the cheek, and handed her the latest changes. The electricians were busy setting the lights for the scene he had prepared the day before. He peered through a viewfinder, making minor adjustments in the composition of the shot.

When he raised his head, he saw Slim smiling at him.

"That smile of yours doesn't fool me," Danny joked. "Underneath, you worry all the time—that's why you're pulling your hair out."

Slim's hand instinctively went up to his enlarged bald spot. "I've got a surprise for you," he whispered.

"That's just what I need, another surprise."

And then he spotted her, standing on the edge of the set.

As he stared, Slim said, "Danny, I want you to meet your mother."

Margaret Dennison came forward, her eyes glistening.

He embraced her. She felt so thin and frail in his arms. There were deep lines in her drawn face.

It had been years since he'd seen her. He only made perfunctory calls on holidays, and occasionally sent short antiseptic notes with the monthly check. To these he always received a warm, grateful reply. Now he felt so guilty. Finally he stammered out, "I'm so glad to see you. Every time I made plans to visit you I got mired in a movie."

"I understand, Daniel. I've seen them all."

"At the Rialto?"

"Of course."

"Yes. That's where it all started," said Danny as he sat her down in his director's chair. Her dress seemed too big for her fragile frame and her slip was showing. He squatted down beside her. "I'll never forget those Saturday matinees."

"Neither will I."

"And now 'Look at me, Ma'—like Cagney—'I'm on top of the world.' "

Margaret squeezed his hand.

"We're ready, boss," Slim interrupted.

"Don't let me hold you up, Daniel."

"Don't worry. Stars never rush to the set. . . . Take care of my mother, Slim, while I create a masterpiece before her very eyes," he chuckled.

"Are you comfortable, Mrs. Dennison? Anything I can get you . . . coffee?" Slim was most solicitous.

"No, no, thank you. But maybe you'll tell me what is happening. I've never seen a movie being made. This looks like a saloon . . ."

He started to explain, but she didn't seem to be listening. She watched, fascinated, as Danny spoke softly but intently to the actors playing the greedy rancher MacMurtry and his wife.

"Quiet, everybody!" yelled Slim over Mrs. Dennison's head. "We're rehearsing!"

MacMurtry spoke: "I've had enough—let's stop it now."

Mrs. MacMurtry: "No. We can't go back. Sober up, please. We've got to finish it, Mac."

MacMurtry: "You're right—we're in too deep. There's no turning back."

Mrs. Dennison's face came alive. " 'I am in blood/Stepp'd in so far, that, should I wade no more,/Returning were as tedious as go o'er.' "

Slim looked at her strangely, not understanding.

"That's the theme of *Macbeth*," she explained, teacher to student. "The dilemma of a man who's crossed the point of no return. He can't retreat. He has to keep moving toward certain disaster."

"Hm, I see," Slim said, looking at his watch. "Ready for a break?"

Danny returned with two cups of coffee.

"Daniel, you're such a hard taskmaster," Mrs. Dennison exclaimed as he handed her a cup of coffee, "making the actors repeat the same lines over and over. It must be exhausting for them."

"That's why they make a lot of money."

She giggled. "And who are those people on the set now?"

"Stand-ins. They stand in the spots so the electricians can adjust the lighting properly."

"Why don't the actors do that themselves?"

"You just said they must be exhausted."

She giggled again, squeezing his arm. She was acting like a happy schoolgirl. Danny was delighted that she was enjoying herself.

As they were leaving they bumped into Milt, who had a rendezvous with Darlene in Danny's office. In the Continental manner he reserved for older women, Milt kissed Mrs. Dennison's hand. "I see where Danny gets his good looks."

She beamed.

"Milt is my best friend," Danny said.

"Yeah," Milt deadpanned, "that's why I let him keep ninety percent of my money."

Danny laughed at Mrs. Dennison's puzzled expression. "He's just joking, but some agents mean it."

―――――――

That evening, he took her to dinner at Chasen's in Beverly Hills.

"To the woman who played the most important role in my life," he toasted her with champagne.

"You have given me such a wonderful day, Daniel." Her eyes were misty.

Danny couldn't get over how much she had aged. Her lipstick

didn't quite follow the lines of her mouth, and she had lost her patrician look of refinement.

He ordered a "Hobo" steak for both of them, a Chasen's specialty. "Medium rare?"

"Oh that would be fine," she said, nodding.

Over the rim of his champagne glass he studied this woman who had done so much for him. She looked sad. On the set she was giggling, and now she was so solemn. Her pupils were hot black spots, and her hand trembled as she raised the glass to her smudged lips.

"You feeling all right, Margaret?" It felt strange to say her name after so many years.

She looked up at him, and in a low voice he could barely hear above the din of the restaurant, she said, "If I have committed any sins against you, Daniel, please forgive me."

Danny was startled. "How can you say that? You have done more for me than any person alive."

She smiled faintly as she took another sip. "I hope so. I would like you to remember any good deeds I may have done."

She's talking so strangely, Danny thought. Maybe it's the champagne. "Is anything wrong, Margaret?" he asked again.

"Nothing," she said with a wan smile. "I'm so proud of you, so proud of your success. But I'm feeling a little tired, and I have to catch an early plane back home tomorrow."

"But Margaret, you just got here! You haven't seen my house yet. There's a lovely guest room for you—"

"Oh thank you, Daniel, but I must go back."

"Why don't you stay awhile and rest? You look tired. Please."

She smiled sadly. From her battered handbag she removed a small package wrapped in pale-blue paper and tied with a lacy ribbon. "I want you to have this, Daniel. It's a little book someone gave me when I was young. I didn't pay much attention to it then, but lately I've found myself returning to it over and over. Will you please read it carefully and think about what it says?" She looked at him with those intense eyes again; she seemed to be pleading. "Consider it an assignment from your old teacher."

Danny took the package, not knowing how to respond. When he said good-bye, he promised to visit her soon. But he didn't have a chance. A week later he got a call from her minister telling him that Mrs. Dennison had died; she had cancer and had made the visit to California against doctors' orders, knowing it was her last chance to see him.

It was then, struggling with grief and guilt, that he opened the little package. It smelled of lavender, like she always did.

The book, a sixteenth-century morality play, was in German on one side, *Jedermann,* and English on the other, *Everyman.*

He found the archaic English hard to follow; it was much easier to read the German. "God spoke: Summon All Creatures to Come and Give Account of Their Lives," it began. The protagonist Everyman faces the final reckoning. As God's messenger, Death, waits, he desperately calls on his friends to testify on his behalf, but all of them— Pleasure, Beauty, Strength—fail him. He opens his treasure chest, but his accumulated wealth is useless. His only salvation is his friend Good Deeds, but Good Deeds finds little to say in Everyman's favor. The moral of the play: Take inventory of your life now—be sure you have done enough good deeds—the final reckoning always comes sooner than you expect.

Danny lowered the book and absentmindedly riffled the pages. He was disturbed, but he didn't know why. "Take an account of your life"? Is that what Margaret Dennison was trying to tell him? Was that the inheritance she left him? This was a book for an old woman with cancer who knew she was going to die. He wanted something that would erase the unhappiness that seemed to tinge everything in his life, even the good moments. Could the key be in this book? He doubted it, yet *Everyman* stayed in his thoughts.

CHAPTER 6

1986 | Brighton, England

olonel Johnson, standing erect and smiling, was waiting for them at the train station. "In a moment you will be greeting your new home," he declared, holding the car door open while the two women lugged the heavy bags and put them in the trunk.

GREENFIELDS INN, the sign said. What a lovely-sounding name, thought Luba as they drove within view—so peaceful. It was a rambling, four-story Victorian building with eighteen guest rooms and many terraces.

In the front seat, Colonel Johnson was explaining to Magda that because of her vast experience in food service she would be responsible for the cooking and catering. He planned to take over the public-relations end of the business. There was much to be done; the season had just started.

By the second week, the hotel was fully occupied. Magda slaved in the kitchen preparing breakfast for three dozen people. Most guests were at the beach during lunch, but many would want sandwiches to take with them. Then she'd have to start dinner.

During the day all the rooms needed to be cleaned and the beds made. That was Luba's job. He promised to hire additional help, but he had not yet found the right person. Meanwhile, he insisted on perfection, military precision. He criticized everything as not good enough and not fast enough. He could get quite unpleasant when displeased. But in front of the guests he always wore his smiling mask, constantly referring to his "wonderful wife" and his "beautiful daughter."

Luba was glad of one thing—she had a room of her own. It was on the fourth floor, where the smallest, cheapest guest rooms were, and hers was the tiniest of all. It wasn't a room really, only a converted supply closet, but it was hers.

At the end of the third week, he took it away. It was Saturday evening, and Luba was dead tired; she couldn't wait to finish working and stretch out in her little room. She was helping her mother wash the last of the dinner dishes when Colonel Johnson walked into the kitchen. "Luba, clear out your things," he ordered.

She looked at him, perplexed.

"On the double. We have a guest for your room. Put your clothes in our bedroom closet. You can sleep on the couch in my office." And out he went, resuming his smile.

"Why didn't he say the place was full?" Luba exploded.

Magda silently continued washing the dishes.

"Couldn't he say, 'I'm not giving my daughter's room away'? No ballet lessons. No swimming. And now no room! What's next on his goddamn schedule?"

"It's the season," Magda said finally. "He's nervous. He's trying to make it a success. Luba, darling, please be patient."

"Patient? We've been slaving here a month. He keeps talking about extra help—where is it? It's easy for him. He puts on his white jacket and just stands there grinning. He's great at playing the host—and counting money."

Magda slammed down a pot. "Stop it! I don't want to hear any more. We're in a strange town. I want to make a good life so we—"

She broke off. Colonel Johnson was standing in the doorway. She hadn't heard his rubber-soled shoes.

"No foreign language is to be spoken here, ever!" he snapped. "Here we speak English. And that's an order!" He gave them a hard, long look as if to underscore his words, turned sharply, and left.

Luba tried to contain her anger. How could her mother have been so wrong about this man? How could she? Of course Magda desperately wanted it to work out; she couldn't admit another failure.

All right—I'll help her in any way I can, Luba decided. No matter how difficult it is. Obediently, she went to move her things.

The office had a large, old-fashioned rolltop desk—Colonel Johnson's domain. He worked there every day, going over the bills and bookings; and he kept it securely locked, the key secreted in his vest pocket, which he always took care to button down. Luba saw him patting the pocket often, as if making sure the key was still there.

The second night Luba slept on the hard couch there, she was suddenly awakened by blazing lights. She opened her eyes to find Colonel Johnson working at his desk.

"What's happening?" she asked drowsily.

"Don't interrupt me when I'm working," he snapped.

Luba watched him counting money—a large pile of cash that he seemed to count over and over—all the while muttering something about "laziness" and "incompetence." Colonel Johnson didn't believe in savings accounts or safe deposit boxes, having lost his fortune when the British granted their colonies independence and the Africans nationalized the banks. Luba wondered how much money was already stashed in that rolltop desk. When he was through, he shut the top, carefully locking it and depositing the key in his vest pocket.

That was the first, but by no means the last, of many nocturnal visits.

One time he burst into the office, dressed in full military regalia, yelling, "Get up! Get up! It's the Queen's birthday—get up! We assemble at zero-five-hundred hours."

Totally dazed, Luba stumbled downstairs, where Magda was struggling to attach the Union Jack to the lanyards of the flagpole. He commanded them to stand at attention while he raised the flag.

"We honor the flag at every national holiday," he declared after the ceremony, following them into the kitchen.

Holy shit! Luba thought. Does it have to be at the crack of dawn? She glanced up at the wall clock. It was a little after five, two hours

earlier than they needed to be there, and they were already working—
he wanted a special breakfast to commemorate the occasion.

Colonel Johnson paced the kitchen floor, observing them with
impatience. Suddenly he smashed his fist into the mound of butter
balls. "They must be done properly!" he yelled.

They quickly began reshaping the butter as he continued to berate
both of them. Magda didn't look at Luba.

Three hours later, he was in the dining room, wearing his uniform,
his medals prominently displayed, his trousers creased, shoes shined.
"Good morning"—"How did you sleep?"—"My lovely wife has prepared something special this morning." He smiled his ingratiating
smile.

That afternoon, he decided that all the supplies should be moved
from the basement to the attic, where, he said, no one could steal
them.

Who the hell would want to steal toilet paper? Luba wondered as,
for the tenth time, she climbed the steep iron staircase that led from
the fourth floor to the attic. But, true to her vow to be patient, she
said nothing.

When she scrambled up, exhausted, for the last time, she found
him there, carefully putting away his uniform in the large trunk that
held his military memorabilia. He snapped the ornately carved lid
shut, saluted the trunk, and walked out as if she weren't there.

At last the season came to an end. A cool September wind blew in
from the sea, dissipating the heat of the summer. The hotel was
nearly empty. Things would change now, Magda said; Colonel Johnson would relax. The hotel had been filled during the entire summer,
so they must have done well, although he didn't say a word about it—
he never discussed money with them.

Yes, things changed. They got worse.

He insisted on running the hotel on the same routine. With many
vacant rooms, Luba still had to sleep on the couch. He ordered that
the linens in the empty rooms be changed even though no one had
slept in the beds, and the floors polished though no one had scuffed
them. "We must be prepared at all times for guests," he said.

He's crazy, Luba thought. He *must* be crazy. As if answering her
thoughts, Magda said, "He's hoping to get a large group of beer
distributors—a convention." She quickly glanced at the door. Whenever they spoke Polish, they were fearful he might overhear them and
blow up again.

His nighttime visits to the office were now more frequent. He would enter, put on the lights, and walk about the room noisily, muttering complaints.

Luba decided she must discuss it with Magda, but suddenly, the interruptions stopped. Luba was grateful. Then one night, undressing for bed, she had a strange feeling that she was being watched. She strode to the door and yanked it open. There was Colonel Johnson in a crouched position; he had been peeping through the keyhole. "I'm checking the locks," he said, straightening up quickly, and he walked away.

Luba lay on the couch, listening to the torrential rain. Since the incident last week, she had placed a towel on the doorknob to block the keyhole. She was miserable. The anger building within her was hard to restrain. She searched her thoughts for something pleasant. She tried to conjure up a carousel, the horses going round and round. The sound of the calliope was blocking out the din of the downpour, and Valentine was almost coming into focus, when suddenly she heard a loud thump and then something scraping against the floor, as if furniture were being moved around. Clearly now, she heard sharp cries of pain. It was her mother.

Luba sprang out of bed, threw on some clothes, and ran down the hall. She reached their bedroom door—it was locked.

"You fucking dirty cunt—I'll kill you!"

Was that the impeccable Colonel Johnson talking? She had never heard him utter a foul word.

"Please, please stop!" Magda was begging.

He was beating her. Luba pounded on the door. "Magda! Magda!"

There was a sudden silence, then a snarl: "Go back to your room." The beating resumed. Luba could hear what sounded like leather slapping against flesh, and her mother's whimper.

Luba pounded on the door again.

"Get away, you bitch!" he yelled. "I'll kill her if you come in!"

She ran out into the rain. Her bare feet splattered through the puddles as she raced to the police station. She was soaked to the skin and her wet hair was hanging in strings around her face by the time she got there. She rushed into a green-tiled room. "He's killing my mother! He's killing her! Please!!"

"Now, now, just calm down, little girl," said a policeman from behind a desk high on a podium. He was fat and bald with a thick mustache that made up for the hair he lacked on top.

"Help her—my stepfather's killing her!"

"I'm sorry," the policeman said, shuffling some papers calmly. "We can't interfere."

"Don't you understand?!" Luba said, looking wildly around the room for other policemen who might listen. "He's killing her!"

"We have no jurisdiction in family disputes."

Luba was speechless. Even in Poland the police would have come to investigate.

Noting her accent, he added, "That's English law."

A tall young sergeant, standing nearby, came over. He looked kind, and for a moment Luba thought he might help her. "Would you like some tea?" he asked in a polite voice.

She stared at him. He seemed embarrassed; his face was red above the boyish mustache that was just beginning to sprout on his upper lip. "Some tea?" he repeated with a smile.

She was incredulous—a man was killing her mother, she was pleading for help, and he was offering her tea.

"It's nice and hot," he added.

Shaking her head, she walked out of the building and slowly retraced her steps.

When she reached the hotel, shivering from cold, she found the front door locked. Fortunately a while back she had hidden a spare key in a flower box holding some plastic geraniums. Once inside, she held her breath and listened. The house was deathly quiet.

———

In the morning Luba cornered Magda alone in the pantry. "How long has this been going on?" she asked in a low voice.

Magda's eyes were full of fear. "Let's not talk about it, Luba. I'm fine."

"Fine?" Luba exclaimed with a sarcastic laugh. "He's nuts. Let's get out of here."

"Where will we go?"

"Anywhere!"

"He's my husband. Things will get better—you'll see," Magda insisted, and seeing Colonel Johnson approach, she quickly returned to her pots and pans.

The colonel came in slowly, looking at both of them as he walked around the worktable in the center of the kitchen. He stopped, glanced down, and pulled out a handkerchief from his vest pocket to brush some dust off his shoes. Carefully, he folded the handkerchief and put it back. He placed both hands on the table, his fingers spread

out, leaned over, and stared at Magda. "We speak English here—
remember? Only English. Do you understand, Magda?"

"Yes," said Magda softly.

"Speak up! Do . . . you . . . understand?" He measured out
each word precisely.

"Yes, yes," Magda said more clearly.

Luba turned away so that he couldn't see the angry tears forming in
her eyes.

————

With a red crayon, Luba slashed away at the sketchbook she propped
up against the closed rolltop desk. In her rage she had drawn a satanic
caricature of Colonel Johnson. She clenched her teeth. She was in a
whirlpool, helplessly spinning around with Magda. She had to get
out. They both had to get out.

It was an unusually warm day for the end of September and Luba
was perspiring—from the heat or from the hatred, she didn't know
which. She put down her sketchbook and took off her blouse. She
went behind a screen in front of the sink, turned on the faucet, and
started to sponge herself with cool water. Then she heard the door
open. He was in the room.

She stood there, saying nothing, hoping he would leave. She
couldn't make out what he was doing on the other side of the screen.
She leaned in to hear better. Maybe he had left.

Suddenly, from behind her, a hand clasped one of her breasts. "I'll
help you," he said.

She whipped around. He was naked and had an erection. He
started rubbing her wet body with his hands.

"Don't you touch me!" She pushed him away, hurriedly reaching
for her blouse. He tore off the page of her sketchbook with his
unflattering likeness and waved it at her as he danced around screeching, "Dirty girl—dirty little cunt!"

He ripped up the paper, throwing it in the air like confetti. He
whirled around and around more rapidly, rubbing his cock, letting
out a rapid stream of insults. "Cunt, asshole, shit—piss—dirty—dirty
girl."

She ran out of the room as he climaxed.

Bewildered by what had happened, Luba tried to avoid Magda.
How could she tell her? What could she say? Magda would remember
Chaim and think that Luba was betraying her again.

Luba set the tables for the evening meal, slamming down the silver-
ware. Before long Colonel Johnson came in from the kitchen wearing

his standard little white jacket. He looked at her quizzically. "Why are you so upset?" Without waiting for an answer, he walked out.

———

Throughout the fall and winter it was more of the same—a period of calm followed by more violence. Magda tried to hide the new bruises and Luba pretended not to see them. Magda's face was never bruised; somehow, in his crazy rages, Colonel Johnson never left marks that could be seen by his guests.

In order to avoid him as much as possible, Luba took to spending all her spare time in the attic, her sanctuary. There, curled on top of Colonel Johnson's military trunk with her sketch pad in her lap, she tried to block out what was going on in the rooms below. But the fanciful drawings of carousels and horses that had always helped her pass the time in Kraków now gave way to harsher images—shadowy silhouettes glimpsed through the chain-link fence of San Sabba, dead fish on the riverbank, the ocean view blocked by the heavy iron trusses of a fire escape.

Luba's absences seemingly went unnoticed; Colonel Johnson simply ignored her. Then it happened again.

Luba was in the office, kneeling on a chair, plucking her eyebrows at the little mirror, when she heard a key in the door. In the mirror, she watched him slowly enter in his full military dress. He stood by the door at attention and then unzipped his fly. He began to stroke himself. She stared at his reflection.

As he got close to her, she turned and grabbed his cock. He jumped back as if he'd been stabbed. Holding on, she backed him up against the wall and hissed, "Come on, let's fuck!"

Petrified, he slithered along the wall, whimpering, "Dirty girl—cunt!"

And then the pent-up anger boiled over, and she pounded him with her fists. "You goddamn fucking runt! Don't you touch my mother again!" She kicked him. "You little shit! I'll kill you!" She was amazed at her own violence. He didn't fight back. Exhausted, she stopped, leaving him there huddled against the wall, muttering obscenities.

She picked up her coat and walked out of the hotel. Outside the air was fresh and bright. She took a deep breath, but the depression sitting on her chest like a heavy boulder refused to lift. She looked around. Crocuses were already in bloom—spring would come early this year. It was the first warm March afternoon, and the residents of Brighton were happily taking advantage of this perfect day.

Walking on the promenade, she passed the young sergeant who

had insisted that she have a cup of tea. He tipped his helmet and greeted her cheerily: "Good day—how are things going?"

She didn't answer and continued walking past the happy mothers pushing perambulators along the promenade. On a bench, insatiable lovers clung to each other against the backdrop of gentle waves tipped with silver. She deserved to be loved like that—not to be fighting off a disgusting pervert. Magda deserved to be loved too. She had scrambled so hard to get them out of Kraków. She had been so proud of Colonel Johnson, certain he was the answer to her prayers for a happy future. What a cruel joke!

He was totally mad. And where would his madness lead? Magda went about her job in a state of numbness. When Luba last tried to persuade her to leave, Magda just shook her head. "We don't even have the money for a train ticket."

"I have it."

"You have money? You didn't steal it from his desk, did you?"

"I would if I could open it, but the bastard never lets go of the key. I just don't give him all the tips I get."

"But Luba, even if we left, where could we go? Back to Kraków?"

"Yes! That was a hell of a lot better than this."

Magda winced.

"Look, Magda—we could go to London. Remember that woman I met in Weymouth? Lois, from the escort service? I still have her address and phone number."

"An escort service is just like walking the street."

"So? What's wrong with that? It pays well."

"Never. Never again."

Looking out across the ocean now, Luba wondered if it was her fault. Maybe life would be better for Magda if she left. Her gloomy thoughts were interrupted by a faint, familiar sound. She ran along the promenade toward the source, and there it was—a miniature carnival on the beach. The tiny carousel was spinning children round and round to the accompaniment of a tiny calliope. Their laughter carried over the melody.

Valentine—where are you? He was the only bright thought in her dreary life, safely hidden in the corner of her daydreams. At night, when she lay on her couch, he would come out smiling, reassuring her, swinging around the stanchions of the revolving merry-go-round, his eyes never leaving her as she went up and down, up and down, over the hill into ecstasy, the calliope song echoing in her mind:

Ride, ride the carousel and reach for the golden ring. . . .
Never to finish, but begin again, life is a circular thing.

She turned around and went back to the hotel.

———————

Spring had won the battle and routed the last vestiges of winter with a victory cry of thunder and lightning. It rained hard that night. Luba, lying on the couch in the office, pulled the blanket around her and waited for Valentine to come strutting again across her mental horizon.

Her reverie was interrupted by violent screams. Even the roar of the storm could not muffle them.

Luba jumped up and dashed down the hall. The yelling reached a crescendo just as she turned the knob. The door was unlocked. She saw Magda rolling on the floor, Colonel Johnson over her, beating her with his belt. They were both naked. He was screaming, "You dirty woman—you filthy whore—you cunt!"

Luba leaped on his back and tried to pull him away from her mother. He threw her off with amazing strength, his face contorted with rage. "Get out of here!" He rushed to the closet and ripped Luba's clothes from the hangers. "Get out!" he hissed again, grabbing her shoes, her suitcase, and heaving everything through the open door. "Get out for good!"

Luba stood paralyzed. He brought his purple face within an inch of her nose and yelled, "Do you hear me, cunt?!"

Calmly, Luba spoke to her mother. "Come on, Magda—come with me." Magda stumbled up, but Colonel Johnson grabbed her by the neck. With his other hand he snatched up a pair of large scissors from the dressing table and held the points at Magda's breast. Everyone stood frozen, transfixed in a murderous scene caught in wax at Madame Tussaud's.

Then, distinctly, in a stony voice, he said to Magda, "I'll kill you if you move."

"Please go," Magda whispered.

Luba looked at the two naked bodies glistening with sweat; Magda's was covered with welts, a small trickle of blood slowly moving down her leg. She saw the blade of the scissors partially concealed by her mother's breast. She tried to sound composed. "If you put that down, I'll go."

Slowly, he moved the scissors away and tossed them on the bed. Tears were streaming down Magda's cheeks. "Please—please go."

Luba took the scissors and walked out. The door slammed behind her and a key turned in the lock. There was no other sound but the pouring rain. She gathered her things and put them in the suitcase. Numb, she went down the hall. I told her to leave a long time ago. I did my best to help her. What more can I do? She fought back the tears. But I tried, goddamn it, I tried. I've got a life to live too. I'm nineteen—my life can't end here.

She walked out into the night. This time she did not go back. She caught the first train to London.

CHAPTER 7

1968 | Beverly Hills, California

anny had been with Milt and the Famous Artists Agency for almost fifteen years, but he had never been invited to the annual dinner party given by Charlie Grossman, the head of the agency. Even Milt, in an office two doors away from Grossman, had never been invited. The exclusive list of sixty or so was circulated among gossip columnists and defined the Who's Who of Hollywood. This was the first time Milt and Danny made the list. Milt was overjoyed, even bought a new tuxedo, but Danny was irked that his name on the invitation was misspelled as "Denison."

With Milt driving, Danny next to him, and Sarah spread out over the backseat trying not to wrinkle her endless yards of taffeta, they pulled up to 2000 Coldwater Canyon. A valet took their car, and they ascended the stone steps leading to the front door, Sarah constantly admonishing Milt not to step on her dress.

Danny was surprised at the modesty of the house. Muted colors, mostly beige tones, gave the simply decorated rooms a quiet elegance —the perfect backdrop for a magnificent collection of Impressionist paintings—Monet, Vlaminck, Matisse, Chagall, and several others that Danny could not identify.

Charlie Grossman came up to them, and for the first time Danny spoke to the man whose agency collected 10 percent of all his earnings. To avoid any mistakes, Milt quickly injected, "This is Danny Dennison, one of our real important clients, Charlie."

Grossman patted Danny on the back, as if he'd known him for many years. "Get yourself a drink, Danny," he said. "Make yourself at home." And he sauntered off to join Jack Warner and Darryl Zanuck, two of the moguls, who hated each other in private but appeared to be the best of friends in public. Like the three musketeers, Danny, Milt, and Sarah ambled down the long hallway, peering into each room resplendent with celebrities. It was quite a turnout—Joan Crawford, Rita Hayworth, Katharine Hepburn, all the studio heads. Miniskirted Shirley MacLaine was laughing loudly at something her brother, Warren Beatty, had said from across the room. Jane Fonda, oblivious to all others, was holding hands with her French husband, Roger Vadim. But no matter how many stars were in a room, all covert glances went to Elizabeth Taylor, who was making a point of ignoring Richard Burton.

As dinner was announced, everyone funneled outside to the candlelit garden, following Governor Ronald Reagan and his wife, Nancy.

Peacocks strutting in the garden competed with the peacocks sitting at the tables around the pool. Each table was adorned with a centerpiece of orchids and set with fine delft china. Danny found that his name on the place card still had one *n* missing. To his right sat Mrs. Chandler, "Buff" to her friends, the founder of the Music Center, home of Los Angeles opera, ballet, and theater. The chair on his left was empty; the place card said MISS STEPHANIE STONEHAM. Great, he thought—nothing better than being squeezed between a dowager and a spinster for the evening.

On the other side of the empty chair sat Adolph Burns, a former optician and current head of MTT, chatting with Mrs. Chandler across Danny's plate as if Danny were invisible. He was wearing wire-rimmed glasses, and Danny wondered if he had filled his own prescription. A sudden hush interrupted their conversation; Burns peered over Mrs. Chandler's head and smiled. Danny twisted in his chair to follow his gaze.

A woman was walking down the stone path. She turned heads as she passed, and no wonder—she was the most beautiful creature Danny had ever seen. Tall and slender, with shoulder-length golden-blond hair, she seemed to float gracefully between the tables, and she was coming straight toward him. Adolph hopped up to greet her, kissing her on both cheeks.

"Stephanie, my dear, I was afraid you had decided not to appear tonight."

"Of course not." She lowered herself gracefully into her chair.

Danny stared at the flawless bare shoulders, his eyes inadvertently following her long milky-white neck to a cloud of blue chiffon draped over her full breasts.

She looked at him with misty gray eyes, and picked up his place card. "Denison?"

"Yes, but with a double *n*."

She smiled.

"And you're Stephanie Stoneham," he said, reading her card.

"How clever of you."

"Are you an actress?" he pressed on.

"My God, no!" she said with a husky laugh. "That's the last thing in the world I ever want to be."

So beautiful and no desire to be an actress? Danny assumed that every beautiful girl in Hollywood was there to become a star. Out of the corner of his eye he saw the majordomo whispering to Adolph Burns, who then immediately got up.

Stephanie turned. "Are you deserting me?"

"My darling, they tell me I have to take Agnes home. The cocktail hour was a little too long for her—again," he added wryly.

"Oh, I'm sorry—do give her a kiss for me."

"I will. And don't forget—Friday evening at our house."

"I can't come, Adolph. I have to be in Long Island."

"Too bad—we'll miss you. But be sure to tell J.L. that we look forward to getting together with him in the south of France." He left without ever seeing Danny.

As Stephanie sipped her wine, ignoring the soup, Danny tried to resume their conversation. "Do you live in Long Island?"

"No, no—my father is having a party for Princess Margaret—he insists that I be there."

Was she putting him on? She might be beautiful, but she sure was a bullshitter.

When the main course came—salmon with rice and asparagus—she ate nothing, concentrating on dividing the rice into little piles. Pondering what to say next, Danny watched her long, delicate fingers nervously playing with her fork.

Then suddenly she rose. "I have to mingle a bit and find myself a ride home," she said.

"Mingle with me, and *I'll* take you home," Danny said quickly.

Her eyes met his. He could feel her taking him in, and he sensed she liked what she saw. "Why not?" she said. "I'll be ready in a little while." And she left.

Then Danny remembered that he had no car—he had come with Milt and Sarah. Where were they? Mrs. Chandler, addressing no one in particular, had just launched into a description of a recent Music Center operatic production. His eyes furtively searched the garden until he caught sight of Milt waving to him. When Mrs. Chandler paused in her monologue to take a breath, he slunk off.

"Milt, who is this Stephanie Stoneham I'm sitting next to?"

"You don't know who she is?"

"Well I know she's full of crap, but she's beautiful—I like her."

"She's the daughter of J. L. Stoneham."

"J. L. Stoneham?"

"Yeah, the ball cutter of Wall Street. One of the richest men in the country."

Danny was stunned. "She's really going to Long Island?"

"I don't know, but I think that's where her father lives."

"And having dinner with Princess Margaret?"

"If she says so."

Danny had always prided himself on detecting people who put on airs. Yet she had told him the truth, and he hadn't believed her.

He looked around, but she was nowhere in sight. People were beginning to leave and he thought that maybe someone else had taken her home. Then he felt a tug on his sleeve. "Are you planning to leave without me?" Her eyes were smiling and she looked more beautiful than before.

"Of course not—just making arrangements with our driver." He motioned Milt over.

"Hello," Milt said, taking her hand. "I'm the agent for this brilliant young director. He's so successful I have to moonlight as a chauffeur." And Milt burst out into his usual cackle.

Getting into the car, Danny caught Sarah eyeing the classic, understated perfection of Stephanie's chic chiffon dress. In contrast, Sarah was a gaudy apparition in her ruffled taffeta with bows that bounced on her generous bosom.

Milt was in a jolly mood, and Danny was relieved to have him jabbering away; he felt uncomfortable trying to talk to Stephanie with an audience up front.

They left Coldwater Canyon and drove down Rodeo Drive to the Beverly Wilshire Hotel, where Stephanie lived.

"Did you hear the one"—Milt was chortling even before he started —"about the drunk who goes ice fishing?" Without waiting for an answer, he went on. "He cuts a hole in the ice and sinks his line and waits. Then he hears a loud booming voice above him: 'THERE ARE NO FISH DOWN THERE.' " Milt delivered the line in a loud, booming voice, turning around to catch the reaction in the backseat.

"Milt, watch your driving." Sarah, annoyed, had obviously heard the joke many times before.

Undeterred, Milt continued. "So the guy gets up, moves over a couple feet, and cuts another hole. He hears the voice again. 'THERE ARE NO FISH DOWN THERE.' So he looks up and asks, 'Who is speaking?' And the voice answers: 'THE MANAGER OF THE ICE-SKATING RINK.' "

Milt convulsed in laughter and Sarah reached over to grab the wheel in case he lost total control. "Bob Hope you're not," she sighed.

Stephanie was laughing as raucously as Milt. Danny loved that she seemed so uninhibited. Before they reached the entrance to the hotel, he got up the courage to gently press his leg against hers. She didn't respond, but she didn't move away. At the door, he bid her good-night in a gallant fashion, kissing her hand.

Inside the car, Milt was chortling, "You're learning from me, *boychik.*"

Sarah sighed again. "Milt, Casanova you're not either."

———

The next day, Danny hurried down to the florist and selected a bouquet of white roses to be sent to Stephanie. On the card he wrote:

Before they wilt, call me. Danny Dennison (with two n's).

Then he walked over to Milt's office, which Sarah had recently
decorated in an Oriental motif; even the chessboard looked Chinese,
and the latest starlet photo had a new bamboo frame.

"I can't get her out of my mind," Danny confided to Milt, looking
out on the traffic of Wilshire Boulevard below.

"You better try," said Milt, " 'cause J. L. Stoneham won't let you
near her, and he's one mean son of a bitch."

"What are you saying?"

Milt scratched his neatly trimmed beard and walked over to him.
"Danny, everybody knows the story. His own father was in the hospital, dying. He turned over the family fortune to J.L. But—you'll never
believe this—the father recovered. Did he give the money back? No
way! The old man died of a broken heart, abandoned without a
penny. Now I ask you—is that a mean son of a bitch or what?"

"I'm not interested in J.L. I'm interested in Stephanie. When is she
coming back?"

"How the hell should I know?"

Just then, Milt's secretary interrupted: "Mr. Schultz . . . Ace
Films just sent over these papers for Mr. Dennison." Milt grabbed the
documents with a big grin and patted the futon couch, motioning for
Danny to sit beside him. Together, they quickly flipped through the
contracts—for Danny's next movie, his sixth, based on *Much Ado
About Nothing* and called *Something for Nothing.*

Milt's chubby finger pointed to a clause granting a large increase in
salary. He beamed. "Now you can build that tennis court and pool
behind your house. . . ." He turned the page. "And look at this—for
the first time you get credit *over* the title: 'A Daniel Dennison Film.' "
He turned to the secretary. "Make duplicate copies—Mr. Dennison
will want to frame this." Danny only shook his head. When the secretary left, he buried his face in his hands.

"Danny, I'm proud of what I've negotiated. You aren't happy?"
Milt couldn't keep the hurt out of his voice.

"You did swell, Milt. It's just that something for nothing is the story
of my life. I get paid good money for movies that say nothing. But
who cares?"

"You're wrong, Danny—people do care. They like your movies. For
two hours they forget their problems. That's important—"

"Oh Milt, you don't understand—"

"*Boychik.*" Milt put his arm around Danny's shoulders. "A lot of guys would be damn happy to be in your shoes, to have your job, your talent."

Danny just rolled his eyes.

"Yes! I'd like to see what Kazan or Wilder would do with the kind of scripts you have to turn out."

"That's just it, Milt. It's junk. I want to make a film that means something."

"Here we go again."

"Yes! Not something for nothing; something that makes a difference."

"I get it, *boychik*. Artsy-fartsy. What's that thing you had me read—*Fellowman?*"

"*Everyman.*"

"Yeah. That's something? That's nothing. No characters. Good Deeds—that's supposed to be a character? No plot. It's just one long sermon."

"I know I don't have the right fix on it yet, Milt. But, believe me, I have a feeling in my gut—it has a universal message. It—"

Milt threw himself back on the futon in exasperation and looked over at Danny. "Kafka again."

"What?"

"Listen, I had a client." He sat up again. "A very talented director. He gave me the same *boubameisa*. Wanted to make a film based on Kafka's stories. I was just starting out, so I let him push me—I put it together. He made it—and you know what? A fucking disaster."

"What kind of a story was it?"

"It was about a Jew—remember I told you, 'Don't do any Jewish stories; nobody gives a damn'? Ahh, but this guy had a universal message too. It still ended up a piece of shit. I want to save you from that."

"But I'm doing shit now! I want to do something good. I'm not talking about a Jewish story—"

"Look, I don't want to argue with you, Danny. Please let's leave it alone for now, OK?"

———

The only way Danny could leave it alone was by thinking about Stephanie. He thought about the long column of her neck, the golden hair brushing against her bare shoulders; he replayed the moment when her misty eyes locked with his. A week later he heard from her.

It was almost eleven when he got home from the studio and found a message under his door:

I come in—you go out. Call me. And thanks for the flowers.

Did she send the note over by messenger or was it possible she came by herself? Danny couldn't believe it. He looked at his watch. Was it too late to call? He took a chance.

"Hello?" That voice was unmistakable.

"Oh, I'm sorry to call so late . . ." he began, but she interrupted.

"No, no, it's not too late—come on over for a nightcap." A little surprised by her invitation, he showered quickly, threw on a pair of slacks and an oxford-cloth shirt, and sped over to the Beverly Wilshire.

She was waiting for him in a satin robe the color of champagne, which blended perfectly with her golden hair. He couldn't help wondering if she was wearing anything underneath.

"I just got back, and I need a strong drink to get Long Island out of my system."

"I'll join you."

She poured them each a double Scotch, and then sat down beside him.

"So you didn't have a good time?"

"The usual time—I was in bed sick. Oh, how I hate him."

"Who?"

"My father. Whenever I see him I get sick."

"But why—isn't he good to you?"

"Sure—if I do what he wants, I get everything. See this lovely apartment?" For the first time Danny looked around the dimly lit room at the starkly modern furnishings, all white leather and crystal. "It's his. If I don't obey, he'll have me evicted."

"Are you serious?"

"He's done it before. I can never meet his standards. No matter what I wear it's wrong; no matter what I say it's dumb. I can never be what he wants me to be. I hate him." Tears began to form in her eyes.

Danny put his arm around her. "Don't be upset. Let's forget him. I like you just the way you are, Stephanie."

Her teary face immediately brightened. "No one ever said that to me before," she whispered, and with a coquettish smile she moved closer to him. "I'm so glad you're here, Danny." She kissed his ear. The touch was feather-soft and sent an electric wave through him.

He turned his face, and their lips met. Eagerly, his tongue explored every part of her mouth as she unbuttoned his shirt. Those long nervous fingers that had mesmerized him at the dinner table now traveled down across his chest, unbuttoning his belt, stroking his erection.

Then she turned out the lamp and slid down from the couch. The only illumination in the room was a streak of light coming through a partially opened door. In its soft glow, he watched her stretch out on the rug and languidly, with both hands, open her robe. Her naked body was devastatingly beautiful.

He reached down and let his hand glide over her silken hair and throat, lingering on her firm breast, its nipple hard against his palm. He lowered himself beside her and found the soft, moist spot between her legs. As he caressed it gently, she bit her lower lip. "Oh Danny . . ." she moaned, turning her head from side to side, "take me . . . take me."

He rolled over on top of her, and she spread her legs wider to admit him, clinging to him fiercely with both her arms. Danny felt his chest crushing her breasts, but she only held on more tightly. "Now, Danny . . . now . . ." she moaned as his thrusts quickened. He felt strong, all-powerful. A torrent poured out of him.

Breathing heavily, he lay on top of her quivering form. Her arms still held him fast.

The next morning she threw a few things together in a bag and drove back with him to his little house on Tower Road. Danny was floating on an unreal feeling—this beautiful socialite was moving in with him.

He was astonished to discover that she was a gourmet cook. When he came home from the studio, wonderful exotic aromas would be emanating from the kitchen. She ordered fresh flowers, bought new lamps and rugs. And then she surprised him with an aquarium filled with tropical fish in brilliant hues. It didn't seem like the same house.

In the mornings he would wake up and turn to look at her, fast asleep, her hair like a golden veil covering her angelic face. Often, coming home from the studio, he would walk in the door to hear her calling his name—and he'd run upstairs to find her stretched out in the tub, her eyes beckoning him from under hooded lids as she handed him the soap. Sex was wonderful with her; she was so submissive, childlike, she made him feel omnipotent. So why did he hesitate when she suggested that they get married? Danny couldn't understand his indecision. He was thirty-six years old. He had never been so strongly attracted to a woman before. Surely, this was the real thing. Why not get married?

But everything was moving too quickly for him. And between the beautiful moments were episodes when her mood swung violently—she would be at the point of tears, and suddenly laugh hysterically. She was unpredictable. She pleaded with him to marry her, but he put her off.

It all came to a head a month later when he got a phone call from J. L. Stoneham.

A gruff voice said: "I'm completely against it."

"What are you talking about, Mr. Stoneham?"

"My daughter is very impulsive and she doesn't know what she's getting into. I don't want her marrying an actor."

"I'm not an actor, Mr. Stoneham. I'm a director."

"It doesn't matter—you're part of that Jew industry."

"I'm not a Jew," he said too quickly.

"But you're contaminated."

"What are you saying?"

"You will never marry my daughter."

Stunned, Danny replied, "Don't you think that's something between Stephanie and me?"

"No!" J.L. snapped. "I've dealt with you fortune hunters before."

"Listen, Mr. Stoneham . . ." Danny was seething, but he wasn't allowed to finish.

"Let me warn you that if you marry her, neither of you will get a dime—"

"Mr. Stoneham, I can't believe—"

"—but if you stay away from her I'll see that you get *more* than a dime."

"Are you trying to bribe me?"

"Everything has a price, sonny. Take the deal."

"You don't have enough money to buy *everything*." Danny slammed down the receiver.

The next night he and Stephanie were married in Las Vegas.

———

There was no reaction from J. L. Stoneham; his silence was almost ominous. If it bothered Stephanie, she said nothing about it. They were happy, and they looked it. Whenever they walked into the Bistro restaurant all eyes would be on them. The beautiful couple—Danny, tall, energetic, darkly handsome, Stephanie a slender, golden column beside him.

Stephanie liked being seen with Danny in places frequented by the upper crust. She even arranged to have him sponsored into the exclusive Westside Country Club so that he could play golf with her friends.

The only negative note was that his marriage with Stephanie had a cooling effect on his friendship with Milt and Sarah. After the first gefilte fish and borscht dinner, there was no doubt that the two wives were not destined for a bosom friendship. But Danny and Milt made up for it by getting together more frequently, just the two of them.

J. L. Stoneham finally broke his silence in a letter from his lawyer, advising Stephanie that he was taking legal steps to disinherit her:

MR. STONEHAM WISHES TO INFORM YOU THAT HE WILL HENCEFORTH CEASE TO ACKNOWLEDGE YOU AS HIS DAUGHTER.

This put Stephanie in a tailspin. Danny came home from scouting locations and found her practically unconscious; apparently, she had been drinking for several days.

When she became coherent, Danny tried to reason with her. "Stephanie, we knew this would happen. Why are you so upset?"

"But he took *everything* away from me."

"So what? We don't need his money—I make enough."

"Don't you see? It's not the money. It's like I never had a father—it's like I'm a bastard child."

"Oh Stephanie, that doesn't make sense."

But he couldn't reason with her; she insisted that she had been abandoned, and she couldn't cope with that.

As quickly as it came, her deep depression disappeared, and she seemed gay again. The next crack in the smooth surface came a month later.

Stephanie suggested they give a small dinner party. Danny was pleased. He would show off their lovely home. Stephanie would enjoy preparing the meal, something she did so expertly. He invited Art Gunn and several other important people in the industry.

The morning of the dinner party he discovered nothing had been arranged. Stephanie was unnerved completely. She went on her second drinking binge.

Furious with her, he shook her by the shoulders. "Pull yourself together!"

"I can't, I can't," she sobbed.

"What's so impossible about a dinner—you do it so well. . . ."

"I can't!" she repeated, pulling away from him and running upstairs. The bedroom door slammed.

He stormed out of the house. Greatly embarrassed, he had to ask his secretary to call all those invited and make the excuse that his wife was ill.

He returned to the house that night determined to have it out with her. But she was gone—no note, nothing. For two full days he was frantic with worry. Then she reappeared.

"Stephanie, where the hell have you been?"

"Long Island."

"You saw your father?"

"No." She began to cry. "He wouldn't let me in. I had no place to go."

Danny hugged her to him. "Stephanie, of course you had a place to go. Your place is here. This is your home. I was so worried the last two days. I missed you."

"Did you really?" She brightened, cuddling against him.

Sex was never better than that night.

Danny resolved to be more patient with her, to try harder. He played tennis with her, went out more to parties. It seemed to be working for a time, until a letter arrived from J.L. inviting Stephanie to Long Island—without her husband. Overjoyed that her father had not abandoned her after all, Stephanie went immediately. Danny covered his hurt, not wanting to mar her happy state; maybe a reunion with her father would stabilize her. But Stephanie returned from the trip more unhinged than before, though laden with expensive jewelry. Danny winced when he thought of how dearly she paid for it.

Now she drank more than ever. One evening when he came home from the studio, he found her half dressed, her hair in disarray, her lovely face smeared with makeup, rambling on about her painful childhood.

For the first time, Danny heard the story—a living nightmare. Stephanie had never told him that her mother had committed suicide. That was when her father became a pillar of granite and took over Stephanie's life completely, demanding total obedience. If she showed a bit of human weakness, he demeaned her, calling her spineless, weak, like her no-good mother. He used money to punish or reward her.

Danny listened patiently, letting it all pour out of her, until, exhausted, she flopped in a chair. He came over and knelt beside her.

"Darling, I wish I could help you, but I can't. You need to see a psychiatrist."

She pushed him away and stumbled to the bar. "I've seen too many of them," she said, pouring the remains of a bottle into a glass. "They all want to lock me up."

"But you're unhappy—you need to sort things out."

"No!" She gulped down the Scotch.

"You need help, Stephanie. Please. For me." He went to her and took her hand.

"Leave me alone!" She shook him off, her angry eyes piercing him. "You're the one who needs help."

"Now listen to me, Stephanie—"

"No, no, *you* listen to *me*! You're the one who's unhappy; you sort things out—always moaning about making a great picture, and ending up with another piece of crap."

She stumbled out of the room.

That hurt him deeply. It was too true.

For several days there was no communication between them. Danny slept in the guest room. He knew he had done all he could. It wasn't her fault, and it wasn't his. It just would never work. He had to end it.

Driving home from the studio, he was determined to tell her there was no other way. She could stay in the house; he would move out. He would accept the blame in divorce proceedings.

He walked in to find Stephanie, her back toward him, feeding the tropical fish. When she turned around, he was absolutely stunned. Her hair was neatly combed, her makeup immaculate, and she was radiant.

Danny didn't know how to start. She did. "I'm pregnant," she said.

———————

All was peaceful now. Stephanie had stopped drinking. She was happy transforming the guest room into a nursery.

One day when he came home from the studio, he found the driveway blocked by a giant moving van. Two workmen were struggling with a tall grandfather clock. He had to wait for them to get it through the doorway before he could enter the house.

"Over there in the corner," Stephanie directed the movers. Danny looked on in astonishment—the clock barely cleared the ceiling.

"Will you explain this to me?" Danny asked when the movers left.

"It's for the baby!"

"What are you talking about?"

She was excitedly winding the key in the face of the clock. "I read about it in a magazine," she gushed, breathless from the effort. "Babies love the ticking of a clock—it makes them think of their mommy's heart."

"Wouldn't a little alarm clock do?"

"Oh no." Her face was beaming. Pregnancy was doing wonders for her looks, he thought. "Only the best for *our* baby."

Danny grinned. In Stephanie's book, the best also meant the biggest and most expensive. But what the hell.

Bing-bong! Bing-bong! The clock chimed the hour—every hour. Danny hated it.

He tried to concentrate on his script while Stephanie watched television in the bedroom. Suddenly he heard her scream his name.

He rushed upstairs, frightened. "What is it?"

She was smiling. "Give me your hand."

Perplexed, he approached the bed, holding out his hand. She placed it over her stomach, and he could feel the baby kicking, trying to get out. Danny broke into a sweat.

Stephanie's smile vanished at the sight of his pale face. "What's wrong?"

He wrenched his hand away, rushed into the bathroom, and threw up.

"Are you all right?" she called out.

"Fine . . . I'm fine." He came out wiping his face with a towel.

"What made you sick?"

"Nothing . . . nothing. I'm so happy about the baby."

"You're not. It's me. You find me disgusting!"

"Don't be silly."

"I'm fat, I'm ugly—it makes you throw up."

"Of course not, darling. The studio commissary is just getting worse," he tried to reassure her, as he hugged her, fighting against a second wave of nausea. But he couldn't tell her that feeling the baby's movements in her belly took him back to San Sabba. How would you begin a story like that? But if he loved her, why couldn't he trust her with his secret? Wasn't love trust? Maybe he didn't love her.

All such disturbing thoughts disappeared when the baby girl was born. Danny now had a new purpose for living—to protect this little life, so pure, so innocent, to help her grow, to always be there. Watching that tiny bundle of pink wrinkles through the nursery window, he vowed to make sure no tragedy ever marred her tiny face. He wanted her to have everything she could get out of life.

He couldn't wait to get the baby home. They both agreed they didn't want to hire a nanny; they would take turns getting up in the middle of the night to change diapers.

Little Patricia, named after Stephanie's mother, seemed perfectly content when they put her in her new crib. She fell asleep immediately.

Danny kissed Stephanie gently on the mouth. "Now you lie down and rest; you've had a hectic morning," he urged in his perfect-father-and-husband role.

"I'm not tired, darling."

"Please, Stephanie, lie down for me." He guided her toward the bed.

"All right," she acquiesced, "if you lie down with me." She winked at him. "You're safe, darling—the doctor says I can't fool around for a week." They both laughed and stretched out on the bed.

"I've never been so happy," Stephanie murmured in his arms.

"Me too."

"Oh!" She sat up suddenly. "Who should we ask to be Patricia's godparents?"

"Gee, I never thought about it."

"I'd like to ask Beatrice—I haven't seen her in a long time, but she was so nice to me at Foxcroft. . . . You decide who the godfather should be."

"That's easy. It has to be Milt."

"But it can't be Milt."

"Why not? He's my best friend."

"He's a Jew."

Danny clenched his jaw. "What have you got against Jews?"

"Nothing. But we're Episcopalians. The godparents have to be of our faith. You know that, Danny."

"Yes, of course," he said as he closed his eyes tightly.

Stephanie was chattering away about someone named Ted Rosemont from the Westside Club.

"Yes, that's a good idea," Danny said in a dead voice.

After the christening was over, he had only a vague recollection of a tall, portly minister dressed in white pouring water over a bawling Patricia. He had to restrain the urge to take the baby and run out of the church. Later, at the reception, Ted Rosemont took him aside.

"Be sure to come to the club meeting next week." He leaned toward Danny. "A few radicals are trying to change the bylaws. But I say, you open the dikes, you let in the kikes."

Danny had to move his head away as Ted's laughter sent a shower of saliva into his ear. He looked at Ted's white-capped teeth. He couldn't resist. "By any chance, Ted, are you a fellow member of SAE?"

Ted's laughter spat up again. He grabbed Danny's hand in the secret handshake.

Danny had a splitting headache by the time the reception was over.

———

Each day was measured by the little things Patricia did—her first smile, the gurgle that sounded like "Daddy," the tight squeeze of her tiny hand around his finger.

Arriving home he always headed straight for the nursery. One evening, as he walked in, he tripped over a new tricycle. A tricycle for an infant? Had Stephanie gone mad? He walked into the baby's room and was dumbfounded to find it filled with other toys and playthings, equally inappropriate. He was even more surprised to see a nurse seated by his sleeping daughter's side. A nurse? Stephanie took such joy in taking care of the baby herself.

"Where is Mrs. Dennison?" he demanded.

The reply jolted him: "She's with Mr. Stoneham, out by the pool." A feeling of foreboding overcame him. His heart beat fast as he walked up the stairs to the patio.

He paused at the door. Stephanie's back was to him; she was leaning over, listening to a silver-haired man who sat very erect.

So that's him.

They didn't notice Danny. He heard Stephanie say, "But Daddy, why would you have Ted Rosemont manage Patricia's trust fund, instead of her own father?"

"Because Ted's a solid businessman, a bank president, and because, my dear, I have too many questions about your husband and you have too few answers."

Danny coughed as he opened the screen door. Stoneham turned around. "Ahh, Mr. Dennison," he said. "Come sit down." Danny felt like he was a guest in his own home.

He walked over and kissed Stephanie. She said nothing.

Stoneham continued: "I was just explaining the provisions I've made for my grandchild."

"Mr. Stoneham, I can provide quite well for my daughter."

"I'm certain you can, Mr. Dennison." The thin lips barely parted. "But you must see—Stephanie does—that as the heir to the Stoneham fortune Patricia should have all the advantages we can give her."

"Well, yes, but . . ." Danny was at a loss.

"I've arranged a trust for her education, for child care, for medical coverage . . . and other incidentals as they arise."

"That's very generous of you, Mr. Stoneham, but I would prefer—"

"No thanks are necessary," Stoneham cut him off again.

Danny felt as if a bulldozer had just passed over him.

"And of course, you have no objection to my seeing my grandchild."

"No, I don't object to that."

"I've hired a specially trained nurse to facilitate her trips to Long Island." He turned to Stephanie. "So then we'll see you next week."

"Yes, Daddy," she said meekly.

"I'll send the plane." He consulted his watches, one on each wrist, and before Danny could utter another word, he strode out.

Stephanie sat motionless as if trying to avoid Danny's gaze.

"Is this what you want?" he finally said.

She nodded, her eyes brimming with tears.

Danny was furious at himself. Why didn't he speak out? Why did he let J.L. manipulate him?

Well, it wasn't too late. He would set down some rules of his own. J.L. was welcome to visit Patricia in her own home anytime. But Patricia's visits to Long Island would be limited to J.L.'s birthday and Thanksgiving.

How he dreaded those holidays. He missed his daughter terribly and was always so delighted to have them both home again. He and Stephanie took great joy in being with Patricia. Their favorite time was Wednesday—the nurse's day off.

On one Wednesday he brought home a teddy bear. He walked in the door and called out, "Patricia—where are you?"

Little Patricia, four years old now, came running down the steps. "Here I am, Daddy!"

Danny pretended not to see her. He walked around the room calling, "Patricia!"

His little daughter—golden-haired like her mother—ran after him and grabbed one of his legs, giggling, "Here I am!" With Patricia clinging to his leg, Danny continued to call her name.

Stephanie was standing on the landing, watching with a smile.

Patricia desperately hung on. "Daddy!" she shrieked, full of glee as his long leg swung her about the room.

"Well, I guess she's not home—I'm going to have to take this teddy bear back to the store," said Danny, heading for the front door. As he opened it, he interrupted her shrieks and laughter by suddenly discovering her.

"Oh, there you are!" He swept her up, high above his head, and looked at that happy red face, the sparkling blue eyes filled with laughing tears.

He brought her little body close to his chest. "I thought you left me."

"No—no—no—" squealed Patricia. She put her arms around his neck tightly and pressed her soft cheek against the side of his face.

He held her close and carried her outside by the pool. The sky was a beautiful California blue, dotted with gentle puffs of white. He was content as he walked about, Patricia clinging to him and the teddy bear.

"I love you, Daddy," she whispered in his ear.

"I love you too," Danny said, kissing the little turned-up nose. "Promise you'll always be my little girl?"

"I promise, Daddy."

"Always?"

"Always."

———

Danny's continued dissatisfaction with his work was dulled by the happiness of his home life; it was his cocoon, his protection against the rumbling events of the world—the Vietnam War, Watergate, the fact that the man he admired the least in the movie industry won an Oscar.

It wasn't that he was a failure. As a matter of fact, his career shot up like a rocket. Because of Patricia, he decided to make a movie that kids would like. He dreamed up a comedy based on *The Prince and the Pauper*. The chief characters were two teenage girls, one rich, one poor, who switch places for a week. It was a hit and started a new trend in the industry—teen-oriented movies.

He became one of the top directors at Ace Films; his films always made money. Long ago he had abandoned hope that he would ever come up with the right angle to turn *Everyman* into a movie. But it didn't matter. He had Patricia.

He relished driving her to school on his way to the studio. J.L. had convinced Stephanie that Patricia should attend a private academy, the John Thomas Dye School, with other privileged children; Danny had wanted her to enroll in the Hawthorne School with the neighborhood kids. The first time he left her at school she cried, and all day long Danny found it hard to concentrate on his work, holding back the impulse to call her teachers. He was relieved that she soon adjusted.

Each morning they had a special ritual. As Stephanie helped her get ready for school, Patricia would sing the song Danny had taught her, *"Steppin' out with my honey . . . never felt quite so sunny . . ."* She would dissolve in giggles when Danny came in, scooped her up under one arm, bellowing, *"Steppin' out with my baby . . . it's for sure not for maybe that I'm all dressed up tonight . . ."*

In the car, little Patricia would sidle up next to him and rub her cheek against his to check if he had shaved. She'd purr like a little kitten if his face was smooth, or squeal, "Oh Daddy, your face is rough . . ."

Those moments were precious to him.

One afternoon Danny received a call at the studio—Patricia had been in an accident. Petrified, he raced back to the house in time to meet the departing doctor. Patricia had fallen out of the car while Stephanie was driving her home from school, but he was reassured that her injuries were superficial.

He rushed into his daughter's bedroom and found her sleeping peacefully with a bandaged forehead, the teddy, his head also bandaged, tucked under her arm.

In the living room, Stephanie sat on a couch, a half-empty bottle of Scotch next to her chair, a full glass in her hand.

"I don't think this is cause for a celebration," Danny said through clenched teeth.

"I'm upset. Daddy called and he—"

"I don't give a fuck about *Daddy*. How did Patricia fall out of the car?"

"She leaned against the door, but I wasn't going fast—I was slowing down at a stop sign."

"People don't fall out of locked doors."

"Apparently it wasn't locked," she snapped back.

"Maybe if you didn't drink every time 'Daddy' called, you might remember to press that little button that locks it."

"Don't talk to me like I'm an imbecile."

"You *are* an imbecile. If you can't—" He was interrupted by the sound of sobbing from Patricia's room. He went in and knelt beside her bed.

"Don't cry, darling." He wiped her tear-stained face with his handkerchief. "Daddy loves you."

"Do you love Mommy too?"

"Of course I do, darling."

"Why are you yelling?"

"We're just both a little upset at what happened to you."

"It wasn't her fault, Daddy."

After the accident, Danny and Stephanie started to drift apart. Whenever Danny was away filming, Stephanie would take Patricia to visit J.L. on Long Island. Danny would never go there, and this arrangement satisfied both of them. The pattern continued. Danny spent more time with his work—the trend in the industry was now toward greater realism, locations away from studio back lots—and Stephanie and Patricia spent more time on Long Island. J.L. even hired a private tutor for Patricia.

Danny would later remember how empty the house seemed on Thanksgiving of 1980 when he returned from location. He almost cried when he saw the teddy—raggedy now, one ear torn in half, a button-eye missing. This was the first time Patricia hadn't taken him along.

But Danny hadn't really noticed how much Patricia had slipped away from him until the sunny morning of her twelfth birthday. She burst into his study, wearing her riding clothes, white jodhpurs and black boots. "I'm getting a horse! A horse, Daddy! Of my very own!"

"What are you talking about?" Danny put his script aside and pulled her down on his lap.

"J.L. is giving me a horse for my birthday—a dapple-gray mare!" She hugged him tightly.

"That's wonderful, Patricia, but where would you keep it?"

"In Long Island."

"Long Island? Then you won't have much chance to ride."

"Oh yes I will. Every weekend. J.L. is arranging for me to go to school back East."

Danny felt his mouth go dry. He couldn't respond—her eyes were glistening with such happiness.

"And look at this, Daddy!" She raised her hand to his face. "Isn't it beautiful?"

Danny looked at the thick band of solid gold encircling her slender wrist. Obviously, it had cost thousands of dollars. The present he had given her—a little girl's watch with a picture of a teddy bear on the face—seemed insignificant in comparison.

"I want to show it to Mommy!"

When she slipped off his lap, Danny felt she had slipped away from him completely.

———

It was sad but inevitable. Finally, he and Stephanie agreed on a legal separation. The grandfather clock now stood silent with Stephanie no longer around to wind it. She and Patricia spent almost all their time on the East Coast. He didn't miss Stephanie so much, but the longing for his little girl was sometimes unbearable.

He counted the days until the end of the school year, June 24, the date Patricia would fly in to spend her usual three weeks with him— just the two of them together.

How surprised and pleased he was when, soon after she arrived, she asked, "Daddy, can I go to the studio with you? I want to see how you work."

She was fascinated with filmmaking. She read every one of his scripts. She asked questions and made suggestions—very intelligent ones. Danny was proud of her.

On the last day of her visit, as they drove home from the studio, she seemed pensive.

"What are you thinking?" Danny asked.

Looking out of the window, she answered, "I want to be just like you. I want to make films."

Danny couldn't respond, he was so overcome with emotion.

"You really are my little girl, aren't you?"

"Always, Daddy." She kissed him.

This beautiful fourteen-year-old girl didn't say, "I want to be an actress." She said, "I want to be a filmmaker." She had a talent for writing, a creative sensitivity. But she also had a delicacy that bordered on fragility that sometimes worried him.

"Daddy—" She startled him out of his reverie. "I want to go with you on location this summer. May I?"

"Of course you can." He tried to hide the ecstatic feeling that was soaring within him.

But as soon as she returned to Long Island, she called.

"Daddy, I'm so upset. . . ."

"What is it, dear?"

"Well . . . I . . . I . . . was looking forward to being together with you on location. . . ." Her voice was cracking.

"What's wrong?"

"It's not J.L.'s fault, Daddy, honestly . . ."

Danny just listened, his heart sinking. He should have known better.

"But he arranged this safari in Africa . . ."

"Africa?"

"Yes, we're studying gorillas in school . . ."

"So you won't be able to join me."

"He went to all this trouble . . . as a surprise . . . invited my whole class . . ."

"I understand, darling," Danny said, his heart aching. Of course, he thought—J.L. wouldn't want to lose her to the "Jew industry."

"Let's do it next summer, for sure, Daddy."

"Of course, darling."

It never happened.

CHAPTER 8

1987 | Brighton, England

 agda arched her spine and rubbed her lower back with the palms of her hands to ease the pain. The relief was temporary; the pain came back as soon as she looked down at the boxes of soap piled outside the kitchen door. She had already carried six boxes, one at a time, up the three flights of stairs, taking the longer and more difficult back staircase. Colonel Johnson did not want her lugging things through the lobby.

This was the job that Luba used to do. Magda stretched again and looked out across the sea. Where was Luba? How was she? In the six months since Luba had left, Magda received only one letter from her daughter. Oh, how happy she was to get it.

The mailman had been late the day it came, and Colonel Johnson was taking his afternoon nap. Magda took the stack of mail into his office, intending to leave it there, when she recognized the handwriting. Her hands unsteady, she tore the letter open and devoured every word.

> *Dear Mama,*
> *I miss you very much. You'd love London. Lois is so nice. We share an apartment and it's lovely. The best news is that I got a job as an extra in a movie and, if things go well, I might even become an actress—*

Suddenly, the letter was ripped out of her hand. "Did I not forbid you to have any contact with her?" Colonel Johnson crumpled the letter in his fist. "Luba is gone. She does not exist." He pushed her down on the couch that used to be Luba's bed. Magda was trembling.

From the desk he grabbed pen and paper and slammed them down in front of her. "Write exactly what I say—and in English." She had to kneel at the coffee table in order to write as he dictated:

> *Dear Daughter,*
> *Everything is going fine and I am very busy. I don't have time for letters. It would be better if you didn't write.*

When she finished, he took the paper from her. "I'll mail it for you," he said and walked out.

Magda wearily got up and retrieved Luba's crumpled letter from the trash can. Carefully, she smoothed it out and hid it in her apron pocket.

For months, her only contact with Luba was that wrinkled-up letter, which it seemed like she had read a hundred times. Yesterday, overcoming her fear, she finally wrote a letter to Luba. She poured out all the humiliations she had suffered. She begged for Luba's help. What should she do? See a lawyer? Run away? Luba would know what to do. She stole a stamp from the reception desk and asked a departing hotel guest to mail the letter for her on the way out of town. She was sure Luba would get it; Luba would find a way to respond.

Now she ignored the pain in her back and reached down to pick up the next carton. The trip to the attic seemed longer each time. It was late in the afternoon, and soon she would have to start preparing supper for the few guests who were there for the low autumn rates;

she had to hurry. The load seemed unbearably heavy. Maybe Colonel Johnson was still taking his usual nap. She drew in her breath—she would take the shorter route up the main steps. She started through the lobby. It was too late to turn back when she saw him, neatly dressed as usual, with a folded handkerchief precisely placed in his breast pocket, quietly talking with some guests in a corner of the room. She froze.

With a pleasant smile he approached her. "Darling," he said with a lilt in his voice, "what are you doing carrying that heavy box? Let me have it."

Taking the carton, he graciously bowed to the guests. "Will you excuse me for a moment?"

Magda followed him in silence. As soon as they were on the second floor, out of the guests' view, he thrust the box at her with such force that she doubled over, and he slapped her.

"You bitch," he hissed between clenched teeth. "I told you to use the back stairs. Finish and get back to the kitchen. And don't be late with supper—*kurva!*"

Magda moved as quickly as she could. The steep climb up the iron staircase was the hardest, the steps high, narrow, and slippery. Once she reached the attic, she slumped on the box and wept. *Kurva*— whore—how that word hurt. Would she never escape it? He had forced her to translate into Polish all the epithets he hurled at her in English and now he relished spitting the foul words at her in rapid succession, his clipped British accent giving them a cold, metallic sound. *Kurva* was one of his favorites. If he only knew how close he came to the mark, Magda thought bitterly. She bowed her head. She had sinned in Kraków. But how long must she endure the punishment?

His voice behind her made her jump. "This belongs to you." He held her letter to Luba between his thumb and forefinger as if he were holding dirty underwear. "Insufficient postage," he smirked. "Maybe tonight you will translate it for me?"

A tight knot began to twist in Magda's stomach.

"You seem to have trouble following orders." He put the letter in his pocket. "I told you—your daughter does not exist. Luba is dead." He leaned forward, speaking in a hiss: "Do you understand? Dead. Dead. Dead!"

The pain in her stomach was beyond endurance now. She doubled over, breathing hard, watching this strange, cruel man, her husband. He was standing at the top of the stairs balanced on one leg, carefully brushing off a speck of dust from his highly polished shoe.

Then the knot within her snapped. Like a crazed animal she sprang up and hurled her body against him. His arms flailed wildly as he fell backward. She shut her eyes and heard the sound of his head hitting the steps. When she looked again, he was a small heap lying on the floor below.

She waited. He didn't move. Slowly she went down the steps. Blood was pouring out of a deep gash in his head. He wasn't breathing. He looked like a broken doll—harmless. How could she have been frightened of him?

Magda was surprised at the calm that overcame her. The pain in her stomach had disappeared. She looked around. None of the smaller rooms on the top floor were occupied this time of the year.

Quickly she retrieved the blood-spattered letter; then she unbuttoned his vest pocket and took out the key. She hurried down the steps to his office and unlocked the rolltop desk. She rummaged around until she found what she was looking for, a roll of money wrapped in a rubber band. There was also a small bundle of unopened letters, all from Luba. She slipped the money and the letters in the pocket of her apron and hurried out to the kitchen porch. She picked up another carton and walked through the lobby, greeting a couple of guests she passed.

When she came to the inert body of Colonel Johnson, she put down the box and buttoned the key back into his vest pocket. Then she let out the loudest scream she could muster.

London

urring contentedly, the gray Persian cat curled up at the base of the thrift-shop music stand that served as Luba's easel. She smiled down at the little animal; she was incapable of sticking to her resolution never to get attached to another pet. When her roommate, Lois, moved out, Luba begged her to leave behind this cuddly little creature that had become her constant companion.

Careful not to knock over the old barstool she used as a mixing table, Luba stepped back and frowned. The likeness wasn't very good; she seldom painted with oils. She hoped she would have a chance to see him again soon and study his face more closely. Danny was such a strange man.

When he had picked her out of the dozen girls auditioning for the role and then asked her for a date, she assumed that was the price; wasn't a night in bed what all directors expected? But even over drinks, she realized that Danny was different. There was something about him—some hurt, some wound, a vulnerability—that reached inside her. Making love with her had made him unhappy—she knew that. Yet she wanted to see him again.

Now she concentrated on Danny's eyes, trying to capture that sad look she found in them. She stepped back again. The shape of his face was right, but something didn't work about the way she had painted his black curly hair. She had done the face only, putting it on a body of a carousel horse running free through thick grass—she had once seen a Greek painting of a similar animal with a human head. Suddenly she realized what bothered her; excited by the thought, she quickly changed Danny's short curly hair to a long flowing mane. That did it.

Luba was looking forward to Monday, when she would see him again. It would also be her big day, her first speaking role. She hoped it would lead to more movie work. It was exciting and paid better than entertaining out-of-town businessmen, which is what she had been doing ever since she came to London six months ago.

Luba would never forget that momentous day when, alone for the first time, she stepped off the Brighton train and was poured out with the flow of passengers into the bustle of London. She was so glad she had kept the little piece of paper with Lois's name and phone number. Immediately she went to a pay phone, but she only got Lois's answering machine. She left a message: "This is Luba, the girl you met in Weymouth? I hope you remember. I'm in London looking for a job—I'll call later."

She counted her money. The train ticket had consumed one quarter of the meager savings she had accumulated from tips. What was left would take care of her for only a couple of days. She knew what to do, and she wasn't going to waste any time. She picked up her little suitcase and started walking in the direction of the river.

As she got closer to the port, her steps quickened. She rounded a corner and stopped—before her loomed a large merchant ship. Two sailors were walking toward her. She smiled at them, and a familiar happy feeling overcame her.

Suddenly she felt a sharp stab in the ribs. She turned to see two women in black miniskirts and thigh-high black boots. "Move it, sweetie," the taller one with the scarlet lipstick said, while the shorter one blocked the sailors' path.

Luba picked up her small suitcase, and was about to cross the street, when she spotted two other women, also overly made-up, giving her dirty looks. It wasn't going to be easy.

She walked into a pub and headed for the pay phone. She tried Lois again. This time she got her.

"Of course I remember you, Luba. Where are you?"

"Down at the Battersea."

"Gawd! What are you doing there?!"

"I need some money and I thought—"

"Are you crazy? Look—you have my address?"

"Yes."

"Get in a cab and come over."

Lois welcomed Luba into her two-bedroom flat as if she were a long-lost friend. Soon Luba was sipping hot tea, comfortably settled against one of the large colorful cushions that were scattered over a beautiful Kirman rug. "Gifts from one of my Turkish clients," she laughed as Luba gazed around the cozy room. "There is an extra bedroom if you need a place to stay. . . . I'm hardly ever here and you could look after my cat." The Persian kitten had already made himself at home on Luba's lap.

After she refilled Luba's cup, Lois grew serious. "Listen carefully, Luba. The port is out. It's dangerous."

"Yes, I know. I ran into a couple of real tough girls—"

"That's not what's dangerous."

"What are you talking about?"

"AIDS!"

Luba looked at her. "But only gays get that."

Lois rolled her eyes in astonishment. "I don't believe you. Where have you been?"

Patiently, she went into a long explanation. Luba listened, aghast. "Remember, Luba," she finished, "you have to be very selective about your clients. As I see it, the richer, the safer. That's why I work with an escort service—they only handle the best customers, all rich businessmen."

Full of gratitude, Luba moved in with Lois and started working for the escort service. Through one of her new customers, an executive with Pinewood Studios, she got her first acting job as an extra. She found the movie world very exciting. Of course, you couldn't earn a living being an extra—to make real money, you had to get speaking parts.

And soon enough she needed more money than ever. Lois left to live with a Japanese industrialist, and the burden of paying the rent was completely on Luba. But she enjoyed having the whole place to herself; she even started calling the second bedroom her studio.

The ringing of the telephone interrupted her thoughts. Maybe it was Danny returning her call—she had left two messages at the hotel over the weekend. She wiped the paint from her hands with a rag and went into the living room to answer it.

It was Dorothy from the escort service. "Mr. Brauner tonight, businessman from Munich. Room five-twenty, the Savoy, nine P.M. Eat first."

Luba wasn't looking forward to the "date." It wasn't like Kraków; it wasn't fun anymore. You couldn't pick your own customers; you had to see doctors. Acting in the movies might be a pleasant change and a way out.

She hung up the phone and looked at her watch—five o'clock. She had been painting for hours, so absorbed she had forgotten about lunch. She better fold up and eat something.

She carefully replaced the caps on the tubes of paint, and tucked each tube in its slot in the paint box. Oils were expensive. The box went on the top shelf of the hall closet, where she stored other paintings she had done, some framed, some not, but all neatly matted —drawings of carousels, landscapes, cats, dogs, wild horses. There were just a few portraits of people: Magda sitting at a table smiling, Josef confidently walking the high wire, and Valentine leaning against the stanchion of a carousel.

She went into the kitchen, put some leftovers in the oven, and made herself a cup of tea, then sat on the windowsill. Outside, a steady drizzle made the sidewalk glisten under the streetlamps. She watched people hurrying along under umbrellas, dodging the spray of water from the wheels of passing cars. She felt cozy, happy, with the kitten for company, while the weather seemed so bleak outside. How luxurious to have the whole apartment to herself.

She thought of Magda. This was the first time they'd been apart, and she couldn't say she really missed her. At last, she had been cut loose. Immediately, she felt guilty. How was Magda making out in Brighton without her? Luba had written to her several times, but Magda wrote back only once—a short note in English. Obviously, Colonel Johnson had dictated it.

She should go to Brighton and see what was happening. Once she had called and hung up when Colonel Johnson answered. Now, on an impulse, she picked up the phone—she would demand to speak with Magda.

An operator came on: "The number you have dialed has been disconnected."

Salzburg, Austria

anny jolted up to a sitting position and shook his head violently to rid himself of a nightmare. His toes bumped against the cold brass at the foot of the bed. All beds seemed too short for his six-foot-two-inch frame. He blinked his eyes and looked around the room, which was dimly lit by shafts of light coming through the sides of the closed curtains.

As his eyes widened, they focused on a brochure on his bedside table: *"Hotel Schloss Fuschel—Das Schloss von Herr von Ribbentrop."* Whatever had possessed him to fly out of London yesterday and come here to Austria, to Salzburg, to the former mansion of Hitler's best friend? He closed his eyes. The memory of two nights ago filtered through his thoughts. He rewound it like a spool of film and played it again.

After the image of Rachel receded into a silent scream, he had sagged beside Luba in a cold sweat. His head was spinning, and he shivered.

"Did you like it?" Luba asked softly, resting her head on his arm.

"Yes," he said, gently smoothing her hair from her forehead. "You were wonderful, but I don't feel like myself . . . probably drank too much."

He raised himself on his elbows, then, wary that the dizziness might return, made his way cautiously toward the bathroom. He felt better after he threw some cold water on his face and wiped his body with a wet washcloth. Coming out into the hall, he steadied himself against a wall in the semidarkness and nearly knocked down a picture hanging there. He took care to straighten the frame, and then the feeling of unreality gripped him again. He was staring at a pen-and-ink drawing —so finely detailed it could have been a photograph—of his father's crucifixion. A sharp ringing started in his ears.

"Where did you get this?" he asked hoarsely.

"What?" she called from the bed.

"This picture."

"Oh, it's just something I drew when I was at San Sabba."

The ringing was so loud he could barely hear himself. Blood was rushing through his body. He leaned against the wall, still holding on to the picture frame. "You were in the concentration camp?"

"No, no," she said with a laugh. "I'm only twenty." She got up and slipped on her robe. "I was there when it was a refugee camp—years after the war."

"What's that got to do with the drawing?"

"I saw this crucifix made by some Jew who died there."

Danny gripped a chair to steady himself, fighting back a feeling of nausea as he watched her comb her hair at the mirror. The face reflected back to him was Rachel's. He had to get away.

"I'm tired," he said in a low voice. "I better go home."

"Do you want to see me tomorrow night?" She came over and put one soft hand on his shoulder.

"I might have to go out of town," he said flatly. "I'll call you."

"Please do." Her eyes were smiling.

Once back at the Dorchester, he lay awake for a long time. What right had she to invade the most private part of his life? San Sabba! For him, it had meant the end, death. Of course, for Luba, it had represented a beginning, life.

He felt compelled to put distance between himself and this strange girl. That was when he picked up the telephone and rang for the concierge to order a plane ticket for Salzburg; the day before he had seen a poster advertising the Salzburg production of *Everyman* with Klaus Maria Brandauer.

And here he was now.

A loud knock on the door startled him. "*Guten Morgen,* Herr Dennison." An old waiter came in with a breakfast cart.

Wisps of steam curled up from the coffeepot as the cart was wheeled into the center of the room. With Teutonic efficiency the waiter placed a chair at the table and in one smooth motion pulled the drapes open. The early-morning light—reflected off a small lake already dotted with white sails—illuminated the room.

The waiter went to the door, turned, and almost seemed to click his heels as he said, "*Ist alles in Ordnung?*"

It annoyed Danny that the waiter assumed he understood German. Where were you during the war? he thought. Did you hustle old Jews along to the gas chamber? Or did you work the crematorium detail?

The door closed on his unanswered questions, and Danny got out of bed, stretching his naked body. He walked over to the window and looked out across peaceful Lake Fuschel. The beautiful setting made him angry. Von Ribbentrop must have been very happy here.

He sat down at the table and poured himself some of the rich mocha. He lifted the delicate china cup to his lips, then set it down sharply. Why had he come here?

Of course he had always been curious to see *Everyman*. Since Mrs. Dennison had given it to him, he had read the play many times. He still kept alive the dream of finding a way to make it into a movie. But what a time to come—just when all preparations were completed for *London Rock*, his fifteenth film. It was a sudden impulse—Luba had disturbed him.

Jedermann would not start until five o'clock in the medieval town square of Salzburg, fifteen kilometers away. He had plenty of time. He would have a late lunch at Der Goldene Hirsch, a highly recommended restaurant.

He put in a call to Milt. After a few rings he heard his friend's voice on the tape machine: "All work and no play makes Milt a dull boy. After six days, even God had to rest. So, please leave a message, and either God or Milt will return your call."

"Milt, don't try to get me in London this weekend. I'm now in Salzburg to see *Everyman*. Remember? Yes—*Everyman!*"

Restless, he decided to take a walk. As he was rummaging in his suit bag for a shirt, he picked up the two letters the concierge had handed him the evening of his date with Luba. He still hadn't opened them.

He walked around the lake, his fingers nervously tapping the letters in his pocket. He kept putting off reading them.

He watched the white sails glide along the lake and listened to the muted happy voices in the distance. Children were playing on the bank, young girls giggling as they chased each other, boys skimming stones across the water.

Danny lowered himself on a grassy slope. He could feel the letters hot against his skin. Finally, he took them out of his pocket; he leaned back and looked at the two envelopes, one in each hand. He could guess the contents of the one from Stephanie. Sure enough, she was taking up the six-week residence in Reno to obtain a divorce. But he was still afraid to read what Patricia had to say. Abruptly, he sat up and tore open the envelope.

She started off so pleasantly, telling him about the blue ribbon she had won in a horse show. Then he read the bottom paragraph, the real point of the letter. The chilling words seemed to have come from J. L. Stoneham's lips:

After the divorce we will be living with J.L. in Long Island. He has been kind enough to ask to adopt me. This would make everything so much simpler for us all, and it would in no way minimize the affection I hold for you.

Danny read the lines over and over until he couldn't read anymore. It was his own fault—he knew that well enough. He had immersed himself in his work, and, in the process, lost his family. He had neglected Stephanie, but more important, he had neglected Patricia. He had opened the door for J.L. to take over.

But why would J.L. want to adopt Patricia? To change her from his granddaughter to his daughter? It didn't make sense. She was already his heir; she lived in his house; she was under his influence and control. Adoption would accomplish only one thing—destroy the last frail link between Danny and Patricia.

He thought of her now—a beautiful young woman of seventeen. She had loved him, clinging to his leg, shrieking with laughter as he walked around the room pretending not to see her. That was a golden moment, a time of innocence before the world tumbled in with school and rules and decisions, and the corrupting influence of a wealthy grandfather. He leaned back on the grass and looked up at the cloudless sky. Those moments with Patricia were so precious. Remembering them was painful. She was so young, so full of life and love, and so trusting. Had there ever been such a time in his childhood?

Oh, yes—on the farm, milking the cows with Rachel, watching Mameh in the kitchen, tagging along with Tateh. When he was the age of the little boys playing on the edge of the lake, Tateh had taught him how to skip flat stones on the surface of the water.

He picked up a stone and threw it. It plopped beneath the surface. He found a flatter stone and gave it a hard underhand throw. It whirled across the water. Five skips! A good omen.

He glanced at his watch, surprised to find that it was ten minutes after three. Too late for lunch. He went back to his room, showered, changed, and ordered a limo.

Speeding along the well-manicured landscape to Salzburg, Danny stared at the fat red neck of the driver. It was covered with prickly white hairs, and bulged over the collar.

"Where were you during the war?" he heard himself say, shocked that he couldn't contain the pent-up anger within him.

The driver turned toward him with watery blue eyes and smiled. "No speak English."

"I bet you don't, you Nazi son of a bitch!"

He saw the chauffeur's back tense up, but the man said nothing. Danny's hatred carried him into the heart of the city.

The car stopped abruptly, too abruptly. The driver opened the door, a grim expression on his face. The slam was extremely loud behind Danny as he walked into the town square.

It was twilight, that moment when God holds His breath. The setting sun bathed the colorful Gothic buildings in a golden light, their sharply pointed rooftops drawing jagged lines against the crimson sky and casting dark shadows over the cornices, where pigeons nestled. In the cobblestoned square, a temporary stage had been constructed. He took his seat. The chairs around him were quickly filled with tourists speaking different languages, but German cut through all the voices. It irritated him until the performance began. Then, suddenly, German sounded beautiful, and Danny was surprised how easily he could follow a language that he had tried to block out of his mind for so many years.

God was speaking to Death, His messenger: "It pains me that Everyman cares only for worldly riches, living for his own pleasures. Go thou to Everyman and command him in My name to make a reckoning."

The twilight deepened, lending a magical quality to the setting. Danny was touched by the agonies of the protagonist, a man who realizes with despair that his life has been frivolous and worthless. How pitifully Everyman reached out to all those around him, trying to atone. When he slammed the cover of his treasure chest, the sound startled a flock of pigeons, and they swooped off in unison into a sky tinged with orange light.

Poor Everyman: "O Death, thou comest when I had thee least in mind."

As the light grew dimmer, silhouettes of men appeared on the rooftops of the buildings. They cried out accusingly, "*Jedermann!*" Their voices, echoing around the square, seemed to be calling directly to Danny.

What had he accomplished in life if tomorrow he were to die? He was not the man his father had been—a true artist. His father had been strong, but Danny knew he was weak. He was still Moishe, a frightened child. Even though he was successful, he felt he was getting away with something. His body didn't fit inside his skin somehow. He didn't like himself. Danny couldn't remember a time when he liked himself.

The next morning he took an early flight to London. As the plane made its descent into Heathrow, he unwound his long body and peered out of a window. Somewhere in that large, sprawling city beneath the mist was Luba.

She scared him. In one orgasm, she had brought all his dead memories to life.

She had only one day's work in the movie, and then she must be out of his life.

CHAPTER 9

1987 | London

anny walked onto the set, all the emotions of his turbu-
lent weekend safely suppressed. He felt no reaction
when he saw Luba—costumed for the part of a Cockney teenager in tight miniskirt, skimpy halter top, and
beehive hairdo. He greeted her in a curt, businesslike manner. She
only smiled.

After explaining the scene, set in a mock-up of a fish-and-chips
joint, he positioned her and the demure little girl playing her cousin
side by side at the counter, each munching a fried fillet. When Bruce
Ryan, the star, walked in, Luba was to look at him, nudge her young

companion, and loudly whisper in a Cockney accent, "Hey, ain't he sexy!" Then, to the ten-year-old's question "What's sexy?" Luba was to reply: "Someday you'll find out."

Although it was a simple scene, Danny had difficulty making Luba lose herself in the character. She spoke the lines like a mature woman instead of a giddy teenager. She wasn't self-conscious, just aware, too aware, quietly watching everything around her.

"Are we going to be here all day?" Bruce grumbled as he made his entrance for the fifth time.

"Keep that swagger when you walk in," Danny called out to him placatingly. "Act like you own the place."

"I do," answered Bruce. His two hangers-on—a little skinny guy with a punk haircut and bad skin, and a tall fat guy with a punk haircut and bad skin—laughed too loudly at the joke. They sat on the edge of the set, one on each side of Bruce's leather-covered chair as if guarding a throne.

Danny walked over to Slim, whose receding hair had by now given way to total baldness. After thirty years together, through early television, through nine westerns and five teen features, Slim could easily read Danny's mind. "She ain't gonna make it," he muttered.

Danny sighed, "Set up for a master shot, Slim, and have Luba come to my trailer."

Luba seemed perfectly calm as she walked in and sat down facing him. "You don't like it," she said.

This wasn't the typical nervous actress fretting about her first scene —not a trace of anxiety, no beads of sweat disturbing her makeup. Nothing seemed to bother her. "No, no, it's fine," Danny said, "but it can be better. Think about the scene. Here you are, talking to a little girl who knows nothing about sex—"

"Why not?" Luba interjected.

"Why not what?"

"Why wouldn't she know about sex? *I* did."

Danny raised his eyebrows. "At ten?"

"It was nine." And she matter-of-factly told him of her relationship with Felix.

"Amazing. How long did it last?"

"Over a year. On and off."

Danny let out a soft whistle. "Once a week?"

"Sometimes more."

"More?!"

"My mother was interrogated by the police often that year. Felix was a friend. He didn't mind staying with me."

"I'll bet he didn't." Danny found himself intrigued by the straight-forward way she described the sexual details.

"It was a new game for me, better than playing with dolls."

"You would rather play with thumbs?"

Luba's answer was a mischievous grin.

"It amazes me that he never said to you, 'You mustn't tell—' "

"He never did. It wasn't necessary."

Danny studied her. She looked very young, childlike, except for the eyes—the eyes still mesmerized him as much as they did when he first met her. There was kindness in them, and also a wisdom borne of having seen more than a child's eyes should see. The expression in them was so like Rachel's. . . .

Luba interrupted his thoughts. "You know, Danny, I've heard about children that have been exposed to sex at an early age. I think at first they're intrigued, then they get frightened they'll be punished, and they feel guilty. But that never happened to me."

"You never felt guilty?"

"I couldn't see a reason to."

"That's rather mature—"

"People don't realize how sensual children are. They have feelings, I mean, sexual feelings. Adults forget that kids can respond."

Danny wanted to know more, but he tried to sound casual. "Did you, uh, respond when you were playing with him?"

"Yes . . . no . . . I guess I didn't quite know what it was, that feeling—but it was exciting."

"Did he try to do more?"

"I was too little. He would just rub it between my legs."

Luba amazed him. She described this sexual initiation as if she were talking about what she had for breakfast. But Danny found himself becoming aroused.

"When I couldn't be with Felix, I stayed with my aunt. Her Turkish husband taught me to kiss."

"He what?"

"It was nice."

"I thought you were past that. Didn't you ever kiss Felix?"

"Not like that!"

"My God! You mean you learned to suck a cock before you learned to kiss?"

She nodded, laughing. Her mirth was infectious. Danny liked how completely at ease she made him feel. No one had ever talked with him so openly about sex. "Luba, Luba—that's a beautiful name."

"It means *love* in Polish."

"Are you Polish?"

"I was born there."

"How did you get out?"

"That's a long story—"

There was a loud knock, followed by Slim's "Ready when you are, boss!"

Danny wanted to hear more, but called out, "Thanks, Slim—I'm on my way."

_____

Danny tried the fish-and-chips scene one more time. "Print it," he said, but his look told Slim this one was destined for the cutting-room floor.

"That's a wrap!" Slim yelled.

As Danny was leaving the set, discussing the next day's work with the cameraman, he noticed Luba waiting for him by the door.

He walked over. "Good work, Luba. Thanks."

She didn't react to the false compliment. "Would you like to see me tonight?" she asked.

"I've got to look over the rushes."

"Well, if you get done early, I'll be home."

He was tempted to forget the rushes as he warmed to her provocative smile.

"I've got lots of stories to tell," she added softly.

_____

Sitting alone in the screening room, Danny could not concentrate. As soon as he pushed Luba out of his mind, disturbing thoughts of Patricia rose to the surface. He could barely focus on the screen. But finally the rushes were over. It was after ten when he got back to his Dorchester suite. He ordered some cold smoked salmon from room service, but when it arrived he couldn't eat it.

Ever since returning from Salzburg yesterday, he had wanted to call Patricia, but he was afraid. How could he make her understand? Could he find the right words to tell his daughter that she was the dearest thing in his life? Would she believe him, after all the time they had spent apart? Would she understand that it would kill him to lose her?

He looked at his watch—it would be around 5 p.m. in Virginia. He picked up the phone and asked for the Stoneridge Academy. He hated this boarding school full of lonely girls with trust funds and phony titles, abandoned children of divorced jet-setters; he had wanted her to live with him and attend Beverly Hills High. He should have overruled Stephanie.

The school office informed him that Patricia was away for a few days.

"Where did she go?"

"I'm sorry—we can't divulge that information," the officious voice said.

"Goddamn it! This is her father!"

There was a momentary silence. Then the voice recited: "Patricia has gone to Long Island. She will be back tomorrow."

That's a hell of a trip for a "few days," thought Danny. But not so far when a private plane picks you up and flies you back. He put in a call to Long Island.

"Stoneham residence," a butler with a trace of a British accent answered.

"I'd like to speak to Patricia, please."

"Who's calling?"

"Her father."

"Just a moment, sir."

Danny waited a long time. He began to think he had been disconnected.

"She's in the middle of a tennis game with Mr. Stoneham. Please call back in an hour."

Danny tried to control his fury. "Will you please tell Patricia that her father's calling—from *London.*"

"She is busy, sir," the butler repeated, speaking very slowly, as if explaining it to a moron. "Mr. Stoneham says she cannot be disturbed."

Danny slammed down the receiver. An hour later he called again.

This time the voice said, "She is in the middle of dinner with Mr. Stoneham; she cannot be disturbed."

Danny slowly hung up the phone and lay back on the bed, breathing heavily. He'd never win. He should have fought earlier, but he had ignored too many things that were happening around him. He lay there quietly for a long time. He had no strength to move.

———

All the extras were in costume and ready; they sat quietly around the disco set watching Danny go through the movements that Bruce Ryan would be making. He tried hard not to look at his watch too often as he waited for Slim to come back.

"He's still in makeup and it's gonna be a while." Slim's face showed his annoyance when he finally reappeared out of Bruce's trailer.

"What's taking so long?" Danny asked patiently.

"You ought to see him—he looks like shit."

"Coke again?"

"What else? The makeup man just finished covering up the circles under his eyes. *That* took an hour."

"Damn! We'll be lucky if we get a shot before lunch."

Slim crossed his arms and rocked on the balls of his feet, grumbling, "He can't act, but for three million bucks he can be on time. You ought to kick his ass."

Trying not to raise his voice, Danny said, "Let me handle the actors, Slim—that's *my* job."

"Right, boss," Slim bristled, "I've done mine." He spun on his heels and stormed off.

Danny slumped in his chair. Slim didn't understand actors. He couldn't see that Bruce's obnoxious bravado was hiding a frightened kid, afraid of being stripped naked before the camera, scared to death of making a fool of himself. Danny hated Bruce, yet he understood him too. A bricklayer's son from rural Pennsylvania, Bruce had a macho physique and yet a slightly feminine quality; the combination gave him on-screen charisma. But despite his popularity, success, and money, Bruce was insecure. Maybe it was because he had never finished high school and thought himself dumber than everyone else. He always imagined that people were making fun of him behind his back, which was sometimes true.

Finally, after two hours, Bruce sauntered out onto the set.

"Places, everyone!" Slim called out.

"All right, Bruce." Danny approached him. "You sit here looking toward the dance floor. On action, hold it for a beat, walk toward the camera, and say your line."

"I ain't gonna say it," Bruce mumbled.

"What do you mean?"

"I ain't gonna say it," he repeated louder.

This time everyone heard him, and they stopped and stared.

Danny was incredulous. "May I ask *why* you 'ain't gonna say it'?"

"It's a stupid line!"

Danny picked up the script and read the line over. "What's wrong with it?"

"I ain't gonna say, *'I'm your mother's little helper.'* It makes me sound dumb."

"Come on, Bruce. Don't you get it?" Danny was trying hard to sound pleasant. "It's a play on the famous Rolling Stones song."

"Never heard of it."

In exasperation Danny threw down the script. "I see why you're the star of *London Rock*—you've been living under one."

The extras burst out laughing.

His face flushed, Bruce pointed his finger at Danny. "You change that line, or I change directors."

He stormed off the set, his sidekicks following.

Danny knew he had gone too far. Usually he could control himself, but he had allowed his own problems to spill over into his work; he had humiliated Bruce knowing how sensitive the actor was to jokes at his expense. He nodded to Slim, who was rubbing his bald scalp.

"Lunch, one hour," Slim announced. Everyone rushed off the set, but Danny wasn't in a hurry. He knew he would have to eat crow.

When he got to Bruce Ryan's trailer, the actor was waiting for him.

"Look, Bruce. If you don't like saying the line, then the line is bad," Danny said in a tired voice. "You've got to be comfortable with what you say. My job is to make you look good, and—"

"Cut the shit," Bruce snapped. "What's the new line?"

"What would you like to say, Bruce?"

"I don't write."

Danny bit his tongue. He was tempted to ask if Bruce could even read.

"I'm paid to act."

Far too much, thought Danny, but all he said was "Enjoy your lunch. We'll find the right line."

"Call me when you get it."

Danny flashed him his most ingratiating smile and left. "I hate that prick," he muttered to himself as he walked out onto the busy studio street. He resented the power that stars had. Ryan's last two pictures had made a lot of money for the studio. If it came to a showdown, Danny would be the one replaced. Ryan was hot, he was a star, and he would remain in the picture in spite of Danny's past successes.

Actors in different costumes were hurrying past him on the way to the commissary. Girls in can-can outfits, soldiers, sailors—they all looked happy, even the guy in the science-fiction monster suit.

Danny had to get away; he headed for the back lot, a graveyard of abandoned and dismembered sets. As he passed a row of staircases, he wondered how many different scenes had been played on those steps and all the steps like them in the deserted back lots of the studios of the world. Errol Flynn dueling his way down a staircase;

Douglas Fairbanks leaping with sword in hand from balustrade to chandelier; Clark Gable carrying Vivien Leigh up the steps at Tara. He had those memories from his childhood, when he went to the Rialto with Margaret Dennison and thought how exciting it would be to make movies. Right now it didn't seem exciting at all. Right now all he felt was anxiety, tension, pressure, stress.

He was ready to hear a story.

———

Luba threw on her clothes as she raced to answer the doorbell—God, she still had to put on makeup and comb her hair—Danny's driver was so early.

She flung the door open. Standing before her was a woman, gaunt, pale, the clothes hanging on her thin frame, traces of tears staining her puffy cheeks.

"Magda!"

Paralyzed, Luba could only stare at her mother. Magda seemed to have aged years since they parted.

"Come in," she finally managed. "I'm so glad to see you." She hugged her mother and felt a strange stiffness. "I tried to call you but the phone was disconnected." Magda said nothing, so Luba kept chattering away: "Your note was so short. You said you were fine, but I was never sure if you were really OK."

"He only let me write that one time." Magda's voice was wooden.

"That bastard. How did you get away?"

"He's dead."

"Dead?"

"He fell down the attic stairs," Magda said barely above a whisper as she bent down to pick up her bag.

"Couldn't happen to a nicer guy. He deserved—" Luba broke off. Her mother's expression told her not to continue. She took the bag from Magda and led her into the spare bedroom.

"This is for you." Magda pressed a roll of bills wrapped in a rubber band into Luba's hand. "That's all there was. I looked everywhere."

"What about the hotel?"

"The bank took the hotel."

"Well . . . be glad that it's over. Get settled . . . relax. Tomorrow I'll get this painting stuff out of the way. Now I'll make you something to eat, OK?"

Magda nodded and wearily sat down on the bed.

In the kitchen, waiting for the soup to heat up, Luba counted the cash—only 300 pounds, barely enough for one month's rent. What had he done with the rest? There must have been a few thousand. As she stirred the pot, her mind kept searching the nooks and crannies of Greenfields Inn. Where could he have hidden it?

Magda was more tired than hungry. She sipped two spoonfuls of the soup and pushed the bowl away.

Luba helped her get into bed and made sure Magda was asleep before she left to meet Danny. She was relieved to escape from the apartment. She was disturbed by her mother's appearance, by her beaten-down attitude. Maybe she shouldn't have left her alone, but she couldn't wait to see Danny. She leaned back against the cushions of the limo; it seemed to be moving so slowly.

―――――

"Luba, was there ever a man you didn't feel sexually attracted to?" Danny asked after their lovemaking was over.

"Let me think."

Danny began to laugh. "This isn't a quiz. Take your time."

Stretched out next to her on his king-sized bed at the Dorchester, with an iced bottle of Polish Wyborowa vodka that he had specially ordered, Danny got lost in Luba's past.

"Yes," she said finally. "Josef."

"The father in the wire act?"

"I loved him. He was proud of me. He encouraged me. I became part of his family. All the others groped, like animals smelling something. I sensed it—even if they didn't make a move, I felt it. Josef was the only one who could sit me on his knee, hug me, and nothing would ever—"

"Don't you think you provoked the others?"

"To a point. But it was always there. I was very precarious—"

"You mean *precocious*?"

"Yes, that's the word. I always dared to find out, no matter how it ended, even if it was a disaster—and I've had my share of those. But I don't want to talk about that." She closed her eyes.

Danny felt completely at ease with her. Maybe Milt had been right —he had always been too uptight about sex. But Luba showed him a sensual freedom beyond anything he had ever known. She was turning out to be the antidote to everything. With her, he could forget about Bruce Ryan, who had a suite on the floor above, and all the day's problems. He had left Salzburg planning never to see her again, but now he felt he couldn't do without her.

After she left, Danny lay awake for a long time. Luba was a survivor. She had guts, she fought back, she adjusted. How do you know what you'll do to survive until you are put to the test? Didn't his sister Rachel become a whore at San Sabba to survive? But in the end, she died. Why—when survival was assured? Was it the thought of being known as a Nazi's whore and bearing a Nazi's bastard child that drove her to destroy herself? Or was it seeing David so brutally murdered? David had wanted to marry Rachel; he loved her. But did she love him? Perhaps she preferred the commandant, who drove off and left her behind. She didn't rush up to David's bleeding body; she went back to the commandant's room. Did she look at the bed where she had spent so many hours with him before she ended it all? Questions in the wind that would return no answering echo.

Luba might have the answers. She would have understood Rachel. But Luba would never have committed suicide—even under those circumstances, he was sure.

He wanted to see her the next night. He had an insatiable desire to know every detail of her life.

———————

He was awakened by an insistently ringing phone. "Who the hell is this?" he demanded.

"How are you, *boychik*?" Milt bellowed in his ear.

"Oh Milt"—Danny smiled in spite of himself—"at two-thirty in the morning it could only be you."

"Damn, I always get the time wrong—England is ahead, Japan is behind, not the other way around," the agent cackled.

"It took you long enough to return my call from Salzburg."

"I was afraid you'd want to talk to me about *Everyman*."

"Wrong. I want to talk to Art Gunn about *Everyman*. I found the perfect angle. It'll be about an artist who corrupts his talent for profit."

"Whatever you say."

"So you'll set up the meeting?"

"You got it. Now . . . I don't want to change the subject, but how's *London Rock* going?"

"Lousy, but it's the least of my worries."

"What's the problem?"

"Ahh, it's hard to talk about it."

"Go ahead—you can tell me," Milt said, becoming serious.

"J. L. Stoneham."

"That prick—what now?"

"He wants to adopt Patricia."

"That doesn't make sense! She's your daughter!"

"That's not what Stoneham thinks."

"It doesn't matter what *he* thinks—what does Patricia think?"

Danny fell silent. Leave it to Milt to ask the only relevant question he couldn't bring himself to answer. He couldn't say, even to his best friend, that he was afraid Patricia didn't want him for a father.

——————

The next day Bruce was still himself. He sat on his throne glowering at everyone. One of his sidekicks, the little guy, kept snapping a yo-yo until Bruce grabbed it and threw it in a trash can.

They reshot the disco scene with a new line: "I'm the big man, and you're my little helper."

"Cut!" called Slim, and then, hiding behind his clipboard, he put his finger down his throat. Danny had to smile.

"I'm glad you're not mad at me," Slim said. "Sorry I blew up yesterday."

"Forget it—after thirty years of marriage we're entitled to a squabble."

Bruce interrupted. "Why do we have to go to Portugal?"

"You've read the script, Bruce—for the rock concert in the bullring and the fiesta on the beach."

"I hate countries that don't speak English. The only word I know in Spanish is '*sí.*' "

"Bruce," Slim broke in, "they don't speak Spanish in Portugal. They speak Portuguese."

"Portuguese—what the hell is that?" Bruce lumbered off, cursing under his breath.

Slim whispered to Danny through his teeth: "You mind if *I* kick his ass?"

——————

After the day's work, Danny escaped to his sanctuary—his room at the Dorchester, where fire crackled in the hearth and Luba waited. Her presence alone seemed both to calm and invigorate him at the same time. Everything else suddenly disappeared.

She nestled against his chest. "How did things go at the studio today?"

"OK. But I can't wait till this is over."

"When will you be going back to America?"

"Oh, not for a while. After we come back from Portugal we still have a few days' work here, and then we're through."

"I've never been to America."

"You haven't? You ought to go sometime."

"You don't know how lucky you are to be an American. Ever hear of anyone running *away* from America?" She didn't wait for his answer. "Everyone in Poland dreams of getting there. I was only thirteen when we left, but I remember— Ah, you don't want to hear more about that. It's a dirty story."

"Not at all. Your story is very honest. Fascinating. And you tell it better than Scheherazade."

She laughed, savoring the compliment. "I'll tell you more."

"Tell me what you did during the day."

"Today?"

"No, in Kraków."

"Oh, we're back there." She rearranged the pillows and made herself more comfortable against Danny's shoulder. "I went to school. I was very bright, but I was bored. Only at night I wasn't bored." Luba started to laugh.

"What's funny?"

"There was a guy my mother brought home, an American. I was in my cot, the lights were out, and my mother was saying in Polish, 'Jesus, this guy thinks he's Hercules. I hope he gets it over with soon —I'm wiped out.' But she said it in a way that sounded like she was in ecstasy. I had to stuff the pillow in my mouth not to laugh out loud."

"Would she also tell you if she was enjoying it?"

"Sure. One extreme to the other."

"So, even if you were in the other bed she might say—"

"She wanted to share. It was a lonely life. She was hoping to get out of Poland—she never forgot Adam. There were not many things she could share with other people, nobody she could trust. So, that was one way of sharing."

"It must have been a hard life."

"We've had our ups and downs, but we always stayed close."

"What's the secret?"

"Secret?"

"The two of you have been through so much—how did you stay so close?"

Luba was yawning. "I always knew Magda was looking out for me, and she always knew that I was looking out for her," she said sleepily.

"But *how* did you know?"

"Mmm?"

"You're falling asleep on me—I asked how did you know she was always looking out for you?"

"I felt it. . . . She felt it. . . . No matter what . . . we never gave up on each other."

She hugged her pillow and closed her eyes. Danny got up, careful not to disturb her, and walked over to the window. The rain was coming down in sheets and the wind was swaying the trees in Hyde Park. He stood there, fervently hoping that, across the Atlantic, Patricia would feel that he would never give up on her—no matter what.

He looked at Luba, peacefully sleeping. A warm feeling toward her flowed through his body. It frightened him. He couldn't allow himself to create another problem by falling in love with her. He needed all his emotional strength to struggle for his daughter. He looked at Luba again—that warm feeling for her was still there. He turned away.

———

Luba had coaxed Magda out of the apartment so she could have some time alone to paint, but she just couldn't find the right light. Three times she had spread the newspapers in different spots on the living-room floor and set up her equipment. Giving up, she finally moved her music-stand easel to the edge of the Kirman rug and put her paints on top of the TV. This would have to do. Her model, patiently waiting on the windowsill, was purring away.

Still, she couldn't get started. Thoughts of Danny interfered. She knew something was wrong. She hadn't heard from him in two days and they had been together every night for weeks.

Danny had changed her life. Now she had no interest in returning calls from the escort service, though God knows they needed the money. But she wanted to keep each night free for him. She knew she was being stupid. On Monday he would be leaving for Portugal, and he hadn't even mentioned taking her along. Then, in a couple of weeks, the film would be over. It would hurt her to see him go out of her life—he had reached deep into her heart, a place that had only belonged to Valentine. Danny was the first person who really wanted to know everything about her, wanted to know *her*. Maybe she was a fool, but she was in love with him.

She wanted to immerse herself in her painting to drive such thoughts from her mind.

She was totally absorbed at last when Magda entered the apartment with two large bags of groceries. Luba tried not to listen to her mother's prattling, reluctant to interrupt the trance of pleasure that painting always brought her.

"Luba, can't you stop painting for a moment?" Magda came in from the kitchen.

"What?"

"I was caught short at the cash register. I had to give the butter back. You didn't give me enough money."

"I gave you all I had."

"It wasn't enough."

"I just paid the rent. I won't have any more until Dorothy from the escort service calls."

"But didn't you see—there are two messages from her by the phone."

Luba whipped around, knocking over the little jar of turpentine that held her dirty brushes.

"Oh Luba, look at this mess."

"I see it!"

Magda grabbed a towel and kneeled down on the floor. "It'll never come out." She scrubbed the rug violently. "This beautiful rug is ruined. Please don't paint—"

"But I want to paint."

"Not in the living room."

"Well, I used to do it in my studio, which is now your bedroom."

Magda stopped rubbing, and looked at Luba, her eyes wide with hurt. "Oh, I'm sorry," she said in a tremulous voice.

Luba's anger evaporated. She put her arms around her mother. "Magda, Magda, please. I'm just a little tense. And I'm worried about you. You don't want to do anything, you're afraid to leave the apartment—I have to push you to go to the market. It would do you good to get a part-time job."

"I can't."

"Restaurants are always advertising for help and—"

"I can't, I can't . . ." Magda was now sobbing in Luba's arms.

"But you're good at that."

"Please don't make me—I can't."

Luba didn't say any more. Magda couldn't be reasoned with ever since she came back from Brighton. What had happened there? Magda didn't talk about it, and Luba sensed it was better not to ask. She just held her tight and rocked her as if she were the mother and Magda the daughter, and then she put her to bed.

───────

The night before he left for Portugal, Danny broke down and called Luba. He decided to take her to a Chinese restaurant. He felt it was the least he should do. He had introduced Luba to Chinese food, and she loved it; she had become adept at using chopsticks (Danny still used a fork), and she was much more adventurous about ordering the more exotic dishes. While he stuck to wonton soup, spareribs, and fried rice, she ordered Szechuan black beans and Peking duck.

During dinner, Danny, usually the insistent interrogator, was quiet. "How was your day?" Luba finally asked, but he just kept munching on his spareribs. "Well," Luba said in a mock baritone, mimicking his voice, "I'm glad you asked . . . I had a wonderful day. Bruce Ryan brought me flowers and—"

"What are you babbling about?" Danny broke in.

"You didn't answer my question, so I answered it for you."

"I'm sorry," said Danny. "I had a rough day."

"Tell me."

"I don't want to talk."

"I'll talk, then—I'll tell you a story."

"I don't want to hear it—right now, I've got too many stories in my own life." He got up and went over to pay the cashier. He knew he sounded harsh, but it was difficult for him to say good-bye.

Luba was shaken. He seemed so irritable, so distant. What had happened? He was always so eager to hear new details about her life.

"Let's walk in the park," she suggested as they left the restaurant; she was anxious not to have the evening end. She pulled him to the crossing. They ran to the other side, barely avoiding a collision with a large tour bus.

Luba laughed. "Must be Stash driving."

"Who?"

"Stash was a tour guide in Kraków. He was the one me and my mother shared."

"What?"

"Didn't I tell you?"

"No—I want to hear about this."

At last she had his interest. They walked in the park for a while, Luba telling him the story. Then he stopped her and pulled her down on a bench next to him.

"But how did it happen the first time?"

"I just jumped in bed while they were making love."

"You what?"

"Yes," said Luba. "My mother was upset . . . she was saying I shouldn't be there, or she shouldn't be there. . . . She was fighting it. But she gave in. It seemed quite normal. Believe me, Stash had been thinking about it for a long time, and now it was happening. It was exciting."

Luba squeezed Danny's hand. "Wouldn't you find it exciting?"

"What do you mean?"

"Magda on one side, me on the other, you in the middle?"

"Are you perverted?!" Danny exclaimed, but he felt a tingling in his groin.

Luba laughed; she knew he had found the thought stimulating.

Embarrassed, Danny got up abruptly. "Let's go." He hoped that Luba couldn't see his face in the dim light.

They left the park and were now walking along a shopping street which was sparsely populated at that hour.

Suddenly she cried out, "Isn't he beautiful?"

She was standing with her face pressed against the glass of a pet-shop window, staring at a miniature poodle. "Look, his fur is like a baby lamb's."

"I'll buy him for you."

"Oh no. These dogs are too expensive—it seems the smaller the dog, the higher the price."

"I can afford it."

"No."

"But you like it."

"But I don't want it."

"Wouldn't you like this one as a memento—so you won't forget me?"

She didn't answer.

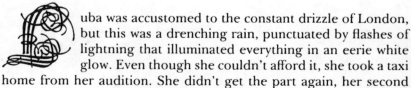

CHAPTER 10

1987 | London

uba was accustomed to the constant drizzle of London,
but this was a drenching rain, punctuated by flashes of
lightning that illuminated everything in an eerie white
glow. Even though she couldn't afford it, she took a taxi
home from her audition. She didn't get the part again, her second
rejection in two days. She was getting tired of trying to be an actress;
she preferred to stay home and paint. She barely had enough for the
fare, and when the taxi pulled up to the curb she made a dash for the
front door to avoid the driver's dirty look at the five-pence tip. The
door was locked—who the hell had locked it? She stood in the down-

pour, searching for her key and getting angrier by the second; her clothes were now soaked, her shoes full of water. She hit the doorbell.

It seemed a long time before she heard Magda's voice over the intercom. "Who is it?"

"It's me—open up, goddamn it!"

She hurried up the steps, kicked off her wet shoes in the hallway, and threw down her dripping jacket. "I need some hot tea, fast," she yelled.

"Just in time," a deep male voice answered.

She walked into the living room and caught her breath.

A strange tea party was in progress. There were two men with Magda—the older of the two, with a handlebar mustache, seemed to have ignored his waistline a long time ago; the younger, tall and slim, had a slim mustache to match. This odd duo sat stiffly in their chairs, sipping tea.

The young man rose when Luba entered. "We seem to be always meeting in the rain," he said. He looked familiar. Of course—he was the young policeman she talked to at the Brighton station the rainy night she ran to get help. He stuck out his hand.

"You wet, Luba," said Magda, awkwardly pronouncing the English words; Magda seldom spoke English to her daughter.

"Yes—you need some nice hot tea," the young officer said, smiling so aggressively his upper lip rode up like a curtain above his gums.

The older man, who filled every inch of the largest armchair in the parlor, nodded his head at her. They were not dressed in their police uniforms, but even in plain clothes it was obvious who they were. They looked so much like the police in Brodki, right down to their mustaches. Magda handed Luba a cup of tea, kissed her on the cheek, and said in a flat voice, exaggerating each word, "They think somebody kill Colonel Johnson."

Luba's mind was racing: He fell down the stairs . . . hit his head . . . what had Magda omitted?

"No, no, no," interjected the fat officer. "We just want to ask some questions, that's all." Then, addressing himself to Luba, he said, "I'm Captain Ferguson of the Brighton Police, and this is Sergeant Sweeney."

Sergeant Sweeney bowed. "I've had the pleasure of meeting the young lady before."

Luba looked from one to the other. "What's this all about?"

The captain cleared his throat. "Oh, we're just finishing our investigation on the death of your father."

Luba cringed. "He was not my father—he was my stepfather."

"Of course," said the captain. "Where were you when your father . . . ah . . . Colonel Johnson died?"

"I was here, in London."

The young sergeant edged forward in his chair. "You do remember the evening you came to our police station?"

"Yes," said Luba, and then added, trying to sound pleasant, "you offered me a cup of tea."

"That's right," said the sergeant, glancing at a notebook in his lap. He uncrossed his legs and crossed them again. "And, if I recall correctly, at that time you said, and I quote, 'He's killing her.' " He narrowed his eyes as he stared at Luba. "I assume you were referring to your stepfather and your mother?"

"Yes," said Luba.

Magda interrupted with a forced laugh. "Luba is good girl. Always worried about Mama. We have arguments. Husband and wife have arguments. Sometime, loud voices. My daughter, very scared."

The young sergeant turned his attention to Magda. "Then, he *wasn't* trying to kill you?"

Magda forced a laugh again. "No, no, no. My husband very good man. Nervous about the hotel—new business for him. He want to make good job."

"I still don't understand," said Luba, trying to conceal her growing alarm. "Why are you here?"

"We just need a few answers so we can close the file," the fat man said. "There are a few . . . ah . . . shall I say . . . *peculiar* aspects to this case. For one thing, as we've already told your mother, the coroner's report tells us that the fatal injury seems too severe to have been caused by the impact of someone falling down the stairs."

Luba concentrated on the two little puddles of water at the policemen's feet.

"And our examination indicates that the head of the deceased impacted on the middle step . . ." He paused as if to underline the significance of his statement.

"What does that mean?" Luba asked.

The captain set down his teacup. "Reconstruction of the body's trajectory indicates he *could* have been pushed—violently."

"Who would do that?" Luba was finding it difficult to breathe regularly.

The only sound in the room was a soft rustle as the young sergeant flipped the pages in his notebook. The captain addressed Magda: "Do you know how he hit his head, Mrs. Johnson?"

"I don't know. I not there. I see nothing. I tell you all I see—my husband dead and I very upset."

"When was the last time you saw your husband *alive?*"

Magda sighed. "I *told* you—when I bring up the box to attic. He stack the box. He very neat man."

Luba just sat there holding her cup of tea and listening to the thumping of her heart. The captain started coughing, and nodded to the young sergeant to continue.

"And then what did you do?" the sergeant asked.

Magda sighed again. "I told you—I go for next box. I carry up to attic and I find him, Colonel Johnson."

"Your husband?"

"Yes, my husband, Colonel Johnson. I find him on the bottom. Dead."

"How did you know he was dead?"

"I no sure, but I touch him, he no move. I get scared, and I yell for help."

"Was anyone around?"

"Yes, we have few guests."

"And did anyone see you going up the stairs?"

"Yes, yes, Mrs. Henry. She ask me if box not too heavy. I tell her no, no, I use to that."

The young sergeant consulted his notes. "That's right, we have Mrs. Henry's statement," he said, holding up the page for the captain to see, but the captain's eyes never left Magda's stoic face.

"You left Brighton rather quickly after the funeral. Why?"

Magda bristled. "My husband dead. Bank take hotel. I'm very sad. I come to my daughter. What you do?"

The captain smiled at her. "Now, now, Mrs. Johnson. We ask the questions. All we want from you is honest answers."

"But that's what I give you, over and over! That's what I give you!" There was still anger in her voice.

The young sergeant piped up: "We know this is difficult for you, Mrs. Johnson, but we have a job to do. Just a few more questions, and we'll be finished."

Luba took her first sip of the now cooling tea, and watched her mother intently.

The two policemen exchanged glances. And then the captain resumed: "Did you have a happy marriage?"

"Yes, yes. We have argument, like other people. We worry—hard job running hotel. My husband want to take care of me and my daughter—"

"But your daughter left home—isn't that right?"

Luba tried to help her mother. "We didn't get along too well. I felt that I was an added burden, and if I left, things would be much better between my mother and my stepfather."

"And were they?"

"Yes," Magda said. "My husband don't get along with Luba. He no have children, he no understand young girls. We decide better Luba go to London."

The young sergeant, still flipping the pages of his notebook, seemed to have reached the last page, Luba observed with relief. He raised his eyes in her direction. "I want to ask one more question about that night you came over to the station. You thought he was *killing* your mother?"

"Yes, I was upset. I had never heard them have such a violent argument, and it scared me."

"Was that all it was—an argument?"

"Yes," said Luba.

"Was there any physical violence?"

"Of course not," she snapped.

Magda sat silently. The rain was coming down steadily, and occasionally one could hear a rumble of thunder. The cat came over to Luba, rubbed himself against her leg, and meowed softly; he was hungry—it was past his feeding time.

The fat captain broke the silence. "Did he leave you much money?"

"No," said Magda. "Nothing. The bank take over everything." Tears formed in Magda's eyes. "Why you ask us such questions? I not in country very long. I not married very long. I love my husband. He good man. This terrible accident ruin my whole life. Now you in my house and ask me questions like I kill man I love." She was crying softly now.

Luba looked at her mother with secret admiration. My God, she thought, she should be playing a part for Danny. She's got me convinced.

The sergeant started folding up his papers and the captain hoisted his porcine proportions out of the armchair. He waddled over and took Magda's hand. "I want to thank you for your patience. I'm sorry we've disturbed you, and I hope this will end our investigation."

The younger man, his rosy face smiling, approached Luba. "It's nice to see you again. Perhaps when you're in Brighton sometime we can chat again over a spot of tea."

Luba didn't respond.

"Well, hope all goes well for both of you," the sergeant added.

"Thank you," Luba said, looking away. She waited until she heard the door close behind them. Then she went into the kitchen, the cat following at her heels, came back with a rag, and mopped up the two little puddles of water where the policemen had sat. She fed the cat and then sat down across from her mother. Magda hadn't moved; she was weeping silently, head down.

"Is that the way it happened?" Luba asked in Polish.

Magda covered her face with her hands. Luba waited.

Wearily, Magda leaned against the back of the sofa, her eyes closed. She took a deep breath, then, very softly and very slowly, she spoke. "I couldn't take any more—I was at the point where I was going to kill myself. . . . Oh Luba, he stood there, on one skinny leg, at the head of those stairs, like an angry black crane that scared me once in Brodki. I couldn't go through another night with him. . . ."

Magda opened her eyes and gazed up at the ceiling. "He seemed to fly through the air . . . oh Luba, Luba, I did a terrible thing, and God will punish me."

Her shoulders quivered as tears streamed down her cheeks. Luba knelt on the floor beside her. "Don't cry, Mama. I should have killed him myself. It's OK. No one but us will ever know. You've got me to look after you. We're together, and that's all that counts."

The doorbell made them both jump. They looked at each other. "They've come back," Magda whispered, her face white with fear.

"I'll get rid of the bastards," Luba said, patting her hand.

At the downstairs door stood a rain-soaked messenger boy holding a wicker basket. "Miss Johnson? This is for you."

Luba could hear little whimpers coming from inside. The attached card read: *Luba—so you won't forget me—Danny.* She peeked under the cover at the squirming ball of white wool.

Hiding the card in her pocket, she took the basket and walked back upstairs. "Magda, a present for you."

She placed the basket on her mother's lap and opened the lid. The little poodle jumped out and immediately began licking Magda's cheeks.

Lisbon, Portugal

lim had arranged for the film equipment to pass through customs in advance so that when the *London Rock* chartered jet landed at the Lisbon airport, the crew could immediately go to location. Everything was proceeding very smoothly, Danny thought with pleasure. Filming on location always put him in a good frame of mind. Even the hurt that was inside him whenever he thought of Patricia seemed duller. Stephanie, J. L. Stoneham, Luba—all were lost somewhere in a haze of London fog. He knew he had made the right decision—to spend the eight days in Portugal without Luba. She was becoming an obsession; he needed to put distance between them.

Now Danny waited his turn to pass the customs security check, watching with amusement as Bruce swaggered through ahead of him like a cowboy walking through a saloon door. His two companions filed by next, and suddenly the security alarms went off. Bruce whirled around and froze. The guards, talking and gesticulating rapidly, led Bruce's two sidekicks away.

Slim rushed over and followed them to the customs office. When he came out, he was scratching his bald pate. He motioned Danny to the side. "Bruce's boys were carrying some cocaine in their shorts. Wrapped in tin foil—can you believe it?"

Danny rolled his eyes. Of course—the tin foil set off the metal detector.

"What'll I do, boss? They're under arrest."

"I better contact the U.S. ambassador and see what can be done to get them out of this mess," said Danny. "You take care of Bruce." He pointed to his star, who stood alone, looking lost. "Get him to the hotel before the customs people decide to look in his shorts. If we lose him, we lose the picture."

———

With the assistance of the ambassador, Danny managed to assuage the Portuguese authorities. Bruce's boys would be released and shipped back to London after Ace Films paid $30,000 in fines, which Art Gunn—spitting with anger over the telephone—agreed to wire immediately.

By the time he unraveled the mess, Danny was exhausted. He slumped in the backseat as his limousine took him down wide, tree-lined boulevards past villas and palaces. The driver pointed out the home of the world-renowned painter Nuno Adolpho, which was set high atop one of the seven hills of the city. Tired as he was, he couldn't help but marvel at the Moorish-style architecture that gave the city an *Arabian Nights* feeling. They turned down a narrow cobble-stoned street into Terreiro do Paço, the famed Black Horse Square, where Slim had rented him a charming little house with stone steps leading down to the River Tagus. What a delightful place, Danny thought, looking forward to a good night's sleep in this peaceful setting.

He got out of the car. Sitting on the front stoop was Bruce Ryan.

"I want my stuff," he demanded.

"What stuff?"

"Stuff, goddamn it! Coke. I don't work without it."

Danny shook his head in astonishment, glancing around to see if any pedestrians had overheard. "Bruce—are you crazy? How am I gonna get it?"

"You figure it out."

"We're lucky that we got—"

"Lucky, my ass. If I don't have it by tomorrow, I'm outta here."

"OK. I'll call customs and tell them that stuff is yours and you want it back."

Bruce gave him a frightened look. "Come on, Danny—this is no time for jokes."

"What can *I* do?"

In a timid voice he pleaded, "You gotta help me. I need it, Danny—I need it."

Hunched over, Bruce walked back to his car. He's just a scared small-town kid from Pennsylvania, Danny thought. He felt sorry for the poor bastard. But where could he get Bruce cocaine? Maybe Nuno Adolpho, who, it was widely known, had experimented with mind-expanding drugs, could help. Did he have the nerve to go see a famous artist and ask for dope? He had to try.

————

Adolpho's home was a rambling, pink-stucco villa, protected by a high wall. It was a bizarre structure, built on many levels. The butler asked him to wait in the *sobrado,* an entrance courtyard from which staircases led to upper balconies draped with ivy and exotic purple flowers.

Adolpho came waddling down the steps with outstretched arms, the sleeves of his floor-length caftan swishing the air like the wings of a bird. "My neighbor!" he greeted Danny. He was a short, roly-poly character with a cherubic face as smooth and red as an apple and snow-white hair that fell to his shoulders. "How gracious of you to visit me!"

"I don't want to interrupt your work, *maestro*. I just came to pay my respects."

"Never an interruption. My house is your house!"

"Thank you, *maestro*. I hope your work schedule will permit you to visit us during our filming."

"With pleasure, Mr. Dennison, but only if you will allow me to host your cast here."

In spite of Adolpho's graciousness, Danny found it difficult to bring up the subject of cocaine. When he did, the artist couldn't have been more understanding. The cordial meeting ended with Adolpho saying with a smile, "What are neighbors for if not to lend each other a cup of sugar?"

─────────

He had averted a major crisis, Danny thought as he stretched his muscles, slowly waking up in his canopied bed. The sun pouring through the window was so bright it hurt his eyes. He smiled with satisfaction. He felt vigorous, strong, on top of the world for a change.

He could smell coffee somewhere below. He jumped out of bed and with a spring in his step headed down the stairs. It was a lovely house, each of the three floors a separate whitewashed room with its own tiled fireplace. The ground floor had a living room, almost identical to the bedrooms above, plus a large kitchen. And that's where, seated at a table next to the red-brick wood-fired oven, he found Slim sipping a cup of steaming coffee.

Slim handed Danny a cup. "You did a great day's work yesterday, boss. I didn't want to wake you."

"Everything ready for this afternoon?"

"All set. And wait till you see that bullring. It looks like a big coliseum, Moorish architecture—fantastic!"

"Are we gonna have enough extras to fill it?"

"Are you kidding? Half of Lisbon is lined up now. They don't often get a chance to see a movie being made."

"How's Bruce?"

"Stoned. Don't tell me where you got the stuff, but if you can get enough to keep him going for a week, we'll swing it."

"No problem." Danny refilled his cup—coffee never tasted so good.

"So we'll meet at the bullring in an hour," Slim said, getting up. He was almost out the door when he pulled an envelope from his pocket. "I forgot—this came for you this morning." He handed Danny a telegram.

Danny ripped it open absentmindedly.

THANK YOU FOR THE POODLE. HE'S WONDERFUL. I MISS YOU. PLEASE CALL ME. I HAVE MORE STORIES TO TELL. MAGDA JOINS ME IN SENDING LOVE— LUBA.

It made him tingle with anticipation. He laughed at himself—a tower of Jell-O. But why not invite her to Lisbon? He could handle it. In two weeks he would be back in California anyway, and Luba would be out of his life forever. So what would be the harm? "I miss you," her message said; he had to admit he missed her too. In so many ways she was unique. And sex with her was extraordinary; she was a master, slowly leading him along the rising scale of sexual experiences, introducing him to something new each time. Always she took him higher and higher. He'd discovered a sexual drive he didn't know he possessed. He wanted to see her. And what was Magda like? He felt he knew so much about her from Luba's stories. Impulsively, ignoring the little voice in the back of his head that reminded him of his recent resolutions, he wired them two round-trip tickets.

When Danny got back from the next day's shooting—which had gone very well for a change, with a less cocky Bruce—a pleasant aroma was wafting from the kitchen. He headed there and stopped in the doorway.

A woman was at the stove, and, with much clatter, was pouring ingredients from several small pots into a large soup kettle, continuously stirring with a big wooden spoon. She was about the same height as Luba, but with a fuller, riper body that mirrored the promise of Luba someday. Not a bad promise. She wore her thick dark hair in a long, single braid down her back. Suddenly she became aware of him. Looking over her shoulder, she gave him a warm smile. "You Danny." It was a statement, not a question.

"Yes. Welcome, Magda." He extended his hand.

Without interrupting her stirring, she switched the spoon to her left hand, wiped her palm on her apron, and shook his hand. "Luba tell me many things about you."

"Nice things?" Danny grinned.

"Oh, very nice."

Danny watched her stirring. How old could she be? Forty? Forty-five? She was very attractive.

Luba came hurrying in from the living room with a vodka martini. "So you two have met."

"Yes, finally," Danny said, taking the drink and kissing her gently on the forehead; her hair was braided in two pigtails. "You two look like sisters."

Magda glowed. "Tonight you eat gołąbki—good Polish food." She fished a steaming cabbage out of the pot and held it up for their admiration.

The stuffed cabbage proved delicious, and Magda, delighted that he liked it, chattered in her broken English all through dinner. How pleased she was to be in Portugal . . . how wonderful to see so much sunshine after the dreary days of London . . . Then she exclaimed, "But I miss my little dog so much!"

"Huh?" Danny, his mouth full of gołąbki, looked at Luba.

She kicked him under the table. "Magda loves the poodle you sent her."

Danny caught on. "Oh, oh—I'm glad."

"Yes, thank you, Danny, very much. But I lonely for him."

"You've just arrived and you want to go back?"

"No, no, but he only a puppy . . . he so sad all alone."

"Don't worry—Mrs. McKeever promised to take good care of him while we're away," Luba said.

"What did you name him?" Danny asked.

Magda blushed and hesitated, looking at Luba.

"She named him Danny," Luba said.

They all laughed.

After dinner Magda turned in early, while Luba and Danny lingered over coffee. "I'm glad you invited her," Luba said. "She hasn't been herself since her husband died. That's why I gave her the dog you sent—she needed cheering up."

"You think she's all right up there?"

"Sure, but why don't you check on her?"

Danny wondered if there was a deeper meaning in the suggestion, but Luba just continued sipping her coffee. He climbed the stairs, hesitated a moment, then knocked.

Magda was in her nightdress and seemed a little flustered when she opened the door.

"Are you comfortable?"

"Oh, yes. And thank you that I come with Luba."

"I'm glad you're here." Danny didn't know what else to say. "So you love little Danny?"

She stepped back, wide-eyed.

Danny realized she had misunderstood. "I mean Danny your dog."

"Oh yes, yes. He my boyfriend. Thank you again."

He looked at her, the outlines of her ripe body clearly visible through her nightgown. This was the woman Luba had described— the woman who had walked the streets in Kraków, object of every man's desire. Aware of his gaze, she picked up her robe.

"Sleep well," he said softly, going out and closing the door.

Later that night, lying in bed, listening to *fado* songs from a nearby café, Danny caught himself fantasizing about being in bed with both of them—Luba and Magda, mother and daughter. The thought intrigued and scared him at the same time. He pushed it away, and nudged Luba. "Tell me a story."

Luba giggled.

"What's funny?"

She mimicked him: " 'Tell me a story.' You're like a child, but instead of Little Red Riding Hood, you want to hear about fucking."

"After little boys grow up, they prefer those stories."

"Some little boys prefer them *before* they grow up."

"What are you talking about?"

"My newspaper boy," she said slyly. "He comes over every Sunday morning to be paid."

"What's with him?"

"He's cute, about fourteen. I usually just wear a robe"—then she lowered her voice—"I let it open a little. . . ."

"And he looks?"

"Of course! It excites him. He turns red. And while I'm paying him, his crotch is bursting."

"Did you ever—?"

"Maybe," she teased.

"And what happened?"

Her head popped up from the pillow. "Why do you ask so many questions? Let me ask *you* a question for a change."

"OK—go ahead."

"Have you ever sucked a cock?"

"Don't be stupid!" Danny said indignantly.

"If you had, would that make you less of a man?"

"Are you serious?"

She settled back on her pillow. "Men are so mixed up about sex—macho image. Some men put on women's clothes from time to time, or makeup, and go for women. When men wore fancy clothes, lace cuffs, wigs, and beauty marks, weren't they still men? The Greeks used women just to have kids—they thought love existed only between men."

She had a point, Danny had to admit.

"Danny?"

"What?"

"Someday you ought to suck a little cock."

"Oh, go to sleep."

While Danny was off filming, Luba and Magda would pass the time relaxing, strolling the streets of the city, enjoying the sights, sunbathing by the River Tagus behind their little house. Lisbon agreed with Magda. She was getting a healthy glow from the sun, and her outlook on life seemed rosier too. Luba wasn't worried about her anymore. But now it was Magda's turn to worry about Luba.

"Are you falling in love with Danny?" Magda asked her point-blank one sunny afternoon as they sat on the dock, their feet dangling in the water.

"Oh, I'm just having a good time."

"I know you, Luba. You haven't acted this way since Valentine. You don't care about anything except Danny."

"Don't you like him?"

"I like him, but in a week he'll be going back to America, and you'll be left behind. Don't fall apart like you did when Valentine disappeared."

"Maybe he will ask me to come to America with him."

"Luba . . . Luba, that's a fantasy."

Luba watched the ripples her feet made. "Remember that Polish proverb? 'Life without fantasy is like a pond without a fish—just a puddle of stagnant water.'"

"I'm trying to give you good advice and you talk poetry. Don't get hurt, Luba—just don't get hurt."

On Sunday, the company's one free day, Adolpho invited cast and crew to a cocktail party on the terrace of his beautiful villa. Danny urged Magda to join him, but she said she was too shy at parties and insisted on staying home.

Adolpho was a very amusing host as he mingled with his guests, inviting them to the *boa mesa*, a buffet table laden with various regional Portuguese dishes and dominated by a huge baked cod, the country's favorite fish. Not that the crew needed much urging—they devoured the food as if they hadn't eaten for days.

When Adolpho spotted Danny, he enveloped him in his purple robes, and, stepping up on his toes, kissed him on both cheeks. "My dear neighbor, do you need a cup of sugar?"

Danny laughed, throwing a glance over at Bruce Ryan, who was hugging the corner of the room. Ill at ease without his sidekicks, Bruce seemed to be searching the room for a replacement. Danny was about to approach him when he saw the actor sidle up to Luba at the bar. He patted her backside with a leer. "You got a nice ass."

He's the height of sophistication, Danny thought, and then he heard Luba answer, "So do you."

Danny winced and walked away. He wandered through the part of the house that was clearly Adolpho's gallery. The whitewashed walls were covered with the artist's strange paintings, which were large, dramatic, and very colorful—elephants on long spindly legs, seascapes crowded with stick figures.

Absorbed, Danny wasn't sure how long he'd been away from the party when he heard Luba's voice behind him. "Isn't his stuff incredible?" She didn't wait for an answer. "Can you believe that these wonderful works of art come from that roly-poly man? He's a genius. Look . . ." She led him by the hand to a painting of lambs and lions, with the lambs twice the size of their predators. "What an imagination . . . point of view . . . Did you ever see such wild colors?" She pulled him in a different direction, to a painting of a wheat field on fire. "Now that inspires me."

Stimulated by what she had seen, Luba continued babbling. It was not until the evening's end that she had run down, like a toy whose spring had finally unwound.

They walked home from the party, each in a pensive mood. Luba's cigarette, a bright ember in the dark, glowed with each puff. In the distance a dog was howling at the full moon. Luba stopped to listen.

Danny looked at her questioningly. "What is it?"

"For a minute it sounded like Blue Boy."

"Huh?"

"Blue Boy, my dog."

"What happened to him?"

"We had to leave him in Milan. I wanted to keep him, but I couldn't. I can still see him jumping against the bus, barking his heart out as we pulled away. He was a mistake. It was a lesson. Parting is too painful; you can't afford to become attached."

"Is that the real reason you gave Magda the poodle?"

She nodded, and he put his arm around her.

"You think about Milan, and your most poignant memory is a dog. What about people? Didn't you leave friends behind?"

"Oh yes, but they had a chance. The dog had none."

"You love dogs."

"Yes, and now Magda does too. She got angry at me for picking up Blue Boy, but now she understands. Your gift helped her." She took a deep puff on her cigarette. "You have a dog back home—in California?"

"No, I don't."

"You should, Danny—dogs are wonderful. They spend their whole life waiting, just waiting for the one they love. They wait to be let out, wait to be let in, wait to be fed. They wait for affection. And how they appreciate that! They give it back, always. All they want is to give you love. Even if you beat them, they can't stop loving you."

Magda was already asleep when they walked into the dark house. They went to bed, and for a long time they both lay very quietly. Finally, Danny broke the silence. "Luba, are you asleep?"

"No, Danny."

"You know, Luba . . . I love the thoughts that pour out of you—"

"You do?" She snuggled closer to him.

"Such beautiful thoughts—about dogs, life, sex . . ."

She giggled.

"Don't laugh. It's true—you've taught me a lot, especially about sex. Every time I have sex with you it's new—it's like the first time."

"Do you remember your first time?"

Danny didn't answer.

"Tell me about it—what was it like?"

"It's getting late. Go to sleep."

"I told you about mine. Come on—did you play with your thumb?"

"No," Danny chuckled. "I think it might shock you if I told you."

"Shock *me*? You're kidding."

He took a deep breath. "I had sex with my mother."

Startled, Luba raised her head. "I don't believe you."

"See—I told you you'd be shocked. But she wasn't my real mother."

"Tell me more."

"She adopted me after my parents died. It was a wonderful introduction to sex." He turned away. "I never told anybody this."

"Danny . . ." She molded her body against his. "What you just said means a lot to me. You trust me. I believe you never told anyone. I never told anyone things I've told you."

Troia, Portugal

 hen the troupe moved to Troia for the last two days of shooting, Magda decided to return to London. She enjoyed the visit, she said, but she was worried about her new puppy. Luba stayed on.

The first evening, over dinner on the veranda of their suite in the Aparthotel Magnoliamar, Luba held Danny spellbound as she told him how she had seduced Chaim on the riverbank.

"Was it like that one?" Danny pointed to where they could see the River Sado flowing to meet the Atlantic Ocean.

Luba laughed. "Danny, in the heat of passion, all riverbanks look alike. But maybe we should check it out."

With a mischievous grin she kicked off her shoes and raced down the steps to the beach. Danny followed her with a glass of port that the hotel owner had lauded as the best in Portugal.

As they strolled the beach barefoot, sharing the port, Danny coaxed her to continue the story. "What did Magda say when she caught you in the act?"

"Nothing. We didn't talk for two days, and Magda wouldn't listen to Chaim's explanations."

Danny laughed as he took another sip. "I can hear him now— 'Magda, I'm sorry, I apologize. It's my fault, not hers. She reminds me of you. I was thinking of you.' What could the guy say?"

"But she was more angry with *me*. And she was right. I wanted to hurt her, but as soon as I did, I was sorry."

"Did she get together with Chaim again?"

"*We* got together."

"My God! I'm going to make the first X-rated TV serial out of all this. When?"

"A week or so later."

"You maneuvered it?"

"I had to, because Chaim was too timid."

"Timid?!" Danny hurled the empty port glass into the waves. "Oh, of course . . ." His voice was full of mock sarcasm. "He was just a shy guy having a romance with the mother and then he fucks her daughter—"

"Do you want to hear this or don't you?"

"I'm sorry," he said, suppressing a laugh. "I really do."

"He wanted to take us out for dinner to celebrate our new life."

"You arranged that?"

"Oh, no. *He* wanted to take us out. *I* arranged to have the dinner in our room."

"You scare the hell out of me. I'm going to keep away from you," Danny said, sprinting off toward a grassy dune.

She caught up to him. "Please don't do that." She gave him a gentle kiss.

They sat down on the grass, Danny a little out of breath. "And what did your mother do?"

"She refused. She was still hurt. But I told her we were leaving, Chaim was in love with her, he had to see her just once more."

"So she gave in finally?"

"That's right."

"And she cooked the dinner?"

"Yes, but he brought the—"

"Don't tell me—the fish!"

"Of course. A large bass."

Danny sprang to his feet and began to improvise with flourish. "I see it clearly—late afternoon. He went out and fished, this time alone. The sun was low on the horizon. He felt guilty, berating himself: 'What am I, some kind of pervert? Her daughter! I'm never going to do anything like that again.' "

"Do you want to tell this story?" she asked with a throaty laugh.

"No—no—no! Let the celebration begin! I want to hear the episode that gets the series renewed."

"Then don't interrupt. After dinner, the wine bottles were getting empty—"

"And when Magda drinks, it relaxes her, yes?"

"Yes!"

Danny began to pace. "I wish I were shooting that scene tomorrow."

Luba scowled.

"I'll shut up. But how did it happen? How did you maneuver it?"

"I went over and kissed Magda on the mouth."

"And Chaim's jaw dropped a little?"

"I thought you were going to shut up."

"But did you really kiss her? Did you—"

"I kissed her."

"And?"

"And she tried to pull away."

"But not too hard."

"She had too much wine, and she liked it."

"And Chaim watched?"

"I thought his eyes were going to pop out of his head!"

"Then?"

"I called him over."

Danny flopped down beside her. "You do scare the hell out of me. You were fourteen!"

"Going on fifteen."

"And you loved the power of manipulating the whole situation." He mimicked her: "Chaim, come here."

Luba grinned. "I just looked at him."

"Holy shit! You should be a screenwriter! This series'll run for five years! We'll get Sophia Loren to play Magda. A nationwide search for the girl to play your role. I'll test hundreds of them."

"I bet you will."

"It's brilliant! I see it so clearly—'Chaim, come on—kiss Magda'!"

Luba nodded impishly.

"People are like puppets to you—you pull the strings."

"While he was kissing her, I kicked my shoes off, pulled down his pants, and there we were."

"Chaim must have been reeling—and not for a fish!"

Luba made a face at his bad joke and went on. "He was excited—he didn't know which way to turn. Then Magda lay down on the bed."

"You *both* seduced Magda!"

"It had to be that way."

Danny sighed, visualizing the situation. "How was Magda feeling?"

"She didn't feel betrayed."

"Oh, Chaim, how I envy you! He never had a night like that—ever! Nor have I."

"It was a little good-bye gift."

"Well, say good-bye to me!"

"Good-bye, Danny!" She burst out laughing.

"I mean it, Luba. Let's all get together. Let's pretend we're in Milan, Kraków, wherever."

"I thought you said that's perverted."

"I said that? Well—scratch it."

"Someday . . . I promise." Her eyes locked on his as her hand began to unbutton his shirt. "Tonight you'll have to settle just for me." She pushed him down on his back and slipped off his trousers. Then she stood up and whipped off her dress; underneath she was naked. In silhouette against the dark sky heavy with stars, a crescent moon over her shoulder, she seemed like an ebony statue.

She kneeled, and let her fingers trace the muscles on his chest, moving slowly down over the outlines of his body. Her hands cupped his erection and guided it into her mouth. She gently caressed it with her tongue. When she felt it begin to throb, she straddled him and slowly impaled herself on his cock.

"Feel good, darling?" she whispered.

A satisfied moan was Danny's answer, and he began to move up and down.

"No, no—don't move," she said in a husky voice, picking up the rhythm he had set. "Just lie still—look up—count the stars." She giggled softly. "Count slowly—and before you get to ten you'll see a comet race across the moon."

—————

Back in the hotel room, spent, Danny stretched out on the bed beside Luba. He held all the air in his lungs for a moment and then exhaled. "Happy?" he asked.

"Very." In the dark, Danny couldn't see the contented expression on her face; she had found another way to please him.

He pulled her closer and cradled her in his arms.

"Ooh, I like this," she said. "It makes me feel safe. Like when I was walking the tight wire and fell and Josef caught me."

"I know what you mean. When I was a kid I fell off the roof of the barn, but no one caught *me.*" He chuckled softly. "Then my sister picked me up, brought me in the house, and put me to bed. It's nice to be taken care of."

Sleepily, she muttered, "Tell me more . . ."

He kissed her hair. She snuggled up closer and drifted off to sleep.

Danny stayed awake. He wanted to tell her more. He wanted to tell her that she made him feel safe enough to remember the things he had blocked out for forty years. There were so many beautiful memories too—why had he robbed himself of those? She made him want to remember. Was it because she reminded him of Rachel?

She was such a strange gypsy, filled with mystery. At one moment she scared him with her brashness; at another she disarmed him with her vulnerability. She was always honest; she said exactly what she felt, exactly what she thought. *Shame* was not even in her vocabulary. He lived with it every day.

CHAPTER 11

1987 | London

The magical influence of Lisbon rapidly dissolved in the jet stream of the British Airways flight en route to London, where the final scenes would be shot at Pinewood. One more week and it would be over. Danny wasn't in a mood to talk. He let the script he was marking fall in his lap, leaned back, and closed his eyes, pretending to be asleep. But he was acutely aware of Luba's presence next to him.

He had a deep feeling for her, deeper than he had realized, and he couldn't cope with it. She frightened him too much. Somehow she had found a weak spot in the wall he had erected around himself. She made him feel too comfortable, too relaxed—he forgot to keep his guard up. It was so easy to tell her about Mrs. Dennison, about falling off the roof at the farm. He almost told her more.

She was supposed to be the storyteller, he the listener. But he broke the rules. And now she knew things he had never told anyone. What other secrets of his life could she extricate from him?

He opened his eyes and saw Bruce Ryan, in the row across from them, looking appraisingly at Luba. Bruce winked. Luba winked back. Then she glanced over at Danny, who started writing notes in his script again.

"Don't mind him," said Bruce. "He's always working. I don't think he knows how to play."

Danny chose to ignore his remark, but he was annoyed at Luba.

"Do *you* know how to play?" Bruce asked suggestively.

"I think I do," she said.

"Yeah, I bet you do."

Danny watched them out of the corner of his eye, remembering Bruce's advances at Adolpho's party. Then an attractive stewardess brought Bruce a drink and diverted his attention.

"You got much more to do, Danny?" Luba asked.

"Not much," he answered without lifting his head.

Luba studied him. He seemed totally engrossed in his work, but the pulsating vein at his temple told her he was very tense. Something was bothering him again. He was not at all like the man who had plied her with questions last night.

Since their affair began, she had told him so many things. At first she tried to hold back. But he was insatiable, insistent; he wanted to know everything. And the more she told him, the more she enjoyed confiding those secrets only she and Magda shared. She had a need to tell him. And finally, Danny was beginning to open up to her too.

From Heathrow Airport, Danny took Luba in his limousine to her apartment. As the driver unloaded her bags from the trunk, Danny brushed Luba's cheek with his lips. "Be sure to kiss Magda for me."

"I will." She nodded. She was leaning against the car, looking up into his face. The sun of Portugal had bronzed her skin so it glowed with health. A breeze ruffled her hair, a few wisps straying across her smiling eyes. My God, she is beautiful, he thought.

He reached into his pocket and extracted an envelope.

"What's this?" Her smile disappeared.

"Some money—I know you need it."

"But Danny, with you I don't do it for money. I love you."
Danny bit his lip. He almost said, "I love you too." It would have
been so easy. It almost slipped out.
"Don't you understand?" she said, searching his eyes. "I love you."
He kissed her lips gently. "Consider it a loan. . . ."
She gave his hand a quick squeeze. "I'll let you know if I need it."
She left him there holding the envelope.

——————

The concierge handed him his messages and mail. There were four
calls from Stephanie in Reno—all within the last three days. He
crumpled them into a ball and threw them away. There was also a
large envelope, postmarked Long Island; in the corner were six or
seven names—a law firm. A shiver went through him. He stuffed it in
his pocket and walked toward the elevator, not even hearing the
operator greet him. When he finally got to his room, he was perspiring. From his pocket he took out the envelope, blotched with dark
stains from his sweaty palms.
He ripped it open—pages of legal documents covered with the
mumbo-jumbo phrases of expensive lawyers. Adoption papers. All
the places that required his signature were carefully marked with blue
crosses, and the pages with paper clips.
J. L. Stoneham's angular signature stood out, glaringly, on the
lines just above the crosses, and in a few places he caught Stephanie's
perfectly formed Foxcroft script.
He slumped down on the couch. That son of a bitch! Here was a
man who could skillfully manipulate the stocks of a company to skim
off the profits and leave it squashed like a bug; the acquisition of a
young girl must seem simple compared to a hostile takeover. Danny
could see who was going to be the bug squashed in the process.
It gave him a twisted feeling down in his guts to see it so neatly
typed out: PATRICIA D. STONEHAM.
D! Was that the last morsel left to him?
By signing these papers he would relinquish all legal rights to his
daughter. Is this what Stephanie wanted him to do? Is this what
Patricia really wanted? How did J.L. convince both of them?
His head pounding, he picked up the adoption papers, and a pread-
dressed envelope with rows of stamps fell out. J.L.'s team had taken
care of every detail. The old man left nothing to chance. All he
needed was Danny's signature to close the deal.
Well, fuck him! He can't treat this like some corporate raid! I'll *never*
do it!

Danny ripped up the pages and threw them in a wastebasket. He could hardly breathe. He opened the window and inhaled deeply. Across the street in Hyde Park, a group of girls was getting ready for a race, their parents cheering them on. Happy families sharing a happy time—Danny couldn't bear to watch.

He threw himself down on the couch and buried his head in a pillow. What was Patricia doing at this very moment—attending classes?—riding her horse?—maybe taking a walk? He imagined her racing with a group of girls, himself at the finish line rooting her on. Patricia was inching ahead. He let out a yell of encouragement. The racers momentarily disappeared around a wooded bend, but when they came back into view, Patricia was gone. Off to the side he saw J.L.'s black limousine driving away with a girl's hand outstretched through the back window. Was she waving good-bye to him or urging him to follow? The other girls were nearing the finish line. Leading them was a smiling Luba, running toward him with outstretched arms . . .

The telephone rang.

It had an insistent ring, demanding to be answered. "Mr. Dennison, it's your wife, calling from Reno, Nevada," the operator said.

He looked at his watch—one o'clock. That would be five in the morning in Reno. She must be desperate. "I'll take it."

"Danny?"

"Yes, Stephanie."

"I've been trying to get you for days." He could tell from her voice that she was drunk.

"I was in Portugal, working."

"Don't they have phones there?"—and then without a pause—"I hate being stuck in this shitty place for six weeks."

"Then leave. I don't need a divorce. I'm satisfied with the legal arrangement we have."

"But if I don't go through with the divorce, Daddy says he'll cut me off without a penny!"

"It's your choice."

"Why does he mess me up every time?"

"Ask *him*."

"He won't talk to me."

"Why don't you call him when you're not drunk?"

"I'm not drunk!" she shouted.

Danny knew he couldn't reason with her.

She started to sob. "Patricia won't talk to me either. He's turned her against me. Now he's bribing her with clothes and trips. He's ruining her—"

"STEPHANIE!" he yelled, and that stopped her. "If you weren't so damn drunk, you'd remember *you* were the one who signed the adoption papers!"

Now he could hear her whimpering. "He . . . he threatened to have me committed to a mental institution. . . . He said I was an unfit mother. . . . I'm all mixed up. Come here . . . get me out of this place. Please, Danny."

Sorry that he yelled, Danny tried to humor her. "Stephanie, you'll feel better once you get some sleep."

"I don't want to sleep!"

"Most people are asleep at this hour."

"And I don't want this Gestapo companion he sent me . . ."

"Just try to go to sleep, Stephanie."

". . . I think she's a dyke."

"Stephanie, call your doctor."

"I don't want a doctor . . ."

Her voice trailed off as Danny hung up the phone.

Syracuse, New York

 beefy man in a plaid suit walked down the hallway of St. John's Orphanage and removed his fedora before knocking on the door to the mother superior's office. A young nun poked her head out. "May I help you?"

"I'm here to see the mother superior."

"Who may I say is calling?"

"Mr. McCrachen." He reached into his breast pocket and extracted a large white envelope. "I'm here on behalf of the Stoneham Foundation."

London

Everyone was pleasant on the set Monday morning, as if good behavior would get them back to sunny California sooner.

Even Bruce Ryan was smiling. He came over with a copy of *The Hollywood Reporter* and pointed to a story about a new Sidney Sheldon best-seller. "I just bought the rights. You know the book?" he asked Danny.

"Yes, I read it. It's terrific."

"That's something you could direct."

The novel would make a good film, but Danny wasn't sure he could take that much more of Bruce. He searched his brain for something nice to say. "It's the perfect role for you," he said finally. "Let's talk about it in L.A."

"What happened to that girl who was flirting with me on the plane?" Ryan smirked as they walked toward the set.

He is right—she did flirt with him, thought Danny. But she is a whore, he had to remind himself. Instantly he knew what he would do. He looked directly at Bruce and calmly asked, "You like her?"

"Yeah," said Bruce with a leer.

"You got her."

Bruce caught Danny's arm and stopped. "What d'you mean?"

"Leave your door unlocked—ten o'clock. Just be in bed. She'll be there."

"What . . . what . . . Are you sure?"

"Are you willing to risk leaving your door unlocked?"

They both laughed.

The work went well that day. In the afternoon, Danny called Luba.

"Danny, what happened? I tried to reach you last night—are you angry?"

"Of course not. I had some problems. Are you free tonight?"

"Am I free? For you, I'm always free."

"Come to my room at the Dorchester. The car will pick you up at nine. They're waiting for me. 'Bye."

And he hung up.

The waiter placed the coffee on the table in front of the fireplace and left. Danny poured her a cup, talking all the time. She ignored the coffee and took a swig of vodka instead. She listened to him quietly as he outlined exactly what he wanted her to do. "The door will be unlocked. Just walk in, close the door, go to the foot of the bed, and look at him—don't say a word."

"Not even 'Hello'?"

"Don't be funny."

Luba got up with a sigh. "Are you having that much trouble with him?"

"He asked for you, Luba."

She took another swallow from the bottle.

Danny continued. "Go to the foot of the bed—"

"Don't you do enough directing during the day?"

"This is important."

"I'm listening."

"Keep looking at him, take all your clothes off, then pull the cover off him, slowly—and go down on him."

She looked at Danny curiously. "You really want me to do this?"

"Yes, I do."

"I just can't figure out why."

"It's up to you, Luba."

She took one more swallow and put the bottle down. "Room eight thirty-five?"

He scrutinized her carefully. "That's right."

She looked at her watch. "Well then, I'd better be going. I don't want to be late." She gave him a strange half-smile over her shoulder as she left.

When he heard the door click shut he wanted to call her back. Why had he done it? To show off? To let Bruce Ryan know this beautiful girl would do anything he wanted? He hated the bastard. His hand reached for the phone. He could still call the room above and stop it. But he didn't. He had to go through with it. He needed something drastic to save himself. He couldn't let himself fall in love with a whore.

Danny took off his robe and stretched out on the bed. He closed his eyes and searched desperately for some pleasant thought—anything to take him far away from the present.

He was fourteen again, playing down by the railroad not far from the orphanage. He started climbing up one of the tall iron posts that supported the loading platform, feeling his crotch rubbing against the cool iron. Just as he reached the top, he felt a strange, pleasant sensation overtake his body, a warm wave. It centered in his cock, and he leaned back, pressing it against the post, and looked up at the blue sky. He squeezed against the post in jerks.

"Oh God, I could die," he whispered to himself.

He almost fell off, but he hung on and slowly slid down to the ground. He felt numb.

After that he masturbated often. Not by stroking his cock with his hands, but by rubbing it against a towel, as he was doing now.

The lights were off. He slowly rubbed up and down, playing out his new fantasy—Luba and Magda, the three of them together.

———————

How long had Luba been standing there? He didn't hear her come in. He quickly pulled the covers up.

She flicked on the bathroom switch; the filtered light fell into the bedroom. "I hope you're happy now. I've done it." She poured herself a drink from the bottle on the bureau. "Just like you directed me. First I pulled the covers off him—"

"Was he naked?"

"No, he was wearing a nightgown." She walked toward the ice bucket.

"You mean pajamas."

Luba turned to look at him. "No, he was wearing a black negligee."

"A woman's negligee?"

"Do they sell *men's* negligees?" Luba asked dryly.

Danny was speechless. The rugged Bruce Ryan in drag? "Is he gay?"

"You tell me. He sure is peculiar."

"Did he enjoy it?"

"Hard to tell. He was talking all the time." She took a long sip. "What did he say to you?"

"He wasn't talking to me. He was on the phone."

"The phone?"

"He never stopped talking, except for a few seconds when he came. Then he went right on talking."

"Who was he talking to?"

Luba took another sip. "Some guy."

"Bullshit," said Danny. "It must have been a girl."

"Whatever you say, but he kept calling her Jim."

"You're making it up."

"That's the way it was."

"He sure fooled me."

"Why are you so surprised? I told you—some very rugged men are gay. What I can't figure out is why you sent me up there to do it."

Resting his head back on the pillow, Danny said very softly, "To see if you would."

"I'd do anything you asked me to do."

"You did it because you're a whore!"

She didn't raise her voice. "You just found that out?"

"You'd do anything, wouldn't you?"

She looked at him steadily. "If you asked me to."

"You're a *kurva*—isn't that what they called you in Kraków? That's why you'd do anything! What about the newsboy?"

She didn't answer.

"And I saw you and Ryan getting it on while my back was turned."

She poured herself another drink. "You're mad at me, because I did what you asked me to do."

He sat up abruptly. "Did you have to do it so quickly—without any argument?"

"Oh, don't be silly, Danny."

Yes, he felt silly, and he didn't like it. "I want you to leave," he said, trying to regain his dignity, which was hard sitting up in bed in only his pajama top.

"Please, Danny, why are you so upset?" She walked toward the bed. "I don't want to leave."

"Get out of here!" he shouted as she came near.

She stopped, bewildered. "What's the matter?"

He glared at her, as if to stop her from coming closer. "You didn't *have* to do it."

"Danny, you're not making any sense."

Between clenched teeth, he said, "You're a fucking whore!"

"And what are *you*, Danny? Tell me! I do what you want me to do and you're mad. I'll tell you what you are," she said, looking him straight in the eyes. "A fucking *phony*!"

He sprang out of bed, grabbed two 100-pound notes from the night table, and stuffed them down her dress. "Get out!"

She stood there for a moment looking at him in his pajama top with his privates dangling. He felt ridiculous and threw himself under the covers again. She raised her glass and toasted him. "Sleep well, Colonel Johnson." She placed the glass down, and walked out with great dignity.

"Colonel Johnson"? What the hell did she mean? And then he

remembered the story of the man Magda had married. "Bitch," he muttered.

Slowly he got out of bed and reached down to pick up his pajama pants. He stopped. In the light from the bathroom he could see the two 100-pound notes lying on the floor.

CHAPTER 12

1987 | Los Angeles

anny had not called Luba before he left. That part of his life was over. He would never see her again. He was grateful to be on a plane that was speeding him away from her.

His legs slightly cramped, he sat motionless, staring blankly into a sky filled with puffy clouds and drinking his third martini. After a while, feeling drowsy, he charmed an attractive stewardess into taking out the armrests of the four middle seats in the economy section and lining them with blankets. Unsteadily, he moved toward his makeshift bed and stretched out his long body.

He put his arm over his eyes to block out light and reality, wanting to plunge into a dreamless sleep. But his jumbled thoughts raced on as the plane streaked through the stratosphere. Luba had disturbed what had lain dormant within him for so long. My whole life has been a lie, he thought. When did I pass the point of no return?

" 'I am in blood/Stepp'd in so far, that, should I wade no more,/ Returning were as tedious as go o'er,' " he mumbled, seeking an answer to a question that now pounded in his brain. Why did he cling so desperately to a silly child's lie? Moishe's lie—constructed to save him from drowning in the bloody river of his memories. In the alcoholic haze of his mind, he saw himself struggling in a whirlpool of red water. Suddenly all was black. Faintly he saw a silvery light in the distance. It grew larger as it came closer, and when it flashed by him he saw his father's crucifix. He tried to make out the face of the man on the cross, but huge white cumulus clouds engulfed him. They were soft to the touch, and made him feel safe. Then, with a crash of lightning, the clouds turned dark, ominous—black roiling smoke from tall Salzburg chimneys. He heard voices in the darkness crying, "Everyman! Everyman!" He raced across rooftops, sweating and trembling, and came face to face with Luba, stark naked, laughing and yelling in his face, "Phony—phony!!!" He lifted his hand to slap her, but she easily eluded him, running along the roof ledge. He pursued her, shouting, "Whore! *Kurva!*" Just as he reached out to grab her, she disappeared around a chimney, and he toppled off the building.

Falling through the air, he saw a large mirror shatter below into billions of pieces. They became the swirling sparks of his father's torch. The sparks grew into a red flame that illuminated his sister Rachel, naked on a bed of human skeletons. The commandant, in his uniform, was standing over her. His shiny black hobnailed boot kicked one of the skulls. The thump reverberated through Danny's head as, with a sudden jolt, the wheels of the plane hit the tarmac at Los Angeles International Airport.

He woke up sticky with sweat, and gratefully took the hot washcloth the stewardess offered him to wipe his face. He lay still for a few minutes. Finally, he unwound his stiff body, stretched, and peered out of a window. Nothing was visible through a blanket of smog. He wondered what was waiting for him inside that murky layer.

The studio limousine pulled out onto Sepulveda Boulevard and they headed for Beverly Hills. Danny sat wedged in the corner against the window.

"Is Tower Road off Coldwater?" asked the driver.

"No, Benedict Canyon. Near the Beverly Hills Hotel."

"Thank you," the driver said politely. He was young and good-looking, probably another out-of-work actor.

"I'm an actor," he said as if reading Danny's thoughts. "I've admired all your pictures, Mr. Dennison."

"Thank you. How long have you been driving?"

"Three months, sir, but I'm up for a good role at Paramount."

"Well, I hope you get it," said Danny, and he closed the partition.

It depressed him to talk to young actors. They were all so naïve, filled with enthusiasm and confidence. Little by little, the enthusiasm would seep out of them to be replaced by desperation.

The women were more depressing than the men. They would bounce into his office, their belts tightly cinched, wearing blouses with several buttons unfastened to reveal a little too much of their pushed-up breasts.

Those who made it were always insecure, like the gorgeous Sylvia Koch, star of his film *Buffalo Land*. Before each take she would look at the camera as if it were a god and plead, "Make me beautiful." And if she believed it, maybe it did.

Those who didn't succeed—most of them—fell prey to agents and producers who dangled promises of movie roles as they took them to bed. The older ones were the saddest—with makeup carefully concealing the lines under their eyes, the scars of a badly done face-lift still visible—accepting little gifts of perfume, scarves, dresses, and then money. They became whores, and they didn't even know it. Luba knew what she was; she didn't pretend to be something else. She was honest, and that honesty gave her strength—strength he wished he had. Why was she always creeping into his thoughts? Forget her, he told himself again.

But aren't we all whores—selling something? Goddamn it! He wasn't going to sell his integrity anymore, be a nursemaid to Bruce Ryan. For once he would harness all his energies to make a film he would be proud of.

The car was passing the Beverly Hills Hotel. He looked at his watch —five-thirty. Right now the Polo Lounge was crowded with deal makers, all trying to second-guess what the public might buy in the constant quest for a blockbuster. But insecurity always led them to play it safe with violence, sex, and horror. Could his hope to make *Everyman* stand a chance?

The limousine pulled up into the driveway of his house. A sleek silver Ferrari he didn't recognize was parked beside a battered old

Ford Mustang. He caught a glimpse of racquets and tennis balls in the Mustang's backseat. That must belong to Bob, the tennis pro. He had offered Bob the use of the court while he was gone. I've got to start working out, Danny thought, and instinctively his hand went to his stomach.

"Just put the bags at the front door," he said, getting out of the car.

"Yes, sir," said the driver, hurrying around to assist him.

He slipped him a $20 bill. "And I hope you get that part."

"Thank you," the driver said gratefully.

Danny walked around the side of the house and up the terrace steps to the tennis court. Bob wasn't there. A few yellow balls were lying on the court near the automatic ball machine.

When he came around to the front, the limousine had left, and his two suitcases and garment bag were lying by the door.

He walked into the house, dropped his bags, and headed for the living room. As he passed the aquarium, he noticed that two of the tropical fish were floating on the top, upside down. It made him sad; he had spent hours hypnotized by the beautiful colors and movements of these fish. He had arranged for someone to feed them. Damn! You can't trust anyone, he thought.

He went up the steps to his bedroom and was hit by a strong, pungent odor—pot. The shades were drawn, and the room was in darkness. He quickly pulled up the shades and opened a window. Then he saw them—Stephanie and Bob—fast asleep. The sheet didn't quite cover Stephanie's breasts.

Danny stared at the two of them. It must have been one tiring tennis game.

He kicked the bed violently, and Bob's eyes popped open. Stephanie murmured something but didn't wake up. Bob's eyes grew larger as he recognized Danny; he scrambled out of bed, mumbling incoherent apologies, picked up his sweaty tennis clothes and sneakers, and backed out of the door.

Danny never took his eyes off Stephanie. Still asleep, she rolled over, exposing her naked bottom. He heard Bob stumbling over the bags. Stephanie didn't stir, and Danny whacked her bare ass. She groggily twisted around and focused on her ex-husband.

"What are you doing here?" she asked in a thick voice.

"This is my home, Stephanie—remember?"

"Well, it's my house too!"

"No, darling—if you recall, you just divorced me."

Stephanie said nothing and rubbed her eyes.

"Please feel free to use the tennis court, but would you mind doing your fucking at your own place?"

"With Patricia in the next room?"

Danny stiffened. "I thought she was at school?"

"We're at the Beverly Wilshire."

"Get dressed," Danny said abruptly and left.

He went downstairs to the corner of the living room where framed photos covered the wall—a pictorial history of his daughter: as a baby in her pink crib, learning to walk across the lawn, splashing in the pool with Daddy's hands under her tummy to keep her up, on her first pony with the trainer holding the reins. He stared at the photo of the three of them on the beach at Malibu, where they had celebrated her tenth birthday.

We really looked happy, but were we ever happy?

There was a more recent photo of Patricia on his desk; it had been taken a couple of years ago, when she was fifteen. She wore shorts, revealing long, slim legs just like her mother's. She had Stephanie's face, her creamy white skin and golden hair—milk and honey. She was beautiful. He hadn't seen her in four months. He longed to talk to her. Did she still want to make films? Did she have a boyfriend? How little he knew about his own daughter.

He circled the telephone, not knowing how to talk to her, what to say. His eye caught the bookshelves below the fish tank—a row of neatly bound scripts in black leather, fourteen volumes. He didn't need to count them. He had done that often enough. More than a dozen films, and tomorrow he would start editing his fifteenth. He wasn't proud of a single one of them. A neat row of compromises.

He sat down by the phone and started doodling on his calendar. It would take him a month to edit *London Rock*. Today was October 3. He stopped.

He looked at that square—today was Yom Kippur, the holiest of holy days. This was the day of atonement, when the Book of Life was indelibly sealed. In it was inscribed who shall live and who shall die, who by water and who by fire. He remembered that day on the farm when the family was fasting. Little Moishe was so hungry. He sneaked into the chicken coop and quickly grabbed one of the eggs from beneath a clucking hen. He had just tapped a hole in it and was sucking out the yolk when he saw Tateh at the barn door watching him. Tateh didn't scold him. He took him out in the fields and explained that he must fast and spend every waking hour of Yom Kippur taking stock of life, begging forgiveness for past sins. It frightened Moishe, the thought of God watching him suck an egg when he was supposed to be praying. The fear took away his hunger. Now Danny was gripped by that same fear. But how much greater were his sins! He was seized by an urge to pray. He hadn't prayed in so long. Please God! he managed. Forgive me. Help me save my daughter.

He picked up the phone and dialed the Beverly Wilshire. But when he asked for Patricia Dennison, he was told that no one by that name was registered. Then he realized his error. "Mr. Stoneham's suite, please." After two rings her voice answered.

"Patricia!"

"Yes." There was a pause.

"This is your father."

"Oh Daddy, you're back."

"Just got in," he continued in a cheery voice.

"How did *London Rock* go?"

"It would have gone better with your help."

"Oh Daddy—" She sounded like she was going to cry. "I wanted to be there with you so badly, more than anything else on earth."

"I know, darling. I'm sorry it couldn't be arranged."

"Well, it's just that J.L.—"

"You don't have to explain."

A buzzer sounded in the background.

"Can you hold on, Daddy? Someone's at the door . . ."

After a moment she returned. "Mr. McCrachen's come to get me. J.L.'s waiting for me in the car. He's always so annoyed when I'm late."

"I understand. Let's have lunch tomorrow, darling."

"Oh, I'd love it, but I'm leaving with J.L. for San Francisco right now. I'll be back next week," she added quickly.

He tried not to sound disappointed. "That'll give me a chance to get the cutting started. How about next Wednesday?"

"Whenever you say, Daddy."

"I'll come to the hotel, and we'll have lunch at the El Padrino."

"Great."

"One o'clock, then? I'm so anxious to see you, Patricia."

"I want to see you too. You don't know how much I've missed you, Daddy."

He heard the click of the phone before he could say good-bye. But he realized she had to hurry—J.L. was waiting. She *did* seem happy to hear from him, he reassured himself as he crossed to the door to retrieve his luggage.

He carried the bags up into the bedroom and set them on the

crumpled bed. Stephanie was fully dressed now, sitting at the vanity table, outlining her lips in that coral lipstick she always wore.

He stood behind her. This woman had been his wife for nineteen years. She still had firm breasts, a flat tummy, long sinewy legs; how could she abuse herself with drink and still look so well?

"Some welcome home," he said.

"What the hell am I supposed to do?" she asked his mirrored reflection. "We're not married."

"I'm not criticizing the act, just the choice of place."

She spun around. "You're not even jealous, are you?"

"No."

"What the hell did you marry me for? Did you ever love me?" Her voice was very low.

"Please, Stephanie, we'll talk when you're sober."

"I'm not drunk."

Danny unzipped one of the bags, thinking of an answer to her question. Did he ever really love her, or had he just used her to protect the facade he had constructed?

She stood up and leaned against the vanity table. "Let me hear you say it just once—"

"Say what?" He raised his head. Her face had a sad expression.

"Say 'I love you'—even if you don't mean it."

He pretended to concentrate on emptying his suitcase. "Maybe we both married for the wrong reason," he mumbled.

She said nothing. He couldn't look at her.

"I'm afraid." Her voice was hollow.

"Of what?"

"My father," she answered simply.

"Now that's silly. You're a grown-up woman."

"No, I'm not. And you know it. My father never let me grow up, and you didn't help much either."

"Now it's my fault?" Danny snapped.

She looked at him sadly. "It's both our faults."

Danny didn't know how to talk to her when she was so calm. Usually she would get into a hysterical crying fit or drunken rage when they attempted to have a discussion, and he wouldn't have to confront her assaults with logical responses. "You're drunk" was a convenient end to every argument.

She continued in that low voice. "But I'm grateful to you, Danny. You gave me whatever happiness I ever had in life. It's just that I expected too much—I thought you were strong enough to save me from my father." A far-off look came into her eyes. "You know when I loved you the most?"

He sat down on the corner of the bed.

"When you were at your weakest." And for the first time she smiled. "When you were uncertain, disappointed in your work, talking about finding a way to make that film—what was it called?"

"*Everyman*," he said softly.

"That's it. Are you ever going to do it?"

"I hope so—I've got the angle now."

"Tell me about it—I'm a good listener."

"I'm too tired to talk."

The sun was already behind the trees surrounding the tennis court. It was beginning to get dark in the room.

She walked over and sat down on the bed beside him. "Danny, let me help you."

He looked at her in amazement. "Help me?"

"Yes, like the song says—'*Let me try again.*' I know I'm the one who really needs help. God knows, my father has told me often enough. . . . But if I could help *you* in some small way . . . I'd like myself more."

Danny got up, walked over to the window, and watched the twilight. "Just help yourself."

For a long time she studied him, her head tilted to one side. "I'll try." She got up, picked up her purse and sweater, and left the room.

He listened to the clicking of her heels on the hardwood floor. Then she stopped. He heard a whirring sound—she was winding the grandfather clock.

"Thanks for the use of the pad," she called out as she shut the door behind her.

The sound reverberated through his body and echoed in his mind —the closing of the door to his life with Stephanie. Another compartment locked away. How many doors remained open?

The Ferrari peeled out of the driveway, gears grinding. Then the sound dissolved. It was quiet, very quiet.

Outside, the approaching darkness now battled the last vestiges of a brilliant sunset. On the other side of the tennis court a brown hill cut across a fading orange sky. A Turner painting. The leaves, moving gently in the breeze, were tinted by the setting sun.

He felt so alone. Tomorrow morning he would pick up the trade papers, *The Hollywood Reporter* and *Variety*. First he would look at the obituary columns to see if others had died who were younger. He was reassured whenever someone died much older; it gave him hope that he would live long enough to do something worthwhile. He was only fifty-five. He was not an old man. He would get in shape again, cut down on rich food and play tennis. Damn it—now he'd have to find a new pro.

He walked over to the vanity where Stephanie had sat. He put the lights on around the magnifying mirror. The lines in his face were deep, the hair at his temples gray. He looked carefully at the little wrinkles around his eyes.

He didn't feel old when he was with Luba. Her youth seeped inside him. With her, he could become young again.

Bing-bong! Bing-bong! the clock chimed—a hollow sound, echoing his loneliness. He couldn't bear the feeling. He called his best friend.

———

It didn't take Milt long to drive over. He burst through the door, his hands raised in mock surrender. "I did it—I set up the meeting with Art Gunn. *Everyman* gets its chance Tuesday at two, and I don't want to hear a word about it."

Danny almost hugged him. "Thanks," he said as Milt barreled past him into the kitchen.

"For what? I'm your agent; it's my job." Milt was slamming the empty refrigerator and reaching for a can of beans.

"Thanks for coming over."

"*Boychik,*" said Milt, struggling with the can opener, "I should thank *you.* You saved me from Yom Kippur—let Sarah fast!" He dug into the can with a spoon. "We were on our way to the synagogue when you called—I told her it was an emergency," Milt gurgled with his mouth full. "It was! I was starving!"

Danny chuckled despite himself.

"But you don't have any food—that's the trouble with you WASPs."

"I'm sorry, but I just got back."

"Don't worry about it," said Milt, gulping away. "This is great, and I hate beans."

Danny had to laugh.

"Good—you're laughing. On the phone you sounded like you were going to die. What the hell happened?"

"Everything and nothing."

"Oh, I see," said Milt. "Now I know the whole story."

They settled down in the living room. Danny leaned against the mantel and watched Milt sprawl out on the couch. Milt always came whenever he called. He didn't ask why. He was the only person in

Hollywood Danny felt he could count on. How strange that his best friend was a Jew.

"How's your sex life?" Danny asked, getting on Milt's favorite topic. "What's her name—Yvette?" He found it hard to keep up with Milt's stable of starlets.

"Don't ask . . ."

"What do you mean? You had a fight?"

"No, I don't see her anymore."

"Why?"

Milt adjusted his spectacles and picked a few beans out of his beard. "She became a porn star."

"A *what*?"

"You heard me—a porn star."

"I can't believe it. I thought you were getting her small parts in some good movies."

"That's right—*small* parts. But she couldn't wait. She was anxious to be a star. She made it."

"Milt, are you sure?"

"I saw the tape: *Around the World in Fifteen Minutes*. She did things in that she never did to me."

Danny suppressed a laugh. "Forget it, Milt—you had fun while it lasted."

"Yeah," Milt said, dreamily looking off in space. "I did." Then, turning to Danny with a smile, he said, "Did you hear about the town that was so small, the only hooker was a virgin?" And he cackled.

Danny shook his head. "Poor Milt—it takes you so long to get over a disappointment."

Milt cackled again. "Danny, I met a new girl—"

"Here we go again."

"No, Danny. *This* is different. *This* is serious."

"OK, tell me."

"Marilyn is the greatest thing in my life," Milt sighed. "She's on location now in Tucson, starring in this picture I set up. I'm running out of reasons to tell Sarah why I have to go to Tucson." He looked at Danny hopefully.

"Let's get it straight, Milt—I have no reason to fly to Tucson."

"Don't worry, *boychik*—we'll find one."

"I was afraid of that." Danny grinned and plopped into a chair.

"Danny, she is the classiest dame I've ever met. A beautiful girl—rich family—her father is the head of a stockbroker's firm."

"Is J. L. Stoneham a customer?"

"What?"

"Never mind—go on."

"She fell for me, honestly. I tried to avoid it. But she was having trouble with her part and asked me to help her . . . evenings."

"I'll bet you helped her."

"Well, she came on strong, really strong, for such a classy dame. I couldn't believe it. She really had a crush on me—me, a Jewboy from the Bronx. She was tired of her debutante life, and those silly boys from fancy colleges."

"She have a house on Long Island?"

"No," answered Milt, puzzled by the non sequitur. "She needed someone like me, down to earth, talented, to save her."

Danny stole a peek out of his half-closed eyes. Milt was very serious.

"I told her I was too old for her, but she brushed that aside. She is lovely—a young Dina Merrill. I'm hooked. We're having a great romance. Oh Danny, when I'm in bed with her I feel half Gentile."

"That's terrific," Danny said weakly.

"But she's jealous," Milt added with pride. "Went into a rage once when Sarah called. She doesn't want to share me with anyone." He sighed. "I envy you. You're divorced. I got Sarah like an albatross around my neck."

Danny puffed out his cheeks and exhaled with a gust. "We all carry an albatross, Milt."

Milt stared at Danny. "You got a problem?"

"Yeah."

"So you didn't ask me here to talk about my love life?"

Danny didn't answer.

"All right, tell Miltie."

"It's Luba."

"That London girl you told me about?"

"Yeah."

"Oh no, Danny. I thought you broke it off."

"I tried, Milt, believe me. I'd be ashamed to tell you what I did to break it off. But I can't get her out of my mind—I think I'm in love with her."

"In love with her? Danny, you can't be serious. I told you on the phone—she'll only bring you trouble. She's a whore!"

"Knock it off, Milt," Danny said sharply.

"Danny . . . Danny." Milt tried to placate him. "*You* said it yourself—she is a whore. She's probably fucking somebody this very minute."

CHAPTER 13

1987 | London

obby Thomas's coal-black body was glistening with sweat. He groaned and rolled over, jabbing Luba's back with his knees. She winced. "Easy, Bobby." But he was already out.

His wife, Alice, threw a sheet over him, then motioned for Luba to follow her out of the room as she gathered up the crushed capsules of amyl nitrate with a piece of tissue. Once they were in the bathroom she flushed them down the toilet.

"Boy, I don't know where he gets all that energy," sighed Luba.

"Well he ain't got much right now," said Alice, sitting on the bidet.

Earlier that night, Bobby Thomas had given a comedy performance to a howling audience at the Palladium. After the show, they had stopped at Tramp's for a few drinks, and now they were in his hotel suite at the Savoy. It had been a wild night, wilder than usual. Bobby was tireless, switching from Alice to Luba, and finally taking both on together.

Without seeming to hurry, Luba slipped on her clothes. Fully dressed, she waited as Alice combed her hair. Finally she blurted out, "Gee, I don't think I have any change. I need some money for a taxi."

"The car's downstairs," Alice said with a scornful smile. She continued to comb her hair, humming to herself.

Luba gritted her teeth, knowing that Alice was waiting for her to beg.

"Well, if you could spare something, I certainly could use it . . ."

The humming stopped. The smile never left Alice's face as she reached for her purse lying on the marble counter and pulled out two crisp 100-pound notes. She handed them to Luba. "Don't bother saying good-night to Bobby." She blew Luba a little kiss and disappeared into the bedroom.

Luba stood there for a moment, pensive in the dim light of the luxurious bathroom with its sunken tub in the middle. The dressing table was littered with fancy baubles from Tiffany's and Cartier. It was hard to resist the temptation.

With a deep sigh, she walked out the side door. She knew the suite well. She went down the long quiet hallway. The elevator man seemed very polite—too polite. "Good evening, madam."

In front of the hotel, the doorman ceremoniously tipped his cap as he opened the door of Bobby's stretch limousine. Luba glanced at her watch—4:15 A.M. The driver took off immediately, not saying a word. It was obvious he was annoyed.

To hell with him, thought Luba. I'll talk to myself; I'm better company.

She was tired of Bobby and Alice. It might have been more fun if they weren't such tightwads. Celebrities often acted as if you should pay them for sex. Danny was generous, but she would never take money from him. She felt a pang of sadness. It was hard to imagine that she'd never see him again.

The car came to a screeching halt in front of her apartment. "Good night, Joe," she said, but she couldn't decipher what he mumbled back. He drove off as soon as she shut the door.

She fumbled for her keys, then wearily trudged up the two flights. It had been a full day, a full evening and night, and now it was almost dawn. She flipped on the light and was accosted by the shrill yapping of the frightened poodle.

Magda came out of her bedroom, half asleep.

"Geez, Magda, why the hell don't you keep the dog in your room—he's such a nervous ninny."

"He's just a puppy—he'll get better," said Magda, taking the dog in her arms. She hugged him and kissed him on the nose. "Little Danny" was everything to her—all the company she needed. Now she stayed home more than ever, a complete recluse. Luba never had any privacy, something she relished when she was painting.

In the bathroom, Luba took off her clothes, looked in the mirror, and saw that the hair along her face was stuck together with sweat and semen.

"Ah, the hell with it," she grumbled. "I'm not going to take a bath." She wiped her face and hair with a towel, threw off her clothes, and came out nude.

Her mother was still standing there. Luba ignored her and walked into her room. Thank God they each had their own.

Magda called after her, "Luba, Mrs. McKeever came up for the rent again."

Without looking back, Luba said, "In my purse in the bathroom." She closed her door and fell back on the bed. When she first came to London, she felt guilty about leaving Magda behind. But in a short time, she began to like living alone, having an extra room for her studio. She had been tied to her mother for too long. And now they were bound together again, except this time the financial burden was totally on her. Magda had brought 300 pounds with her. Only 300 pounds after slaving for that bastard for two years. Where was the rest of it? He must have saved more than that from a hotel packed all season and the two of them working for nothing.

The door opened. Luba didn't move, hoping her mother would think she was asleep.

"Luba . . . Luba . . ."

Luba sat up and faced her mother. "It's late. I'm tired—what do you want?!"

The bills clasped in her hand, Magda warily advanced into the room. "Two hundred—it's not enough for the rent."

"So what can I do?"

"We promised—we're a month behind!"

"That's all there is," Luba snapped and turned into her pillow.

"We've got to get the money," Magda persisted.

"Any suggestions?"

Timidly, Magda said, "You could sell a painting—Mrs. McKeever wanted to buy one of them. That would take care of some of the rent."

"No!"

"But you've got so many in the closet."

"I said no! They're mine!"

"Then how are we gonna get the money?"

"How about *you* getting it!" Luba yelled as she sprang out of bed. "You go out, see if you can get more. You're the teacher!"

She was now opening and slamming drawers, looking for a cigarette. "Maybe I'm not good enough! That's all I could get! Why don't *you* peddle your fat ass for a change?"

Magda stood there helplessly.

With her back to her mother, Luba lit a cigarette and inhaled deeply; she couldn't stem her anger. "Why the hell did you have to come back? Goddamn it, every time you have a problem, I have to pay. The hell with it! I've had enough."

Luba never heard her mother leave the room. When she turned around, Magda was gone. Luba snuffed out her cigarette violently and threw herself back on the bed. She tried hard to fall asleep, but she couldn't. It was so easy to hurt someone you loved.

Magda had been a good mother. She left Brodki for Kraków to make a new life for both of them. She was strong, capable. Once they had escaped, she counted so much on her marriage to Colonel Johnson to be the salvation. But he broke her spirit.

Luba imagined her mother hurrying down the steps, leaning over the battered form of her dead husband, removing the key from his buttoned-down vest pocket. She did it for me, too. She must have been so frightened. Luba admired her mother; she was a survivor. No one would ever know how much they had shared together. Not even Danny.

Her guilt growing, she held her breath and listened carefully. She heard nothing.

She got up and walked quietly into her mother's room. It was dark. She crawled into bed and put her arms around Magda. "I'm sorry, Mama—I didn't mean the things I said." Magda just lay there, motionless. Luba shook her gently. "Come on, Magda—wake up." And with a giggle she added, "I'll help you."

She rolled Magda on her back; there was no resistance. A chill went through Luba's body. She quickly turned on the lamp and knocked over an empty pill bottle.

Magda's eyes were vacant, her mouth partially open.

For a moment, Luba was paralyzed. "Magda!" she screamed, and slapped her face.

A strange guttural sound escaped her mother's lips.

Luba slapped her again and again. Magda was barely breathing.

Hollywood

anny couldn't remember the last time he had walked into Art Gunn's office with this much apprehension. For years now, whenever he wanted to do a new film, Milt would set up a meeting, and usually after he got a few sentences out of his mouth, Art would cut him off with "Go ahead." But this time he would be proposing something foreign to Art Gunn's taste; things might not go so smoothly.

"Sit down," said Art from behind his huge desk. "What do we talk about first—*Paris Rock* or *Rome Rock*?"

Danny's jaw dropped a little, and he glanced at Milt for help.

"Knock it off," said Milt. "We're here to talk about a new movie that Danny wants to make—*Everyman*. You know that."

Art took a big puff on his cigar, ignoring the ashes dropping to his tie. "All right, I'll listen." He glanced at his watch. "Just don't take long."

Through the cigar smoke, Danny couldn't see the expression on Art's face clearly. Over the years, Art had lost some hair and gained some weight, but his abrasive manner stayed the same.

Danny began in an even tone. "This is the one movie that's been building up in my gut for years."

"Sounds too dramatic already."

"Please," interjected Milt, "do you have to criticize before you hear it?"

"You're right. I'm listening. Give it to me in three sentences."

Suddenly, Danny's mind was blank. He didn't know how to begin. At home, in his study or lying in bed, it was all so clear. He could visualize each scene. Now he saw nothing. He got up and started tentatively, "I've made fifteen movies for Ace Films. . . ."

"Money-makers, too," Art muttered through his cigar.

"You never had to read my scripts . . ."

"I can smell a good one."

"You trusted me . . ."

"That's right."

Danny leaned forward. "Well, do you still trust me?"

Art sat motionless, his eyes darting from Danny to Milt. A small pile of ashes had now accumulated in the crease of his tie. "Why do I have the feeling I'm being blackmailed?"

"Do you trust me?" Danny persisted.

"Sure," answered Art, after a moment of hesitation. "But is it gonna make me money?" he snorted, and the pile of ashes slid down his tie and disappeared behind the desk. "Give me just a little hint."

"This movie will appeal to everyone—it's about taking inventory of your life."

"Well, if you're gonna talk about inventory, I'll bring in my accountant," Art chortled.

"Please!" Milt jumped up.

"OK, OK, no jokes—I'm listening."

Danny cleared his throat. "I'll give it to you in three sentences. As the film opens, we see an artist on his deathbed. He takes inventory of his past, and we see how he has corrupted his talent. He vows to make amends, but it's too late."

Danny stopped and sat down.

Art looked owl-like from Milt to Danny. "That's the movie?"

"Yes."

"It don't smell like a hit to me."

"It's a universal theme," Danny insisted, trying to conceal his annoyance.

"That's been in your gut for years?"

"Yes."

"A little bicarbonate would've gotten rid of it."

"Goddamn it!" Like a jumping jack, Milt was up again. "I won't have my client insulted."

"Take it easy, Milt."

"Let me remind you"—Milt shook his finger at Art's cigar—"this man stood in this very spot years ago trying to sell you a movie for kids based on *The Prince and the Pauper*. You didn't like that idea either —until the returns came in. How many millions have you made on teen flicks since then?"

"Please," said Art, spreading out his chubby hands to quiet him, the cigar now a stub clenched between his teeth. "That was years ago. This is now. But go ahead, Danny."

Danny remained silent.

"Hey, Danny." Art grinned. "You mad?"

"I'm goddamn mad." Danny got up and approached the desk. "I've paid my dues. I'm not going to beg to make a picture. I quit."

"You *what*?" The stub fell out of Art's mouth.

"I'm through with Ace Films."

Danny spun on his heel and headed for the door. Milt sprang out of his chair and blocked him. "Now calm down, Danny."

Art lumbered around his desk. "You can't leave—we got a contract."

Danny whirled around. "Fuck your contract—I'll find a studio to make my movie."

Art grabbed Danny's shoulders with both hands. "Now stop. You found the studio—Ace Films."

Danny let Art lead him to the sofa. They both sat down. "I'll make the deal." He put his arm around Danny. "Limited budget. And you gotta stick to it."

Danny began to relax. There was something unique about Art— just when you hated him, you began to like him.

Milt pulled up a chair to face them. "I'll draw up the papers."

"Not so fast." Art glared at Milt. "We cross-collateralize it with *Paris Rock* . . ." He took out another cigar from his breast pocket and trimmed it with his teeth. "And *Rome Rock.*"

"*Rome Rock*?!" Milt yelled. "What the hell are you talking about? No way!"

"OK, OK," said Art, putting a flame to his cigar. "I'm a fair man. We'll cut out *Rome Rock*—the Italians would probably screw it up anyway."

Danny wasn't listening; he was ecstatic. He could start making *Everyman*, a film he knew would be his masterpiece.

———

"*Boychik*, I never saw you so mad," Milt said as they left Art's office.

"I was fighting for my life."

"You scared me. You sounded like you really meant that 'I quit' crap."

"I did."

"Are you crazy? If Ace Films turned it down, what other studio would take it?"

"I could sell it to Columbia."

"Columbia! They change studio heads faster than Zsa Zsa Gabor changes husbands. Begelman, Price, McElwaine, Puttnam, Dawn What's-her-name . . . Nobody's there long enough to finish telling the story to. And now the Japanese might take over."

"Well, at least when they screw up they commit suicide."

Milt's uproarious laughter was interrupted by the valet, who pulled up with his Mercedes.

Driving up Gower Street, Milt mumbled, "I can't remember that play *Everyman*—I read it so many years ago, but the spiel you gave Gunn . . . inventory . . . death . . ."

"Don't tell me—you don't like it either."

"It's not that," said Milt, shaking his head, "It's just that . . . I don't know . . . Reminds me of Kafka."

Danny looked at him quizzically.

"I told you about it—that film Joe Epstein made."

"Oh yeah, one of your first clients. What was that about again?"

"You don't want to know. Some story about a Jew standing at the door of the judge's chamber trying to find out his crime."

"And what happens?"

"Nothing," said Milt. "That's the story."

"But that's silly."

"Danny, you're a Gentile. You have to be Jewish to understand it. Joe was *too* Jewish."

"But *Everyman* isn't a story about nothing. It has—"

"*Boychik,* I love you, but to me this project sounds too intellectual." He put up his hand to keep Danny from interrupting. "But it doesn't matter what I think. I make the deal—you make the movie. All that matters is that Art Gunn gave you the green light. So go ahead and run with it."

Beverly Hills

 anny wore his favorite tweed jacket and tailored open shirt. He was excited and nervous about seeing Patricia. On Rodeo Drive, he paused in front of a fancy gift shop displaying a large, overstuffed teddy bear in the window. On impulse, he walked in.

No salesperson was in sight; he became impatient as he waited. He finally attracted the attention of a supercilious clerk who disappeared into the storeroom for a long time and then emerged to announce that "the teddys" were sold out, but he deigned to allow him to purchase the one in the window.

Danny looked at his watch. He hastily threw some money on the counter and hurried out of the store without waiting for the teddy to be wrapped. He ran the rest of the way to the Beverly Wilshire. In the El Padrino room, he looked around for Patricia.

"Danny," a voice called out. He turned to face Bruce Ryan, sitting at a table with his pimply-faced sidekicks and a pretty young girl who was staring dotingly at Bruce.

"Good to see you." Bruce shook the teddy bear's paw. His friends tittered.

Danny thought of him in a black negligee as he said hello and continued on.

But Bruce's arm reached out and stopped his progress. "Sorry that Sidney Sheldon film didn't work out. I fought for you, but *somebody* got Jeff Kanew."

"He's very good. And I'm busy anyway." Danny tried to move away, but Bruce held on.

"What are you working on?" Bruce persisted.

"A project called *Everyman.*"

"You'll do better if you call it 'Every*woman.*'" Bruce laughed, and the others joined in.

Danny forced a smile. He was rescued by Tony, the headwaiter. "Your booth is ready, Mr. Dennison."

With his heart beating faster, he twisted his way through the crowded dining room to the banquette he had reserved. He stopped short.

Looking up at him was the red face and steely eyes of J. L. Stoneham.

"Where's Patricia?"

"Sit down," said the red face. "This is Mr. McCrachen." Seated next to J.L. was a beefy man wearing a plaid suit that did not seem to have enough material to cover his bulk; his thick neck protruded over the collar of his white starched shirt.

Danny sank into the back of the booth, a knot tightening in his stomach. He placed the teddy bear beside him.

"What would you like to drink?"

"Nothing, thank you. I'll wait for Patricia."

"She's not coming," was the blunt reply.

"I beg your pardon?"

J. L. Stoneham raised his martini to his lips, surveying Danny impassively. He took a long sip. His tongue licked off the residue, and he gently placed the glass down.

The other man sat there calmly, a glass of plain water in front of him.

Danny broke the silence. "I have a luncheon date with my daughter."

The red face never changed expression, and the words came softly through the thin lips. "She doesn't want to see you."

Danny could feel his pulse throbbing in his temples. He fought back the nausea that was rising from the pit of his stomach. "Mr. Stoneham, I don't believe you."

A sardonic smile came across the red face as the modulated voice said, "Then you'll have a long wait."

The sick feeling inside Danny grew stronger. Stoneham emptied his glass and darted a look at his companion. A large thick hand placed a bill on the table. As they rose to leave, Danny blurted out: "I'm her father!"

J.L. cocked his head, leaned over the table, and pierced Danny with his steely eyes. "That mistake can be corrected."

Danny grabbed for J. L. Stoneham's throat. "You bastard," he muttered hoarsely.

He never saw the beefy man's hand strike out; a viselike grip held his arm down to the table.

J. L. Stoneham seemed oblivious of nearby diners who were turning their heads. He straightened his tie; his voice became a whisper. "Listen, you bum. Mind your manners and remember—you're divorced."

"I divorced your daughter, not mine. I never signed those papers."

"But Stephanie did. You better see a lawyer. She has custody, and I'm the child's legal guardian."

Danny thought he would black out. Suddenly, the pressure was released from his arm. He heard the shuffling of feet. He kept his head down.

The waiter came over, picked up the empty martini glass and the $20 bill.

"Would you like to see a menu, sir?"

Danny didn't raise his head. "I'll have a double vodka on ice."

After the second drink, the queasiness left his stomach, though he could still feel the pain in his forearm.

He looked over at the blank face of the teddy bear on the seat beside him. As the waiter placed another drink in front of him, he asked for a piece of paper and an envelope.

Sipping his third drink, he tried to think of something to write. By the time he emptied the glass, he settled for:

Patricia dear
Never fear
Daddy's near!

Leaving some money on the table, Danny got up, clutching the teddy bear. He realized he was very drunk. He made an effort to walk carefully out of the dining room. Tony, the headwaiter, eyed him apprehensively.

Unsteadily, he walked over to the reception desk and placed the envelope and the teddy bear before the clerk, trying to enunciate clearly. "Please leave this for Patricia Dennison."

The clerk took the envelope, and with a slightly annoyed look at the drunk swaying before him, said, "Just a minute, please."

Danny pressed both hands on the counter in an attempt to stand in a dignified manner. The teddy bear's blank button eyes stared at him.

Returning, the clerk announced in a superior tone that there was no Miss Dennison registered.

"There must be!" Danny slurred.

"I'm sorry, sir."

Danny's fuzzy mind began to comprehend. "Patricia Stoneham?"

"Ah, yes," the clerk replied quickly. "We have a Miss Stoneham." He pulled a pen out of the desk holder, scratched out Dennison, and scribbled Stoneham.

Danny's eyes focused on *Stoneham* blotting out *Dennison*. He tried to hold back the prickly tears that stung his eyes.

———

When the cab brought him home, he didn't enter the house; instead, he stumbled up the terrace steps to the tennis court. He filled up the ball machine with a basket of old balls and plugged it in.

The mechanical arm began to spit the balls at him. He picked up a racquet. Each time he swung he saw the head of J. L. Stoneham coming at him. He smashed the balls with all the force he could muster, watching them sail over the fence and into the woods.

Finally, the machine was empty. He felt he had demolished J. L. Stoneham and his burly companion. With a victorious yell, he threw his racquet into the air and ran forward to leap over the net, but he tripped and sprawled on the other side.

He came to at the sound of a voice yelling his name. "Danny— Danny—sorry I'm late!"

Dressed in tennis whites, Milt came hurrying around the house and halted at the sight of Danny squatting on the court and rubbing his hands against his shirt.

"What the hell are you doing? I thought we had a game."

Danny looked up at him through bleary eyes.

"Are you drunk?"

The answer was obvious.

Danny got up and staggered toward the house. Milt picked up Danny's jacket, turned off the ball machine, and followed him.

Danny was at the back door, looking through his pockets for the key. He couldn't find it. Impatiently, he kicked the window and smashed the glass. He stuck his hand through and opened the door from the inside.

Milt hesitated. He had never seen his friend in such a state. He shrugged and delicately stepped over the shards of broken glass. In the kitchen, Danny put his head under the spigot for a long time, then wiped his wet head with his shirttail.

"Pretty early in the day for drinks. Have you had lunch?"

Danny's head was still buzzing as they moved into the living room. "No," he muttered. "I've been stood up." He stretched out on the sofa, his hands behind his head, and stared at the fish tank. "That's just the way I feel," he said.

"Like what?"

"Like those dead fish." He pointed at two more floating belly up.

Milt took off his glasses and rubbed the lenses. "What's the problem?"

"You don't wanna hear it, Milt. And I don't wanna tell it."

"Come on, *boychik*. You listen to all of my problems—tell Miltie."

Danny breathed deeply. "I'm in a mess, Milt, a real mess." And he let it pour out, all that had happened at El Padrino.

Suddenly his torrent of words ceased. He lay there with eyes closed.

When he flicked them open, he saw Milt looking down at him through his glasses. "You know what, Danny—your father-in-law gave you some good advice—"

"What?"

"He said see a lawyer, right? That's exactly what you should do. Find out where you stand. I bet Steve Gordon can figure out some way around this. Call him."

Danny gave his agent a faint smile. "You're a good friend, Milt. I almost feel better."

"And besides a lawyer, you need some food. You stay here—watch the ball game—" He tossed the TV remote control into Danny's lap.

"I'll fix you a sandwich, if I can find something to eat in this *goyishe* house."

Danny flipped through the channels, hunting for the ball game. Despite his mood, he had to smile at the terrible clatter coming from the kitchen. He decided to get up to help Milt when the sound from the TV caught his attention.

"Greed is all right. Greed is healthy. You can be greedy and still feel good about yourself." The self-satisfied grin of Ivan Boesky lit up the screen. A crowd cheered. The announcer's voice came on: "That was Mr. Boesky two years ago addressing the UCLA graduating class. Today Mr. Boesky faces a prison sentence on charges of insider trading—"

"Look at that, Danny—now there's a man with problems!" Milt was carrying a plate of rye bread onto which he had dumped the contents of a sardine can.

"Why did he have to steal?" Danny mumbled. "This guy and his pals were making millions a year legally."

"Yeah, but everybody wants more."

"I guess you're right, Milt—it's never enough."

Milt looked at his watch. "Talking about 'never enough,' I gotta meet Marilyn. *Boychik*, you'll have to eat alone." He rushed toward the door, then rushed back. "You got her number, right?"

"Right. If Sarah calls I'll tell her you just left, and I'll sound the red alert."

"You're a pal."

"How is it going?"

Milt grabbed his crotch, laughing, "The greatest!"

Hearing Milt's car speed away, Danny got up slowly, looked at the plate, and picked up one of the sardines in his fingers. It reminded him of his dead tropical fish, and he put it down. He walked over to the tank, and removed the floating fish. He poured some food on the surface for the four survivors, which swam up and sucked in the crumbs.

The TV droned on. Danny caught random words—junk bonds, poison pills, hostile takeovers . . . The new vocabulary of corruption. Suddenly he heard: "This is Mr. Ted Rosemont, the former president of the Security Bank of Los Angeles, entering Lompoc Federal Prison—" He whirled around. Well, if it wasn't Stoneham's fair-haired boy. His all-American smile seemed a bit weak as he walked in chains between two federal marshals. "Mr. Rosemont was found guilty of embezzling funds in excess of five million dollars. He will serve two years in prison."

Danny turned the TV off, but the show lingered in his mind. Boesky, Rosemont—petty thieves compared to J.L. That bastard was smart. He knew how to steal within the law.

Danny walked into the kitchen and threw the sardines down the garbage disposal, thinking of J.L.'s red face, his tongue licking off a bead of martini from his thin, purple lips.

That son of a bitch ought to take inventory. His day of reckoning will come, and then his bursting treasure chest won't save him.

Danny wiped his hands on a dish towel. Damn! He slammed his fist on the counter. *Everyman* was a morality play about greed, the perfect parallel. Why hadn't he seen it before? It wasn't about a corrupt artist. He had been confused by his own guilt.

At last he knew where *Everyman* should be filmed—on Wall Street.

———

Danny drove into the parking lot of 1888 Avenue of the Stars and, with the usual difficulty, found a spot in the underground parking garage. He repeated the number to himself—4-2B—knowing he was likely to forget it and spend hours looking for his Jaguar in the maze of ramps and automobiles. As the elevator ascended to the eighteenth floor, he felt his anxiety rising with it. He entered the reception room of the law firm, which had almost as many partners as the one representing J.L., and without delay was ushered into Steve Gordon's office.

It was plainly furnished, but the imposing floor-to-ceiling rows of heavy, leather-bound books conveyed an oppressive feeling. Danny laid out the situation, pacing the rug in front of the tall windows, oblivious that the ocean view was unobstructed by smog on this crystal-clear day. Then, bracing against the back of an armchair, he asked, "Can I get my daughter back?"

Steve was hesitant, seeming to weigh his words very carefully. He walked over and put his hand on Danny's tense shoulder. "First, why don't you come over here and sit down?"

Danny didn't move. "Look, Steve—I don't want to hear a lot of damn legalese or get tangled up in all that Latin spaghetti."

"Calm down." Steve's eyes softened. "I'm a father too; I know how you must feel. How old is Patricia now?"

"Seventeen."

"Please—do me a favor and sit down."

Danny let Steve steer him to the couch.

"The answer to your question is that there isn't very much you can do."

"I have no legal rights?!" Danny burst out. "You mean Stephanie signed my rights away too?"

"Danny, what Stephanie did has no real bearing on the issues involved here."

"Then why can't we sue? I want to fight that son of a bitch—even if it takes every dime I've got."

"It would take more than that, and it would only get you hopelessly tangled up in that legal spaghetti you hate. But it wouldn't get you your daughter back." Steve spoke in a low monotone. "All right—if we do what you say, we go to court. Imagine what would happen. Patricia would have to take the stand. She's seventeen, Danny, almost the age of maturity—any judge, no matter what the legal arguments, would ask her to make a choice. Do you want to put your daughter through that?" Danny's jaws were tightly clenched, and his facial muscles began to twitch involuntarily as Steve went on. "As your friend more than your lawyer, I advise you not to take legal action. Don't force your daughter into a corner."

"Isn't there anything I can do, Steve?"

"Yes. Be patient. Try to maintain contact with Patricia. Let her know you love her no matter what. She'll come around on her own."

"Stoneham doesn't want her to see me. He keeps her like a prisoner. I have a hard time getting a phone call through."

Steve put his arm around Danny's shoulders. "You'll find a way. Don't say you heard it from a lawyer, but it wouldn't be the first time a father's love won the case."

On the way out of the building, Danny stopped by Milt's office two floors below. Milt had jumped camps some time ago and now had an elaborate suite of offices with PCA. Danny seldom visited Milt's lair and was always amused at Sarah's touches. The Santa Fe decorating motif was in vogue, and Milt sat behind a rough-hewn table with crooked legs—it looked like it was going to fall over at any moment.

He was on the phone. "I started with the pawn to king-four . . ." He waved Danny in. "Irregular opening?! I had you in trouble with doubled rooks . . . 'queen's gambit'? What the hell is that?" He motioned for Danny to sit down. "All right, all right, I'll be at your house for dinner . . . yes, Wednesday." He hung up.

"See what happens when kids grow up, Danny." Milt peered at him from behind a lamp made out of a piece of petrified wood. "I taught that little bastard how to play chess—now he treats me like a dummy. And talking about kids—how did it go with Steve?"

"You were right. I feel much better. Thanks."

"*De nada.* Anything else I can do for you?"

"Yes—give me your undivided attention for five minutes."

Milt pushed the phone button. "Hold my calls." He leaned back in his Navajo-blanket chair. "I'm all ears, *boychik.*"

"Milt, I made some drastic changes in *Everyman.* The film will open with a board meeting being conducted by the top corporate raider of Wall Street."

"Didn't they do that movie?"

"What movie?"

"*Wall Street.*"

"Milt, this is different—just the beginning and end take place on Wall Street."

"But it sounds like something I've seen—"

"Just listen. All through the titles, we hear a screaming ambulance siren. Chairman of the board Edward Everyman has just collapsed from a heart attack. Paramedics are rushing him to the hospital. From there, we tell Everyman's life story in flashbacks as he lies on his deathbed."

"What a downer. You got any sex in it?"

With a forced smile, Danny said, "For you, Milt, I'll put in some naked girls."

"That'll be an improvement. Then what happens?"

"Scenes from his life. People in poverty because he closed down factories. I'm still working on this part. At the end, Everyman realizes all the harm he has done because of his greed, but it's too late. Then I want a climactic ending—in his death delirium, he sees himself as a young man standing in the heart of Wall Street, where he collapses and dies. What do you think?"

"Well, at least it's timely. Every night on TV—"

"That's it exactly, Milt. It's *today.*"

Happy that Milt understood at last, Danny got up to leave.

He was almost out the door when Milt yelled, "Hey, Danny! This movie should bring you and your father-in-law closer together." His cackle carried down the hall.

———

Putting the key in his front door, Danny could hear the muffled ringing of his phone. Maybe it was Patricia. She must have his note by now. He fumbled with the lock and was out of breath by the time he picked up the receiver. "Patricia?"

"No, Danny, this is Stephanie." Her voice was very calm and very low.

"Where's Patricia?"

"Out with J.L. As usual."

He again felt that dull pain in the pit of his stomach. "Did she get the teddy bear?"

"Yes, I made sure she got it."

"Thank you. Did she like it?"

"Very much."

The pain in his belly lessened.

"The reason I called, Danny . . . I thought we might have dinner and talk. I could come over and fix something. You always said I was the best—"

"Stephanie," he interrupted. He would appreciate a good meal; she was an excellent cook. But he heard himself say, "Thanks, I'm not hungry."

"I'm sorry—I thought it would be nice to get together before I leave."

"Where are you going?"

"India."

"India? What for?"

"To get away from J.L.'s army of psychiatrists."

"Maybe they will help."

"I've been drowning in fancy psychiatrists all my life. I need something else. I read about this Buddhist monastery on a mountaintop. Maybe I can find some answers there."

"Stephanie, aren't you going too far? Think this out."

"I have, Danny—I need to find peace in my life."

Danny wondered if she was drunk. "But a Buddhist monastery doesn't make sense to me."

"No religion ever made sense to you."

"What's that mean?" he asked defensively.

"You haven't been in a church since Patricia was baptized."

Danny felt his irritation growing. "You're just running away. You should be here. Patricia needs you."

"There's nothing I can do for Patricia. It's too late. J.L.'s got his hooks in too deep."

"But she's still our daughter."

"Is she?" her voice cracked, and she hung up.

Danny sat there looking at the telephone. He wished he hadn't been so hard on her. She was trying. But India sounded like such a desperate move. He was worried about her, and almost called her back. Instead, he phoned a florist and ordered a bouquet of white roses sent to her. Stephanie loved white roses. He didn't include a card.

———————

The next day, Danny went back to the Beverly Wilshire Hotel, determined to see Patricia before J.L. whisked her away to Long Island in his private plane.

For a long time he stood in front of El Padrino, looking out through the revolving door at the new section of the hotel across the driveway. Suddenly, he saw him. Accompanied by his beefy bodyguard, J.L. was walking briskly, his hand on Stephanie's arm. She tried to pull free twice, clearly annoyed at the firm grip that guided her to the waiting limousine. Poor Stephanie, a grown woman treated like a recalcitrant child. Would this happen to Patricia someday? When the car drove off, Danny ran across the courtyard and took the elevator straight to J.L.'s suite.

Patricia answered his knock. Her pale face broke out into a wide grin as she threw her arms around him, "Daddy, Daddy!"

She ran over and grabbed the teddy bear. "I love your present. It's just like the teddy I used to have when I was little."

"I hoped you'd remember." He looked at her, so like her mother, almost a woman, yet so childlike with the teddy in her arms.

"Oh Daddy, I'm sorry you had to cancel our lunch. J.L. gave me your message. But I understand how busy you are."

Danny was stunned. He wanted to scream, He's a goddamn liar!— but he said nothing. It would only bring more confusion into this fragile girl's life.

She propped the teddy against the vase of flowers that Danny had sent to Stephanie. "Teddy loves sitting in the garden," she giggled.

"It's a beautiful garden, lovely flowers."

"Yes, they belong to Mom. I don't know who sent them—there was no card—but they made her very happy."

Danny settled next to her on the couch. "Where *is* your mother?"

"Oh, J.L. took her to the doctor. Mom didn't want to go."

She removed one of the blossoms and began twisting it nervously in her hands. "Mom is so unhappy. And she's always arguing with J.L. I don't know why—he's so kind and he just wants to help her."

"Darling, sometimes things are more complicated than they seem."

The flower petals were falling to the floor. She looked down. "Daddy, I understand about the divorce. I really do. J.L. explained it to me." She looked up at him sadly. "But we can still work on a film together, can't we?"

"Of course we can, darling."

"J.L. doesn't like movies much, but maybe you could explain to him how they're made—he doesn't really understand. Why don't you talk with him, Daddy?" She looked at her watch. "He should be back any minute."

"Maybe some other time, darling. I really must get back to the studio." He gave her a tight hug. There was an awkward pause. "Take good care of teddy."

"I promise, Daddy."

"And just never forget that I love you very much, no matter what happens."

"I love you too, Daddy."

"And will you always be my little girl?"

"Always."

"Always?"

"Always."

Taking the elevator down, Danny wiped away the tears forming in his eyes. Thank God he hadn't lost her. Now he had reason to hope that they might be close again like in the old days.

The elevator door opened on the ground floor. Standing in front of him, dead ahead, was J. L. Stoneham. Both men stood motionless for a moment.

J.L. broke the silence. "I don't make idle threats. I'll destroy you."

CHAPTER 14

1987 | North Philadelphia, Pennsylvania

randpa! Grandpa!" The little black girl jumped off her bicycle and raced up the front porch steps.

"Now what is it?" The portly man wiped the beads of sweat from his ebony brow and went back to carving the wings of a wooden airplane. He never stopped rocking on his glider.

"Somebody important here to see you!"

The old man squinted over the little girl's head at the beefy man in the plaid suit carefully picking his way past the geranium planters made out of old tires. "Important, is he?"

Coming closer, the beefy man extended his hand. "My name is McCrachen, and I'm looking for Tyrone Luis."

"You found him."

"Were you in the Forty-fourth Paratroop Squadron in World War Two?"

"I'm guilty," Tyrone guffawed.

"You mind if I ask you about some of your war experiences?"

"Sit down," Tyrone said, making room on the glider.

Beverly Hills

 fter two sets of tennis with his new pro and twelve laps in the pool, Danny felt good inside and out. He found himself whistling as he walked into his study, his favorite room in the house. After Patricia was born, he had it built adjoining the master bedroom on the second floor, and he loved working here instead of in his office at the studio. He enjoyed the freedom of pulling back the sliding door to gaze at the trees or take a quick dip in the pool or work out his frustration on the tennis court.

Lily Kane, the assistant Milt found for him, was getting the word processor ready for their next work session. He liked this intelligent young woman, a recent graduate of his alma mater, the USC cinema school. She was attractive, with rosy cheeks, blue eyes that always seemed to sparkle, and shiny brown hair. Her wholesome body made you think of those paintings of French peasant girls laughing in the sun.

"You're in a good mood this morning, Mr. Dennison."

"Yes, and let's try to keep me that way."

She laughed. "Shoot."

He started dictating. "The scene is a stockholders' meeting. A steelworker is addressing Edward Everyman, the chairman of the board. He says, 'You want to smash the Ten Commandments and worship the golden calf! You want—' "

"Excuse me," Lily interrupted. "Isn't that a little pompous for a steelworker, Mr. Dennison?"

Danny looked at her coldly.

"Oh Mr. Dennison, please don't change your mood." She winked at him.

He grinned. "OK, let's try for something better, but for God's sake stop calling me Mr. Dennison—it's Danny."

"Yes, sir, Danny."

"That's better. How about: 'A few of you rich guys make a lot of money at our expense. There is only so much money out there. When you get richer, we get poorer.' "

"Oh, I like that," Lily broke in.

He studied her face—no makeup, just a soft line around her eyes, blue eyes that sometimes seemed green, innocent, yet full of intelligence. She was excellent at her job. Her questions were never trivial; they always made him think and weigh more carefully the words he put in Everyman's mouth.

Danny walked around the study, dictating as she typed. "The chairman of the board speaks: 'You clearly don't understand that I have an obligation to the stockholders of this company.' And the steelworker yells, 'But you're the biggest stockholder. It's your own fat ass you're looking out for.' Now, the chairman jumps up in a fury and shouts back, 'That's capitalism! What do you want—communism?!' "

Lily broke in again. "But Mr. Den— Danny, isn't the chairman right?"

"Lily, I'm trying to expose people who abuse capitalism by getting rich exchanging pieces of paper. What do these stock-market manipulators manufacture or produce?"

"They produce capital so that directors like you can finance your movies."

"Oh, a USC smart-ass—"

Not the least bit ruffled, she expectantly waited for his reply.

Danny sat down next to her. "Listen—I'm talking about corporate raiders, who destroy. They don't build up companies, engage in research, or develop new products. They take over, sell off the assets, and make a huge profit. I know. That's what my father-in-law does—he's the master of the game."

Lily studied him intensely, digesting what he had said. "How do you stop them?"

"I don't know, but I want my movie to focus a spotlight on the problem. I want to say that the day of reckoning has come, time to take inventory—what are we doing, where are we going, what do we want out of life? I want to make a movie that asks these important questions. I'm tired of making crap like *London Rock*."

"I saw a sneak preview of *London Rock*—I liked it."

"You did?"

"I thought it was light, but very amusing."

"Well, you must hate working on *Everyman* then."

"No, no. I've never worked on a project as exciting as this. *Everyman* could be a classic." She looked at him with admiration.

Danny felt a flush of color coming to his cheeks as she turned back to her word processor. He watched her graceful long fingers dancing on the keyboard.

Aware of his gaze, she raised her eyes. "What's wrong?"

He smiled. "Nothing's wrong. As a matter of fact, I was just thinking of that Robert Browning poem: 'God's in his heaven—All's right with the world.' "

You *will* do it!" J.L. commanded. "The driver will pick you up here at the hotel, and you *will* be ready on time, and you *will* keep your appointment!"

He had been badgering Stephanie for half an hour. The subject—always a sore one between them—Stephanie's refusal to keep regular appointments with her psychiatrist.

"But Daddy, please. *Pleeease.* I don't want to; I can't. He'll only send me to some institution. He threatened to the last time. Just this once, let me try to work out my own life."

"I don't want to hear about India again. I know what's best for you."

"I've seen doctors all my life." Her voice was rising, hysterical. "I've been in sanitariums." She was screaming now. "None of it has made me into what you want me to be!"

J.L. started to leave the room. "I've had enough. You're just like your mother."

"And look what happened to her."

Standing at the door, J.L. took in a breath through clenched teeth and looked at her with contempt.

"Daddy, Daddy, why can't you accept me the way I am?" Stephanie pleaded. "I'm a grown woman."

"You're not a woman—you're a child, and you need help."

Stephanie ran across the room and grabbed his arm to prevent him from leaving. Her eyes mirrored desperation. "I won't do it, Daddy. I have a family, a child, a husband—my husband will help me."

Stoneham looked at his daughter with a slightly twisted smile. "Stephanie dear, you've lost your grip on reality. You don't have a husband—or a child."

She let go of his arm and crumpled to the floor.

"I'm taking Patricia back to Long Island this afternoon. You'll stay here until you come to your senses."

The door slammed shut behind him.

New York

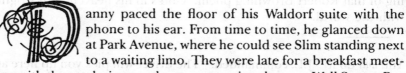 anny paced the floor of his Waldorf suite with the phone to his ear. From time to time, he glanced down at Park Avenue, where he could see Slim standing next to a waiting limo. They were late for a breakfast meeting with the set designer, who was expecting them on Wall Street. But Danny had to get through to the Stoneridge Academy in Virginia. Didn't they ever answer the phone? Finally, someone picked up. Patricia wasn't there, he was told; she had taken off early for Christmas vacation to ski in Gstaad. He was disappointed; he had hoped to continue the warm conversation they'd had at the Beverly Wilshire, maybe even spend the weekend with her.

When Danny finally emerged from the hotel, Slim was looking at his watch pointedly. "Boss," he said, "you're the one who said let's start early." Danny didn't answer as they hopped into the car. The driver, clearly used to carting bankers around, had laid a copy of *The Wall Street Journal* on the backseat.

They had sent the set designer ahead to scout locations on Wall Street and to arrange permission to shoot there on a Sunday, when the stock exchange was deserted. Now he and Slim were ready to nail down the arrangements.

Looking out the tinted window, Danny imagined how he would transpose the tall spires of Salzburg's Gothic cathedrals into the skyscrapers of the World Trade Center. "This is the scene, Slim, that will really make the film. When I shoot—" Danny nudged him. "Hey, can I have your attention?"

Slim's eyes were glued to the front page of the newspaper in his lap. Danny followed his gaze to a headline that read:

STONEHAM BUYING
ACE FILMS STOCK;
TAKEOVER FEARED

Danny grabbed the paper. The article said that J. L. Stoneham had started buying out Ace Films stock, causing its price to rise twelve points—an apparent first move to take over the company. He reached for the car phone. He woke Milt up in Los Angeles.

"*Boychik,* I don't know—I don't know—I haven't read it yet."

"Where the hell does this leave me?"

"Hold it, keep cool. It could just be a false rumor. Let me talk to Art Gunn—I can't see him just rolling over."

"Everybody has a price."

"*Boychik,* a studio still has to make movies."

"Milt, Stoneham wants Ace Films so he can crush me."

"Come on, don't get dramatic. There's gotta be cheaper ways to crush you. He doesn't need to spend half a billion dollars!"

"You don't know him."

"OK, OK. Remember—you have a contract. Don't panic, and do what you're doing."

Over breakfast Danny barely managed two coherent sentences as Slim discussed the locations with the set designer.

When they got back to the Waldorf, Slim put his arm around Danny's shoulders. "I wish I could do something, boss."

"Thanks. You know, I've been trying to figure out how to make this movie for twenty years. Now I got the angle, I got the money, and my father-in-law screws me up."

Slim patted his back, muttering, "It ain't over till it's over."

Dejectedly, Danny walked down the long corridor to his suite. He opened the door and stopped with a jolt.

Seated on the couch before him was the beefy man in the plaid suit.

"What the hell are you doing here?"

"Mr. Stoneham owns this hotel." The beefy man rose to his feet and extracted a thick wad of papers from his breast pocket. "I am here to deliver a message from him."

"Deliver it and get out!"

"Mr. Stoneham says he will drop all attempts to take over Ace Films if you will sign certain documents."

"Tell Mr. Stoneham to go fuck himself!"

"Thank you." The beefy man carefully refolded the papers and replaced them in his breast pocket. He brushed past Danny on his way out the door.

Danny couldn't sleep that night. His hatred for J. L. Stoneham almost gagged him. He felt powerless, alone, isolated. He needed someone to talk to. He picked up the phone.

When he heard her voice, he felt tongue-tied, but finally managed, "Luba—this is Danny." There was silence. He thought she had hung up. "Are you there?"

"Yes, I'm here."

"Luba—sorry it took me so long, but . . . ah . . ."

"But what?"

"I owe you an apology."

"Let's forget it."

There was an awkward silence.

"I miss you, Luba," Danny blurted out.

"I shouldn't, but I miss you too."

He became tongue-tied again. "Well . . . I was just thinking that . . . I'm in New York for a few days . . ."

"Oh, you're not far away."

"Three hours by Concorde. . . ."

There was a long pause. "Please come, Danny—I want to see you."

"I'll only be able to stay for the weekend."

"Then stay here."

London

 uba seemed genuinely glad to see him. She hung up his clothes, took out his pajamas and toilet case.

"Where's Magda?"

"She's been sick."

"Oh, no—"

"She's much better now; she's recuperating with some friends in Weymouth."

"I'm sorry to miss her."

"She'd be sorry too—she became very fond of you in Portugal."

"She did?" Danny studied her face, but it revealed nothing more.

"Now, get yourself cleaned up, and I'll fix you some food. I'm almost as good a cook as Magda."

"OK. Do you need any help in the kitchen?"

"You're more help in the bedroom," she laughed. "Wash up and fix yourself a drink."

Danny explored the apartment—he had hardly noticed it the one time before, in the dark. He felt comfortable here. It was small, modest, immaculate, and there were geraniums in the windows.

On a table, he saw photos of Luba trying to look older, and Magda trying to look younger. They were both very pretty. They should have been rich in Kraków.

He poured himself another drink and lay down on the rug.

Luba came in carrying two lighted candles, placed them on the dining table, and turned out the other lights. "I'm glad you're here, Danny."

"So am I." He put his glass down beside him on the floor and stretched out. "So tell me a story."

Luba started to laugh so hard tears rolled down her cheeks. "You came three thousand miles for a fairy tale?"

"You can't laugh yourself out of it."

Luba wiped her eyes, shook her head, and said, "Danny, you'll never change."

The oven timer buzzed in the kitchen. "Saved by the bell . . . your story will have to wait."

He made a pouting face.

While she busied herself in the kitchen, Danny wandered around the room. In the corner he found several large canvases turned to the wall. He picked one up. "Oh my God!" he exclaimed.

Luba poked her head out of the kitchen, wondering what had disturbed him.

"Portugal!" He was staring at a painting of two naked silhouettes standing on a beach, behind them a huge purple sky sparkling with a thousand diamonds, in front of them a blanket of waves reflecting the starlight. He chuckled.

"What's so funny?" Luba asked defensively.

"No, no, it's not funny. It's terrific. It's us! But where is the comet racing across the moon?"

"Please put it down," Luba mumbled, turning back toward the kitchen. He watched her through the doorway as she occupied herself slicing bread.

"It's very well done," Danny said, coming closer. "You have a special talent—I hope you realize that."

Luba wasn't used to hearing compliments about her paintings; she never showed them to anyone, except Magda. She stood at the kitchen counter, looking down at the bread, not knowing what to say.

Danny gently placed his hand under her chin and lifted her head. She was blushing.

"You're embarrassed—really embarrassed," he said in astonishment. "I think this is the first time I've seen you this way."

"No one was supposed to see it."

"You know, you amaze me. You can stand naked in front of anyone, without blinking an eye, but you blush when someone says something nice about your painting."

"You don't understand—this is private," she said stiffly, breaking away from him. "Go away and let me finish dinner."

He went back to where the canvases were stored. He picked up one after another, amazed at her prolific talent. Then he gasped. The last one was a gray stallion galloping through tall grass, but with the head of a man.

Luba walked in with two bowls of soup. "Danny, please leave them alone. Let's eat."

"But it's me! And you made me a satyr."

"I don't even know what that is." Luba busied herself folding napkins.

"Well, in Greek mythology a satyr was a kind of god, half human, half animal, usually associated with sex orgies."

"I wasn't thinking of that. Sit down before the soup gets cold."

Danny obeyed, but he kept looking at the painting. "You know what that reminds me of? A stallion we had on the farm when I was a kid. I'll never forget the first time I saw him mating with a mare." He chuckled. "I didn't even know what he was doing back then. My sister and I couldn't take our eyes off him, until my mother made us—" He stopped abruptly.

"Go ahead . . . made you what?"

"No, I'm talking too much—the soup's getting cold."

"Where was it?"

"Ahh . . . what?"

"Where was the farm?"

"Oh . . . ah . . . in Syracuse."

"Was it a big farm?"

"No, medium size."

"Did you have many horses?"

"What is this? A third degree? Stop bugging me—let me eat."

But he didn't have much appetite. He pushed the soup aside after two spoonfuls. He had gone too far again. How did she trick him into revealing so much?

Luba was baffled by his quick change of mood. He didn't like the soup. He was upset. She'd have to find a way to take his mind off whatever was bothering him.

A bell was ringing. It filtered through Danny's sleepy head. His eyes opened, and he saw Luba looking down at him. She was sitting cross-legged on the bed, naked, sipping a cup of coffee.

It rang again.

"Who's that?"

Luba took another sip of coffee. "It's Rick."

"Who the hell's Rick?"

"The newspaper boy. The one I told you about, remember? It's Sunday. He wants to get paid."

The doorbell rang more persistently. "He's getting anxious," Danny said.

"Yes, I better let him in." She walked toward the door, ignoring her robe on the floor. From the other room Danny could hear her talking through the intercom. "Rick? Come on up." Then the buzzer released the door catch.

Danny sat up and took a long sip of coffee. He felt awkward. Should he get dressed? Put on his pajamas? He did neither. He took another sip.

In Portugal he had been angered—and titillated—by Luba's reference to the paper boy. Now, he only felt oddly uncomfortable, straining to hear the conversation in the living room.

"Rick," Luba was saying in a lilting voice, "so nice to see you." He couldn't make out what the boy said.

"I was asleep. Didn't even get a chance to grab a robe. Like some coffee?"

"No thank you," said a high-pitched Cockney accent.

Danny felt silly sitting in bed listening like an eavesdropper. The talking stopped. There was silence followed by a throaty laugh from Luba. He heard some movement. He wanted to sneak a look. Then Luba continued, "Oh Rick, Mr. Dennison is here."

"What?!"

"You wanted to meet him. Come on."

"No—no—no," said the frantic boy.

Holding him by the hand, Luba led a tall, slim teenager into the bedroom. Danny couldn't believe his eyes—the boy was completely nude too! My God, he thought, how does she maneuver everyone so quickly?

"Danny, this is Rick. He wants to be an actor. Don't you think he has possibilities?" She spoke as if they were all fully clothed and in the middle of a cocktail party.

"Hi, Rick." Danny hoped his voice sounded nonchalant.

" 'Ello, Mr. Dennison," the boy murmured, trying to twist his body and arms to hide his erection.

"He keeps himself in good condition by running on his paper route. Don't you, Rick?" Luba continued. "He's got a good body, no?"

Danny opened his mouth but could say nothing. Rick made some incoherent response.

"And he's not fully grown! He's going to be very, uh, big." And she smiled wickedly at Rick and wet her lips. "We've become good friends, haven't we?"

As he made a sound of assent, she turned toward Danny, pleading, "You must help him—please, Danny, will you?" Then, turning back to the naked newspaper boy, she added, "I like Rick."

There was a momentary silence. "Oh, you know what Rick likes?" Luba picked up a capsule of amyl nitrate from the bedstand. In one quick movement, she broke the amy and pushed it against the boy's nose. Rick breathed in deeply. "I like it too," said Luba, taking a whiff as she pulled Rick down on the bed between them. "Don't you?" She pushed the capsule up to Danny's nostrils.

Danny did. He relaxed as the tingling warmth went to his head and through his body. Rick lay there, breathing deeply, his cock reaching toward the ceiling. "Isn't that beautiful?" Luba murmured, quietly touching it.

She took Danny's hand and placed it on Rick's cock. Danny was jolted, but he liked how it felt—hard, pulsating. In his tingling mind, he felt that he was touching himself.

Almost maternally, Luba whispered, "Rick, I know what you want." She put her nipple to his mouth and reached for another capsule. Danny looked over at Rick devouring her breast.

"Isn't he a nice boy?" she cooed. Another amy snapped. Her tongue reached for Danny's mouth as they both took a deep whiff. Then she slowly pushed Danny's head toward Rick's cock. Suddenly, that firm, young cock was in his mouth. Rick groaned softly. Danny's head was spinning. What am I doing? he thought. But he didn't stop. A flush of excitement went through his body as Luba gave him another whiff. He caught her dark eyes, and raised his head. "I want to see you fuck him," he said hoarsely.

"Oh yes," murmured Luba as she eased Rick's body over on top of hers.

Opening her mouth wide for Danny's hard cock, she said, "Give it to me." She started sucking on Danny with sounds of contentment.

Danny felt an electrical current go through the three of them as he watched Rick ram into her. He leaned back against the headboard, his cock reacting to the massage of Luba's tongue. He could see the boy's round ass go up and down as Rick pounded away.

When it was over, Luba said in a soft, pleasant voice, "Rick, you're going to be late for the rest of your collections."

Without a word, he got up and went into the other room. As he dressed, she called out pleasantly, "I'll pay you next week."

They heard the door close.

Luba looked at Danny with adoring eyes.

He lay there quietly, his arm across his eyes. "God—what have I done?"

"What do you mean?" asked Luba, giving him an affectionate kiss, and running her fingers through his hair.

"I feel like a pervert."

"Oh, come on," Luba laughed.

Danny said nothing.

She laughed again, showering him with kisses. "Let me make you some fresh coffee." She left the room.

He jumped out of bed and packed his bag quickly.

"Nice and hot," said Luba, walking back in. She stopped. "Where are you going?"

"I'm leaving," he said, avoiding her eyes. He put on his clothes.

"What's wrong, Danny?"

He didn't answer.

"Danny, are you upset by what happened?"

He still didn't answer.

"I thought you'd enjoy something new and different. Here, have a sip of coffee—you'll feel better."

He didn't take the cup she offered.

"Danny," she said with a smile. "Sucking one little cock doesn't make you a cocksucker."

He struck her across the face with such force, the coffee sailed across the room. She stared at him in disbelief as he picked up his bag and stormed out the door.

There was no taxi in sight. He paced the street angrily, wanting to get away as quickly as possible. Milt was right. A whore will bring you nothing but grief. He was dumbfounded by Luba's deft handling of the whole situation. He was ashamed of his quick cooperation. That bitch could get him to do anything.

As his rage against Luba subsided, it was replaced by self-loathing. How could he have done it? How could he sink so low?

He remembered Tateh telling Mameh that sex was an important part of life—but should sex be as important as Luba made it? He had never done such a thing—never thought of it—and was frightened that he found it exciting. Maybe the perversion was his. He had a sinking feeling that the weakness was within him.

He could see the stork on the roof of the barn, wings outstretched, one leg raised, the other planted on the peak of the roof. His father had told him that the bird would fly away when he became a man. Danny knew the bird was still there.

CHAPTER 15

1987 | Los Angeles

 anny came off the polar flight at LAX with his carry-on bag over his shoulder and walked directly to his waiting limousine. He was surprised to find Milt pacing in front of the car. *"Boychik,* I tried to reach you—I guess you went down to Virginia to see Patricia—"

"Yeah, I did, but she wasn't there," Danny lied, unable to confide even in his best friend what had happened in London. "What are you doing here?"

"I bring good news."

"Good news?"

"I talked with Art Gunn. You have nothing to worry about. Art is fighting it—no way is Stoneham gonna get the studio."

"Cut the bullshit—it's not making me feel any better."

Milt let out a sigh. "OK, Danny. I'm exaggerating a little bit. But let's say the worst happens. Stoneham takes over the studio. You have a contract. He has to honor it, and then once the movie is in the can—"

"He doesn't have to distribute it."

"Of course he does. He'd have a tough time explaining to his board why he didn't distribute a film that cost millions of dollars."

"Come on, Milt—you know the facts. If Stoneham's willing to spend half a billion to crush me, what's five million more to kill the film—peanuts."

Milt didn't respond immediately. He seemed preoccupied with watching the other cars on the San Diego Freeway. "OK, Danny. But it hasn't happened yet. You've got time to make the film. These takeovers don't happen overnight. Lots of reasons it may not go through—SEC regulations, stockholders' objections, proxy—"

"It will go through. And I'll be through."

"Boychik, you're too tired to think straight. Let's talk again after you've had a chance to rest, clear your head. Then I'll even buy you dinner at Spago's. OK?"

Rome, Italy

he beefy man shifted impatiently in the metal folding chair.

"I'm sorry to have kept you waiting, Mr. McCrachen." The Red Cross worker hurried into the room, carrying a thin folder. "But I had a hard time finding the information you need."

"I see you've found *something."*

"Well, the only existing record on the liberation of the San Sabba Concentration Camp isn't very helpful. Very few children survived. Only six, in fact—four girls and two boys, neither by the name Daniel."

"Are you sure?"

"Yes. Of course it's possible the record is incomplete. But the only

names are a seven-year-old David Solomon and a twelve-year-old
Moishe Neumann."

"That's all?"

"I'm sorry."

Beverly Hills

 anny drove up the steep incline that led to the parking
lot behind Spago's. Two days of hibernation—feeding
the fish, walking around the house, and mostly sleeping—had lessened his pessimism. Milt was right; he
wasn't through yet. There was enough time to make the film, and if
Everyman was as good as he knew it would be, nothing could stop it
from being distributed, somehow, somewhere.

As he made his way into the parking lot, he saw the usual flock of
fans, paparazzi, flashbulbs popping, young and old, men and women.
Fans never ceased to amaze Danny. How could they spend so much
of their time just waiting and waiting for momentary contact with a
star? Where did they get the money to buy the pictures and books
that they clutched, hoping for a signature? He remembered being
with Bruce Ryan when a fan approached with a large color photo.
Danny couldn't help asking, "Where did you get that?"

"I bought it," said the fan, "for six dollars."

And that was just for one photo! Others had stacks of them. How
could they afford to spend that much money and what did those
signatures mean to them?

Wolfgang Puck, the congenial Austrian owner of Spago's, led him
to his table in the far corner, where the wide windows overlook
Sunset Strip. "Mr. Schultz called to say he'd be late—he suggested
you have a Jewish pizza," Puck said, as a waiter brought over a pizza
made with lox, cream cheese, and caviar. It was delicious. Danny
ordered a vodka to wash it down and settled in to wait.

He liked Spago's. It was noisy, but the tasty food, prepared in the
open kitchen, had made this the "in" place of the moment. He took a
sip and looked around: A starlet was leaning over a producer, hoping
the view of her breasts would land her a part; a top macho star
surreptitiously held hands under the table with his male lover; a
fading movie queen sat smoking a cigarette in a silver holder, trying

hard to look glamorous; gawking tourists waited endlessly for a table as the celebrities passed them by.

At the center table sat two studio chiefs in an intense discussion, while their bored wives played with the food. Neither of these men, both former agents, had ever made a movie, and yet they determined what movies were to be made. If they guessed wrong too often, they would be replaced. But they wouldn't be out of work long; among Hollywood executives, failure often became a step up the ladder of success.

At another table sat Harry Moss, a business manager indicted for absconding with his clients' funds. He was awaiting trial, but he wasn't crying in his soup—he was slurping it with relish.

Danny took another sip. He didn't mind waiting. It gave him a chance to relax and observe.

Across the room he recognized billionaire Jonathan Shields, costumed as usual in silk shirt, ascot, and dyed Hitler mustache. His guests smiled and listened to his inane banter with rapt attention. They must be hoping some of his money will rub off on them, Danny thought. Nothing will rub off.

Suddenly, through the din, Danny heard loud applause and cheers. Beaming and waving, Larry Pressman entered with his wife. People came over to shake his hand as Danny looked on in amazement. Larry Pressman, president of World-Wide Pictures, had recently been convicted of forging directors' signatures and cashing their checks, but the studio still wanted to retain him as their chief executive. An eminent psychiatrist had been engaged to convince the court that he was mentally ill—temporarily. Milt had heard a rumor that Pressman protested this defense strategy but was finally convinced with the argument: "Either you're sick, or you're a crook. If you're sick, you can run a studio. If you're a crook, you go to jail."

Such hypocrisy, sham, dishonesty, Danny thought—*Everyman* would deal with all that was surrounding him. It didn't just exist on Wall Street; it was here, and everywhere. His movie would show it. His movie would make a difference. A warm electric current went through his body, the pleasure of anticipation.

Milt, out of breath and full of apologies, broke into his euphoria. "I ordered you a vodka and cracked crab," Danny said as Milt sank into his seat and grabbed the last slice of the Jewish pizza.

Milt's usually neat beard seemed bedraggled, and the cheerful glint in his gray eyes was gone. "You look awful," Danny said. "What's with you?"

Milt gulped. "Sarah kicked me out."

"What?"

"Two days ago—the same night I picked you up at the airport."

"Because of Marilyn?"

"Yeah—she found out."

"Those are the chances you take."

"Don't I know it."

"So now you're staying with Marilyn?"

Milt closed his eyes and shook his head. "That's over too."

"Wow, Milt—a lot's been happening."

"Danny, you won't believe it . . ." The waiter brought their order, and Milt fell silent for a moment as he concentrated on breaking open a crab leg. "I should have known something was going on. She's been acting funny ever since the preview. The picture was a bust, you know."

"So I heard."

"After that she was always out on auditions, never returned my calls, breaking dates." Milt was absentmindedly munching on his crab. "I was desperate the night Sarah threw me out—I went to her apartment. She wasn't home. I waited outside—three hours! She drove up—with John Washington."

"John Washington? The black actor?"

"Yeah, a *shvartza*."

"Don't be a racist."

"I'm not, but he is a *shvartza*. She saw me—she came out. He stayed in the car. 'What do you want?' she asked. 'What do I want? I want you, Marilyn.' She stared at me. 'I left my wife for you.' And then she said it: 'Milton, it's all over.' Oh Danny—" Milt lowered his head. "I didn't want her to see me cry. I didn't know what to do. I tried to go back to Sarah. I called her—she wouldn't talk to me. My kids won't talk to me. You'd think they'd understand—I mean, they're adults!"

Danny looked across the table at Milt, pale, hunched over, distraught, but still gulping down his drink and reaching for another crab.

"What should I do?" asked Milt with his mouth full.

Danny suppressed a smile. "Remember, Miltie—a problem is a point of view. If you get the right point of view you solve the problem. Don't call your wife—write to her."

Milt stopped chewing. "Write to her?"

"Yeah, tell her what a fool you were. Tell her how much you miss her and that you've broken off with—"

"But she knows Marilyn dumped me. It was in Army's column."

"So scratch that. Just write that now you know you want only her—and *this* is important—but you know it's too late."

"Too late?"

"Yes. You can never recapture the wonderful moments you had together in the Bronx." Milt looked sharply at Danny, who continued, "You hurt her and you understand she wants no part of you after what you did. You accept that." Milt tried to interrupt. "No, no—let me finish. You can't face her again after behaving the way you did. Tell her you must have been crazy to risk her love. For the rest of your life you want to make it up to her. Tell her you're writing because you're too ashamed to talk to her. Send the letter and don't call her for five days."

"Five days?" Milt asked weakly.

"Yes."

"All right, Danny. I hope it works."

"I do too," said Danny, feeling good that he could come up with such clever advice.

"Thanks a lo—" A piece of crab fell out of Milt's mouth, and he turned red.

"What's the matter?"

"There," Milt choked out.

"Where?"

"There!"

"Who?"

"Him—there he is with Marilyn."

Danny turned to see the handsome black actor pulling a chair out for Marilyn, a picture of sophistication in a white silk dress that clung to her perfect body. They were both laughing.

Paralyzed, Milt continued to stare at them, his mouth agape.

"Let's go, Miltie." Danny threw down some bills, pulled his friend out of his chair, and rushed him out of the restaurant. Walking through the parking lot, Danny put his arm around Milt. "You're lucky it's over."

"Yeah," Milt said without conviction.

"I mean it, Miltie."

"Sure . . . sure."

"Believe me, it could never last."

Milt let out a sigh. "Maybe you're right."

Danny gave him a squeeze. "Come on—tell me a joke."

"I don't feel like it." Milt shook his downcast head.

"Please, Miltie—just a little one."

"Well, OK."

"Now you're talking."

"What's the difference between a first and a second marriage?"
Milt paused for emphasis. "The first time the orgasms are real, but
the jewelry is fake." He cackled softly.

Chuckling with him, Danny said, "I'm not worried about you, Milt
—you have a sense of humor; you'll be all right."

Danny walked him to his car. "Where are you staying?"

Milt suddenly looked pathetic, like a little boy going to camp for the
first time. "In a hotel."

"Stay with me, Milt."

"No thanks—I have the penthouse suite at the Beverly."

———

Danny drove home pleased that he had succeeded in making Milt feel
better. Why hadn't he realized before that helping others gave you
such a good feeling and took your mind off your own problems?
Maybe that's what Stephanie was trying to do when she asked to help
him with *Everyman*. He should call her. He had never responded to
her note thanking him for the flowers. *"White roses! Could only be you.
Call me—I'm lonely,"* she had written. Poor Stephanie. He wanted to
help her. Maybe he was wrong about India. Maybe they still could be
friends. He remembered Stephanie's exposed breasts when he
walked into the bedroom. They had had wonderful sex together when
they were first married.

He dialed the hotel. "Mrs. Dennison, please." After a long wait,
listening to inane music, he was told there was no answer.

"Is she still registered?"

"Just a minute—I'll check with the front desk."

More Muzak. When he was finally told she was indeed still there, he
asked to leave a message.

"Just a minute—I'll connect you with the message service."

The silly music came on again, and he hung up.

———

Stephanie heard the ringing. She raised her head from the table and
knocked over the empty bottle of Scotch. She got up, almost falling.
Someone must be at the door, she thought through her drunken
haze. She wrapped her robe more tightly around her and raked her
fingers through her tangled hair.

No one was at the door, but the ringing continued. Bewildered, she
looked at the phone. But by the time she reached it, the line was dead.
She felt dizzy. She leaned on the nightstand to steady herself, and the

fragile table teetered and fell over—lamp, phone, framed photos, vials of pills all crashing to the floor.

"Oh I'm sorry . . . I'm sorry . . ." She dropped down and picked up one of the little pictures. Through the cracked glass she saw the smiling faces of Danny, Patricia, and herself on the beach at Malibu. She sat on the floor staring at the picture. *"Steppin' out with my baby . . ."* she began to sing, *". . . can't be bad if it feels so good . . ."*

London

uba was in the kitchen opening a can of tuna that she had stolen from the supermarket. This was not the first time in the past month that she'd had to steal food. But there was no alternative. The cat, smelling the fish, impatiently rubbed his fur against her ankles. She gave him the empty can to lick and started mixing the salad. She could hear Magda puttering in the living room, the poodle yapping away. The tranquilizers the doctor had prescribed made Magda feel better, but the two-week hospital stay had used up all of their money—in spite of national health care.

Now, when she needed the money so badly, the escort service wouldn't use her—she was considered unreliable.

Desperate for cash, she had finally agreed to sell the seascape Mrs. McKeever had admired. Once she did it, she wondered why she had resisted for so long. It felt good. She wasn't giving up a private part of her life; she was sharing it. And she enjoyed receiving payment for something she had created, even if the money covered only two weeks' rent. She was pleased with the compliments that Mrs. McKeever showered on her in the hall: "My sister just loves your painting." And "The plumber was here today—he paints too—and he said that was superb workmanship."

The cat licked the can clean, and Luba picked him up and walked to the window. Out on the street, Rick was delivering the Sunday paper. He looked up, but Luba moved behind the curtain. He was the reason that Danny had gone out of her life. But it wasn't his fault, and it wasn't hers either. She had been certain that Danny would enjoy the new experience. And he had. Why was he so angry? She raised her hand to her cheek; she could still feel the sting of his hand.

Rick stood in front of the apartment building for a long time, and then continued on his way. She put the cat down and went outside to get the newspaper.

On the front page was a picture of a blown-up airplane—yet another tragedy, all those people killed. Was it chance or fate? She turned the page, and her eye caught a photo of a beautiful woman. The words jumped out at her: MRS. STEPHANIE DENNISON—SOCIALITE —SUICIDE— A maid had found Stephanie in the hotel suite with an empty bottle of Scotch and an empty vial of pills beside her.

Luba rushed upstairs to call Danny. After four rings his machine picked up. She almost hung up, not knowing what to say, then she blurted out, "Danny, I'm here for you. Call me."

Beverly Hills

anny got up early Sunday morning and plugged the phone back in. The answering machine told him there was one message left during the night. As soon as he recognized Luba's voice he turned the machine off. He was proud of himself; he didn't hesitate in the slightest. Luba was not going to disrupt his concentration now. He put on his tennis clothes and headed for the court.

Danny liked to approach each movie like an athlete—in shape; for *Everyman* he wanted to be in superb condition. Sweat was pouring down his face as he slammed tennis balls from the automatic machine.

"Danny!" someone yelled. He stepped on the pedal to stop the machine and saw Milt approaching him with the morning newspaper.

"What's up?" Danny grinned at his friend.

Milt wasn't smiling as he handed him the paper. "She must have done it the night before, while we were at Spago's."

Danny read the short account, then lowered himself into a lawn chair and closed his eyes. When he finally spoke, his voice was hoarse. "My God, Milt. Where do you think they took her?"

"The morgue, I suppose. That's usually what police do."

―――――

The clerk at the morgue looked sleepy. "My name is Dennison. I'm here about my wife, Stephanie Dennison."

"Oh," the clerk said, "to identify the body?" He consulted a note-book. "Two forty-eight."

They followed him down an antiseptically tiled hallway to a metal door. A gust of frigid air rushed out when the clerk opened it. He led them to drawer number 248 and pulled it out.

Danny braced himself.

The drawer was empty.

The clerk scratched his head. "Let me check." He leafed through some papers on a clipboard hanging from a dirty string. "Oh, the deceased was checked out four hours ago, shipped to a funeral home in Long Island, on the orders of J. L. Stoneham."

Danny slowly walked away.

Milt put his arm around him. *"Boychik,* she was a troubled girl, and you did everything you could."

Danny sat in silence as Milt drove him home. How ironic that while he was trying to reach Stephanie with a strong desire to make love, she was probably already dead, lying alone in a hotel suite waiting to be discovered. She had reached out for him—she wanted to help him with *Everyman.* She wanted to cook him dinner. Maybe she wanted to make love, too.

"Milt, you think she'd be alive now if I had let her help me?"

"I don't think so. It was in the cards—nothing could have stopped it."

"I wish I hadn't talked her out of going to India."

"Don't blame yourself, *boychik.* It's not your fault. It's nobody's fault. It's just the way things work out."

"But it's so sad. She was abandoned—rejected by everybody—even me."

"You did everything you could for her."

"I don't know, Milt. The last time I saw her, she asked me to say 'I love you'—"

"And what did you say?"

"Nothing."

"Boychik, why the hell didn't you say it?"

"Maybe because I never did love her."

Milt sighed.

Out of the car window Danny saw people buying Christmas trees in a parking lot. Christmas in Los Angeles—so strange. Red-faced Santas in sleighs pulled by reindeer were suspended above streets barren of snow. He remembered shopping for a tree with Patricia—the squabbles they had, Patricia always choosing one that was too tall to get into the house. Every year Stephanie prepared a Christmas feast topped off with her special plum pudding. There was always mistletoe. . . .

How ironic, he thought. 'Tis the season to be jolly. What a sad Christmas this will be for Patricia.

———

Danny's frantic phone calls to Long Island got him nowhere. The clipped British voice of the butler imparted the news—too politely— that Patricia was attending a church service for her mother open only to family members. Obviously, J.L. didn't consider him a part of the family. The butler condescended to give Patricia his message.

He waited by the phone for hours. That evening she called. He would never forget her hysterical cry, "Daddy, Daddy, what shall I do?"

As he tried to soothe her, the phone clicked off. He was stunned. He dialed again and the same British voice told him bluntly, "Miss Patricia is not available," and hung up. He dialed repeatedly. A continuous busy signal was the only response. Desperate, he paced the room. That poor girl, his own daughter, was crying out for help. He had to do something.

He took the first plane for New York, a charter helicopter to Long Island, then a taxi to J. L. Stoneham's mansion.

"This is where the Stoneham place starts," said the driver to Danny's reflection in his rearview mirror. Huddled in a thin topcoat, Danny looked at the high stone wall as the taxi sloshed through the snow. When it came to a stop, he paid the driver and stepped out. There was no traffic on the quiet street as the taxi sped off, spinning up a spume of gray mush.

A high iron gate festooned with colorful Christmas wreaths blocked the entrance to an immaculately clean winding driveway— even the mounds of snow on either side seemed antiseptically white.

Danny opened the intercom box, aware of the closed-circuit camera eye looking down at him, and rang the buzzer.

Almost immediately, a polite woman's voice came over the speaker. "Merry Christmas, may I help you please?"

"This is Daniel Dennison. I'm here to see my daughter."

"Just a moment, please," came the cheery female response.

He waited, stepping from one foot to the other, the cold seeping up through his shoes.

A gruff man's voice now came through the speaker. "I'm sorry— Miss Patricia can have no visitors." The intercom clicked off.

Danny hit the buzzer again. The pleasant female voice returned. "Merry Christmas, may I help you please?"

"I'm here to see my daughter," he yelled, "and I'm not leaving until I see her!"

There was no response.

Danny hit the buzzer again and again. No response.

He looked up and down the neatly shoveled sidewalk that ran along the wall. Near the service entrance, he noticed a large trash container. He dragged it against the wall and stepped on it. Yes, he could reach the top. As he moved his hand over the edge to get a firm grip, he felt a sharp sting of pain. When he pulled himself up, he saw blood spurting from a deep gash in his icy cold hand. The entire top of the wall was imbedded with jagged pieces of broken bottles. "That son of a bitch," Danny muttered as he wrapped his hand in a handkerchief. He let himself down on the other side into two feet of snow, and began to trudge through a large garden of boxwood hedges trimmed in the shapes of animals, all snow-capped in white. His pants were soaked and his loafers filled with melting snow.

Suddenly he heard barking, and a pair of large black rottweilers came plowing toward him. But before they could reach him, someone yelled, "Halt!" and the dogs stopped in front of him, up to their bellies in snow, snarling and baring long fangs. Two uniformed guards approached with drawn guns. "What the hell are you doing here?" asked the taller one.

"My name is Dennison. I want to see my daughter, Patricia."

The other one pulled out a walkie-talkie, but Danny didn't hear what he said because his words were muffled by the growls of the dogs. He clicked off. "You better leave now, Mr. Dennison, or we'll have to call the police."

"Call them," Danny said stubbornly. "I have a legal right to see my daughter."

The guards exchanged glances, and the one with the walkie-talkie turned away and again communicated with someone. After a long exchange, he put his walkie-talkie into a holder on his belt. "Follow me, Mr. Dennison."

The now-familiar beefy man appeared at the front door of the mansion and politely escorted him inside to a large, book-lined room; in the center, twinkling with hundreds of silver bells, stood a huge Christmas tree, reaching up to the twenty-foot ceiling. The beefy man pointed to the red velvet sofa, but Danny remained standing. His hand was throbbing. He looked down and saw that drops of blood were falling from the soaked handkerchief onto a priceless Oriental rug. He shoved his hand in the pocket of his coat. Through the hidden stereo system a soft voice was singing, "*Noël . . . Noël . . . Noël . . .*"

Patricia walked into the room.

Danny was ripped apart by the anguish and bewilderment he saw in her young face. He wanted to take her into his arms, shower her with kisses, tell her how much he loved her—anything to erase that look—but he just stood there, paralyzed.

"Patricia, I'm here," he said stiffly. "I don't know what to say . . . I'm sorry." He reached out to her.

She backed away. Her eyes were wild and desperate. She looked so thin and somehow taller. So different from that little girl who had laughed with glee as she clung to his leg.

"It's me, your father."

She just stared.

He waited. She said nothing. "Darling, this has been a shock for both of us. But let's give ourselves a chance to heal. Then we'll get together and talk. OK?" He could not keep the pleading tone out of his voice.

Tears were streaming down her cheeks now. She let out an anguished cry and collapsed in hysterical sobs.

He moved toward her, but two men bolted into the room and tackled him. They yanked him to his feet and pulled his arms up behind his back. The pain was excruciating. A large woman in a white uniform herded Patricia out.

J. L. Stoneham entered the room. "You have upset Patricia enough. Get out."

"She is my daughter. I have a right to see her."

"You have no rights. You will never see her again."

"You took Patricia away from Stephanie, but you can't take her away from me!"

J.L. dismissed the guards with a motion of his head. Alone in the room, they confronted each other. Stoneham broke the silence. "I told you I'd destroy you. And by the time I'm through with you, you'll wish you'd never been born—you Jew prick!"

Danny froze.

"Oh yes. I know everything about you—San Sabba, your adoption —you're lucky you didn't end up in the oven, you kike." Danny's head reeled. J.L.'s lips twisted into a smile—he was enjoying the moment. "You thought you pulled the wool over everybody's eyes," he continued. "Well, I'll see that the world knows your dirty little secret."

Dazed, Danny stood rooted to the spot. This man had unearthed a lie buried halfway across the world.

"I'm dreaming of a white Christmas . . ." the soft voice filtered through.

Danny took a deep breath. "I don't care what you do," he said hoarsely. "I only care about my daughter." His voice grew stronger as he moved toward the granitelike figure. He shook his bloody fist. "Do *you* care about her? She's breaking apart. She needs medical attention."

"She'll get the best money can buy."

"You think your money will fix everything. Will more gold bracelets and horses make her forget her mother? You killed Stephanie—"

"That's enough!" Blue veins were standing out in Stoneham's red neck.

"You destroyed your own father. You killed your own wife—"

"I said that's enough!"

"What kind of a monster are you?" J.L. took a step backward. "Do you think I'd let you do the same to Patricia? *My* daughter—my half-*Jewish* daughter?"

J.L.'s narrow eyes widened. "I'll kill you if I have to," he rasped out.

Danny came closer, towering over Stoneham. "Go ahead, you bastard," he said through clenched teeth, "because I'll never give up."

"Get out! Get out! GET OUT!" J.L.'s face turned purple.

The guards rushed in and grabbed Danny. Stoneham was breathing heavily.

As the guards pushed Danny out of the room, he saw Stoneham crumple into an oversized leather chair. Danny's last image was of J.L. staring at the floor where the blood had soaked the carpet.

By the time he boarded the 747 at Kennedy Airport, Danny felt his head was about to burst. It was as if heavy iron bells were tolling inside, and yet they could not obliterate Patricia's screams. He had to think, had to figure out a way to get her out of J.L.'s clutches.

"Jew prick"—with those words J.L. had ripped down the facade that he had so carefully constructed over the years, a facade that he'd believed was impenetrable.

How would Patricia react when she found out her father's secret? Would she say—as he did so many years ago—"I don't want to be a Jew"? Never had Danny felt so helpless, so impotent.

"Merry Christmas," the stewardess said.

Suddenly, he had a strange compulsion to laugh until he cried, and to cry until he was too exhausted to think.

CHAPTER 16

he cat sprang up on the table and rubbed his body against Luba's arm, but she gently pushed him aside. Undaunted, he carefully stepped between the piles of bills in front of her until his soft paws found a sheet of paper that he deemed suitable to curl up on.

Luba groaned. A hell of a way to start the New Year! How could there be so many bills? She had done a drawing of Mrs. McKeever's sister's dog for 100 pounds and sold a small sketch to the plumber for 25, but all that was far from enough. Gently dislodging the cat, she picked up a note from Dorothy regarding a rendezvous with a rock

group that evening. Luba hated to do it, but she had to. At least she
was back in Dorothy's good graces. She crumpled up the message,
tossed it toward the wastepaper basket, and missed; the cat chased
after it and started batting it around.

She added up the bills that still had to be paid. Where would she
get the money? Luba knew that one evening with some young rock
singers would not solve her problem. There was one possible solu-
tion that kept creeping into her mind. What did she have to lose?

————

The next day, without telling Magda where she was going, Luba took
the bus to Victoria Station and bought a round-trip ticket to Brighton.

Greenfields Inn looked bleak and deserted in the chilling drizzle of
winter. A FOR SALE sign on the unkempt lawn instructed interested
buyers to contact the Royal Bank of Brighton. Luba glanced around
—the street was empty this time of year—and approached the entrance. The door was locked. She reached into the flower box, which
still held a bright red plastic geranium. The key was there.

She had an eerie feeling as she walked down the cold corridor of
the empty house, her footsteps making a hollow, echoing sound. She
knew the money had to be here somewhere. Colonel Johnson would
not have hidden it anywhere else. She had thought often enough
about it, mentally searching each room of the hotel. The best bet, she
decided, was the basement. It must be the basement. She remembered the day she first thought him insane when he made her move all
the supplies from the basement to the attic. He clearly didn't want her
going down there. But where in the basement could it be hidden?

She paused at the office door and looked in. Involuntarily, she
shuddered. Slowly, she entered the room of her nightmares. The
rolltop desk was open and bare; his white monkey jacket was hanging
neatly on a coat tree. She wondered what he was wearing in his coffin.
Of course, if he had anything to say about it, he'd want to be buried in
his uniform. She gasped. It had to be!

She moved quickly up the carpeted staircase. She dreaded to think
what Magda must have felt the last time she went up these steps
carrying that box of soap. It was now late in the afternoon, beginning
to get dark. She switched on the hall light, and, resisting an urge to
see if there were any bloodstains at the base of the iron steps, went up
to the attic. At the top, she looked at the boxes of soap and toilet
paper still stacked there. How often she had come up here to hide and
sketch until she was chased away by Colonel Johnson.

There it was on the right against the wall, the wooden trunk on which she had sat so often. She yanked at the heavy top—it was locked.

She ran down the stairs to the kitchen, startling a mouse, which scurried across the floor. In a drawer, she found a mallet and an ice pick, and rushed back. This had to be it; she was certain. Breathing hard, she placed the ice pick against the hinge and started beating it with the mallet. The hinge gave way easily. She lifted up the heavy top. Lying there, neatly folded, were Colonel Johnson's military uniforms, his cap on top. She lifted them out of the trunk. Underneath was a saber, a strange African voodoo doll, a field helmet, and a riding crop. She took them all out and stared at the empty chest. Nothing. She couldn't believe it. She had been so sure. As she bent down to replace the objects, she hesitated. The bottom of the trunk was higher than the base. She leaned over and felt around. In one corner, her finger touched a small tab. When she pulled on it, the floor of the trunk moved. Underneath lay a metal box. She grabbed it with a surge of triumph. It was locked. With a smile, she picked up the mallet.

"Who's there?" a male voice yelled.

Damn! Quickly, she pushed the false bottom back in place, dumped everything inside, except the metal box and one uniform, and closed the trunk. "Who's up there?" The voice was getting closer. She wrapped the box in the uniform and hugged it to herself. She started to go down the iron steps. Looking up at her was a policeman.

"Oh my God—I'm so glad it's you, Sergeant Sweeney—you frightened me."

"Miss Johnson! We do meet in the strangest places. What are you doing here?"

Luba cocked her head and smiled provocatively. "I might ask the same of you." She descended the steps and came close to him.

"I saw the lights, Miss Johnson, and I came in to turn them off."

"Sergeant Sweeney, I hated coming back here alone, but my mother couldn't bear it. You can't imagine how hard this has been for her." She placed her free hand on his arm, and looked into his eyes.

"But Miss Johnson, the house has been sealed by the bank for the sale. Nothing is to be removed."

"Of course—it's just that Mother, in her grief, forgot to take this uniform. Colonel Johnson wore it when he fought in the Mau Mau rebellion. It's part of our family history," she said, her breast pressing against him.

"Well yes . . . it must mean a lot to her . . . but I'm not sure . . ."

Luba's eyes mirrored deep hurt. "Well, if you must . . . here—take it."

"No, no," he said, "I guess it can do no harm."

As they walked down the hallway toward the main staircase, she made sure she stumbled against him.

He put his arm around her waist for support, forgetting about turning out the light. Luba didn't remind him.

"Would it be inappropriate to again invite you for a cup of tea?" he asked shyly, his face flushed.

"You are very thoughtful, but I must make the London train."

"Let me escort you to the station."

"Oh you don't have to do that."

"I'd like to."

"Thank you. I can't miss it—my mother is waiting at home."

"I hope she feels better soon."

She gazed up at him and squeezed his arm. "It will be a long time before she gets over this tragedy."

"Yes, I can understand that," he said with extreme sympathy. "I hope this uniform brings some comfort to her."

"You have no idea what it will do for her," she said, misty eyes locked on his.

When they got to the train station, the loudspeaker was announcing the departure of the London train. About to step aboard, she turned and kissed him full on the mouth. "I can never thank you enough," she said. She left Sergeant Sweeney standing on the platform, agape.

———————

"Luba, where have you—" Magda stared at the uniform in her daughter's arms. "Where did you get that?"

"From his trunk."

"In Brighton?"

"Of course."

"Luba! Are you sick?"

Luba didn't say a word. She threw the uniform on the floor and placed the box on the table.

"What's this?" asked Magda.

Luba just smiled as she brought out a screwdriver and hammer. She placed the screwdriver into the lock and raised the hammer. "Happy New Year!"

With a crash, the box sprang open and piles of pound notes flew out across the table.

Beverly Hills

he studio was closed for the holiday season, so Danny knew he wouldn't be missed. He could hide. The hysteria he had felt on the plane ride home hadn't left him. He bolted the door, pulled down the shades, unplugged the phone, and tried to drink himself into a stupor. But the vodka did nothing to lessen his fear.

When would Stoneham do it? How would people react? Unmasked as a fraud! What would Milt say? It was too much for Danny to handle. And thinking about Patricia petrified him. Was she on the verge of suicide? What could he do for her? Would he be able to help her even if Stoneham relinquished control? He had no answers.

For all his bravado at the mansion, he knew damn well who had won. Stoneham had trapped him in a whirlwind of tangled steel coils that were spinning into a knot around him, tighter and tighter, until he was inextricably bound, unable to act, unable to move, unable to breathe.

He hadn't eaten, slept, or bathed. He just sat there drinking.

He refilled his glass, ignoring the blinking red light on the fax machine. He wanted to sleep, sink into a dreamless sleep and not wake up. But the red light continued to throb, insistently piercing his closed eyelids. He lurched forward to pull the plug. A message lay in the basket, and one word caught his eye: PATRICIA.

He picked up the paper and strained to focus. The fax was from Stoneham's attorneys.

WE WISH TO INFORM YOU THAT PATRICIA IS IN A PRIVATE SANITARIUM IN CAPABLE HANDS. SHE IS DOING WELL. HER PHYSICIANS PREDICT SEVERAL MONTHS OF TREATMENT WILL BE NECESSARY. IN THE BEST INTERESTS OF HER HEALTH, SHE CAN HAVE NO VISITORS FOR THE TIME BEING.

Danny reread the words SHE IS DOING WELL. Thank God! The message didn't say where she was, but he was grateful to hear something—anything—about her. He was grateful for this crumb from J.L. Maybe Stoneham had changed his mind about destroying another person close to Patricia. Could that really be possible? Or was that only his wishful thinking?

———

Danny thought he was pretty successful in covering up his anxiety as he started preparing to film *Everyman*. For the next two months, he immersed himself in auditions, script changes, set designs, locations, rehearsals. He didn't realize how manic he seemed to others until a worried Slim took him aside one day.

"Hey, boss, why are you so uptight? This is not your first flick."

"Well, this film means a lot to me—I've been trying to set it up for years," Danny said, sloughing off Slim's concern.

"Come on, boss. I know you. Something's eating you. Stoneham's takeover is stuck in the courts. It might never—"

"I don't give a damn about him," Danny said more sharply than he intended. "Let's get going."

Slim was taken aback by his abruptness. "OK, boss." He moved away.

The first scene, shot in an abstract style, went well. Danny used actual footage of the stock exchange and blended it with a foreground scene filmed at the studio—a melee of hysterical traders, their hands clutching pieces of paper, their arms waving, as they cried out, "Old money! New money! Borrowed money! Stolen money! Laundered money! All money! More! More! More!"

When he yelled, "Cut! Print!" Danny got a spontaneous ovation from the crew. As he took a mock bow, his eyes focused on Lily, conspicuous in her blue linen dress, her fresh-scrubbed face beaming as she applauded enthusiastically. She was a tremendous help, indispensable. Sensing he was under pressure, she never asked any questions. She was there when he needed her, always cheerful. He was becoming very fond of her.

———

The first week of shooting ended on Friday evening, giving him the weekend to work on script revisions. Things were going well, but Danny was still edgy. On Saturday afternoon, while looking out the window, waiting for Lily's car to pull up at any moment, Danny noticed a brown nondescript sedan slowly making its way up the street, as if the driver were looking for something.

The car stopped in front of his house, and a man dressed in black got out and walked toward the front door. As he came closer, Danny could see the inverted white collar and the cross around his neck—it was a chubby priest, probably looking for donations.

Braced for the encounter, he opened the door. The shiny, round face before him looked baby smooth, as if it had never been touched by a razor. The bald head was fringed with wisps of ginger hair and it surrounded what looked like a yarmulke of shiny skin. The priest was smiling broadly, revealing a gap between his two front teeth. Danny couldn't quite place where he had seen him before.

"Danny Dennison?"

"Yes."

"May I come in?" he asked as Danny still stared.

"Well, I—"

"I'm Father Callahan." With a grin, he added, "But you knew me as Roy."

"Roy?!" Danny's eyes grew wide.

"Yes, Danny."

Danny threw his arms around him in a tight hug and pulled him inside. "Roy! I never thought I'd see you again." He began to babble with excitement. "I tried to track you down, but the orphanage wouldn't give me any information."

"Yes, I know. I tried that too."

Danny stepped back and looked at him. "How did you find me?"

"I recently saw a movie directed by Danny Dennison—*London Rock.*"

Danny winced. "That terrible thing."

"I liked it. And I remembered Mrs. Dennison would take you to the movies all the time, so I followed a hunch."

Danny just shook his head in disbelief.

"I felt like a detective, but the Directors Guild helped me, and here I am, Danny—a little heavier."

"I knew your parents would fatten you up."

"Oh they succeeded—they couldn't do enough for me. They didn't even mind the few times I wet the bed." And he burst out in a hearty laugh.

"I just can't believe it's you, Roy." Danny hugged him again. "Let's go out by the pool, have a drink to celebrate our reunion. What would you like?"

"A beer, maybe—anything so long as it's not red wine. We get that every Sunday."

They couldn't stop laughing—they were so happy to see each other. Danny busied himself opening the beer bottle for Roy, his hands clumsy, unsteady. He poured a vodka for himself. "To us!" He raised his glass.

"To St. John's Orphanage," Roy chuckled.

Danny made a face.

"I can't tell you, Danny, how often I've thought of those days."

They sat down by the pool and just looked at each other, each seeing the little boy in the face of the man now forty years older.

"Roy, Roy . . . Look at you—I never thought you'd become a priest."

"Well, I knew I'd never be a baseball player." They laughed at the memory of Roy sitting out the games. "But seriously," Roy continued, "it's your fault."

"I see. I get blamed for everything—for your wetting the bed, and now for your becoming a priest."

Roy's head went back in another loud peal of laughter. "Oh Danny, I'll never forget those days—that cigar box, the stories you read to me. . . ." He patted Danny's shoulder affectionately. "Your kindness to me affected my life. It made me want to help others. I've been doing God's work in many places, and now I've been given an opportunity to fill a post in Australia, working with the aborigines."

"Australia! That's a long way off, Roy. Now that we've found each other, couldn't it be somewhere closer?"

"I must follow the path that God has put before me." There was an intensity in his voice, communicating the strength of a man certain of his purpose.

"Your parents must be proud of you."

"I'm sure they are, God rest their souls. But they've been gone three years now, killed by a drunken driver in a car accident."

"Oh, what a terrible thing to happen."

"Yes, but I've come to accept their loss. I only feel sorry for the hapless drunk who must live with his guilty conscience."

"Sorry?! I'd want to kill him!"

Roy's cherubic face crinkled in a smile and he looked affectionately at his friend. "It's not for us to judge; we must only feel compassion."

Danny studied his friend in disbelief. "Don't you ever get angry? Don't you ever hate?"

"Yes, I did—when I was younger. But now I understand—" He broke off. "Let's not talk about sad things. Tell me about your life. All I know is that Mrs. Dennison adopted you, and you became a successful movie director. Are you married? Any children? I see you have a lovely home—you must be very happy here."

Danny got up, walked to the end of the patio, and looked off into the hills. After a moment, Roy followed him. Danny felt a gentle hand on his arm.

"My friend, I hear you quietly screaming. What troubles you?"

Danny gave a bitter snort. "I thought in a confessional you are hidden behind a screen."

"It's just me, Danny—Roy, your friend."

"I've been having a tough time. I'm filled with such hate." His voice came from between clenched teeth. "I hate my father-in-law—what he's doing to my daughter, what he did to my wife. . . . I hate the secrets deep in my gut that fill me with guilt. . . . I wish I could tell you about it."

Roy took both of Danny's hands and clasped them in his own. "Don't torment yourself. Maybe you shouldn't talk now. Think about it—look into your heart. At the right time, in the right place, a higher force will help you."

Danny emptied his glass. "Let's have another drink."

Roy sighed. "Unfortunately I can't. I have to get going right now. I'm leaving for down under this evening."

"I hate to see you go, Roy. You have no idea how much . . ." Danny didn't finish. They walked down the steps along the side of the house.

"We'll see each other again, God willing," Roy said.

Danny had a lump in his throat as they approached the car. He felt exactly as he did when Roy left with his cigar box. He hadn't told him his secret then. He couldn't tell it now. He looked at his friend's boyish face, free of wrinkles, free of troubles. "You're happy."

"The feeling I have is more than being happy, Danny. It's being fulfilled—at peace."

"That must be a nice sensation."

"Yes. It's gratifying to find out what you want to do in life and do it. I'm fortunate."

"And this gives you peace?"

"Danny, one is always at peace when one is true to oneself."

They gave each other a last embrace and Roy drove off. Then slowly, very slowly, Danny returned to the house, Roy's last words echoing in his mind.

———

As he came into the living room, he heard music coming from his study upstairs. Lily must have come in while he was out back by the pool. She always liked to have music in the background when she worked. But he wasn't ready to tackle another *Everyman* scene yet.

He sat down in the living room, thinking of his conversation with
Roy. The music filtered in. It was Lily's favorite Tina Turner tape. He
had never paid attention to the words before.

> *Well the men come in these places*
> *And the men are all the same*
> *You don't look at their faces*
> *And you don't ask their name*
> *You don't think of them as human*
> *You don't think of them at all*
> *You keep your mind on the money*
> *Keeping your eyes on the wall*

A whore's lament. Is that the way Luba felt? But she never took any
money from him. Why?

He got up quickly, brushing away the answer. He had resolved to
push her out of his life; he wasn't going to start thinking of her now.
He went up the stairs to his study and turned the stereo down.

"Oh, I'm sorry it was so loud," Lily apologized, "but music is my
addiction—I've got to cure it."

"No, no—I like music too."

"I saw you at the pool with a priest, and I didn't want to overhear
your confession," she giggled.

"Well, it was almost that."

As she turned on the word processor, she said, "I didn't know you
were Catholic."

"I'm not."

"What are you?"

He looked at her open face waiting for a simple answer and hesitated. "I'm Episcopalian. The priest was an old schoolmate. He has
something in common with you."

"Oh really? What's that?"

"He liked *London Rock* too."

She laughed. "Well, he'll love *Everyman*. Shall we go to work?"

"Yeah. Where was I?"

"You wanted to rework the section where Everyman dumps toxic
waste in a bird sanctuary."

"Yes, I'm going to add a scene where he bribes the park superintendent."

"You mind if I say something?"

"Can anyone stop you?"

She pouted. "I think you're too hard on Everyman."

Danny looked at her quizzically.

"He's so evil. There's a danger of him becoming a caricature."

"Lily, I think I can avoid that pitfall."

"I don't mean to be a smart-ass—"

"So how come you succeed so often?"

She made a gesture as if to punch him. "Seriously—you always say that drama is contrast, light and shade."

"That's right."

"I think you need a Rosebud scene."

"*Citizen Kane?*"

"Yes, remember—he was an evil man too, but on his deathbed he thought of his most precious possession—a tiny sled he had when he was a boy. There was a time when he was innocent."

"Not Everyman." Danny's voice hardened. "He's modeled on J. L. Stoneham, and my father-in-law was never innocent—he was born evil."

Taken aback by his vehemence, Lily sat mutely in her chair.

Danny paced the room, trying to pull his thoughts together. "I don't feel much like working," he finally said.

"Do you want to take a lunch break?"

"I'm not hungry. It's too hot."

"Take a dip in the pool, then. Cool off. I'd like that myself."

"Good idea. There must be a bathing suit for you around here somewhere."

"Oh come on, Danny." She turned off the word processor. "For a guy who writes scenes with naked girls running across rooftops, you're awfully prudish." Then she laughed at his surprised face. "What happened to that old-fashioned American institution known as skinny-dipping?"

"What?"

But she had already disappeared into the bathroom, calling out, "I'll get some towels."

A little unsure of what to do, Danny pushed open the sliding glass door leading from his study to the patio, and stepped out. He hesitated, then threw off his clothes and dove in. Coming up for air, he saw her standing at the edge of the pool, naked. Yes, she was a peasant girl laughing in the sun.

"Is it cold?" she called out.

"It's terrific!"

She made a nice clean dive, and came up beside him. "Oh, you liar —it's freezing!" And off she swam. They frolicked in the water for about ten minutes. It felt so natural. Good wholesome fun.

She jumped out first and ran shivering back into the study. He followed her and watched her rubbing herself with a towel, in rhythm to the music.

She's beautiful, and she knows it, he thought.

"Feel better?" she asked, drying her hair.

"Much."

"Ready to go to work?"

He walked slowly toward her, the water dripping from his body. "I think so," he said softly. "How about you?"

"Almost." She let the towel drop. She reached up and put her arms around him. The effect of her touch was electric.

His hands feverishly caressed her breasts, shoulders, thighs, as he brought her down under him on the rug, his erect cock pressing against her.

His need was immediate, urgent. He pushed into her. She was ready.

The same song he heard before came on again:

All the men come in these places
And the men are all the same

Suddenly, he shriveled up. He tried, but the feeling was gone. He slipped off of her and lay beside her.

"Are you all right, Danny?"

"I'm sorry—"

She put her fingers on his lips. "Shhh, don't be."

"I don't know why—"

"These things happen."

"I'm suddenly impotent."

She turned on her side to face him. "Women are impotent sometimes, but men seldom know it; we can fake it."

"Yeah," he said, "a man can't fake an erection."

"You've been under a lot of stress—juggling a lot of problems—while making a great movie."

"For a smart-ass, you're a very sweet person," he said.

"Danny, let me fix you something to eat—I'm a great cook."

He shook his head. "Why is it all the women in my life want to cook for me? Do I look undernourished?"

"No," she giggled. "I just thought a nice meal might relax you. I could stay the night—we could cuddle—no sex, just affection."

"Thanks, Lily—for everything. But I think I'd like to be alone."

After she left, he threw a robe around himself and walked out on the patio.

He was bewildered. Lily was the perfect woman—beautiful, full of mirth and self-confidence, yet wholesome. He could still see her standing naked at the edge of the pool—fine breasts, a triangular patch of brown between her legs matching her shiny brown hair. He wanted her. What happened?

That goddamn song, reminding him of Luba! It made him angry. He ought to smash the cassette. Then he caught himself. How ridiculous could he be? He shook his head with a wry grin. No matter what happened, he blamed Luba.

CHAPTER 17

1988 | New York

he blades of the helicopter slowly started to rotate. Then, as they picked up speed, they whirled in an invisible blur that matched the spinning thoughts in Danny's head. He did not bring Lily to New York. He couldn't. He felt awkward, embarrassed, although she was still the same sassy girl, eager to please. He left her behind at the studio to prepare the film footage for editing.

The helicopter now swerved past the World Trade Center. Danny looked out the window at the skyline of New York. At least the picture was coming along well; he was anxious to start putting it together.

Despite everything that had happened, he felt strangely content. Maybe this was how his father felt when he had completed his crucifixion.

The helicopter was now hovering over Wall Street, deserted on a Sunday. This would be the final scene in the movie—the delirium sequence. The camera, secured in the open door, was focused on a young man standing on a corner. Danny could see Slim below, relaying his last-minute instructions to the actor.

The makeup man sprayed more "sweat" on Everyman's face; the hairdresser tousled his hair in an attractive manner. Through a bullhorn, Slim shouted, "Everybody clear!" The crew surrounding the actor ran off into a building, leaving a lonely, tormented figure staring up at the heavens.

"Camera ready?" yelled Danny over the intercom.

The cameraman signaled OK.

"Action!" The helicopter swooped to the figure of Everyman, who was now reaching out in all directions, pleading for help. It lingered over the scene and then slowly moved up the side of the building—shades snapping shut on each window in quick succession, rejecting Everyman's pleas—floor after floor to the roof. There, the camera focused on a naked girl, a hidden wind machine blowing out her long blond tresses. She looked down below and called out, "Everyman! Everyman!"

The helicopter banked to the opposite building, allowing the camera to pan across a setting sun and rest on another naked girl, this one with flaming red hair reflecting the rays from a spotlight. She pointed down into the street and cried out, "Everyman!"

The camera now panned down to the small figure below, as Edward Everyman slowly crumpled to the ground, dead.

"Cut!" Danny yelled.

"We got it!" the triumphant cameraman signaled back. Danny gave the order, and the helicopter spun around and headed for the heliport. The early-spring light was already leaving the sky; they finished just in time. He leaned back against the seat and looked down at the lone figure of the Statue of Liberty, a symbol to millions of immigrants escaping oppression in foreign lands—refugees like Luba. Luba had never seen the Statue of Liberty, but she would appreciate it. He imagined her standing below looking up at the Lady, one strong woman to another. The statue's arm, raised in greeting, seemed to be hailing him. And then her lantern lit up. It was a good omen.

London

agda was in the kitchen, stirring the sauce for the *goląbki*. This was the dish she had made for Danny and Luba in Portugal. How happy Luba was then, in love with Danny, who seemed so very warm and affectionate with her. But Magda had worried from the start that it would come to no good.

The little poodle was squirming at her feet; she leaned down and gave him a small morsel of the spicy ground meat. "You like *goląbki* too, don't you, little one?"

Magda remembered how Luba's eyes twinkled when she looked at Danny. Poor Luba. All she did anymore was stay inside and paint, paint, paint. Magda was glad that she managed to convince her today to get out and do the shopping. For so long Luba had tried to get Magda out of the house. But now their roles were reversed.

It made Magda sad that even with their financial worries gone, Luba still couldn't enjoy herself. Colonel Johnson's money made them almost rich. No more shoplifting; no more waiting for the escort service to call. Luba should be happy.

Letting the sauce simmer, Magda wearily sat down in the living room, which was littered with paint jars and boxes of brushes. She looked at the unfinished canvas resting on a real easel that she had bought for Luba to replace the old music stand. Luba barely noticed. What could she do for her daughter?

For so long Luba wouldn't let anyone see her paintings. And yet Magda remembered how happy her daughter was when Mrs. McKeever had bought one, and then the plumber.

She got up and opened the door to the closet where Luba's paintings were stored; it was crammed. She picked up one canvas—the silhouettes on the beach. It seemed to her very well done. How much talent did Luba have? Only one way to find out.

Magda went into the kitchen, turned off the stove, and quickly washed her hands. She took the painting, wrapped it carefully in a tablecloth, and, throwing on her coat, left the apartment.

Clutching the painting to her body, Magda walked back and forth the length of Mount Street, trying to muster the courage to enter one of the fashionable galleries. In the window of Geoffrey's she could see several beautiful paintings. Was she being stupid? She liked Luba's better, but what did she know?

As she peered in the window, she caught the intimidating eyes of a spindly lady staring at her through thick glasses. She took a breath and walked in.

Inside, several customers were browsing among the lithographs. The tall lady immediately approached her as if to block her path. "May I help you?"

Magda let the tablecloth fall to the floor. "This my daughter make. You like?"

The woman's nose seemed to twitch. She barely glanced at the painting. "I'm sorry, madam—we only deal with recognized artists."

" 'Scuse me," Magda mumbled. Dejectedly she stooped to pick up the tablecloth.

"Please wait a moment." A tall man wearing a dark suit and a silk cravat approached, umbrella in hand. His eyes were glued to the painting. "I like it—I like it very much."

"Yes, Lord McFadden, it is very interesting," the spindly proprietress said quickly.

The man's gaze shifted from the painting to Magda. "Who is the artist?"

Beverly Hills

t was midnight before Danny got home from the airport. Every bone in his body cried out for rest—a well-earned rest. The shooting in New York was finally over, and he couldn't wait to start the editing. His bed had never looked so inviting; he snuggled between the freshly laundered sheets, and their comforting whisper was the last thing he remembered before he crashed into unconsciousness.

Through a thick haze of sleep Danny heard someone pounding on the door, but he only wrapped his blanket more tightly around himself. The pounding continued. Resigned, he got out of bed—the clock said one-fifteen—and stumbled to the door in his pajamas.

As soon as he opened it, he wished he hadn't. Standing before him was the beefy man in the plaid suit. His face was expressionless. "Mr. Stoneham wishes to see you."

Danny shook his head in disbelief.

"The plane is waiting at the airport," the man was saying.

"Are you crazy?"

"Mr. Stoneham insists."

"Mr. Stoneham can go to hell."

"It's urgent. You can be back in Los Angeles in twelve or thirteen hours."

Danny tried to slam the door, but the meaty hand held it back.

"It's about Patricia."

Danny felt suddenly queasy. "What's the matter with Patricia? Where is she?"

"Mr. Stoneham will explain. Patricia is fine, but he must speak with you."

Danny dressed quickly and followed the beefy man out to the limo.

At the private sector of the Burbank airport, revved up and waiting, was Stoneham's 707, its name painted in large gold letters: THE PATRICIA. Somehow, Danny resented seeing his daughter's name on the gargantuan belly of J.L.'s plane. The steward quickly led him up the steps through one salon after another: There was a fully furnished office, with computers, telephones, fax machines; another room looked like a library removed from some Tudor mansion; there was a sitting room, a dining room, flowers, bowls of fresh fruit, crystal decanters of liquor. The steward—there seemed to be at least four of them besides the cockpit crew—took him into a lavishly decorated bedroom, where a pair of silk pajamas had been laid out for him. "Before you retire, perhaps you wish something to eat," the steward said. "The chef can prepare a steak, omelet, anything." Danny shook his head.

The steward started to explain the various buttons on the bed's headboard, but Danny waved him away, not listening. Fully clothed, he threw himself down on the bed; he felt fuzzy-headed from exhaustion, and he was trembling with anxiety—what would J.L. spring on him now?

He couldn't believe he was on this plane, lying in J.L.'s bed, on his way to see him in Long Island. The speed of the events gave him little time to think, but he didn't want to think—he just wanted to see Patricia.

He kept pushing the buttons, trying to turn the lights out, but instead he activated the wall-sized television screen before him, which now displayed a map of the United States with a little red plane, glowing like a cigarette ember, making its way across. Danny closed his eyes and tried to doze, but his thoughts wouldn't let him. He opened his eyes to see that the little plane was over Nevada. Below the screen, a series of numbers kept constantly changing: speed 640 MPH, altitude 47,000 feet, remaining flight time four hours and five minutes, external temperature –42. He closed his eyes, and must have slept, because when he opened them again the little red plane had left Nebraska, and the remaining flight time was two hours and ten minutes.

At Kennedy Airport, in the bright morning sunlight, another limo was waiting for him on the runway. The instant Danny got in, it drove off; he let his head fall against the seat cushion. Was it just six hours ago that he was sleeping peacefully in Beverly Hills? Stoneham certainly had a dramatic way of doing things.

The limo stopped, the driver opened the door, and Danny got out. He wasn't in Long Island, but Manhattan—in front of Lenox Hill Hospital at Seventy-seventh Street and Park Avenue. Was Patricia here? The beefy man had said she was fine. He braced himself as a white-clad man led him without a word to the elevators and on to the intensive-care unit.

The darkened room made the screens of heart monitors appear brilliantly alive, their high-pitched beeps keeping time with the jagged lines. There were six beds in a semicircle, only partially obscured by curtains so the nurses could easily observe the patients.

Danny barely recognized J.L. He seemed to have shriveled. His normally red face had a pale yellow tint and translucent green tubes stuck out of his nose and arms. But the watery eyes had not lost their intensity. They pierced through Danny as the raspy voice spoke from the bed. "I don't like you one bit—not one bit."

"The feeling is mutual," Danny said curtly. "Why did you bring me here?"

"Listen and don't interrupt," Stoneham commanded.

They stared at each other. Stoneham took a shallow breath. It seemed to be painful for him to talk. "I want to make a deal—"

"Did you say a deal?"

"I told you not to interrupt," J.L. snapped.

Even flat on his back, he's got to be in control, Danny thought.

"I will withdraw my takeover bid for Ace Films. . . . I will destroy all records of my investigation . . ." He coughed. "Keep your dirty little secret."

Danny winced. He waited—what would be the price?

The raspy voice spat out the words in answer to his unspoken question. "Patricia . . . is never to know . . . that you're a Jew."

Something deep down within Danny started churning. He laughed harshly. "That's funny. A deal I can't refuse? Not long ago, you wanted to shout my 'dirty little secret' to the world. Now you want to guard it." His words were heavy with sarcasm. "I make no deals for Patricia. Do what you want."

"I always do." The lips twisted oddly beneath the green tube.

Danny turned to leave.

"Dennison!"

Danny stopped.

"Tomorrow I'm having a triple bypass. They tell me I have a fifty-fifty chance of making it." J.L. rested his head back on the pillow, as if pooling his energy to speak. "If I don't make it, Patricia gets everything." His voice grew weaker. "There is no one else."

Danny's eyes focused on the drops of clear liquid trickling down through the intravenous tube.

With another sharp intake of breath, J.L. continued, "If it happens, I expect you to look after her."

Danny's heart began to beat faster. Was this life imitating art? He had just shot this scene—Everyman taking inventory, desperately seeking absolution. He almost felt sorry for J.L. "Of course I'll look after my own daughter."

"Don't be so cocky, Dennison. If you don't see my obituary in the Monday paper, assume I'm alive."

Los Angeles

ack at the studio, Danny shook his head, trying to think clearly. It was the third time he had asked the editor to run the opening frames of his film, but he wasn't seeing what was in front of him. His mind kept replaying the events of the last forty-eight hours.

At the moment of reckoning, J.L. had summoned him; his archenemy had offered to keep his secret forever. It was unbelievable.

Milt came barging in with a bottle of champagne. "Did you see this, *boychik*? It's all over!" he shouted, holding up the *Daily Variety*. The headline read:

STONEHAM QUITS ACE TAKEOVER

"What did I tell you—ha, what did I tell you?" Milt grinned. "Like a smart man once said, a problem is a point of view. We got lots to celebrate."

"Does it say anything about his operation?"

"You can't kill that son of a bitch—when he found out the millions he made on the stock rise of Ace Films he must have jumped out of bed." The cork popped open, sending a stream of champagne all over Milt's shirt. "Holy shit—Sarah will kill me."

"How *are* things with Sarah?"

"Danny, you should be proud of me—I've been an angel." He flapped his elbows like wings.

They drank the warm champagne from plastic cups. "Oh—I almost forgot," Milt said. "Art Gunn wants to know when he can screen the rough cut. Can you give me some idea how long you expect the editing and mixing to take?"

"OK—I'll figure it out and get back to you," Danny said wearily; the champagne was acting on him like a sleeping pill.

Milt peered at him over his spectacles. "You look tired."

"I haven't had much sleep lately. I came home and I had to go to New York again."

Milt laughed, assuming he was joking. "Well, don't kill yourself. We've got a lot more celebrating to do. Sarah wants to have you over —you and Lily Kane." Milt winked, but Danny didn't react.

"Miltie," he said wearily. "For the next month I'll be locked up here with this editing machine."

———

Danny was dead tired. Finally, unable to concentrate, he decided he wouldn't get anything done that day, and drove home.

As he entered the house, he saw the red light on the fax machine blinking. He picked up the message:

MR. STONEHAM WISHES TO INFORM YOU THAT PATRICIA'S DOCTORS WILL PERMIT HER TO HAVE VISITORS SHORTLY. SHE IS IN LE MONT SANITARIUM IN LAUSANNE, SWITZERLAND. UPON RELEASE, SHE WILL BE ENROLLED AT THE PREPARATORY SCHOOL THERE, IF THAT MEETS WITH YOUR APPROVAL.

Danny reread the words IF THAT MEETS WITH YOUR APPROVAL. Did that really come out of J.L.'s lips? And at last—permission to see Patricia. His eyes misted over. He read the fax again. Was J.L. a human being after all? Maybe he too was devastated by the suicide of his daughter, and frightened that it could happen to his granddaughter. Maybe he learned something with death peering over his shoulder. For the first time, Danny had almost a warm feeling toward his father-in-law.

He couldn't avoid Lily forever. When he saw her again, she acted as if nothing had ever happened between them, but Danny felt ill at ease. He tried to spend as little time with her as possible during editing. Her sweet wholesome face was an irritant now—he couldn't help but feel that she was pitying him. He would be relieved when her job was finished.

He loved this film. He never tired of watching his favorite scene: the camera panning up from the distraught figure of Everyman to the windows of the World Trade Center—each identical, like the blocks in a giant honeycomb of corruption—coming to rest on the body of a beautiful, sensuous woman silhouetted against an ominous sky.

"Excuse me, Danny," Lily broke into his thoughts. She was peering over his shoulder. "Am I stupid? And don't answer that question," she added with her usual grin. "But why are those girls naked?"

Danny gave her a steely look. "I want them devoid of any materialistic accoutrements." He hated how pompous he sounded.

She returned his intense gaze.

"Lily, they represent the seduction of greed, power, ego. What better way to show a seduction than through a naked woman?"

Lily said softly, "I hope it works."

"I thought you liked this project."

"I do, but . . ."

"But what?" he snapped.

"Nothing, Danny, nothing."

Danny went back to the editing machine, but his mind kept churning around her words—"I hope it works."

———

Kathy was playing the piano—badly. Nothing has changed, Danny thought. She hasn't improved in thirty years. Sarah had not improved in her cooking either. Thank God Jonathan couldn't make it; he was just as obnoxious at age thirty-seven as he had been at seven, maybe more so, because he was also fat and balding.

Throughout dinner Sarah showered her attentions on Milt: "Miltie darling, this is your favorite—gefilte fish."

"Sarah sweetheart, you shouldn't have."

Danny knew that Milt meant it—she shouldn't have. There was nothing Milt hated more than gefilte fish, which he compared to frogs in formaldehyde.

Danny looked around the table. Everyone was eating with such zest. Milt was devouring the gefilte fish with feigned relish, smiling appreciatively at Sarah between bites. What a guy! Was it that long ago that Milt came over to USC to look at his little film? Agents didn't do that anymore; they didn't go out and search for talent—they waited for you to become a star, and then they condescended to handle the deal. Milt still went to USC every year.

Milt caught Danny watching him and grinned. He tapped his wineglass, cleared his throat, and stood up. "Here's to Danny—one of the first clients I ever had in this business. He came to my office, back at Famous Artists, when I was the last one at the end of the hall. He had just made a short film called *Rescued*—wasn't it, Danny?"

"*Saved,*" Sarah broke in.

"Yes, I'll never forget," Milt continued. "I knew he had talent then. And believe me, it makes me feel good to see my faith justified." He looked around the room with a smile. "That ten percent has paid for all the furniture in this room, including the wallpaper." It was hard to tell if he was joking or not. Suddenly, he stopped smiling. "Tomorrow, we will see for the first time a new Dennison film, *Everyman.*" His voice became hoarse with emotion. "Danny, I know that with this film you, my best friend"—his eyes were struggling to hold back the tears; Sarah was already sniffling—"will rise to a new plateau in filmmaking. *Mazel tov!*" He gulped down the wine.

Danny leaned against the wall of the editing room, watching the boy load the cans of film on a dolly. Each was marked EVERYMAN in bold ink. That evening the studio would see the rough cut for the first time. It was now out of his hands. As the dolly rolled away, he had a desire to clutch the cans of film and take them home.

Lily came in carrying her raincoat and book bag. "Well, I guess this is good-bye, Danny."

"What do you mean?"

"My job is through. You don't need me anymore—for anything."

Danny was flustered by her calm directness. "Aren't you going to wait for the reaction?"

"There is nothing I can do about that—good or bad." She smiled weakly.

"Why are you so negative?" Danny's nerves were getting the better of him. He couldn't stop himself.

"I'm not negative, Danny. I sincerely hope they love it."

"But *you* don't, certainly."

"Listen, Danny—"

"Maybe it is better if you leave," he said flatly, busying himself with some papers.

He felt her staring at him. Then she left without a word. He wished he had handled that better. If anything, the conversation had made him all the more jumpy.

When he got home, he paced around the living room as he listened to the messages on his answering machine.

"Danny—I love ya, *boychik.* I'll see you when it's over, and I'm saying a prayer for you."

Danny's hands felt clammy.

He picked up the mail that the day maid had left on his desk. Absentmindedly, he glanced through it, throwing the junk mail in the wastebasket. There was a postcard with a picture of two baby koala bears hugging each other on a tree branch. He turned it over.

The aborigines are wonderful people. I have made many friends. But there will always be only one friend like you. God Bless You.

Roy

Two people he loved were so far away, Roy in Australia and Patricia in Switzerland. As soon as the preview was over he would fly to Switzerland, take Patricia on a hike; maybe they could go sailing on Lake Geneva. Alone together, they could talk at last. What would he tell her . . . ?

Bing-bong! Bing-bong! The grandfather clock was measuring out the hour. Five. They would be shuffling into their seats now. He had suggested an early-evening viewing. He hated late showings, when everyone was filled with food and drink and falling asleep. Five o'clock was the twilight hour, the right time to see *Everyman,* just as he had seen it in Salzburg.

He got up; he just couldn't sit there waiting. He had to return to the studio. There was such a heavy turnout to see his film it was difficult to find a parking spot. He shut off the ignition and sat quietly. Then, on impulse, he left the car and entered a side door, walking slowly down the deserted hallway to the projection room. He glanced at the posters on the walls depicting scenes from important movies: *It Happened One Night, Lawrence of Arabia, On the Waterfront, The Bridge on the River Kwai.* How nice it would be, he thought, to have a scene from *Everyman* join this elite collection.

He pressed his ear to the door. Silence. They were engrossed in the film. He let out a deep sigh, said a silent prayer, and went out.

He tried to make himself comfortable in his car, but he kept fidgeting, glancing at the clock, imagining what scenes they were watching. Finally, it was six-fifty—time for the helicopter shot at the end of the movie.

Soon after, he heard voices. He felt his heartbeat quickening as he got out. Shielded from view behind his car, he watched them leave the building and head toward the parking lot. He strained to listen.

"What was that crap all about?"

"It's worse than *Last Year at Marienbad.*"

"You could put everyone that wants to see that goddamn mess in a phone booth."

Danny stood there, stunned. Then he felt an arm around his shoulders. He looked directly into Milt's soft, sympathetic eyes.

"It wasn't good?" he asked in a childish whisper.

"Danny—" Milt clutched his shoulder firmly. "Sure it was good, too good, but good for what? Who'll see it?"

Art Gunn's voice cut in: "You've spent too much time in Europe."

Danny looked at Gunn, cigar hanging from the corner of his mouth, shaking his head. "We can't even release this masterpiece." With a laugh, Gunn turned to Milt. "Suddenly he wants to win the Cannes Film Festival with a movie that only six unemployed intellectuals in a bistro can understand!"

"That's enough, Art," Milt said protectively. "We'll work something out."

"Of course we will. It was low-budget. We agreed to cross-collateralize it against *Paris Rock.* Don't feel too bad, Danny," he said, walking away.

As the cars started to leave the lot, someone yelled in a loud falsetto voice, "Everyman!" The shout was picked up by another. Danny shrank back in the gathering darkness, listening to the roaring motors of expensive cars and the laughter and cacophony of falsetto voices: "Everyman—Everyman—Everyman."

It was quiet now. Danny felt absolutely nothing.

Milt was still there. "Let's go to Chasen's and get something to eat."

"I'm not hungry," Danny said in a low voice.

"You OK?"

"Sure—and thanks, Milt."

But Milt didn't leave. "Danny, your film is brilliant."

"Cut it out, Milt."

"It is, Danny, but brilliant movies aren't salable now. They want blood and guts . . . chainsaws . . . vampires . . . ."

"Or *Paris Rock,*" Danny said bitterly.

Milt took his arm, "Come on, *boychik*—let's go home."

————

At Danny's house, they headed straight for the bar. Milt poured each of them a double vodka. They gulped the liquor in silence.

"I wanted to make a difference," Danny said morosely.

"*Boychik,* you wanted to get even with your father-in-law." Milt quietly refilled their glasses. "Forget it—do *Paris Rock.* Think of the dough."

Half the bottle was gone before either spoke.

"Did *you* like it?" Danny asked.

Milt peered at him through his eyeglasses. "What?"

"*Everyman!*" Danny was irritated.

"Give me another drink."

Danny reached over to pour, and the vodka spilled across the bar. He looked intently at Milt. "Answer me—did *you* like it?"

Milt let out a deep sigh. "Kafka."

"Kafka?"

Milt nodded and took a swallow.

"You compare *Everyman* to the story of some dumb Jew?"

"Stop talking like an anti-Semite." Milt's voice had an edge to it. "I'm telling you because I'm your friend. Your film is artsy-fartsy. It's . . . I don't know . . . a little phony. It misses."

"What the hell are you talking about?"

"Like that Kafka film. It missed too."

"But that was a stupid story—an old Jew waiting to be told what his crime was."

"Kafka's story is a classic."

"Classic?" Danny's voice was laced with contempt. "His crime was that he was a Jew."

"Easy, Danny—don't forget you're talking to *me.*"

"And I don't forget what you just said about the best thing I've ever done."

"Danny, Danny—you want the truth or bullshit?"

"I want the truth."

"I just told you the truth—it's a flop!"

"You're an asshole!"

"So are you!" Milt yelled.

"Don't compare Everyman with a dumb groveling Jew!"

"Well, fuck you, you WASP! Your picture stinks!"

"Shut up! Shut up!" the words came out of Danny's mouth, each phrase rising in intensity until the last one was a shriek: "SHUT UP!"

He towered over the smaller man. Milt's eyes bulged like a frog's behind his thick glasses, his mouth wide open. Without giving him a chance to say a word, Danny yelled, "You want a drink? Here!" He threw the vodka into Milt's face. A piece of ice cracked one of his lenses, but the agent just sat there, hunched up, as if completely paralyzed, the liquid dripping down his face.

Danny raged on. "I don't care what you think. I don't give a damn about you, your girlfriend, your wife, or your kids. And I don't give a shit if your cock is in Marilyn or in Sarah. Get out." Milt didn't move.

"GET OUT!" shrieked Danny, grabbing Milt by the lapels and propelling him toward the door.

Milt stumbled out of the room. "Jew-hater!" he yelled as he slammed the front door.

Danny ran after him. He wanted to shout, "But I am a Jew!"

He couldn't. The words stuck in his throat.

CHAPTER 18

1988 | Beverly Hills

fter Milt stormed out, Danny, gasping for breath, staggered around the room, clutching the nearly empty bottle of vodka. He stumbled against a chair, doubled over, but held on. As he drained the remains his eyes focused on the fish tank. The last four fish were floating on the surface. With an animal-like yell, he hurled the bottle at the tank. The glass shattered and the water gushed out. He watched it running over the neatly bound scripts of the movies he had made. Milt had helped him through every one of them, from the very beginning. Milt was his best friend. They loved each other. How could he have abused Milt that way?

He slumped down into a chair, hating himself more than ever. With his head in his hands, he sobbed, "I'm sorry, Milt . . . I'm sorry." But he couldn't erase the image of his friend's bearded face dripping vodka, staring at him through cracked eyeglasses in horror.

He picked up the phone. He had to beg Milt's forgiveness.

Sarah answered.

"This is Danny. Is Milt there?"

"I thought he was with . . . Oh, he's just walking in. Hold on."

Danny sighed with relief. His friend would forgive him. Miltie would understand. They would patch things up.

"Danny—" It was Sarah's voice.

"Yes."

"Milt says he doesn't want to talk to you—ever." And she hung up.

His chin fell against his chest. It's my fault, he thought. All my fault. Then he heard a buzzing noise—the phone was still in his hand. He replaced it. With an effort, he lifted himself up and walked into the bathroom. He felt hollow inside, completely alone. He picked up a towel to wipe his face and stared in the mirror.

For the first time, he saw himself clearly—a middle-aged man living a lie, a Jew who made it a crime to be a Jew. Luba was right: He was a phony, a complete phony. That's why his film had failed.

London

anny didn't call to tell her he was coming. She might have stopped him, just when he needed her most. Luba was the only one left.

It was raining in London, as usual. He walked out with his garment bag and found a cab. When he arrived at her apartment, he suddenly felt frightened—what if she refused to let him in? Should he have the cab wait? He paid the driver, walked up to the front door, and pressed the button for her apartment.

Magda's voice answered. "Yes?"

"Danny."

She said nothing. He waited. Then the buzzer sounded. He climbed the two flights, and the door opened. He stood there with his wet hair plastered to his forehead; his eyes were bloodshot, a stubble covered his face, and dark shadows circled his eyes. Magda's first words were "Danny, you look terrible."

Avoiding her eyes, he asked, "Where's Luba?"

"I don't know," she answered hesitantly.

"When is she coming home?"

"I don't know."

"I'd like to wait. May I come in?" Magda seemed flustered, but she stepped aside, and he walked into the living room, which was cluttered with Luba's paintings. Some were in cardboard cases, others leaned against the walls. "Are you moving?" he asked.

"No, no—Luba putting painting in art gallery," Magda said with a smile. "On Mount Street."

"Hmm, that's a fancy street."

"Yes, they like Luba's work."

"I like it too," Danny said as he picked up the painting of himself as a satyr. The silence in the room was punctuated by the rain beating against the window. It was now pouring.

"Danny," he heard Magda's voice say timidly. "Please—no hurt my daughter."

"Magda, how could I hurt Luba? She's been wonderful to me. She helped me. I would never hurt her."

"Bullshit!" Luba's voice was strident as she stormed out of the bedroom. "You selfish son of a bitch! You treat me like the cheapest whore and walk out. Who the hell asked you to come back?!"

Danny was startled by her vehemence. "I want to make it up to you," he said softly.

"Bullshit!" yelled Luba. "You got a problem, and you're running home to Mama!"

"You're right, Luba." He made a faint attempt at a smile.

Without pausing, Luba went on. "You drag out of me every secret, wring me dry like a wet washcloth, and throw me away when you don't want me."

"I want you, Luba—I've always wanted you."

"You're so full of crap." Luba threw herself down on the couch. Magda unobtrusively left the room and went into the kitchen.

"I'm sorry, Luba, but my problems—"

"Sure! Everybody's got problems. All God's children got problems."

Magda came back in with a steaming bowl of vegetable soup. She put it down on the coffee table in front of Danny. "Take off your wet coat," she said.

Grateful, Danny obeyed. He didn't want to leave. Magda took his coat into the kitchen to dry.

The soup tasted good.

Luba waited until he finished it. "You feel better?" she asked in a more civil tone.

"Yeah," he said, pushing the bowl away.

"Well, I do too. I wanted to tell you off for a long time." Before he could answer she said something to Magda in Polish. Soon he heard the tap running and the dog yapping. "You're a mess. Take a bath and go to sleep. You can use Magda's bed." And she left the room.

Danny got up, took his wallet and traveler's checks out of his coat pocket, and put them on the table. Luba came back with a robe.

"Here." She tossed it to him. "Get some sleep before you fall down."

He pointed to the table. "Take what you need for the rent—"

"I don't need your money—I never did."

"I know, I know." He stood, head down, fidgeting with the robe like one of the boys at the orphanage being reprimanded by the mother superior. He raised his eyes. "Maybe we can use it for a trip. Anywhere you'd like. Let's just go somewhere." Luba didn't respond.

Magda came out of her bedroom carrying a bundle of clothes, the little poodle at her heels.

"I hope I'm not kicking you out, Magda."

"No, no. Luba right—you go in there and rest."

Danny put his long body into the hot tub and soaked. When he returned to the bedroom, his bag was unpacked, and his pajamas were laid out on the turned-down bed. He put them on and crawled in. He was tired, dead tired.

Luba came in with a glass of water and a pill. "Take this—you need it."

He did as he was told. She stood there, looking down at him. He reached up to her.

"No, no," she said. "I don't want to find a corpse lying on top of me."

Danny detected a hint of amusement in her voice. He patted the bed, inviting her to sit down.

She gave in. "But no bedtime stories."

Now he could see that she was smiling.

"How did *Everyman* go?" she asked.

He didn't answer. Luba waited patiently. She took his hand and held it.

Finally, he said in a whisper, "They laughed—they laughed at it."

Luba squeezed his hand.

"They laughed," he said in a louder voice. "They laughed at me." He clenched his eyes shut to hold back the tears.

Luba gently caressed his hand, giving him time to compose himself. "Danny," she said, "things don't always work out the way we want. Go to sleep. Tomorrow we'll go somewhere and talk about it."

"Where?"

"I'll think of a place. Trust me?"

"Yeah," he said in a sleepy voice; the pill was beginning to work.

Luba kissed him gently on the lips. As he dozed off, he thought he heard her say, "I'm glad you're here."

————

Danny had slept ten solid hours. They told him that he fell asleep at nine o'clock, and it was now after seven. He could smell bacon and coffee in the kitchen as he shaved off his stubble. Luba was on the telephone.

They had breakfast in the kitchen. He liked that; it felt cozy. He finished everything on his plate. Then the doorbell rang.

"The taxi's here—let's go," Luba announced.

"Taxi?" Danny asked, looking at the bags by the door. "Where are we going?"

"You'll find out," she said in a haughty tone.

Danny was surprised that Magda was going with them. Both women seemed to be in a jovial mood.

When they arrived at the airport, Luba bought three tickets for Kraków.

"Kraków?" Danny was astounded. "But you fled from there. Aren't you afraid to go back?"

"Why? We're British citizens—free to come and go. You said let's take a trip."

"Yes—but Kraków?"

"It's such a romantic place, Danny. You'll see."

On board the LOT flight, Luba and Magda sat together in front of Danny, giggling and babbling away in Polish. Danny got caught up in the excitement of the trip, and *Everyman* seemed to drift away in his thoughts. He just wished he could understand what they were saying to each other.

Kraków

he cab passed over the Wisła River, and Magda and Luba looked with wide eyes at the places they recognized—Wawel Castle on the hillside above the river, the gold cupola of King's Cathedral, the statue of Kościuszko. They circled the Rynek, and Magda pointed to the colorful flower stalls near Cloth Hall. "Nothing has changed!"

"Yeah! They're selling the same flowers we saw eight years ago," said Luba. "They've been waiting for us to come back."

Their nostalgic joy was contagious. Danny pondered their gaiety—they had risked their lives to escape from this place. But he realized that they also associated Kraków with much happiness. They chose to remember that and not the suffering.

"Stop!" Luba yelled to the driver. They were at the Rondo bus terminal, the starting point for their exodus from Kraków. She turned to Danny with a mischievous grin. "This is where I started my journey to find you."

They checked into the Orbis Hotel, where Luba had arranged for a large suite with a sitting room, two bedrooms, and two baths. Danny was installed in the smaller bedroom, Magda and Luba in the larger one.

"Let's get cleaned up and show you the town," said Luba. Magda added something to which Luba agreed enthusiastically.

"It may come as a surprise to you," said Danny in a jocular tone, "but I don't speak Polish."

"Magda suggested that we have an early dinner at the Koń Morski," Luba explained. "That's the Seahorse Restaurant I told you about—remember, Danny?"

Indeed he did. This was the place Stash had once taken them, and where Luba had her first taste of vodka.

Magda started unpacking right away. As Danny went to his room, Luba followed. She helped him undress, her hands caressing his body. "I never forget a promise," she said.

Danny looked at her. "You mean . . . Magda?"

"Yes—Magda's ready."

Danny's eyes widened. "Now?"

"Soon." She winked. "First we're going out to eat. Clean up."

Danny grinned. Of course—where else could his fantasy be fulfilled but in Kraków? He looked out the bathroom window down at the bustling street. This was the town that Luba had told him so much about. Out there were the streets that Luba and Magda had walked, the cafés where they had met their friends, the police they tried to avoid.

He felt refreshed, eager to walk along the Rynek with Luba and Magda. He had them both now, all to himself. They were all in Kraków together. He would place himself in Luba's hands.

He was taken aback when the women came out of their bedroom. Luba's hair was in two braids, one on each side; she wore a short skirt and a ruffled blouse. Magda wore a longer skirt, cinched with a wide belt; her blouse came off her shoulders and exposed a deep cleavage. No longer a wan, tired woman, she had put on dark mascara and outlined her mouth in very red lipstick; she resembled pictures he had seen of her some time ago. They both looked very sensual and giggled like schoolgirls.

They came up to Danny and put their arms around him.

"We have to share and share alike," said Luba.

"That's right," agreed Magda.

Danny could feel Magda's large breasts pressing against him from one side, Luba's smaller ones pressing from the other.

Impulsively, he kissed Luba and then Magda. Magda laughingly rubbed off the lipstick residue from his lips with her finger.

"Come on," said Luba, as they ventured forth into Kraków. "We're the three musketeers."

The Rynek, a large cobblestoned square devoid of traffic, was crowded with people. A bandstand was being festooned with flowers; giant papier-mâché heads were leaning against the wall; flags were being unfurled from the windows of the surrounding buildings.

"What's happening? A Mardi Gras?"

"We're lucky—tonight is the beginning of the Lajkonik Festival," said Luba. "Kraków celebrates its victory over the Tatars."

"It looks like it's going to be a lot of fun."

"The whole town goes crazy," Luba said, and suddenly she hushed them. Faintly, calliope music drifted in; she listened to it for a moment with a beatific expression. Then she broke out into a grin. "Let's go to the Koń Morski."

Danny felt that he had been there before; it was exactly as Luba had described it. The ceilings were draped with fishing nets and there was an old mahogany bar, whitewashed walls, a clock with the signs of the zodiac. It was still early for dinner, and the place was almost deserted.

Magda ordered a large plate of river carp for all of them. They had not eaten much since they left London. Was it only this morning? "Look," said Luba, "the same musician." A man in a gypsy costume came in with a mandolin. Magda got up and walked over to him. Luba winked at Danny. "Are you glad you're here?"

"Yes, I am." Danny returned her impish grin.

"You'll be gladder—or more glad—or however you say it. You know what I mean?"

It was difficult to believe that it was all happening so easily, so perfectly. He must make an effort to curb his impatience. The waiter brought them coffee and more vodka.

Magda came back, happily clapping her hands like a schoolgirl. "He's going to play my favorite—'Moje Serce.'"

It was a lovely melody. Magda joined in the singing; she had a sweet voice and sang with deep feeling. Danny took Luba's hand. "Tell me the words."

" 'When first you came into my life, I gave my heart to you,' " Luba whispered. " 'Now you've left and know full well I have no heart to give to another. . . .' " She kissed his ear.

"Sto lat!" Magda toasted the musician as the song came to an end. Luba nudged Danny, and they all raised their glasses: "Sto lat!" Magda giggled and pointed to Danny. "Look—he speak Polish." The drinks gave them all a pleasant glow. They left the restaurant, Magda and Luba arguing about what to do next, each pulling Danny in a different direction. Finally, in a burst of laughter, they headed across the crowded Rynek, where the festival was in full swing. Men dressed in Tatar costumes were staging a mock battle on painted cardboard horses.

In the melee, ducking the revelers, Danny lost sight of Luba and Magda. He looked around quickly, calling out, "Luba! Magda!" He hurried ahead, pushing his way through the carousing throng. He approached one happy group and tried asking if they had seen the two women, but they only laughed and said something in Polish. He elbowed his way through the jovial crowd, looking right and left.

"Luba! Magda!" he called out. Some people were staring.

He was beginning to panic when arms grabbed him from both sides. "You can't get away from us!" And Magda and Luba pulled him into a crowded café in Cloth Hall. Tables extended out into the square. A band was playing a polka, and people were dancing.

The manager of the café, a strong, heavy-set woman, kissed and embraced Magda; they had known each other years ago. She brought a bottle of vodka to the table and slapped Danny on the back. *"Amer-ykański*—welcome—enjoy!"

Magda filled the glasses. "One more drink and we take Danny home." They all drank. Men stopped by the table, making remarks that Luba and Magda found very funny, and inviting them to dance. Magda waved them away, filling the glasses again. "One more drink and we put Danny to bed, OK?"

The three of them laughed and downed their drinks.

A young sailor, cap in hand, bowed to Magda and offered her a red carnation.

"Go ahead, Magda—that's worth at least one dance," Danny said.

Magda tucked the carnation behind her ear as the sailor danced her off.

"I'm so happy to see my mother having such a wonderful time."

"Yes, she looks so fresh and youthful." Danny was surprised by Magda's grace; he enjoyed watching her simple happiness. How could Magda have become a whore? How could Rachel? He knew the answer. You do what you have to do to survive—if you have the courage. Would Magda have been a different woman if her husband had not deserted her? Probably she would have stayed a housewife and lived out her life in Brodki. But not Luba. He turned to look at her—she was moving her body in rhythm to the music and clapping her hands. One way or another, Luba would have left.

As the sailor whirled Magda close to their table, she threw the red carnation to Luba. Danny toasted her with his drink. Magda was a good mother. She would do anything to please her daughter. An uncomfortable feeling overcame him.

"Come on, Danny—I'll teach you some Polish steps," Luba said, pulling on his hand.

"No, no," Danny laughed. He took both her hands in his. "You dance. I think I'll go back to the hotel."

"OK—we'll go with you."

"You stay with Magda. I'm tired; I'd like to go to bed."

Her smile disappeared. "But I made you a promise."

"Yes you did, Luba, and I'm grateful. But tell me—why did you wait? Why did you hold out that promise for so long?"

"I didn't want to lose you," she said, searching his face. "I thought that's all I had to keep you coming back."

"No, Luba. I came back because I needed you. And I've learned something . . ."

Her eyes questioned him silently.

He reached over and cupped her face in his hands. "Luba, some fantasies should never be fulfilled."

He got up from the table.

"Don't you want me to go back with you? You'll get lost."

"I'll find my way."

Danny opened his eyes. He was lying beside a sleeping Luba. Her peaceful face wore a faint smile. Was she dreaming of what happened when she quietly slipped into his bed and awakened him with the touch of her naked body? Neither of them spoke a word as they made love gently and tenderly, and then slowly drifted off to sleep.

In the far-off distance, he heard the strains of a calliope. In his mind, the carousel was slowing down to a stop. He could see the gaily painted horses. Some of the paint was scratched. Some of the wood was chipped. He was tired of going round and round. He wanted to get off. He had things to do.

Carefully, he left the bed. He took a shower and dressed. He felt very old, and yet he felt young. A curious feeling. He wasn't sure what it was, but he knew something was about to happen. He felt close to something very important.

He picked up the phone in the sitting room and quietly asked the concierge to confirm the airline reservation he had made the night before. Then he packed his bag.

Luba woke up and yawned. "I thought you'd be knocked out," she said with a grin.

"I'm an early riser," said Danny.

Then she noticed his bag. "Where are you going?"

"Switzerland, I must go to Lausanne."

"Danny—come over here."

He sat down on the bed beside her.

"At the café, you said you learned something, but I learned something too," she said, smiling.

"Ah," said Danny. "What?"

She looked directly into his eyes. "I had fun last night. It was like the old days with my mother. But now I know I'll never be a whore again." Then she laughed. "I might become a famous artist."

"I hope so." He took her hand. "I like you, Luba. You're honest. I come from a place where people are dishonest. . . . I've been dishonest too." He got up and picked up the bag.

"Don't go, Danny." A little fear crept into her voice. She jumped

out of bed and followed him into the sitting room. She stood before
him, naked, vulnerable. "I need you."

"And I need you, Luba. I'm grateful to you."

"Will I ever see you again?" A tear was rolling down her cheek. It
was the first time he had seen her cry.

At the door he said, "Yes—I promise." He grinned. "I'll be back in
London next week."

She ran up to him and threw her arms around his neck. He hugged
her tightly to himself, and realized how easy it was to say something
he really felt. "I love you, Luba—I love you very much." And then he
let her go.

EPILOGUE

1988 | Trieste, Italy

anny leaned back in the seat of the plane and looked at the countryside down below. He watched a tiny train snaking its way along a riverbed. Was that the route Luba and her mother had taken on their exodus from Poland?

Magda and Luba—mother and daughter irrevocably bound to each other when they were captives in Kraków, bound to each other when they were free after their escape. They would never try to sever the bonds that kept them together.

He thought about *Everyman,* but it didn't hurt now. He had done what he had dreamed about for years. It had failed because he couldn't see the corruption within himself. Working in the world of make-believe had helped him sustain a lie.

He had told Luba that he was on his way to Switzerland, but first he had to make another stop. When the plane landed at the Trieste airport, he jumped into a cab. The driver asked, "*Albèrgo?* Hotel?"

"No," said Danny. "San Sabba."

"San Sabba?"

"Yes. San Sabba."

The driver shrugged his shoulders and drove on.

They stopped at a tall, dark building. LA RISIERA DI SAN SABBA, the faded sign read.

Finally, he was back. Life is a circular thing. His mother, father, and sister—all of them had died here. This was the dark place where the ghosts that haunted him without end still lived, the source of memories that gave him no rest and demons that crippled his life. How could he save Patricia while being possessed by them? How could he attend to the living, when he had not buried the dead?

Danny stared at the entrance. There was a different gate now, with a little ticket booth on the side. He got out of the car slowly and purchased an admission ticket from a sleepy old Italian. The first time he had walked down this narrow gravel roadway he was clutching Tateh's trembling hand. Today, the courtyard was empty. He looked down at the cellar windows and found the perch from where he had seen so much horror.

There were no other visitors. The world rumbles on; people forget or deny that it ever happened. Danny had tried to deny it too. Yet here it still was—San Sabba—a place of agony and death.

He walked into the crematorium. Whitewashed walls. There was nothing sinister-looking here. In the next room, he saw two ovens, side by side, with long cradles, each about six feet long. Did they really put bodies in these to be incinerated? Maybe it was for rows of baked bread to feed hungry Jews. The room was immaculate.

He retraced his path and entered a door near the gate. On either side was a box—one with yarmulkes, the other with Hebrew prayer books. He took one of each, and then went down a dark hallway to a room where mock trials to convict the Jews of unnamed crimes had been held.

On the walls were many heart-wrenching photos, paintings, and drawings, some of them by children—birds, flowers, animals, gaily colored memories they carried to their death. Danny walked around until he found what he was looking for. It hadn't changed since his father had welded it together. He stood and stared at it—the crucifixion.

There was the base of nuts, bolts, and gears that Tateh had said symbolized the machinery of the Nazi regime. Welded to the base was the skeletal torso, dull strips of steel forming the chest, partially concealing the shiny piece of copper—*neshamah*—the soul. Elongated arms were nailed to the board with large spikes. The piece of yellowed canvas, once white, still had the blue Star of David. Over the other hand, he could make out the stenciled letters ADONAI. Danny looked at the head, poignant with the agony that Jews had suffered.

For so long he had denied being a Jew. As he looked at the sculpture his father had created, he thought: Perhaps Jesus *is* the Messiah. Why not accept this and release oneself from the burden of a religion that carries with it almost constant torment? Why not glide softly into assimilation and peace? Why cling to age-old traditions and beliefs—an angry God demanding allegiance to a standard impossible to maintain? He had become a Gentile because he didn't want to endure the pain of being a Jew. But he never escaped it.

This angry God of the Jews always exacts His price, but for those who bear the burden He grants a reward. Hadn't He vanquished all the enemies of His chosen people—the Egyptians, the Babylonians, the Romans, the Nazis? Hadn't He granted Jews extraordinary talent in proportion to their infinitesimal numbers—to compose songs that the world sings, to write books that the world reads, to make movies that the world sees?

At last, here at San Sabba, where his family had suffered and died, he realized that there was no escape. There never could be.

I must endure my pain because I am a Jew.

He put on the yarmulke, kneeled down before the crucifix, and closed his eyes. Through the flickering flames of the Sabbath candles he saw the gentle face of his mother, and opposite her the weathered, ascetic face of his father. Their loving embrace had created Moishe. Across the table he saw the full lips, the high cheekbones, hair hanging down each side of her sensual face, those large dark eyes alive and tender—his sister, Rachel.

The three of them had died here before he was Bar Mitzvahed. In front of their memory, he proclaimed what every Jewish boy of thirteen says on that occasion: "Today I am a man."

He opened his eyes and stared at the crucifix. Tears were streaming down his cheeks, and through his tears he whispered, "Tateh, I have forsaken you—you, Mameh, and Rachel. Forgive me."

He opened the prayer book. In a loud voice he chanted, "*Yisgadal v'yiskadash sh'mey rabbo . . ."*—the prayer for the dead that he had denied his family for over forty years.

He wiped his eyes with his yarmulke. He had finally buried the dead; now he could attend to the living. Now he had the courage to tell the world his secret, to erase those worn-out lies.

Finally, he was ready for Switzerland. For Patricia.

As he walked through the gates of San Sabba, Danny could feel the firm grasp of Tyrone's black hand holding his. He stopped and looked back at the tall dark chimney against an azure blue heaven.

Somewhere in southern Germany, an iron stork perched on the roof of a barn flapped its wings and flew off into the western sky.

KIRK DOUGLAS is an internationally acclaimed actor. His credits include nine Broadway plays and seventy-five films, and he has earned three Academy Award nominations—for *Champion, The Bad and the Beautiful,* and *Lust for Life,* which also won him the New York Film Critics' Best Actor award. Through his independent production company, the Bryna Company, Mr. Douglas has brought to the screen such classics as *Paths of Glory, The Vikings, Spartacus, Lonely Are the Brave,* and *Seven Days in May.*

Mr. Douglas is the recipient of the Presidential Medal of Freedom, the highest civilian award, for his service to his country in spreading the message of democracy throughout the world.

His 1988 autobiography, *The Ragman's Son,* received rave reviews and became an international best-seller. He lives in Beverly Hills and is now at work on his second novel.